# THE CLAIMANT

## A Novel of the
## Wars of the Roses

*by*
Simon Anderson

# The Claimant:
# A Novel of the
# Wars of the Roses

ISBN-13: 978-84-937464-9-0

# M
MadeGlobal Publishing

For more information on
MadeGlobal Publishing, visit our website:
www.madeglobal.com

*For my mother,*
*Barbara,*
*who loved to read...*

# CHAPTER ONE

"*WE ARE betrayed! The King still lives and the men of Calais have changed sides.*"

At first it was but a single voice, carried on a chill breeze through the steady drizzle and failing light of an October evening. But then the cry was taken up by others. The stark, unwelcome message gathering strength, surging along the lines of soldiers like a flood tide up a river, impossible to stop and leaving devastation in its wake. As the implications sank in a second shout pursued it through the ranks, precipitating a full-scale panic:

"*ALL IS LOST! EVERY MAN FOR HIMSELF!*"

Sir Geoffrey Wardlow, accompanied by his seventeen-year-old son Richard and a retinue of twenty liveried men, had been stationed on the rearmost 'battle', or division of the Duke of York's army. The force numbered some five or six thousand and was deployed in three blocks, one behind the other, straddling the main road from Leominster to Ludlow close to where it was forced to bend around the long ridge known as Whitcliffe. Too steep for an approaching army to scale in any kind of ordered fashion, the ridge offered protection to the right flank of the Duke's position.

In addition, the rain-swollen River Teme, crossed by the Ludford Bridge, ran in a broad curve around their left and rear, and two bowshots beyond that stood the walled town of Ludlow, its mighty castle one of the Duke's principal strongholds. Sir Geoffrey had left Richard in command in order to seek out an old friend further along the battle lines. They had been discussing the disposition of their troops, said to be outnumbered two-to-one by King Henry's approaching Lancastrian army, and also the recently circulated rumour that the King, against whom they were arrayed that day, was dead. Now that the latter had been disproved, however, the former was of no consequence, especially with the defection of some six hundred Calais garrison soldiers, under their commander Andrew Trollope, to the King's side.

On hearing the cries of alarm the two friends exchanged resigned looks, knowing that the time had come to call it a day and make for their homes as fast as their horses could carry them. Fleeing soldiers began to stream past the two knights, many throwing down their weapons and casting off pieces of armour – anything to speed their flight from the battlefield and the King's wrath. Sir Geoffrey clasped his friend's hands in farewell and wished him '*Godspeed*', then set off to rejoin his men and make his own escape.

It was only when he began to walk the two hundred yards or so back to where his retainers had been stationed that Sir Geoffrey realised just how thoroughly panic had gripped the Duke of York's army. What had been open meadows between the battle lines was now a seething crowd converging on Ludford Bridge, desperate to get away. Men were pressing all around him and he was jostled by common soldiers who under normal circumstances would have treated him with the utmost deference. Three times he was knocked to the ground in the crush and by the third time he had struggled to his feet in seventy pounds of plate armour he was thoroughly disoriented. The rapidly-descending darkness had robbed him of reference points and he began to walk around in circles crying out his rallying call, "*À Wardlow! À Wardlow!*" But there was no reply. The jostling crowd finally began to thin, but then Sir Geoffrey stumbled down a steep bank, almost losing his balance. A cold, wet sensation enveloped his feet and crept up his steel-encased legs as far as his knees. He realised he must have been heading the wrong way in the now all-encompassing darkness, not to the bridge but straight towards the River Teme. Not daring to take another step, in case he should overbalance and drown in his armour, he cupped his hands round his mouth and in near-desperation shouted again. *"À Wardlow!"* Still no answer.

The disintegrating rebel army had all but fled the field by now, leaving only the sound of the river swirling darkly around him and, in the distance, the noise of trumpets being blown – faint at first but slowly getting closer. The King's troops, supporters of the House of Lancaster, were coming.

Sir Geoffrey knew that with the rebel army gone, King Henry's men would soon be spilling over the bridge, somewhere off to his left he guessed, and advancing on the town. Drown, or be captured and throw himself on the King's mercy? He felt his feet begin to sink a little further into the river bed. The cold waters of the Teme would not understand the concept of mercy, but King Henry might.

*"À WARDLOW!"* he roared, his throat tearing with the effort.

*"À Wardlow! À Wardlow!"* came the reply. Relief flooded through Sir Geoffrey's body. His men had not deserted him after all.

*"Over here, by the river!"* he shouted. Disembodied points of light, looking like dancing glow-worms, gradually resolved themselves into flickering torches illuminating indistinct human forms. Strong hands grabbed Sir Geoffrey's arms on either side, pulling him from the cold, sucking embrace of the river bed and up onto firmer ground.

His relief at being plucked from the murky waters of the Teme quickly evaporated, however, as the hands that had dragged him to safety continued to hold him in a vice-like grip. These were not his men. Moments later he realised they were not the King's men either. A tall man wearing a full harness of fine-quality armour approached to inspect his catch, flanked by two torch bearers. He unfastened the leather strap on his helmet – a barbuta with a distinctive T-shaped opening – and eased it off, handing it to one of his men.

Sir Geoffrey recognised his captor even before the latter had pulled off his padded arming cap and ruffled out his shoulder-length crow-black hair. It was the eyes that had given him away. Looking into them now, as they glittered in the torchlight, Sir Geoffrey knew he was a dead man.

# CHAPTER TWO

THE FOLLOWING day, in the pale light of a grey, drizzling dawn, seventeen-year-old Richard Wardlow edged forward as quietly as his full harness of plate armour would allow him from his overnight hiding-place on the roof of a church tower. The sound of a crowd gathering somewhere below had caused his curiosity to overcome his desire to stay out of sight. As he peered cautiously around one of the stone merlons of the tower's battlements, the large body of armed men half a bowshot away on the village green suddenly fell silent.

A man, hooded and bound, was led out from one of the houses, a soldier on either side gripping his arms. Wearing only thin woollen hose and a linen shirt he contrasted sharply with the onlookers, cloaked as they were against the misty chill of the autumn morning. As the man and his escort advanced, the mass of soldiers parted to let them through.

Richard gave a sudden start when he saw what lay at the end of their short walk: a crude wooden block placed in a circle of fresh sawdust. His heart was pounding wildly under his ribs. He had occasionally seen the lifeless body of a criminal dangling from a gallows at a crossroads before, but he had never actually witnessed an execution. His stomach told him to look away, but his eyes were irresistibly drawn to the grisly scene.

When the condemned man and his escort reached the block they turned around, standing with their backs to Richard. Two more men now came out of the house and the crowd began to cheer loudly as they, too, made their way to the central clearing. Dressed in fine civilian clothes they walked with a self-assured air, clearly savouring the occasion. The taller of the two spent a little while talking to the gathering, gesturing from time to time towards the prisoner as if giving voice to some damning indictment, but Richard could not quite hear what he was saying, nor could he get a proper look at his face.

Finally the tall man nodded and took two steps back. One of the guards pulled off the prisoner's hood while the other picked up a short, brutish-looking axe and brandished it in front of him. At this point, Richard was able to see the face of the executioner. He would never forget his ruddy, weather-beaten features, nor the contemptuous leer that the man gave the prisoner as he grabbed his shirt, turned him around and shoved him towards the block. Now Richard could see the prisoner's face clearly.

He suddenly felt sick to the core and had to steady himself against the battlements, having immediately recognised the doomed man as his own father. His hand went instinctively to the hilt of his sword, but any hope of rescue was stillborn – the company below him numbered at least fifty. He was reduced to watching in numb disbelief as his father was pushed roughly to his knees, disappearing from view as the crowd closed in.

Above their helmeted heads the ugly little axe appeared and reappeared as it delivered two powerful strokes. A loud cheer and it was over. The onlookers began to disperse, returning to their fires and their breakfasts.

Richard could now see his father's lifeless body slumped on the darkly stained sawdust, revealed as it was by the widening circle of the departing men. He looked away immediately, fixing his tearful gaze on the flag of St George flapping damply above him on the tower. As the red cross blurred and became one with its white background, fatigue, hunger and the sickening shock of his father's murder ushered him into merciful unconsciousness.

# CHAPTER THREE

A HANDSOME, well-dressed woman in her late thirties sat quietly, lost in thought and gazing into the distance from a window-seat at the front of her fine brick manor house. The day's rain had cleared away, leaving the sun an hour or so to tease out the finer autumn colours from an otherwise grey and brown landscape. The golden evening light that fell across the woman's face flattered her pale, drawn features, temporarily disguising the unspoken anguish beneath. Kate Wardlow put her arm around her mother's shoulder and gently guided her away from the window and towards a table set with supper for two.

This tender little act had become almost a routine in the two weeks since Kate's father and brother had left for the town of Ludlow, almost a hundred miles to the south, accompanied by twenty tenants and household men equipped for war. Her father, Sir Geoffrey, was answering a call for help from one of the most powerful men in England: Richard Plantagenet, Duke of York.

Something very serious was going on – she understood that much. Her father had explained to her before he departed that political rivalries, normally confined to the court, had reached crisis point, and now the magnates involved in the bitter struggle to be the King's right hand man had gone to the country. Each lord was mustering his retainers in his own area of influence and that meant men like Sir Geoffrey turning out to repay previous favours. No one knew what was going to happen or how the matter would be resolved. For those left to fret at home, news would arrive with its usual frustrating slowness, and the best that could be done for now was to pray very hard to any saints that would listen.

As they began to eat, Kate looked at her mother with concern in her eyes and was only partly reassured by the brief, strained smile offered in return. All too soon, Ann Wardlow's gaze fell once again to the table, a distant, distracted expression on her face as she minutely examined its surface, seemingly seeking answers in the grain of its oak boards.

When their meal was finished, Jane, the house servant, cleared away the supper things. Kate caught her eye and with a fleeting frown let her know that she was still worried about her mother. The two girls were great friends, keeping no secrets from each other. Kate had been delighted when her mother had taken Jane into service. Their families were distantly related, although Jane's was considerably less well-to-do, so her parents were happy for her to spend time in a respectable household learning the skills which would make her a good wife when the time came.

To fifteen-year-old Kate it simply meant someone her own age with whom she could talk endlessly about the important things in life, which were clothes, horses and, of course, boys. Ann Wardlow treated Jane kindly, including her in many family activities, and was pleased that Kate had a companion, for the present at least.

But for now, Kate was alone again with her mother who, having dismissed Jane for the night, went to close the wooden shutters across the windows. Before securing the final one she paused, reaching out to touch the intertwined initials on the small centrepiece of coloured glass, unaware that she was now a widow.

# CHAPTER FOUR

"HE IS stirring, Father!" Richard, at first groggy from his deep sleep, became galvanised at the sound of voices. He struggled to his feet, his limbs stiff from spending the previous night encased in cold steel, and for the second time that day his hand went for his sword. Now the odds were fair, but his sword was not there. Nor, after he had twisted his arm around to the other side of his belt, was his rondel dagger. He froze, regarding the intruder on the tower with a wild, terrified look that caused the other to step back in alarm.

"God's mercy, lad, by all the saints we mean you no harm!"

Richard's eyes remained fixed on the man as he cried out in a voice he barely recognised as his own.

"Who is 'we'? How many are you? Did you murder my father? By God I shall kill every last one of you with my bare hands."

At this outburst the man took another step back, but Richard was upon him, his hands around his throat. Seconds later, two more men, one of whom was clearly a priest, dashed out of the small access door to the tower and, with some difficulty, wrestled Richard to the ground.

"I am Father William Foster, vicar of this parish," said the robed figure. "Pray be still, my son, we are not your enemies. The animals who killed ... your father ... departed this place an hour since."

Richard let out a long breath and began to sob. Father William's voice became soft, compassionate.

"We witnessed everything but were unable to resist so numerous a company. We even saw you enter the church but decided to leave you be lest we gave away your hiding-place to those ruffians. I doubt the likes of them would observe the rules of sanctuary. Do not be afraid, you are among friends."

"That you are, lad" said the victim of Richard's wild assault, rubbing one side of his throat. Richard looked at him, only now realising how sturdily built he was. He felt a little foolish – the man could easily have made short work of him had he wished. His stumbling apology was graciously dismissed with a wave of the hand and the man introduced himself as John Stotherd.

"Many of us in this village are like you, lad, fugitives from a battle that never took place. We believed we were there to fight the King's enemies, but when the King himself took the field and raised his standard, we knew we could not continue. God knows what has become of our lords of York, Salisbury, Warwick and March, and without those great men to lead us we must throw ourselves before King Henry's mercy. We have been hiding from his displeasure and from that company of wolves, afraid to return to our own houses until now."

As John spoke, Richard recalled the hours spent preparing the battle lines in front of Ludlow, watching the men digging ditches and planting stakes in the soggy meadows. At first, spirits were high, their numbers having been swelled by the army of the Earl of Salisbury who, less than three weeks earlier, had decisively defeated the forces of Henry's queen, Margaret, at Bloreheath.

He remembered the excitement they had all felt that evening when the Duke of York's new guns had been loudly tested, firing into the gathering dusk at the King's approaching army. But in spite of all their careful preparations the day was not to be theirs. Knowing they were outnumbered, and learning that the King himself had arrived to take the field, morale had sunk. No-one had the stomach to raise a sword against their anointed ruler, however corrupt and self-seeking the members of his court might be. Rumours had even begun to circulate within Richard's hearing that the Yorkist lords had slipped away, deserting their loyal followers. It was even said that the Duke of York had abandoned his wife, Cecily, and his younger sons, Richard and George, at Ludlow Castle, in order to make his escape as speedily as possible.

By nightfall, uncertainty had grown into panic, and Richard had been aware of soldiers running from the field in all directions. In the dark and confusion, amid the elbowing, jostling, heaving throng of men, he had become separated from his father, his squire and the retainers who had marched down with them. He had not dared to try to retrieve his horse which, like all the others, had been left well behind the battle lines out of harm's way. The King's forces had already started advancing on the town, judging by the trumpet calls and shouts in the distance. Woe betide him if he were caught! John's voice interrupted his troubled recollections.

"Let us repair to my house – you must be hungry and thirsty. You are welcome there until you decide what you will do next."

Richard, remembering how deftly his weapons had been taken from him as he slept, put his hand to the side of his breastplate and was relieved to feel the small purse of gold and silver coins secured under his thick arming doublet. He glanced quickly at John, hoping that the man had not noticed this small action. God forbid that these decent people should think they were suspected of robbing him!

Father William spoke. "We shall reunite you with your sword and dagger presently, young man. With hindsight their temporary removal proved to be a wise precaution." His eyes flitted briefly to Richard's side. "Any other possessions you might have about your person are no concern of ours."

Richard felt slightly awkward and said at once to John. "I

thank you for your kind offer, and I must pay you for any expense you incur on my part."

"No lad, I will not take your money, not after you have witnessed such wickedness, and in our own village too. We are shamed by our inaction, but it will take more force than we can muster to bring those dogs to account."

Richard felt a sudden wave of grief as he thought of his father. Father William moved swiftly to his side, offering a supporting arm as his legs buckled under the overwhelming weight of his loss. When he could speak, he asked where his father was, remembering the pitiful, headless corpse lying on the circle of sawdust, abandoned in the cold autumn drizzle.

"First, my son, you must eat," replied the priest. "Then I will take you to your father."

# CHAPTER FIVE

THE CROWDED inn was noisy and things were rapidly getting out of hand. Men were already fighting in one corner; in another, an argument over a game of dice looked set to turn nasty at any moment. The collective sound of sixty drunken soldiers all talking at once, each believing that what he had to say was of the utmost importance, was deafening.

Above this could be heard the shrill giggles and screams of the twenty or so women who had been tagging along with the company, having discovered an easy way to make money out of men who were far from home.

Remarkable it was, then, that as a bedchamber door in the gallery above the large taproom opened and a tall, dark-featured young man appeared, the entire assembly fell silent. Only one of the women, who had failed to grasp the significance of the moment, was still loudly holding forth. She was quickly silenced with a hard slap from her male companion. The blow lifted her off her seat onto the floor, into the spilled beer and vomit, but no-one seemed to care.

All eyes were on the tall, handsome figure. Wearing only

woollen hose, riding boots and his sword belt, he stood unashamedly bare-chested before the men. His fashionably slim legs supported a well-muscled upper body honed by years of weapons training. As he raised his arms briefly to acknowledge the gathering, those closest to him might have seen a scar, only an inch long but deeply coloured, close to his left armpit. Anyone who had tried to take on a fully armoured man at close quarters would know that there are but few places at which to aim a killing blow with a dagger: visor slit, groin, armpit. This man had survived a determined attempt by someone to finish him off, someone whose breath would have filled his nostrils. Someone who meant business...

Half-turning towards the bedchamber, he gestured with a flick of his head. A beautiful young girl, no more than fifteen, but tall, with long black hair and green eyes, quietly took her place by his side, dressed in a long, fur-trimmed robe of dark green velvet. She handed him one of the two silver wine goblets she was holding, and he honoured her with a shallow, stiff bow by way of reply. The exaggerated, formal frown on his face caused the girl to giggle unaffectedly, pressing her fingers to her lips. There was an accompanying ripple of laughter from the soldiers below. The girl was clearly at ease before such a large gathering, and her relationship with the man seemed to be one of comfortable equality, in spite of the ten years that separated them. Finally, the tall man spoke, his words finding eager listeners, "My friends, we have travelled many miles together and faced many trials. You have endured much in my service and very soon you will reap your reward. We are only days from the end of our long journey, and on reaching our destination I shall claim what is rightfully mine. Those who have supported me in this venture, unflinching in the face of danger, unquestioning in their loyalty, will find me a generous benefactor. In view of what lies before us, I propose a toast. *To coming home!*"

As one, sixty pots were raised and sixty voices roared their approval. One of the soldiers then jumped onto a table, turned to face his comrades and shouted. "Three cheers for Edmund of Calais!"

Edmund of Calais acknowledged their acclaim with a long, deep bow, then turned on his heel, offering a hand to the girl as the pair returned to the bedchamber. As the door closed behind them, the men resumed their carousing with renewed vigour, their female companions regarding them with fresh interest at the mention of reward...

# CHAPTER SIX

LATER THAT night Edmund of Calais, also known as the Bastard of Calais (though the latter was a factual description of his status, not an insult), looked out through the open shutters of his bedchamber window. There was a perfect full moon, revealed and hidden in turn as the chill autumn breeze blew dark shreds of cloud across its bright silver face. The weather would be better tomorrow. He looked down at the sleeping form a few feet away, clearly visible in the ghostly light, and smiled to himself.

Bastard he may be to those around him, but Edmund knew perfectly well who his father was - after all, he had ordered and witnessed his execution the day before. The widow, her family and their tenants would not present much of a problem; there were sixty good reasons for believing that slumbering heavily in the room below. He closed the shutters and went back to bed.

# CHAPTER SEVEN

TWO DAYS had passed since his father's murder, and in that time Richard Wardlow's raw, searing emotions had hardened into the kind of cold, vengeful, steely resolve that had no place in the heart of a mere boy of seventeen. Youthful he may have been, but he had aged immeasurably on seeing his father's washed and blessed body sewn into a shroud and placed on a trestle with a candle burning at each corner. Only days before, on the long journey down to Ludlow, he had felt very grown up as his father explained the various court rivalries and political tensions that had led to two opposing English armies being raised and mobilised. Richard had understood the risk his father was taking in supporting the Duke of York against the King, or rather, as Sir Geoffrey was keen to point out, the King's corrupt advisers, but he had also felt intense excitement. This could prove to be his first taste of battle, although the general mood among the more high-ranking Yorkist supporters, with whom his father was involved in frequent earnest discussions, was one of hope that the situation could be resolved by negotiation.

Recent events, however, had changed everything for Richard.

He was growing up far faster than he had bargained for. Now he had his own, private war to fight. From the moment he saw his father's corpse in the chapel, his thoughts never strayed from the image of the tall man whose words he could not quite hear, whose face he could not quite see. He was going to find him and kill him, even if it took him the rest of his life.

Realising this, Father William's comforting tone changed to a fiery one as he lay before the boy the torments in store for him in the realm of the damned. It was no use – the icy look in Richard's pale blue eyes told him his words were in vain. Defeated for the present, the priest turned to more practical matters, suggesting temporary interment of the body in the vault of a sympathetic local family, the Dwyers, until such time as Richard could arrange for his father to be taken home. Richard agreed to this, settling an amount of silver and gold coin on the monks of the local priory to provide for the saying of daily masses for Sir Geoffrey's eternal soul.

Believing that the demands of decency had been met, at least for now, Richard was anxious to pick up the trail of the killers before it went cold, although a company of sixty could not be too hard to locate, provided it had not disbanded, its members returning to their farms, their trades, their families. But where were they from?

Even in times of great stress, the human mind can find itself noticing minute details, mundane and irrelevant to the main horror being played out before the observer's eyes, perhaps, but equally unforgettable. While his father was being vilified and brutally dispatched, Richard had unwittingly committed to memory various aspects of the gathering and it was through these that he was now frantically sifting, looking for any useful clue.

He shuddered to recall that evil morning, but he forced himself to replay the scene again and again, looking for a banner, a standard, a livery jacket or a distinctive badge – anything that might hold the key to identifying who these people were, who their patron was. But there was nothing. A few soldiers had been wearing jacks – multi-layered, thickly padded cloth garments very effective against both sword cuts and long range arrows – but they were simply grubby, devoid of any markings or designs. The rest of the men had been wearing cloaks; after all, his father's last day on Earth had been a cold, wet one. Once again the leering face of the executioner sprang into Richard's consciousness. He understood now why the wretch had looked so pleased with his work; not only had he killed a man of infinitely superior social standing, but he had done it with the full blessing and protection of his master. Richard swore he would kill him, too, but the man had no name, no place.

He came, at last, to the uncomfortable conclusion that this particular company did not wish to be recognised. Following the disastrous events at Ludlow, he could understand those on the losing side casting off anything incriminating and fleeing for their lives, but surely the triumphant supporters of the King had nothing to fear from making their allegiance public?

The armies which had faced each other that day consisted of dukes, lords and earls, with their large affinities, and many retainers, lesser figures, but still rich and influential, such as Richard's father, with their followers. Even before the spectre of impending civil war had loomed like a thundercloud on the horizon, the concepts of law and order had been crumbling. Legal process was highly convoluted, favouring those with deep pockets and good connections; local enforcement was often ineffectual. The strong could take what they wanted from the weak, and those with land and property to protect found it prudent to maintain a reliable body of armed men to discourage hostile incursions by covetous neighbours.

Considerable expense was lavished on equipping and training such companies, their size reflecting both the affluence of their patron and the level of danger expected from day to day.

The Scottish border region suffered the most, to the extent that the immensely wealthy Percy family in Northumberland kept what amounted to a large private standing army. In looking after their own local interests they were also safeguarding the northern gateway to the Kingdom - a fact not lost on either the King or the Percy family.

Henry VI had no regular army as such, save for the Calais

garrison under its captain, Andrew Trollope. These well-trained, professional troops, numbering almost six hundred, had initially sided with the Duke of York at Ludlow, but had returned to the crown at a critical moment. Richard recalled the alarm caused by their defection, and the rapid collapse of Yorkist resolve thereafter.

But these soldiers were the exception. In order to field enough men to meet any challenges to Royal authority, the King relied heavily upon the co-operation and goodwill of the great magnates – goodwill that was bought with grants of land, money, titles and appointments. With such a system, it was not uncommon for self-seeking favourites to benefit more from the King's generosity than men who had done loyal service to the crown – men like the Duke of York, for instance. Not only did King Henry owe him a great deal of money, but the Duke also found himself increasingly excluded from the privileged group of royal advisers.

Sir Geoffrey Wardlow had done his best to acquaint his son with the serpentine workings of the country's politics, having spent time in London attending Parliaments and meeting some of the major figures of the day. Richard wondered if his father had met his murderer moving in such circles. Perhaps theirs was an association turned sour by recent events as they found themselves on opposite sides. Perhaps the tall man envied Sir High's position, or Sir Geoffrey has promised him money or favours that were not forthcoming. The tall man had clearly been out for retribution, the current unrest providing convenient cover for the pursuit of a personal feud. He could justify his actions by claiming to have punished an enemy of the Crown, but having killed Sir Geoffrey what might he do next? Did he seek to profit further from the ill-luck of those who had supported the Duke of York?

Of course! With its landlord dead, and the pick of its men scattered about the countryside, the Wardlow estate was wide open. Richard reeled from the realisation. Twin feelings of triumph and horror coursed like hot lead through his body. He knew now exactly where the tall man and his company of killers were headed. He had to get home quickly.

# CHAPTER EIGHT

TWO TEENAGE girls, one at the reins of a handsome, powerfully built destrier, the other riding pillion behind her, giggled as they exchanged opinions on the best-looking local boys. Kate Wardlow and her friend Jane were making their way along a pleasant, sunlit bridleway at a gentle, unhurried pace. Either side of the road, the oak trees clothing the surrounding hills reflected the lateness of the season in the yellows and browns of their falling leaves. The horse, accustomed as it was to carrying the weight of a fighting man in full plate armour, hardly noticed its double burden as it plodded along the familiar route. Kate's favourite ride involved following the narrow, sunken lane from the family home, down and down, until it met the main bridleway between Nannerch and Bodfari, an important route that not only allowed the traveller to cut through the long, steep ridge of the Clwydian Hills with ease, but also happened to run along the floor of a particularly beautiful valley. To improve safety along the route, the trees had been thinned out so that the edge of the woodland was some fifty yards from the bridleway on either side, making it harder to spring an ambush. Kate was not worried about being ambushed today, however, as she and Jane had an escort.

Following discreetly twenty paces behind them was eighteen-year-old Stephen, one of the estate grooms. He certainly looked the part in his burnished jawbone sallet, named for the shape of its visor, which was currently flipped wide open. Over his padded jack and polished breastplate he wore a Wardlow livery coat of dark blue woolcloth with a seated greyhound embroidered on the front and back in silver thread. His legs were encased in long brown riding boots whose tops were turned down, in what he hoped was a suitably rakish fashion, and at his left hip hung a sharp, single-edged straight sword, its leather scabbard slapping gently against the flank of his well-cared-for chestnut rouncey. At his right hip, a small shield the size of a dinner plate, known as a buckler, and a long, narrow-bladed bollock dagger, so called because of the two ball-shaped extensions that formed the handguard, completed the ensemble.

Stephen's armed presence had been at the absolute insistence of Kate's mother. Ann Wardlow was still worried sick over the absence of her husband and son, and would otherwise have forbidden the girls from taking a morning ride. She had almost refused outright, escort or no, when Kate had told her she wanted to take Rollo, her father's favourite mount, but some expert wheedling, coupled with Stephen's reassurances as to Kate's riding ability, had made her relent, albeit reluctantly.

Kate had won her father's unstinting admiration by forging a special bond of trust with his beloved black warhorse, a magnificent creature trained for both tournament and battlefield. The two were great friends, the girl somehow able to charm the horse to do her bidding, even at a full gallop. Her mother, of course, fretted endlessly every time Kate went out, wishing she would take a pony instead, but the girl seemed to revel in the danger and her father did nothing to dissuade her.

Sir Geoffrey had not wished to risk such a valuable animal on the long, uncertain expedition to Ludlow and had, like his retainers, set out on a rouncey more suited to all-round duties. In any case, if it came to a fight, it had become the custom to go into battle on foot, since a horse presented far too easy a target for any keen-eyed archer with a barb-headed arrow nocked on his bowstring.

Stephen, initially crestfallen at being left out of the Ludlow party, was now glowing with pride at being chosen for escort duty, especially as it involved accompanying the two prettiest girls on the estate. He appeared to be taking his work very seriously, affecting an air of cool detachment, his posture in the saddle relaxed but alert, his narrowed eyes scanning the trees and the road ahead for trouble.

In reality, he was straining to hear what the girls were talking about, since he could have sworn he heard his name mentioned a few moments earlier.

Suddenly Jane turned around in the saddle and looked him straight in the eye. Stephen felt he had been caught eavesdropping and his face began to colour. Jane turned back and cupped her hand to whisper in Kate's ear, then both girls turned and gave him a mischievous look before dissolving in a fit of giggles. The poor lad now glowed scarlet from shoulder to scalp. So much for cool detachment.

As the little group continued on its way they reached a crossroads. Turning right would, as always, take them up the steep, tree-lined track to Caerwys village, then back to the Wardlow's manor house. The five pleasant miles took an hour or two to complete, depending upon how often Kate dug her heels into Rollo's glossy, black flanks. She never, ever failed to be thrilled by the massive power beneath her and Jane frequently had her work cut out staying on board.

Kate's eyes wandered in the direction of the narrow lane that formed the left arm of the crossroads heading southwards. It led invitingly over a wooden bridge above a small stream, then upwards and out of sight over a steep, wooded rise. Kate drew Rollo to a halt, weighing up her choices. She let out a sigh as she thought of her father and brother, gone a fortnight now with still no word. Jane, sensing her mood, gripped her slightly tighter around the waist, resting her head against Kate's shoulder in unspoken sympathy.

"I want to go this way", she said firmly. "It is the road Father and Richard took on their way to Ludlow, is it not?"

Stephen's voice held concern. "Indeed it is, Mistress, but are you sure that's a wise thing to do? There's naught but rough hills, thick woods and little criss-crossing tracks that way for far enough. We may lose our way or meet outlaws."

"Outlaws?!" exclaimed Kate. "I've never heard tell of outlaws in these parts. Are you afraid to go on?"

Stephen's young pride was visibly stung by her accusation. "I am only afraid of what my lady Ann will say if we meet trouble because I didn't do my job properly, Mistress," he replied in a carefully controlled tone, sitting stiffly upright in the saddle to emphasise his manliness, which had clearly been called into question.

"Of course you're not afraid, Stephen. I'm sorry for my remark," Kate said quickly. "It's just that I want to share a small part of their journey so I can feel close to them."

Two weeks earlier, Kate's mother had asked a departing Sir Geoffrey why he wanted to take a narrow, winding road over such difficult, hilly country when the simplest way would have been to ride down the valley to Bodfari and then join forces with Roger Kynaston and his men, who were setting out for Ludlow from Denbigh Castle at the same time and taking the main route south, along the Vale of Clwyd. Kate's father had explained that since he was effectively leaving the estate unguarded while he was away, he would feel better if he made a sweep of the rough country to the south, just to reassure himself that there were no travelling bands intent on mischief. If there were, that was the country that afforded them the best cover. He and his men would have to see them off before continuing to Llandyrnog, the agreed rendezvous for the two Ludlow-bound retinues. Stephen spoke, his voice heavy with reservation. "Well, I suppose we shall be all right just for a mile or so, but then we really should head back, Mistress. It will mean we have ridden a good deal further than usual and I do not wish for your lady mother to grow anxious."

They continued in silence.

# CHAPTER NINE

COMING UP from the south, five mounted soldiers rode slowly in single file. They wore open-faced helmets and plain padded jacks, but no mail or armour, and their weapons were carefully stowed so as not to rattle, the only sound being the muffled thump of their horses' hooves on the earth road. When the lead rider spied the girls and their escort in the distance he turned in his saddle, pressing the side of his index finger to his lips then gesturing his men to get their horses off the forest track and out of sight. Peering through narrowed eyes, he recognised Stephen's Wardlow livery coat. This was it! Minds alert, senses taut as fully-drawn bowstrings, the soldiers quickly followed their serjeant's orders. Their excitement was palpable. They were getting close to the end of their long journey.

The lead scout had realised immediately who the girl riding the warhorse was, having the advantage of information gathered along the way by the rest of Edmund's retinue, which had been taking its time, slowly building up a picture of what lay ahead. Much could be learned at roadside inns, for example, either by the simple expedient of getting the locals drunk, or by waving two days' pay under their noses. Anyone who tried to discourage their friends from divulging sensitive intelligence might find themselves under interrogation, often with a burning candle applied to their bare feet in order to sharpen the memory.

In the case of recognising Kate Wardlow, one young man, a travelling farrier whose work took him all over the district, had clearly been smitten by her on his visits to the estate, waxing lyrical over her distinctive waist-length hair, describing it dreamily as: "All at once red, yellow and gold, dancing in the wind like the flames of an autumn bonfire," before sliding unconscious from his bench under the influence of a night's free ale.

Thus had Edmund of Calais added to his existing knowledge of the estate he intended to seize and the family that held it. He was only too aware that his late father had a legitimate son – he would deal with him personally when the time came. On the other hand, the mother and daughter might prove valuable levers for bargaining against the possibility of armed resistance to the takeover. Edmund was not afraid of a fight, but he did not relish the thought of losing good men needlessly.

One factor in Edmund's favour was his father's recent increasing political isolation. For various complex reasons of loyalty, contract or expediency, many of Sir Geoffrey's neighbours had found it prudent to declare for King Henry and would therefore be less likely to consider helping the Wardlows. After the events at Ludlow, just days before, anyone of rank who had defied the Crown and supported the Duke of York would be lucky to keep their heads, let alone their estates. Things could not have gone better for Edmund, who had been keeping a close watch on developments from across the Channel through a network of spies posing as wine traders.

He had been willing to take a gamble, but much had depended on upon where Sir Geoffrey's true loyalties lay. As it turned out, Edmund had been right – his father had aligned himself squarely behind the Duke, their strong personal ties stretching back to the French wars. It was a decision that was to place Sir Geoffrey firmly on the losing side.

28

How ironic! Many friendships had been forged in the fires of that long and bitter conflict, but the ill-advised one between a youthful Sir Geoffrey and Edmund's mother Elaine, a French lawyer's daughter, had not lasted. Love had blossomed despite them being on opposing sides, but when Elaine fell pregnant, and Sir Geoffrey conveniently found pressing reasons to return to England, she was left alone, disgraced and without provision. Her family turned its back on her for consorting with the enemy and she was forced to make such living as she could in a town far enough away to dilute the whiff of scandal. Hoping perhaps for some future restitution, she gave her son an English Christian name.

From earliest childhood, Edmund could recall times of great hardship, his mother working long hours in unseemly employment, always coming home tired, but always managing a weary smile for her boy. She spoke very little of Edmund's father, only occasionally making some veiled reference to the dangers of "trusting an English knight". Edmund, not wishing to upset her, kept his unanswered questions to himself. For now, just knowing his father's name would be enough. He would find out more, in good time.

Not until he reached twelve, when his mother died exhausted and broken and the light went out of his life, did Edmund begin to understand, begin to hate. Armed with his mother's hard-earned wisdom and what was to become characteristic single-mindedness, he set out and walked the thirty miles to his grandparents' estate. There he introduced himself and, with a breathtaking combination of eloquence and charm, won over his mother's family to the extent that, far from spurning the bastard child they had never seen, they took it upon themselves to provide for the boy's future and even arranged to have his mother's body exhumed from its pauper's grave and re-interred in the family tomb, in a rather belated gesture of guilty reconciliation. It was decided that Edmund was not to live under their roof, but with his mother's uncle in Calais.

Although the town and a considerable amount of the surrounding countryside had been in English hands for many years, there were merchants from other countries living there who realised the trading opportunities afforded by the presence of a large, hungry garrison. The French were not tolerated but Edmund's great uncle had passed himself off as Burgundian upon his arrival many years earlier. Since then no-one had questioned his credentials, nor did the authorities take much notice of the arrival of a twelve-year-old boy in his house.

The town's strategic location meant that, with the right contacts, licences could be obtained to ply a highly profitable trade with England. Edmund's great uncle dealt in wines and it was this business the boy was to learn and, it was agreed, eventually take over, as his guardian was a childless widower.

The wines of Gascony and Guyenne were particularly highly prized by upper class English customers but the loss of those territories to the French in 1453 meant that the export of fine Bordeaux wines to England ceased, at least officially. As Edmund's great uncle explained, however, if people want something badly enough, a way will be found to furnish them with what they desire; priced at a healthy premium to compensate for the merchant's trouble, of course.

By the time Edmund was nineteen, the war that had lasted over a hundred years was at an end. English aspirations to the French throne had finally been extinguished in a crushing defeat before the walls of a town called Castillon. Calais, nevertheless, remained in English hands, life there continuing much as before, save for its merchants growing even fatter now that hostilities had ceased.

Over the years Edmund's great uncle had, with shrewdness, guile and a penchant for interpreting the laws of taxation somewhat creatively, amassed a tidy fortune. It was to this wealth, upon the death of the old man, that a worldly-wise, self-assured Edmund had succeeded. He had all the knowledge, experience and contacts he needed to maintain the wine trade and the comfortable life it had so far given him. For an ambitious Edmund, however, it was not enough.

If he wished to paint for himself the kind of future he had long envisaged, he would require a broader canvas than his great uncle's town house – he would need a fine country estate. He conjured images of exhilarating hunts, huge banquets, dazzling entertainments, perhaps even a royal visit. He would own hawks, hounds and a fine stable, wear beautifully-crafted armour in the latest style and wield the best weapons money could buy. In short, he would become a gentleman.

High ambitions indeed, but Edmund was no daydreaming fool. On his mother's untimely death the germ of an idea had rooted itself in the dark crypt of his brain. He believed he was owed an inheritance, and if obtaining it meant sending the entire Wardlow family to Hell then so be it.

# CHAPTER TEN

THE SERJEANT motioned to his comrades to dismount and perform a flanking manoeuvre, then continued to ride his horse along the narrow track at an unhurried pace until he was in plain sight of Kate and her party. He eyed Kate's horse enviously. It was of the finest stock, clearly an expensive animal, and another reason to feel sure he had found the Wardlow girl and not someone else. Knowing he had been spotted, the serjeant maintained as casual a pace and as nonchalant a posture as he could in order not to arouse too much suspicion. Surprise was essential as he knew his modest rouncey could not hope to stay with such a magnificent warhorse, even two-up, should it come to a chase.

A few paces short of Kate and her friends he tugged gently on his left rein, bringing his horse about so that it stopped sideways on, half blocking the bridleway and hiding the heavy, curving, broad-bladed falchion that hung from his left hip.

"A fine autumn day, is it not?" he said pleasantly, nodding his head in salutation. Kate was obliged to draw Rollo to halt. She looked the man up and down. His clothing was shabby and dirty – he wore no livery coat or distinguishing badge - but his build was lean and energetic and his features were fine, almost handsome, apart from an old scar which ran from his right ear across his cheek to the corner of his mouth, lending him a slightly sinister, lopsided smile. Kate guessed him to be about her father's age. She sensed intelligence, but she also sensed danger. Whatever was he doing out here? Was he alone or, more likely, did he have company? Alarm grew inside her, tightening her throat. "Indeed it is a fine day and although we have enjoyed our ride it is time we turned for home," she managed, her strained voice betraying her fear.

"That is a pity," replied the soldier. "I had hoped you might tarry awhile, for I feel we have much to talk about."

"My mistress has nothing to say to the likes of you!" Stephen had brought his horse alongside Kate's in a protective gesture, his right hand resting on the hilt of his sword.

"Fie, fie my young friends! A little more warmth in your tone would be a pleasing thing," said the soldier, his lopsided smile still in place, "after all, Mistress Wardlow..." He glanced up through the over arching branches into the bright autumn sky, closing one eye against the sun's glare before fixing his gaze on Kate, his smile gone, "...we shall soon be neighbours."

Kate felt completely disarmed by the stranger's words and the calm certainty with which they had been delivered. She fought desperately to control her wildly pounding heart, trying her hardest not to sound utterly terrified. "How so? How do you know my name?"

The soldier studied Kate in her fine dress, with her servant and her escort. In spite of her obvious fear she clearly thought him beneath her, looking down her nose at him from her expensive mount. Perhaps if she had witnessed her father's sudden, violent exit from the world of the living she would have shown a little more respect. He kept his silence, watching Kate squirm, only taking his eyes off her briefly to glare at Stephen, whose horse was becoming restless. Stephen swallowed hard, slowly taking his hand away from his sword hilt and resting it on his reins. When Kate could stand the tension no longer she questioned the man again, trying to put on an air of authority, though it was an effort to keep her voice steady. "Why do you bar our way?"

"I do not believe I am barring your way, Mistress, since you said yourself you were about to turn around and head home," the serjeant replied.

"Do not play games with us!" Stephen warned. "State your business here."

Without taking his eyes from Kate's the serjeant raised his voice slightly. "They want to know our business, lads."

Kate's heart leapt into her mouth and she spun round in horror to see that two rough-looking, heavily-set footsoldiers had silently taken up position on the track behind them, halberds crossed like guards at a castle gate, blocking their retreat. They offered her a mocking salute. At the same time a fourth man emerged from the bushes to her right, addressing Kate in a low, gravelly voice. "A fine horse you have there, Mistress, but don't go gettin' no ideas about diggin' yer heels into him. He won't get far with one of these through his heart."

Kate glanced down and found herself looking at the business end of a loaded crossbow, its powerful steel prod and hempen string straining against the release mechanism. One squeeze of the tickler – the long, ball-ended trigger lever - was all it would take to send a foot-long, half-inch thick, leather-fletched quarrel catapulting out of its groove like lightning. At such short range the heavy, steel-tipped missile would drop Rollo like a stone, possibly even tearing right through him and into Stephen's horse. Kate willed herself to stay calm to avoid spooking her mount. As if the situation were not bad enough, a fifth soldier emerged from the woods on Kate's left, his sword drawn and pointing in the general direction of Stephen.

"Three young rabbits for the pot!" shouted the fifth man, spitting on the ground beside him.

"Aye, nice and tender, just how we like 'em!", added one of the halberd-wielding rearguard. The crossbowman's lips peeled back in a gap-toothed grin as he unselfconsciously scratched his groin. "Plenty for all of us!"

Kate turned back to face the serjeant, the fear showing in her eyes, almost as if begging him for help. He held up a hand. "Stow it lads! I apologise, Mistress, if my coarse friends here offend your delicate sensibilities, but you will discover soon enough that your life of comfort and privilege is about to be altered greatly by recent events."

Her blood ran cold at the serjeant's seemingly prophetic words but somehow Kate found her voice again, although it was unsteady and strained. "What do you mean?" She did not wait for a reply in case it contained bad news, quickly adding, "You should know that my father and brother are, as we speak, returning from Ludlow with twenty liveried men, quite likely along this very road. If you treat us kindly I will speak on your behalf and no harm will come to you".

It was an unconvincing bluff. The leader looked pointedly at each of his comrades, then at Kate, his gaze becoming narrow and hard. "I doubt, Mistress, that your score of men would worry our threescore very much" – here he paused for effect – "especially now that they are leaderless."

As he spoke the words, Kate felt like she had swallowed a lead weight that had dropped straight to the pit of her stomach. Something she had been nursing inside her for two weeks had just died. It was hope. The soldier saw it and, for the first time in his rough, hard life felt a little pity. His tone became flat, serious, no longer taunting. "Know, lass, that your father is dispatched to the next life. He took up arms against his King and it was my master's judgement that he should pay the ultimate price. His lands and property may or may not be forfeit to the Crown but whatever the case my master intends to take possession of all that was Sir Geoffrey's, calling it his own and holding on to it by any means at his disposal. Some of his wealth will come our way and we shall be set up for life - we will do whatever is necessary to earn our reward. Now, come with us and you shall meet your new lord."

"You murdering bastards!" shouted an enraged Stephen,

quickly drawing his sword and urging his horse forward to within striking distance of the serjeant.

*"Oh God Stephen - NO!!"* screamed Kate, but the young groom was already committed to his attack. As Stephen's sword came slicing down towards the serjeant's neck, his opponent unsheathed his falchion with practised speed and in one fluid motion brought the heavy, broad-bladed chopper up and over, severing the boy's hand completely. It fell to the ground, the fingers still tightly wrapped around the hilt of the sword. Stephen stared ashen-faced in disbelief as his lifeblood gushed out of the stump. He began to sway in his saddle but before he could fall from his mount of his own accord he was dragged from it by the fifth soldier, who finished him off on the ground with a dagger thrust to the neck. Not a word was spoken as the boy's body was quickly plundered of any useful items then carried out of sight into the woods. The soldiers retrieved their horses and climbed back into their saddles, one of them leading the riderless horse by its reins.

Kate was too stunned for tears, sitting in compliant, numb silence as a lead rein was secured to Rollo's bridle and she and her mount were led away southwards to God alone knew what fate. Only when she felt a gentle, rhythmic shuddering behind her did she remember that Jane was with her. She found her friend's hands and squeezed them until her knuckles turned white.

# CHAPTER ELEVEN

THREE DAYS earlier, Richard Wardlow had taken his leave of the village from whose church tower he had witnessed his father's cold-blooded murder and among whose inhabitants he had found kindness and sympathy. He had promised to return for his father's body once his "business" had been attended to.

Modest but sincere offers of armed assistance had been rendered unnecessary by the appearance in the village of six of his father's men, including two of Sir Geoffrey's ten full-time private soldiers. They, too, had been in hiding since the debacle at Ludlow and had been cautiously trying to make their way home. Each of them had his own tale to tell regarding the escape from the battle lines, but none could say for sure how Sir Geoffrey came to be separated from them in the confusion of that dark, fateful night.

They were all angered and saddened by the news of Sir Geoffrey's death and had all pledged their allegiance to Richard as his natural successor. In the matter of defending the estate, they agreed that a sound plan was needed in view of the odds involved. They also agreed it was vital to act quickly. Since none of them had been able to get back to where the horses were tethered when panic had struck in Ludlow. It would require a forced march on foot to reach home in time.

The recent arrivals were confident that the rest of their company could be collected on the way home, but even so they would still be outnumbered three to one. Richard knew he could add to his strength the older and younger men who had stayed behind to tend the estate, but from what he had seen, they were up against hardened professionals, most likely veterans of the French Wars to whom killing was second nature. It was going to be tough.

# CHAPTER TWELVE

T HE SMALL brew-house, tucked in between the laundry and the bakery, was, as usual, alive with activity. Steam billowed out through the open top of the door, the swirling white tendrils twisting their way upwards briefly, before dissolving in the blue morning sky.

The sickly-sweet smell of the boiling mash carried over to the manor house, where Ann Wardlow was working alongside Matthew, the steward, as he ran his experienced eye over the household accounts. She loved to immerse herself in the running of the estate, proving a thrifty and capable mistress, much to her husband's satisfaction Sir Geoffrey knew that his household would be in safe hands during his frequent absences. Indeed, during his latest foray the task of keeping family affairs in order had become almost an obsession; Ann harrying lazy farm workers and tardy creditors with unrelenting vigour and doubling the cleaning and polishing duties at the manor in order to distract herself from her fears. It simply would not do for the master of the house to return to a shambles, and return he would.

Those who had dealings with Ann knew her to be well-mannered but forceful, gentle natured but nobody's fool. They might also say that she was a creature of nerves, her pale grey eyes hinting at an unspoken inner turmoil, pale grey eyes that were wide with the fear that she would be left alone in a hard, friendless world. Her husband would come home. He had to, or her mind would snap like a twig under a horse's hoof...

# CHAPTER THIRTEEN

FROM WHAT their stomachs were telling them, it must have been around midday when Kate, Jane and their escort arrived at a clearing, well away from the main bridleway. There was a military-style camp set out; sizeable but tucked away from general view. The only signs of life the girls had noticed from afar were the spirals of greasy smoke weaving their way skywards through the oak, ash and birch trees. Kate at first thought they signified the presence of charcoal-burners plying their trade, but now she could see men, and a few women, tending roasting rabbit carcasses, various stew pots and even what looked like a deer. Large numbers of horses of varying quality – mostly rounceys and hacks, but at least one very fine grey destrier and a pretty blue roan mare – were tethered to makeshift wooden rails or trees as soldiers fed and watered them. As many as a dozen carts and wagons, positioned in a neat row down one side of the camp, appeared to be packed with food stores, bags of arrows, barrels of ale or wine, and an assortment of unidentifiable bundles and boxes, sure signs of a well-supplied company on the march.

The little group made its way between two long, straight rows of tents. Their progress was watched intently by an assortment of some of the most alarming individuals Kate had ever seen. Her abductors, rough though they were, seemed like old friends by comparison. She sensed, however, that these evil-looking men were not about to cross their serjeant, the one with the scar who had first spoken to her. Indeed, there appeared to be an air of discipline about the camp, from the neatness of its layout to the relative lack of noise.

Kate reckoned the number of soldiers feeding themselves, seeing to their horses or fettling weapons, to be around forty. The serjeant had said threescore, so the others could be sleeping or foraging for victuals. Frightened as she was, Kate's only thought was of escape, and the more information she could take back with her, the better. They had to get away and alert the estate, or Stephen would have died for nothing. She knew from brief, stolen glances at her brave friend that Jane was of the same mind.

Finally, at the far end of the gauntlet of staring eyes, the serjeant dismounted, motioning to the girls to do the same. As their horses were led away, they found themselves standing before an imposing conical tent of blue-and-white striped canvas. That was when they first encountered the Bastard of Calais, sitting on a folding chair at a small table set with various items for a midday meal, a silver wine goblet in his hand.

The tall, dark-haired man rose politely, giving the shallowest of bows, and introduced himself simply as Edmund. His English bore just a hint of a French accent. In different circumstances Kate would have considered him handsome, but since it seemed in all probability that he had been the instrument of her father's death, she regarded him with a wild mixture of hatred and fear she was finding hard to conceal.

Edmund cared little for the girl's feelings – she may have been his half-sister but to him she was no more than a potential hostage who had fallen quite fortuitously into his hands, an asset for bargaining when the time came to make his move on the Wardlow estate.

His green-eyed French companion, however, emerging quietly from the tent and taking up position at his left side, looked upon the captive and her servant with great interest. Having lost count of the weeks, even months, she had spent in largely male company, she was secretly eager to talk to girls of her own age, as far as her modest grasp of English would allow. Nevertheless, she could not complain of her treatment at Edmund's hands: he was the perfect gentleman. Generous, tender, considerate, he was also fiercely protective of her honour – something she had willingly surrendered to him over a year ago, when the first swallows were swooping out of a clear blue sky. She knew she was safe. Dangerous though Edmund's adherents were, he seemed to hold them completely in his sway. She also knew he would kill any man who touched her. Two overly attentive followers had paid the ultimate price on the end of his dagger, and the lesson had not been lost on the rest of the company. Mindful of his dark side, she decided to rein in her curiosity and hold her tongue for now.

Edmund bade them sit and join him in some refreshment. Kate, loath though she was to sup with a man she strongly suspected of being her father's murderer, was far too hungry to refuse. In any case any intended escape plan would fall flat were she to faint from lack of food. At a nod from Edmund, his serjeant placed two wooden chairs behind Kate and Jane and pushed them firmly, but not roughly, into their seats. The serjeant then retired to resume his duties about the camp; after all, what harm could a pair of fifteen-year-old girls do?

Another nod from Edmund and his French girl, whose name was Ysabel, took her place by his side, silently distributing the cheese, meat, bread and wine very much, it seemed to Kate, in the capacity of hostess rather than servant.

As they ate and drank, Edmund began to recount both the story of his early life and the events following the Yorkist collapse at Ludlow. Kate was stunned into silence as she listened in horror, disbelief and fascination at the narrative unfolding from his lips. She did not know how much of what he told her was true. Could he really be her half-brother? Could the father she loved have behaved in such a dishonourable way? But her father was now dead and it was clear that if her brother fell into Edmund's clutches, he would be too. God only knew what lay in store for Kate and her mother. She would grieve for her father later. Right now she had to find her brother.

Edmund, by now almost swept away in self-congratulation, delivered the final shock to Kate. He spread out his right hand and began to slide it slowly across the table towards her. She started at the sight of the ring on his little finger. Her father's seal ring! All his estate business was validated by pressing the family design, a beautiful seated greyhound surrounded by rose briars, into the hot, soft wax. It was the cornerstone of all the Wardlow dealings and this murderer had no right to wear it. Edmund saw the horror in her eyes. Leaning forward he said, in a tone of controlled anger. "See the motto on your father's seal - *'prudentia'*? It means discretion. It is a pity he did not exercise more of it with regard to my mother. Had he done so he might still be alive."

It was the final straw for Kate. In less than a heartbeat she snatched up the needle-like, bone-handled pricker she had been using to spear her food and, with tears in her eyes, brought it stabbing down with all her might towards the back of Edmund's hand. He reacted instantly, withdrawing from the danger with the speed of a snake, but he was not quick enough to prevent the sharp, narrow awl from pinning him to the table through the web of skin between his thumb and index finger. Shoving back her chair so that it fell over, she grabbed Jane by the hand and made a run for it as fast as her skirts would allow. Forty paces from the white-faced Edmund, who was still nailed to the table, she paused momentarily and gave a shrill whistle using her fingers. Then she ran for her life again, saying a little prayer to herself.

It was answered. By the greatest good fortune her father's warhorse had not been secured; rather, it had been the subject of a great deal of attention and had, with some difficulty, been led up and down in front of the admiring soldiers while they offered their professional and not-so-professional opinions as to its worth. On hearing its mistress, the horse immediately reared up on its hind legs, kicking out at the face of the man holding its reins and killing him instantly. The crowd around it attempted to flee as it accelerated towards the source of the whistle, knocking several of them flying.

On hearing the commotion and the ever-closer hoofbeats Kate's heart thumped wildly. She risked another stop and looked round to see her beloved mount sliding to a halt a few yards away. Within seconds, she and Jane had flung themselves over its broad back and were holding on for all they were worth as they sped away from the camp. Some of the soldiers prepared to give chase but the serjeant with the scar barked out. "Let them go. We can't hope to catch a horse like that. We can deal with them later."

One of the soldiers had nocked and drawn an arrow but just before he loosed it at what any archer knew was the easy target - the horse – the serjeant struck him on the arm, deflecting the viciously barbed missile to bury itself in a nearby tree.

"Our master will surely seek redress for his injury, but even if it allowed us to secure those who hurt him I dare say he would not thank the man who put a hole in a fifty pound horse."

Half a dozen troopers further down the line had vaulted onto their mounts and begun to chase after the girls. The serjeant was impressed by their enthusiasm but secretly doubted they would ride down their quarry.

*Little bitches!* He thought to himself as the girls disappeared from view. *And to think I almost felt sorry for you. God help you when my master finds you...*

# CHAPTER FOURTEEN

K ATE SPURRED her father's horse on as never before, as though the very Devil himself were hot on their heels. Dirt and leaves flew up behind her mount as its huge, iron-shod hooves beat a thunderous tattoo along the narrow woodland track. Behind her, in the distance, she could hear the angry shouts and curses of her pursuers. She felt shaky and giddy, terrified of the consequences of being overhauled and recaptured. On and on they went, the huge, powerful warhorse thumping along the forest road while the two girls hung on for grim death.

As they rounded a bend in the track, momentarily out of sight of the soldiers, Kate suddenly spied a smaller path going off to her left. Its entrance had been barred by the trunk of a fallen tree - clearly some time ago, as bushes had sprouted up around it almost hiding it from view altogether. Encouraging Rollo with a dig of her heels and a slap of the reins, they soared over the obstacle, then continued pell-mell along the narrow, overgrown track, the overhanging branches whipping at their heads and arms.

After what seemed like a heart-pounding eternity she felt Jane thumping her frantically on the shoulder and in a cross between a shout and a whisper saying, *"They're not coming any more Kate! I think we've lost them. Thank God! I think we got away!"*

Kate eased off and gradually allowed the panting, foaming horse to slow down to a walk, its flanks sheened with sweat. She stole a glance behind and saw that they were, indeed, alone. The girls looked around for any clues as to their whereabouts. The forest had by now closed in considerably, the trees only a few feet from the track on either side, robbing the afternoon of what light there was. Their hearts began to sink at the thought of going deeper and deeper into the gloom and becoming utterly lost, but eventually, to their great relief, the woods opened out again. A few minutes later they came to a wide, shallow stream.

"Why don't we follow it?" suggested Jane. It proved to be a sound move. Normally a ford is met when the road reaches a stream, but in the girls' case they followed the stream until they reached a road that cut across it; a fairly well-travelled road by the look of it. Kate mentally tossed a coin to decide on a direction, then steered Rollo to the right of the crossing and up and out of the water.

"Now what?" she said, but Jane did not have an answer for her. The two friends looked at each other, their expressions betraying their fear. In her all-consuming haste to distance herself from Edmund's inevitable, and doubtless painful, reprisal Kate had sped off not knowing where she was headed. It was entirely likely that Edmund and his followers now lay between them and safety.

# CHAPTER FIFTEEN

NOT LONG after Richard Wardlow and his small retinue had struck out for home they encountered five more stragglers, swelling the little band to twelve. In the early stages of their flight from Ludlow all the men had constantly been looking over their shoulders, deliberately avoiding settlements and main roads. But by and by they had realised that they were not being pursued, after which they found the going much easier on their nerves. The village folk they encountered seemed to exhibit little knowledge of, or interest in, the events of Ludlow and therefore offered them the same hospitality they would to any travellers in need, especially ones with coins in their purses and halfway decent manners.

The remaining eight liveried men however - the rest of Sir Geoffrey's ten fully-trained household soldiers - had had a nasty scare as a result of attempting to escape from the field in a large group and not hiding their distinctive dark blue jackets bearing a silver greyhound on the breast and back. They had realised the day was lost and had begun to make their way out of Ludlow but in the dark and confusion, in addition to becoming separated from the rest of the Wardlow party, they had become disoriented in the poorly-lit, narrow streets and were actually heading straight for the advancing Lancastrian army. It was, ironically, upon realising their mistake, and almost reaching the protection of the darkness on the edge of town, that they stumbled upon a scouting party of liveried men, numbering slightly more than their own.

These were clearly on the King's side, judging from the way they were applying themselves to broaching a large cask of ale, presumably pillaged from some nearby inn. It was becoming obvious to Sir Geoffrey's men that the gentle townsfolk of Ludlow were in for a rough night if the lack of discipline shown by this dozen rowdy, drunken and, above all, armed retainers - who probably felt cheated of a good fight after the Yorkist forces had dissolved into the night - was anything to go by...

Tom Linley, the serjeant in charge of Sir Geoffrey's men and the oldest, most experienced member of the group, whispered to his companions that he intended to try to bluff his way through. After all, if the men they were about to face were some of the levies that made up a large portion of each army – not regular soldiers but men hastily recruited along the way, issued with a distinguishing jacket, a helmet and a weapon, but given little or no serious training – it was unlikely they would be familiar with every single livery badge arrayed on the field that day. Nevertheless, it would require a good deal of nerve. Tom steeled himself before moving confidently into the flickering light of the street lanterns.

"Worked up a thirst trying to find some Yorkists to fight, lads?" he called in passing, keeping up a useful, but not suspicious, pace.

The largest, fattest and most obnoxious-looking of the revellers, presumably their serjeant, turned towards him on hearing his cheery address and belched loudly. "Cowards all of 'em! My boys have marched all the way from Chester just to crack a few rebels' skulls and what do we find? The dogs have all run back to their bitch mothers with their tails between their legs! Well, we shall not be denied *some* satisfaction. We intend to grab our share of booze, booty and any young lasses we take a fancy to. Especially young lasses... We'll give them a victory celebration to remember, eh lads, just like the last lot we wooed. Didn't hear any of *them* complain after we'd finished!". His men grunted their lecherous agreement to this last statement.

"This miserable town is ours tonight along with every woman, every drop of ale and every piece of silver in it and damnation to anyone who gets in our way!"

Tom shuddered inwardly as he thought of the fate of any unfortunate young women who might have fallen into the clutches of these animals, and the horrors that lay ahead that night for the local inhabitants at the hands of an inebriated occupying army. There was little he could do to help the majority of the townsfolk, but spoiling the enjoyment of this vile band supping and jeering in front of him would lessen their suffering just a little.

The stout serjeant suddenly eyed Tom and his small band with a measure of suspicion, fearing perhaps that they had designs on their barrel of ale. Even if they had been convinced by Tom's confident manner that he and his group were on their side, they were thirsty men and did not feel inclined to share their liquid loot. In a tone that Tom felt compelled him to stop or be unmasked, the fat man shouted, "And from where might you and your worthy companions have travelled? I do not recall seeing your greyhound badge among the King's followers."

"Nor I yours, my good and loyal friend..." - the words stuck in Tom's throat as the man was clearly the worst kind of pig - "to be sure there was much confusion on the field today and we regret the flight of our quarry as keenly as you."

Tom felt a bead of sweat trickle down his temple as the fat man fixed him with an unfocused glare, swaying unsteadily on ale-sodden feet. If it came to a fight, he thought, at least his men had the advantage of sobriety, even if outnumbered. In an instant, his worst fears were realised.

"I don't like the look of you. You don't fit right. What do you reckon lads?" said the fat man to his comrades without turning round to face them.

Five or six of the dozen ransackers turned at his words, hands reaching towards scabbards.

"Now!" hissed Tom "Kill them all, kill the looting scum!", deftly drawing his short, straight archer's sword, lunging forward and ramming it with all his might into the repulsive fat man's belly before the latter could unsheathe his weapon. As soon as the serjeant's grotesquely contorted face told him the sword had done its work, he braced the palm of his right hand on the dying man's shoulder and smartly withdrew his blade, looking about him for the next target. He took heart from the sight of his companions getting stuck into the looting party with bloody zeal. If they were to escape the bounds of this ill-fated town with their lives it could only be by fighting their way out.

A sudden chill breeze sprang up, momentarily flaring the street lanterns and illuminating the desperate scene as man battled against man in a brutal hand-to-hand struggle. Steel rang on steel, and shouts and screams, grunts and groans were heard in the near darkness as swords and daggers, fists, feet and falchions found their marks.

Outnumbered though they were, Tom's party had one vital advantage – at the ripe old age of fifty-five their leader was a veteran of the wars in France. Tom had experienced at first-hand the horrors of close-quarter combat and had taught Sir Geoffrey's men well, training them to act quickly as a small but cohesive force and to deal out death with practised efficiency. He had even survived capture by the French, including their barbaric practice of cutting off the first three fingers of the right hand of any archer they found, thus depriving them of the means of drawing a bowstring. What his captors had failed to realise, however, was that Tom was left-handed, so once his wounds had healed and he had found a way of working round his handicap using a leather strap to lash the bow to his wrist, he was still able to send a shaft flying fast and true when the need arose.

Now, he was fighting his own countrymen and by the way their opponents were falling around them Tom's gamble had proved correct – the recently deceased fat "captain" and his band of looters were raw levies, recruited in a hurry with minimal training and no experience of actual fighting other than the unseemly scuffles that were an inescapable part of daily life in these lawless times. No doubt they had been motivated by talk of plunder; always, as Tom himself knew, considered a legitimate bonus on top of a soldier's basic, but often irregular, pay.

But this was *England,* home to both sides in this politically motivated conflict. It was bad enough, Tom thought, for countryman to have to face countryman on the field of battle, but when an out-of-control, armed, *English* rabble took to spoiling and pillaging an *English* town and terrorising innocent *English* folk things had come to a pretty pass indeed.

It was for this reason that Tom, in particular, hacked his way through the looters, Englishmen or not, like an avenging angel, his disgust at what he had seen proving ample justification for breaking the sixth commandment.

The melee was over in minutes. Twelve of what could loosely have been called "the King's men" lay dead, dying or badly wounded. Of Sir Geoffrey's retinue most had but minor cuts and bruises. Only one, Sam Wright, who at sixteen was the youngest and currently acting as Richard's squire, had sustained what might pass as a proper injury, having taken a hefty clout to the face with the knuckle guard of a sword. He was bleeding and could hardly stand, but his comrades supported him on either side and helped him along until he could regain his wits. There was a moment of silence as the group dumbly surveyed the bodies strewn in the narrow, dimly lit street. Apart from Tom no-one had killed a man before, and every member of the party wondered what repercussions the night's actions might have for their eternal souls. But then, as one, and full of new-found respect, they turned their awestruck gaze towards Tom. Old Tom, the war veteran, who had bullied the defenders of the Wardlow estate through endless exhausting training sessions. Old Tom whose name they had cursed when they went home tired, aching and bruised after a hard day's mock fighting and weapons drill. Old Tom who now stood before them, the blood of three men dripping from the blade of his short sword. Their worshipful reverie was cut short by the distant sounds of men on the move – distant, but getting closer. Tom wiped the blood from his blade on the clothes of one of the fallen, sheathing it with a chillingly slick, practised motion and pointing to the far end of the street, "This way!"

# CHAPTER SIXTEEN

IT HAD turned distinctly chilly. Large drops of rain had begun to beat down upon Kate's head and, as her father's horse continued at a steady pace to nowhere in particular, she quickly became soaked to the skin. Turning round in the saddle, she glanced at Jane who was just as bedraggled, tired and cold as Kate herself. They needed to find shelter and, as Kate's stomach gave a painful and audible rumble, she wished she had grabbed some food before their flight from Edmund's camp.

The light was failing – it must be late afternoon, thought Kate, as the woods either side of the route began to fill with sounds different from the familiar daytime ones. Raindrops showered down from the gloomy, leaden sky, trickling steadily down both girls' necks, but the screeches of hunting owls chilled Kate more than the developing downpour.

Her hands felt frozen to the reins. Her clothes, heavy and waterlogged, clung to her shivering body. Kate could feel Jane trembling behind her as her friend gripped her waist tightly. Their situation was desperate - both girls had given up any hope of seeing home again. They trudged on, water running down their faces and dripping from their chins.

Then, eventually, as the trees began to thin, Kate made out through the gloom a short, square stone tower. A church! Shelter at least, and possibly a measure of safety. Kate's soul filled with relief, and, with what strength she had left, she guided her mount towards the welcome sanctuary.

Reaching the porch, the girls dismounted stiffly, Kate securing the reins around a small tree low enough for Rollo to graze, patting his neck and whispering words of thanks in his wet ear as she did so. Then, holding each other for support, the two exhausted companions stumbled over the threshold and leaned on the heavy oak door. To their infinite relief it opened with a loud creak. They made their way slowly to the back of the building and collapsed on the cold, hard floor.

Overcome with weariness, Jane snuggled up beside Kate and was soon asleep. Though Kate's eyes were heavy with fatigue, her brain, relentlessly replaying the day's events, would not let her rest. So much had happened in such a short space of time; so much loss, so much pain. She lay there numb, listening to Jane's steady breathing and the night noises.

The rain still hammered on the church roof. It was only a poor, simple building, but at the far end stood the altar, the symbolic portal through which the priest communed with God. It was to this humble altar that Kate now crawled, having gently extricated herself from Jane's sleepy embrace, placing her friend's head on her folded cape. As she reached it she fell to the floor, stretching out her arms towards the sacred table in an unspoken appeal. As her emotions finally overwhelmed her and a single, racking sob escaped her, the hot tears that coursed down her pale face mingled with the cold rain dripping from her bedraggled hair. Shaking with hunger and exhaustion, Kate wept as she silently prayed for a world she had lost forever.

# CHAPTER SEVENTEEN

"*QUE PENSES-TU, mon beau chevalier?*" asked Ysabel, Edmund's young French companion, idly twirling her long black hair with an elegant, slender finger as she sat opposite him at the eating table, which had been moved inside the tent when the rain had started late in the afternoon. He retorted with a look of feigned disapproval which made the beautiful fifteen-year-old giggle. Wagging the index finger of his left hand he said with mock gravity, "No French to be spoken now my love – very soon you will be the consort of an English gentleman and mistress of a fine estate. You must promise to practice extra hard so that when we receive King Henry and his entourage they will think you the most perfect English lady they have ever seen."

Ysabel responded by leaning across the table, sliding her hands behind Edmund's ears so she could draw his face close to hers, and kissing him lightly on the lips. "If it please you my Lord", she whispered, while Edmund, his eyes closed, smiled to himself both at her delicious French accent and her feigned acquiescence.

As she sat down he opened his eyes again and looked the girl straight in the face, remembering her initial query. "What am I thinking my love? I am thinking that there is one little English *bitch* I would like to see dancing on the end of a rope as payment for *this,*" and here he examined his injured right hand, surveying the dark red stain that had seeped through the bandage, flexing his fingers and wincing at the sudden stab of pain. He looked across at his friend Girard, who had joined them for supper. Girard had been out with a hunting and foraging party for most of the day and had therefore missed the arrival - and the sudden, dramatic departure - of the two girls, not to mention Edmund's painful injury.

"That's the second time a member of that wretched family has stuck me, is it not, comrade?" he hissed. Girard nodded his silent acknowledgement, his expression serious.

"And now it is high time I paid them back!" Spitting the words out like a mouthful of sour wine, he grabbed a slender eating knife from the table with his good hand and brought it slamming down, burying the point a full inch into the wood. Ysabel quickly got up from her seat and went round to crouch at Edmund's side, putting one arm around his shoulders and a cool, comforting hand upon the arm that was clutching the buried blade. Edmund looked into her eyes for a few moments, then began to relax his tensed muscles. He made a motion to stroke her hair with his right hand but remembered with a disgusted grimace the blood seeping through the bandage and aborted the gesture, staring at his hand hovering a few inches from the girl's head as if he didn't quite know what to do with it. Eventually he lowered it gently to the table, letting out a slow, laboured breath through clenched teeth. Girard topped up Edmund's wine and slid the goblet towards his friend. Edmund favoured him with a taut but sincere smile, then took a deep draught, draining the cup in one. He motioned to Ysabel to pour them all some more wine and retake her seat. As he stared out of the tent at the rain falling steadily from a rapidly darkening evening sky, he began to replay in his mind the events that had accompanied his first encounter with a Wardlow.

"Make yourself comfortable my love. I shall tell you the story of how Girard and I fought our first battle..."

# CHAPTER EIGHTEEN

FOUR YEARS prior to the Yorkist army's disorderly flight from Ludlow that October night, King Henry's Lancastrian forces had clashed in earnest for the first time with supporters of the Duke of York in the narrow streets of St. Albans. By the sunset of 22nd May 1455, blood had been spilled and lives had been lost. Not many lives, it was true, but countryman had taken up arms against countryman and Englishman had slain Englishman. Even the King had sustained a slight wound, much to everyone's dismay.

The main business of the day, however, had been the settling of old political scores. While the Duke of York, the Earl of Salisbury and his son the Earl of Warwick survived the proceedings to protest their undying devotion to the King - despite the fact they had been fighting against him only hours before - the battered corpses of the Earl of Somerset, the Earl of Northumberland and Lord Clifford were being taken away for burial, their heads caved in with axes and their bodies pierced with swords and bills after a brave but doomed sally from the temporary protection of a small inn.

Among those present on the King's side had been a tall, dark-haired young man in his twenty-first year. He was a young man with a burning desire for retribution and moral justice, a young man whose mother had known disgrace and low work and whose premature death had left him alone in the world nine years earlier. He was also a young man who had inherited a tidy fortune and could afford to employ many pairs of eyes and ears to monitor any interesting developments in England, political or otherwise, that might further his plan to exchange his comfortable wine merchant's house in Calais for a fine country estate.

At that crucial time, Edmund could only muster six reliable companions to stand by him at St Albans. The oldest had been his great-uncle's servant and a veteran of the wars against the English; the others were two wild, adventurous drinking companions of his own age, with whom he had begun to enjoy the various pleasures his great-uncle's money could bring, and three brutally violent former English Free Company soldiers on a wage that ensured their loyalty.

In the months leading up to the battle, Edmund had learned, through his well-organised intelligence network, of the polarisation of the factions at King Henry's court and the simmering resentment felt by the Duke of York towards his bitterest rival for the King's goodwill, the Duke of Somerset. Knowing of his father's long and close association with York, Edmund listened and waited, positively *willing* the tense political situation to boil over into armed conflict so that he could use the situation as the perfect cover for bringing about his father's destruction.

In order to succeed, his plan required an unfeasible number of chances, possibilities, probabilities and coincidences to come together in one unlikely whole. He was, however, so utterly single-minded that he constantly looked beyond any obstacles, difficulties or disappointments, always believing fervently that the right time would one day come...

He had not for one moment, for example, considered what would happen if the Yorkist faction won some pivotal battle, taking control of, or even killing, the King and thus placing his father beyond reach on the winning side. Nor had he thought for a second of the possibility of his own bloody demise were his plan to reach its ultimate objective – an armed confrontation, one-on-one, with his father.

Edmund was indeed hoping for that heroic, but unlikely, situation so beloved of writers of legends and tales of war and adventure to arise – that somehow in the crowded, noisy confusion of battle he would find his father, deliver a damning indictment regarding Sir Geoffrey's cowardly desertion of his mother and then kill him in personal combat. *Killing him legally as an enemy of the King.*

This last part was hugely important to Edmund. With current political tensions promising to provide the perfect excuse for such an act, he would not have to risk having his father murdered by paid agents – something he could have ordered at any time but was unwilling to sanction. Sir Geoffrey was an important, well-connected figure and any underhand attempt on his life in peacetime carried the certainty of a thorough investigation that might easily lead to the door of a certain wine merchant's house. Fortunately, Edmund was a very patient man.

# CHAPTER NINETEEN

"MASTER RICHARD!"

Tom Linley, beaming with relief, his desperate escape from Ludlow suddenly just a memory, broke away from his men and began jogging towards the boy he had protected since the day Sir Geoffrey had first held the new-born child aloft for his tenants and servants to see. Richard turned around to face the owner of the familiar voice but something in his expression and the set of his shoulders made Tom slacken his pace. The leader of the Wardlows' household men came to a halt five yards from the boy, reading his eyes, his heart beginning to sink. He looked around the dozen-strong group with whom they had just been re-united. Where was Sir Geoffrey?

Richard seemed unable to speak but Tom, now looking at the faces of the men who had been travelling with Richard, guessed something serious had happened. Sensing that his young master would not relish retelling the story of his father's murder, Peter Gamlyn, one of Richard's travelling companions and a trained household soldier, took Tom to one side and broke the news to his serjeant. "Aye, Tom, cold blooded murder it was. Must've been an awful shock for the poor lad to see it at first hand, and him all alone at the time too. He says there's fully three-score of 'em, all handy-looking villains and probably headed for the estate as far as he can make out. But he says they wear no badges so who they are we cannot tell. It goes without saying we're all behind the young master but when we think about losing Sir Geoffrey it's like we've all had our guts ripped out, and even if our homes and families are at risk nevertheless our strength is no match for theirs."

Tom listened to the whole sorry tale, finally giving Peter a heavy nod of acknowledgement. Then he walked slowly away from the group to give himself space to think, time to digest the indigestible.

He paused briefly to place a firm, comforting hand on Richard's shoulder, giving the boy a look of silent, heartfelt pity. He carried on, climbing a little way up the high ridge of the Clwydian Hills to the east, his body language indicating to the others that he needed a few moments alone.

He gazed out over the flat, lush pastures that lay bordering the gently flowing River Clwyd, to the town of Denbigh, just visible in the distance. As he took in the peaceful scene, he turned the circumstances of Sir Geoffrey's death over and over in his mind. Each time, he reached the same conclusion; each time, he confirmed his initial suspicion. Sir Geoffrey's past had caught up with him and killed him. He couldn't be completely certain, however, until he knew more. He would have to be very sure of his facts before he shared his dead master's dark secret with Richard.

Tom's was now a heavy burden. As serjeant of the household men it fell to him to organise the defence – or recapture, depending on who got there first – of the estate. As a close personal friend and long-time servant of Sir Geoffrey, he also had a sworn duty to protect the interests of his dead master's widow and children. *His widow...* God's blood! It would doubtless be Tom who would have to break the news of Sir Geoffrey's death to Ann Wardlow. He feared it would send her mad.

He let out a long, deep breath through clenched teeth, slowly shaking his head and turning his gaze skyward, where he was afforded a brief distraction from his worries as his eyes followed the stately progress of a red kite quartering its hunting grounds.

"Oh, to be in your place, my friend, and you in mine! The troubles in men's hearts weigh them down so that they can never soar above the hills and know true freedom".

"Men are condemned to fight for their freedom, Tom," Richard added, having joined him on the gorse-covered hillside.

"It's your mother I fear for most," said Tom, shading his eyes with one hand as the red kite flew towards the sun. As the bird finally became lost to sight Tom lowered his arm and turned to face the boy. "She will take it the hardest of all".

"I know Tom, I know," said Richard, his tone heavy with the weight of responsibility that had landed on his young shoulders over the past week.

"What do I do now, Tom? Everybody is looking to me to come up with some inspired plan to save the estate, if that is where those murderers are headed. But all I can think about is whether my mother and sister are safe and how I am going to break the news to them."

"Don't fret lad," said Tom. "I was proud to have served your father and now my duty is to you and your family. We shall do whatever it takes to preserve what is rightfully yours."

Richard acknowledged the old serjeant's pledge with a solemn nod of his head, then his expression became troubled. "Rightfully mine..." he said, as if unsure. "Tom, what do you know about attainder?"

Tom had heard of it, certainly, and as his mind sifted through what he knew of it, his brain trying to calculate the implications, a creeping cold began to grip his body. The serjeant's heart leapt into his mouth.

"God's teeth!"

Richard started in alarm at Tom's exclamation.

"Forgive me lad, it was nothing," Tom said, his first thought being to shield the boy from further upset, but he realised that if

Richard knew a word like attainder he probably had a passable idea of its meaning.

"It's all right Tom you don't have to hide anything from me. I thought about it a lot on the way here. Do you think they'll do it? Take away the estate I mean?"

"I don't know," replied Tom, gravely shaking his head. It was clear his new master understood the risk his father had taken in supporting the Duke of York. Sir Geoffrey had already paid with his life for his stand against the King - rough justice indeed - but had he lived he might well have found himself attainted; a punishment almost as harsh, by which a man's property and wealth were seized by the Crown, his name dishonoured and the line of inheritance declared void, thus denying his sons and their sons their rights ever-after and effectively reducing the offender and his family to beggars.

"And if the King doesn't steal away my inheritance, that murdering *bastard* and his pack of dogs probably will! Who is he Tom? Why did he hold such a grudge against my father? I've been racking my brains but I just cannot fathom what is going on."

Tom hesitated briefly, wondering if he should tell the boy what he knew, then replied. "That I cannot answer, Master Richard. All I know is we would do well to take stock of our situation, then make all haste homewards if our endeavours are to succeed. We need to find a horse and send a messenger on ahead to warn our folk."

The two men surveyed the group on the road below, silently making an inventory. All the horses, tethered well back from the fighting lines for safety, had been left behind in the rapid, chaotic departure from Ludlow - a very serious loss to be sure - but desperate men with families and homes to protect could make fifteen miles a day on foot if they had to. Of the ten trained men, four had carried longbows when they set out, three crossbows, the remainder bills, but these unwieldy weapons had been discarded during the escape, being of limited use in the narrow streets of the town and awkward to carry when running for their lives. Richard himself had thrown down his pollaxe before he had turned to flee, lightening his load by half a stone.

The eight who had been involved in the hand-to-hand fighting in Ludlow still wore their padded jacks, breast- and back-plates, and open-faced helmets. The other two had thrown their helmets and plates into a ditch to facilitate flight and were now feeling somewhat naked beside their comrades-in-arms.

Thankfully everyone had kept their side arms - short sword or falchion, dagger and buckler – but for Richard the bitterest blow was having to leave behind some of his plate armour. It had been a gift from his father on his sixteenth birthday, Sir Geoffrey having waited until the boy's growth spurt had finished before commissioning a full harness in the Milanese style. Armour was very dear – the whole thing from top to toe had cost over thirteen pounds – and it had broken Richard's heart when he had been forced to discard the pieces that would impede his progress as he made his way back from Ludlow on foot. Initially, lacking Sam, his young squire, Richard had been unable to reach many of the straps and buckles holding the various parts in place, hence his flight from the town and the precarious climb up the ladder in the church tower had been undertaken bearing the weight of full harness. He had thanked God that night that none of the rungs had been rotten. Assisted in their removal the following day by John Stotherd and his wife, he had left them carefully oiled and wrapped in the custody of Father William against his eventual return, intending to bring them home along with his father's body, though when that would be only God in his wisdom knew.

Richard had kept the breast- and back-plates, including the fauld at the front and the culet at the rear to protect his lower parts, and had clung to his elegantly simple, Italian-made visored sallet as though it were life itself. But the greaves, poleyns, cuisses and tassets which guarded his legs, the upper and lower cannons and couters that covered his arms, and the ingenious overlapping pauldrons that protected his shoulders, although cleverly designed and fully articulated for fighting, had nevertheless proved too cumbersome and impractical for the long journey and had, with great reluctance, been left behind. On top of the death of his father, the loss of such expensive and sentimental items, even though only temporary, weighed heavily on the boy. But Richard had hardened over the past few days and it was with a determined look in his eye that he turned to his father's serjeant – *his* serjeant now – and said in a firm, commanding tone, "Come, Tom, we have homes to save!"

# CHAPTER TWENTY

"OWWWW, MY neck!" Jane's plaintive cry rang round the cold, stony nave of the small church upon whose Spartan, comfortless floor she and Kate Wardlow had spent the night. Remembering she was in a sacred place, she quickly clapped her hand over her mouth to avoid any further unseemly disturbance. Sitting up and rubbing the offending area Jane looked around for her mistress and friend, her eyes eventually lighting on a crumpled form just below the altar. With her concern outweighing her discomfort, Jane walked stiffly to where her companion lay, ashen-faced, almost as if in death, one arm outstretched toward the holy table. It was with great relief that she observed Kate's slow, rhythmic breathing. Bending down, she touched her friend gently on the shoulder and whispered her name.

Kate gradually stirred, her sleep-bleared eyes eventually focusing on Jane's anxious face. She accepted the outstretched hands and rose unsteadily to her feet, her mind still deeply troubled by the previous day's events.

"We must find something to eat," said Jane. "We're both fit to drop. Then there's poor Rollo." She had barely finished speaking when the two girls heard a man's voice just the other side of the church door. They froze in terror.

*"God help us, it's them! They've found us!"* hissed Kate, grabbing Jane by the shoulders, a wild look in her eyes.

"Quick, the tower!" said Jane, pointing to a small door at the west end of the church. But it was too late. As they turned to make a desperate dash for safety, there was the click of a heavy latch and the main door creaked open, silhouetting the outline of a heavily-built man against the morning light.

It was all or nothing now. Kate may have been exhausted but she would go down fighting. Goodness alone knew what terrible vengeance Edmund and his band of thugs planned to reap for what she had done, but she would not surrender to it while she had breath in her body. Seizing a heavy brass candleholder she squared up to the intruder. "Do not come any closer! I claim the protection of the church for myself and my friend. If you harm us you will be damned".

Jane armed herself in similar fashion and took up a determined stance beside her friend. Kate hefted her makeshift weapon to show she meant business.

The shadowy figure stopped in its tracks, clearly stunned by the girls' warlike overtures. Kate's threatening gesture caused the man to start back in what appeared to be a most unsoldierly manner, turning on his heels and running out into the graveyard. This was not the kind of reaction she would have expected from one of Edmund's godless ruffians – far from it – and she shot a quizzical glance at Jane. Her companion looked equally perplexed but both girls maintained a state of high alert, fearing for their lives.

Hearts pounding, bodies quivering, they advanced hesitantly towards the door, convinced that at any moment their adversary would regain his courage, returning with reinforcements to hack them to pieces in a house of God.

# CHAPTER TWENTY-ONE

KATE AND Jane stood frozen to the spot, five yards from the church door, nerves taut as bowstrings, every fibre of their bodies straining to hear what was going on outside. The fleeing intruder's footsteps rapidly receded into the distance, then, after what seemed like a lifetime, two sets could be heard coming back towards the church – slow, deliberate, wary steps. The terrified girls looked at each other and nodded. They took up positions out of sight, either side of the main door, shaking with fear, brass candle holders raised above their heads ready to brain the first two men that set foot inside, sacred ground or not. The footsteps stopped just outside the church porch. A tense, whispered conversation was going on but the girls could not hear what was being said. Then, suddenly, a firm, deep voice. "I ask that you give yourselves up without violence. Please surrender your weapons and come to the door where we can see you."

Kate thought the use of the word "please" by one of Edmund's followers was out of character to say the least, although his scarred serjeant had been surprisingly well-spoken. The girls remained silent, holding their breath, and their candle holders, all the more tightly. Die here, thought Kate, rather than be paraded and humiliated before the nightmare band of ruffians, until her father's murderer took his revenge. Five agonising minutes passed.

"In the name of God the Holy Father I command you to lay down your weapons and step forward peacefully."

Jane, confused, looked across at Kate, but she, sensing a trick, shook her head firmly. Again, the firm, deep voice. "In God's name I shall enter my own church. If you would strike down a servant of the Lord, you shall face damnation in the hereafter."

The smallest doubt now crept into Kate's mind. What if it really were the local priest, come to prepare his house of worship for the day? On the other hand, she and Jane still clung on to the element of surprise – a very significant advantage for a pair of slightly-built fifteen-year-old girls who might have to fight for their lives against hardened killers. She decided to wait…

# CHAPTER TWENTY-TWO

EDMUND HELD out his silver goblet for Ysabel to refill then waited until she was seated beside him once more. He looked at her face for a few moments, watching the reflected torchlight dancing in her eyes, then concentrated his gaze on a knot in the wood of the table as he resumed his battle narrative.

Since the late summer of 1453, Richard Plantagenet, Duke of York, had been ruling the country as its chosen Protector while King Henry had been ill, unable to move or speak due to a sickness of the mind. During his time in power, York had been able to redress some of the wrongs done him by the inept monarch and his self-seeking counsellors. His bitterest rival, the Earl of Somerset, had been placed in the Tower awaiting trial for his misconduct of military affairs in France, while Parliament was now packed with York's supporters.

The Duke had also formed a powerful and mutually beneficial alliance with the wealthy and influential Neville family, principally the Earl of Salisbury and his son, the Earl of Warwick. It seemed that York's star was at last in the ascendant, but then, in January 1455, disaster struck: the King recovered.

Even a Parliament filled with York's friends felt disinclined to deny the anointed monarch his right to rule now that he was well again, thus Somerset, Henry's favourite, was released from the Tower within a month of the King regaining control. He immediately set about forming powerful alliances of his own, aligning himself squarely behind King Henry and his formidable queen, Margaret. The Queen had no love for York – he was of royal birth, with a strong claim to the throne, and she feared that one day he might try to wrest the crown from her new-born son, Edward. As a result of Somerset's political machinations, York and his allies found their positions in London becoming untenable. They withdrew to their northern heartlands, enlisting support against what they felt would be an inevitable attempt to overthrow them.

Having gathered a sizeable army – among them Sir Geoffrey Wardlow and the pick of his household men, but not thirteen-year-old Richard – York and his supporters marched on London to present their case against Somerset in a rather more forceful manner. York, as always, had no desire to fight the King. He sought only to dislodge Somerset as the over-rewarded court favourite and to see him justly punished for his part in the shameful loss of English possessions in Normandy, one of the lowest points of which had been Somerset's personal surrender of the city of Rouen to the French.

It was a measure of the scheming Earl's influence with the King that he had survived this long despite his record of incompetence. Even the loftiest of nobles had cause to fear public opinion as was sharply demonstrated five years earlier, when angry commoners had intercepted the Duke of Suffolk in the English Channel as he tried to escape the country. He, too, had exhibited a woeful lack of ability, backbone or honour during the final years of the war with France. No formal trial for Suffolk, though, just a blow to the back of the neck from a rusty sword on the deck of a ship, his headless corpse dumped on a Kentish beach.

Somerset was caught out by York's sudden advance on London. Clearly his much-vaunted intelligence network had let him down and it was a hastily-recruited army of no more than around two thousand men that hurried northwards through the May sunshine to ensure that any clash of arms happened at a safe distance from the capital.

The King himself was at the head of this force and, on arriving at the town of St Albans, he had the royal standard raised in the main square to show he would fight if necessary, though as a deeply religious man he much preferred negotiating to spilling blood. Some of his soldiers took up defensive positions at the town's gates and along the town's defensive ditch, while Henry remained in the square with the majority of the men.

The Yorkist army, superior in numbers by another thousand, arrived at about the same time, arranging itself along a low ridge to the east of the town. The Duke sent several messengers to the King demanding that he surrender Somerset to him, but each time the King flatly refused, threatening to hang, draw and quarter any who drew a weapon against their sovereign. Thus it was that negotiations crumbled and battle was joined.

The young Edmund of Calais, outwardly composed but secretly beside himself with excitement at the thought of his first battle and a chance - albeit a slender one – to bring down his father, had attached his small entourage to the Lancastrian force stationed in Shropshire Lane, at one of the gated entrances to the town. From this exposed position, in front and to the left of the King's position, he hoped to see, and become involved in, as much of the action as possible.

Fortunately for Edmund, his network of spies had been considerably more efficient than the Earl of Somerset's. The information they sent back to Calais enabled him to plan his short voyage to England and his subsequent rapid advance to join the royal army on its march northwards, almost as if he had had a crystal ball. Edmund believed in paying handsomely for a job well done and his informers had certainly kept him up-to-date with regard to the rapidly unfolding events which led to the encounter at St Albans. He had even been able to predict the precise day on which the two sides would reach the town.

Edmund was impatient for action. His two drinking companions, Bertran and Girard, were equally excited at the prospect of a fight and cheerfully oblivious to the physical dangers they would face. His great-uncle's servant and the three former Free Company soldiers regarded the younger men, accoutred as they were in expensive armour and bearing well-crafted weapons, with concealed disdain. They were certainly appreciative of the generous, and regular, wages paid them by their youthful patron, but neither he nor his cockscomb friends had ever stared war straight in its brutal, ugly face. They doubted any of *them* would live to see the sun set that day.

The Bastard of Calais cut an impressive figure nevertheless. He had so far spent only a fraction of his great-uncle's fortune, but he had spent it wisely. He was encased *cap-à-pie* in the latest smoothly-contoured, highly polished armour from Milan. On his head he wore a *barbuta*; a classically-styled helmet offering excellent protection to the head and neck, but with a T-shaped opening at the front for good vision and free breathing. At his side was fastened a rondel dagger, its long, stiff, triangular blade specifically designed for thrusting deep into the gaps in an opponent's armour. But the crowning glory of the ensemble was his two-handed sword. Too long for a scabbard, he carried it over his shoulder; four-and-a-half feet of finely-tempered, delicately-balanced, razor-sharp Italian steel. He knew how to handle it, too, having taken lessons from a student of the great Hans Talhoffer himself, the finest teacher of swordsmanship in all of Europe. Edmund felt invincible.

Looking around him, Edmund took stock. The Shropshire Lane Bar was a solid, business-like structure with a pair of brick-built watchtowers flanking a large, sturdy oak door covered in iron studs and topped with short spikes. One of the towers contained winching gear for raising and lowering the door as required. This, along with other gates and numerous hastily-erected barricades, worked in conjunction with the town ditch, which ran along two sides of a triangle around the town, the third defensive side being formed by the River Ver. The ditch presented a considerable obstacle to York's army, being some twenty feet wide and eight feet deep, making a direct attack on the heavily-manned town gates an uncomfortable but almost unavoidable necessity.

From where he was standing, ten yards back from the top of the ditch, Edmund could see the Yorkist force, perhaps only three or four hundred yards away - just out of bowshot - spread across the fields in three large groups. Banners and pennants fluttered in the warm summer breeze, and armour glittered. Figures could be seen walking up and down in front of the battle groups gesturing to the closely-packed ranks - serjeants, Edmund assumed - of the many individual retinues which formed the Duke's army - organising and encouraging their men prior to the inevitable attack.

Robed figures, which must have been priests, were making the sign of the cross and even at this distance Edmund could see rows of heads bowed in solemn prayer. The troops around him, too, had heard Mass shortly before taking up their positions, the priests reassuring them that since they fought in the name of God's anointed King, He would assure them of a glorious victory. Ever mindful of the hardships endured by his late mother and unswervingly dedicated to the brutal elimination of his father, Edmund had, by this point in his life, become all but faithless, trusting only in his sword arm and his wits. But he was surprised to see how eagerly even the roughest and most warlike of the common soldiers around him sought the priests' blessings, sinking to their knees in the dirt, heads bowed, meek as infants.

*Still,* he thought, *if it makes them fight...*

The Lancastrian troops in Edmund's vicinity, spiritually reassured and, as was the custom before a battle, heavily fortified with ale, now turned their attentions to more pressing worldly matters, offering their opinions on the Yorkist forces arrayed against them with varying degrees of bravado.

"Is that all the men they could muster? Hardly worth gettin' out of bed for!"

"They've got more archers'n us though, I reckon."

"Aye but archers can't be put to best use in these narrow streets."

"That's true. We'll give 'em something to think about, don't you fear! And when we've nobbled those sons of whores there's all that fancy gear they're wearin' up for grabs!"

Several of the older soldiers, who had served in France, grunted their approval at this last comment. Grim work though it was, stripping the enemy dead of their clothes and possessions provided a handsome boost to a fighting man's wages.

A lad of no more than sixteen, pushing back the slightly-too-large helmet with which he'd been issued, called out tentatively, "I could use a new pair of boots..."

*"THEN MAKE SURE YOU KILL SOMEBODY WHO'S WEARIN' YOUR SIZE BOY!"* roared a huge, grizzled soldier holding a fearsome-looking Italian bill, causing a peal of laughter to erupt from those in earshot.

As the merriment died down distant trumpet calls could be heard.

*"They're coming!"* someone yelled from the top of the gatehouse.

Edmund's heart leapt into his mouth. This was it, this was battle! He looked round at Bertran and Girard. Each saluted the other with a nod of the head, the fire of anticipation glowing in their eyes. Edmund looked out over the ditch.

The two outer divisions of the opposing army were indeed advancing, the glittering points of hundreds of polearms waving to the natural rhythm of the march like wind playing over a field of corn.

It was truly an impressive sight, but Edmund's mind was not to be distracted from its purpose. Somewhere out there, among that seething mass of men, was his father; he felt sure of it. He gripped the hilt of his sword tightly with both hands. The time to avenge his mother's disgrace had come at last.

# CHAPTER TWENTY-THREE

THE LEFT wing of the Yorkist army - a thousand men - drew slowly closer and closer to the Shropshire Lane Bar. Edmund's mouth was dry. He took a deep draught of good-quality French wine, one of his own as it happened, from the leather flask attached to his belt. The T-shaped opening of his helmet meant he could drink, breathe and talk without having to remove it. Within moments of quenching his thirst, another of its virtues - its smooth, glancing shape - was thrown into sharp focus. The advancing host had come to a halt at a distance of around two hundred yards, pausing to allow its contingent of archers - half of the entire force - to raise their crude but deadly six-foot yew longbows and draw their hempen cords back to their ears.

There was a momentary shimmer along the entire Yorkist front as hundreds of fingers let slip straining bowstrings, then a dark, sinuous wave of heavy thirty-inch ash shafts, fletched with white goose feathers and tipped with narrow, barbed heads of iron, rose with a terrifying *"whoosh"* into the summer sky.

*"HEADS DOWN!"* cried one of the lookouts.

Almost without thinking Edmund obeyed the shouted warning

from the watchtower. He bowed his head until he was looking at the heels of the man in front, presenting only the polished crown of his helmet to the incoming threat, and held a steel-gauntleted hand over its T-shaped opening, mindful of his partly-exposed face. It turned out to be a very sound move. He had trained hard for battle but had never experienced it at first hand. Thus it came as a rude shock when one, two, then three speeding arrows, plummeting from their high trajectories, clattered noisily against the top of his helmet and his plate armour - all but harmless at this range to a man wearing good quality full harness, but alarming and disconcerting nevertheless.

Some of the shafts buried themselves in the woodwork of the gate, others smacked harmlessly into the ground around the gatehouse and in the town ditch but, since cover was limited, a good number struck home to an accompaniment of screaming and cursing as the cruel points found homes in the unprotected legs and arms of the poorer soldiers. Only a small proportion of the defenders - wealthy knights and men-at-arms - could afford full armour like Edmund. The rank and file had to make do with just an open-faced helmet and a padded jack. If they were lucky, they might also have a breastplate or even a brigandine made of small overlapping plates riveted together and covered in fabric; good protection, to be sure, but only for the parts they covered. An arrowstorm was for them a truly miserable ordeal.

When he thought the deadly shower had stopped, Edmund dared to look up. The Yorkists had unleashed the long-range volley to show they meant business, then they began to move again. On they came at a steady walk. Several of the troops at Edmund's station began taking speculative potshots at the mass of men. Occasionally there would be a cry of triumph from one of the Lancastrian archers, accompanied by cheers from his fellows, as a distant figure fell to the ground, victim of either a skilful or a lucky loose.

Then, as the range decreased to little more than a hundred yards, the cry *"EVERY ARCHER TO THE FRONT!"* was heard, bringing the defending bowmen scampering out from what cover there was, lining ramparts of the town ditch in their scores, their minds focused on loosing a barrage of ash, feathers and iron that would, they hoped, reap a lethal harvest.

On seeing the men standing ready, one of the serjeants shouted out the familiar commands, pausing briefly between each. *"Nock, draw, LOOSE!"*

As one body, each experienced archer, practised since childhood, placed the notch of his arrow over his bowstring, curling one finger above the shaft and two below. At the word "draw" the hard work began: back contracting, chest expanding, legs braced, every muscle straining to draw the naturally springy limbs of the heavyweight weapon into a perfect arc. With the six-foot bowstave close to breaking under its own power, there remained only a second or two for the archer to gauge distance and elevation by pure instinct before the order to loose allowed him to release the stored energy. His eyes unerringly followed the path of the missile, judging its flight and mentally correcting for the next shot.

The effects of a volley of three hundred arrows upon the slow-moving, densely-packed Yorkist division were dire. At this range, the commonly-used narrow leaf-shaped iron heads, barbed to hinder their removal from flesh, could easily kill if they struck the right spot. Half-a-dozen men dropped to the ground, pierced through the neck, face or chest, never to rise. Five times that number received arrow wounds to their legs or arms that put them immediately *hors de combat*, shouting and cursing in their pain.

The attackers hesitated momentarily, recoiling from the rain of shafts. Then, stung into action by the arrowstorm and not wishing to suffer many more, they came on at a rush, reducing the distance to the gate with alarming speed. The Lancastrian archers began loosing at will, many having switched to close range arrows with narrow, acutely-pointed bodkin heads – long ones designed to pierce through mail rings and short ones to punch into plate armour. They caused serious consternation until the Yorkist force finally reached its goal and crowded round the gate. But then the angle of attack decreased dramatically and it became harder to bring large numbers of bows to bear. Now the balance swung in favour of brutal hand-to-hand combat, although both frustrated sides found it hard to engage in any strength owing to the narrowness of the lane, the steepness of the ditch and the sheer solidity of the iron-studded oaken gate. Nevertheless, as the galling crossfire from the Lancastrian archers pricked them into ever more desperate action, some of the attackers managed to scale the steep face of the town ditch. On gaining the ramparts, they set about the defenders in a fury, eager to pay back the hurt they had suffered.

Although only a few Yorkists made it over the ditch initially, these were the shock troops, handpicked for their size and strength, armed with ferocious seven-foot bills and hungry for revenge. Archers tended to wear less protection than the regular footsoldiers in keeping with their need for freedom of movement and mobility, thus, the arrival of well-equipped heavy infantry precipitated a rapid tactical withdrawal. English bowmen could never be accused of running away from a fight, but equally they did not have a reputation for reckless stupidity, the defending archers scurrying for cover behind their own lines of billmen. The unfortunate few who were too slow off the mark, however, fell screaming to the ground, limbs severed or bodies pierced, suffering the kind of gruesome wounds only an expertly-wielded bill could inflict with its long stabbing point, slashing knife-blade and vicious curving hook. Then it was the turn of the defending billmen to counter, rushing at the enemy with shouts and expletives, intent on smashing skulls and spilling guts. For the next half hour a steady stream of determined Yorkist attackers got to within hacking distance of the Lancastrian position, while an equally determined opposition kept them at bay.

Edmund and his followers had thus far been frustrated onlookers, unable to land a single blow owing to their position on the fringes of the press of fighting troops. Only yards away, but out of reach, they watched men shouting, screaming, jostling and plying their weapons, neither side gaining any real advantage in what looked set to become a bloody, bruising stalemate. To add to Edmund's frustration there was no sign to indicate the presence of Sir Geoffrey and his retinue. Try as he might, he failed to spot any men wearing his father's dark blue livery and greyhound badge. Perhaps they were attacking another part of the town's defences. Then, suddenly, a chance for some action...

*"Look! To our right!"* cried Girard, tapping Edmund's shoulder with one steel-gauntleted hand and pointing along the ditch with the other. Following the line of his friend's arm, Edmund could see, some four hundred yards away, part of the Yorkist centre division scrambling up makeshift ramps. In their scores, they made their way over an undefended section of the town ditch between the two gatehouses and fanned out into the gardens of the closely-packed houses that backed onto it, breaking down fences as they went. It was clear they intended to execute a flanking manoeuvre, but the men at the gatehouses were too busily engaged to notice.

*"Let's go!"* shouted Edmund, grabbing Girard's helmeted head with both hands and staring into his eyes, grinning wildly. Bertran, too, had seen what was afoot, raising his sword with a cry of *"Death or Glory!"* The four veteran followers exchanged knowing glances, still convinced that the three youths would meet their maker before the day was out, and determined that they would not meet theirs.

Nevertheless, as one disciplined unit, the small Calais contingent turned away from the fruitless Shropshire Bar fray and set off at a brisk pace towards the cover of a line of houses a hundred yards away. Its excited young leader was too preoccupied to notice that they were the only defenders heading that way.

Edmund had done his research very carefully with regard to blending in with the other Lancastrian units, dressing himself and his followers in copies of the blue-and-white livery jacket and gold portcullis badge of the Duke of Somerset's adherents.

Earlier in the day, while they were taking up their position, two genuine Somerset troopers had looked the little band up and down with more than a modicum of suspicion. But Edmund, resplendent in his expensive harness, had given them a glare of such ferocity as to make them turn away and busy themselves in other matters, fearing for their very lives.

Now, however, heading unsupported toward a sizeable, rapidly encroaching enemy force, his small, liveried group would stand out like an elm tree in a barley field, hence the seven men took care to stay out of sight, darting from the cover of one house to the next, observing and assessing as they went. At about a hundred yards from the nearest attackers and satisfied that neither side would see them, Edmund motioned to his followers, tugging twice at his jacket and pointing to the nearest deserted cottage. Once inside, they all took off their liveries, throwing them in a heap on a table. The older men took the opportunity to grab some hastily-abandoned bread and cheese, chewing noisily as their leader addressed them in a tone of carefully-controlled excitement.

"My friends, I thank you with all my heart for coming to this place. You all know why we are here, and you all know I will show my gratitude should our mission be accomplished. We run a grave risk walking out onto a battlefield without livery, equally likely to be attacked or accepted by both sides, but remember that we need to move freely and if we are to carry out our task undetected, anonymity shall be our shield. We owe allegiance to neither party. Their quarrel is not ours; their arguments not worth any of our deaths. We shall do what we have to do, then leave as we came."

Although a reckoning with his father was uppermost in Edmund's mind, the excitement of his first battle was hard to suppress, the danger acting as a powerful drug. Ultimately he wanted his father's blood on his sword, but for now Edmund realised anyone's blood would do. He wanted a fight.

Emerging cautiously from the cottage and crouching behind the wall of its garden, Edmund could see the attackers were still in the early stages of by-passing the blockades, breaking down fences and doors to make a way through, he supposed, to the town centre. There, the main body of the King's men stood complacently at their ease, oblivious to the impending threat and confident that the gates, the barricades and the ditch would keep the enemy at bay for as long as they were foolish enough to throw men at them.

Busy as they were, dealing with the various obstacles in their way, the Yorkist soldiers were advancing piecemeal in numerous small, scattered groups, meaning they would be unable to form into a large, cohesive force until they made it to the wider streets leading to the market square.

Edmund realised this gave him the best chance, albeit a brief one, of infiltrating the enemy lines. If his unidentifiable band were seen kicking at fences, hacking at hedges and heading the same way as everyone else, they might go unnoticed. On the other hand, if they aroused suspicion and it looked like coming to a fight, they could either run for cover into the nearest house or take their chances against roughly equal numbers.

Despite getting himself and his men this far Edmund still accepted, very reluctantly, that his father could be anywhere among the three attacking divisions – or nowhere. He might even be ill, confined at home having tendered his apologies for failing to turn up in support of his old friend the Duke of York. Edmund had no way of knowing for sure as even *his* formidable spy network did not extend its activities as far as the northern Marches of Wales. Nevertheless, there was something in the air - a feeling in his bones. His father was not far away; he was convinced of it.

# CHAPTER TWENTY-FOUR

THE CHILLY morning air parted around the heavy brass candleholder with a menacing "*swish*" as Kate brought it down with all her might at the moment she judged the intruder's head would appear round the church door. A deep, rich, bass voice exclaimed, "*Deus servo mihi!*"

"Kate!" shouted Jane, "it's the real priest!" Kate did her best to arrest the flight of the heavy brass holder without breaking her own knees and, as she finally brought the wayward mass under control, she could see that her intended target was indeed a man of God, and a very alarmed one at that.

Priest and girl regarded each other, the former wearing a wide-eyed, open-mouthed expression of confused amazement, the latter a blank mask of utter exhaustion mingled with tearful relief.

Kate went limp and sank to her knees, her makeshift weapon slipping from her pale, slender fingers, and hitting the ground with a resounding '*clang*'. The priest dashed forward, fearing the girl might faint clean away, and grabbed her shoulders to save her from braining herself on the cold, hard floor. As he supported the flaccid, bedraggled burden he shot a sideways glance at Jane sensing that, of these two wildly alarming girls, she was *slightly* more in possession of her wits.

"Oh, Father, forgive us!" Jane babbled. "Her father is dead, murdered by ruffians! They cut down our groom and took us away and we were sure they meant to kill us too. Then we escaped, but they followed us and we thought you were one of them and..."

The priest, a reassuringly tall, well-built, broad-faced man in his mid-forties, gently silenced the babbling teenager with one large, raised hand. "Child, you are safe from harm here in God's house. Clearly you have both suffered a terrible ordeal of some kind. I doubt not the veracity of your story, judging by the determination of your young companion to smash in my skull. Thankfully a premature audience with the Almighty was averted."

"Father... Forgive me... My... father's... horse..."

The priest looked down at Kate, his strong hand still supporting her slight frame.

"Your mount is safe and well child. It must have been my verger feeding and watering him that first alerted you to our presence."

"Thank you," whispered Kate, a little strength returning to her limbs. She began to draw herself unsteadily to her feet. The priest helped her up then guided her to the steps by the font, motioning her to sit and rest. He kept his eyes fixed on Kate but half-turned his head towards the door. "Martin? Martin, I need you here!"

"At once, Father!" came the reply from somewhere outside. A few moments later a man in his late twenties – a rather handsome man, the girls would later agree – came running through the door, juddering to a rapid halt then assuming a more sedate pace as the priest's look of mild disapproval reminded him he was in God's house.

"Sorry Father," he said, in a tone that suggested he was no stranger to mild disapproval.

"Well, Martin, at least it cannot be said that you are not eager to serve the Lord!" replied the priest, with a kindly smile.

"These young ladies are cold, wet and no doubt hungry and have suffered some kind of frightening experience. I think your

Elizabeth would be best equipped to restore the colour to their cheeks."

"I shall see to it at once, Father," said Martin, offering a hand to Kate to help her up from the font steps. As she regained her feet, Jane dashed over to her and the two friends held each other in a tight embrace. The priest looked Martin in the eye, a subtle shake of the head expressing his great puzzlement over who the girls were and what they were doing in his church. Martin signalled his acknowledgement with an equally subtle shrug of his shoulders. As the girls parted from their embrace the priest spoke. "My children, there are a great many important questions I would ask of you, but I feel it would be a singular unkindness to put them to you while you have wet clothes and empty bellies. Martin's wife will, I am sure, make you comfortable in that respect. After that, if you do not plan to gallop off over the horizon to some new adventure, I shall call by presently to learn how you came to be here. Your families will be sorely concerned at your absence. If we can assist you in returning you to your homes, we will."

Dark worries wheeled around in Kate's tired mind like a murder of crows: the shock of her father's death, the whereabouts of her brother, Edmund's intended seizure of the Wardlow estate, her mother's mental state. She tried to make some sense of her situation.

"Where are we Father? What is the name of this place?"

"You are under the protection of St. Berres' church in the parish of Llanferres and I am Father Thomas Crowder."

Kate's heart sank. She had never heard of the place and had not the faintest idea how far it was from her home. The furthest she had ever ventured in her life had been to Rhuddlan with her family to browse its markets and to stay a few days within the walls of its impressive castle, where her father had friends. For all she knew they might be halfway to Ludlow itself.

She tried to calculate how far she and Jane had travelled the previous day. They must have been three miles from home when they were ambushed, then they must have ridden four or five more under armed escort before reaching Edmund's camp. But how much distance they had put between themselves and her father's killers during their headlong flight she could not even begin to guess. Panic began to grip her as it dawned on her just how far from home she was. Her mother would be beside herself at the two of them going missing overnight. Nevertheless, Kate doubted they would be home before another day and a night had passed. Both she and Jane were hungry, exhausted and still reeling from the previous day's terrifying events, and in any case she did not see how they could find their way back to the Wardlow estate, regardless of whether or not they were likely to be captured and killed on the way.

Kate could not conceal her turmoil from the two men and it was clear to Father Thomas that she had as many questions to ask him as he had to ask her. "Fret not, my child. We will honour our offer of assistance as regards getting you home, but save your queries for now and let us not delay in drying you out and feeding you."

"This way, young mistresses, it's not far," added Martin, ushering them out of the gloomy church and into bright early morning sunshine that forced Kate to blink and shield her eyes with one hand. The warm rays felt good on her pale skin, helping to ease the shivering caused by her still-damp clothes.

As Father Thomas walked along behind Martin and the two bedraggled girls he looked about him, taking in the dazzling sun, the clear blue sky and the fiery autumn colours of the trees, remarking to himself how sharp a contrast they presented to the previous day's wind, rain and cold.

The Almighty had laid a healing hand on the angry elements. Perhaps this was a sign instructing His humble servant to do likewise for the fortunes of these poor benighted creatures. He would answer that call. He would make sure they got home.

# CHAPTER TWENTY-FIVE

EDMUND OF Calais emerged from his tent into the same bright autumn sunshine that had dazzled Kate. He was more than a little jaded from having stayed up late the night before with his young companions and a good red wine intent on finishing his battle narrative, but he had awoken determined to make his final, decisive move on the estate he felt was rightfully his.

He was followed closely by Ysabel, who had listened intently as Edmund had told his story into the early hours, only comprehending half of what he was saying but paying close attention because the man she loved was speaking. Limited though her grasp of English was, she could tell by the way Edmund's tone and expression had hardened during the latter stages of the tale that all had not ended well four years ago at St Albans.

It had begun to look as though Edmund's bold plan to discard their identifying liveries and attempt to blend in with the advancing Yorkists might just work. Three times they had encountered small parties of soldiers infiltrating the narrow streets through the backyards and gardens, and on each occasion they were largely ignored since their actions tallied logically those of the attackers.

Minutes later, however, Edmund's heart had leapt into his mouth. Only fifty yards away a group of six men, wearing dark blue livery jackets bearing a seated silver greyhound, appeared through a gap in a hedge. *This was it!* These were definitely his father's men. Signalling to his followers to be on high alert, he could barely contain his excitement. Then, as the two groups began to converge on another gap, a seventh man appeared. He was equipped in expensive full harness in a similar Italian style to Edmund's, but topped with an English-made Coventry sallet with its characteristic pointed top, *and wearing a tabard bearing a seated silver greyhound...*

Edmund had the presence of mind to look around to make sure there were no other invading troops in the vicinity, then hissed his order. *"Archers - now!"*

Each of the three former Free Company soldiers silently drew an arrow from the canvas bag secured at his right hip and, with a slick, smooth action born of thirty years' practice, nocked, drew and loosed his deadly, goose-feathered missile at Sir Geoffrey's unsuspecting retainers. All three arrows struck home with immediate fatal effect. Then, almost before the remaining men that stood between Edmund and his father had time to react, three more arrows sped through the air. One went through its unfortunate recipient's eye, burying itself deep in his brain; another passed through its target's throat, only the fletchings preventing it from exiting out the back. The third, however, struck the last of Sir Geoffrey's bodyguard in the left shoulder. The shattering impact of a war arrow at close range spun the man half round, causing him to drop the bill he was carrying, but as one of the Wardlow's trained household soldiers he was made of strong stuff. Gritting his teeth against the pain, he managed to unsheathe his heavy, broad-bladed falchion. He made a desperate lunge towards the nearest archer, weapon raised, intent on separating bow arm from body, but he was stopped in his tracks as Bertran stepped forward and thrust his sword upwards, just below the man's breastplate.

Edmund's young companion, temporarily mesmerised by what

he had done, watched as his victim sank to his knees. Then he slowly withdrew his now-bloody blade, allowing the dying man to fall face-down on the ground.

Turning to his leader, Bertran lifted up the visor of his helmet and looked Edmund in the eye, as if seeking approval for his action. A second later he fell to the ground dead, his face pierced by a foot-long, half-inch-thick crossbow quarrel shot from the gap in the hedge behind Sir Geoffrey, who was now striding purposefully towards Edmund, his hand-and-a-half sword at the ready.

*"Hold fast. He's mine!"* shouted Edmund, dashing forward to close the gap with his father. This was no time to grieve for his friend, right now his own survival was his first priority. Edmund was struck by how quickly Sir Geoffrey, though visibly taken aback by the sudden ambush, had regained his confidence and initiated a counter-attack – and then he realised why.

*"Damnation! There are more of them!"* he cried, as a further four blue-liveried soldiers appeared in the gap behind Sir Geoffrey, one of them carrying his greyhound standard. Again, the *'thwack'* of a crossbow string and the whirr of its iron nut, spinning round as it released its deadly missile. This time it was Edmund's old servant who took a close-range bolt that penetrated his breastplate at heart level. Five against five now, and everything was happening too quickly. Edmund was a calculating man but even his meticulous planning had not allowed for the potential disaster that was currently unfolding before his eyes.

Struggling to maintain a cool head while his comrades seemed to be falling all around him, Edmund finally reached his father and, with all his strength, brought his two-handed sword straight down over his head, intent on beating Sir Geoffrey to his knees. But his attack, though ferocious, was easily read by his opponent. Sir Geoffrey side-stepped to his right, holding his sword point-down and at an angle so as to parry Edmund's blow. Then he lashed out with his right foot, catching Edmund a heavy, winding blow to the stomach which made him stagger back three paces.

Edmund just had time to curse himself for losing his composure and launching such an obvious attack, before his father followed up with a powerful thrust towards the T-shaped opening of his helmet.

Now was the time for lightning reaction; now was the time to put into practice the techniques he had paid so much to learn at Hans Talhoffer's school. Would his cunning and finesse be a match for Sir Geoffrey's experience in the field, or would the soldier best the student?

As Sir Geoffrey's sword point came rushing at his face, Edmund quickly brought his own weapon up vertically by his right side, then swept it swiftly round to the left, beating his father's blade to one side. He then half twisted his sword so it presented its edge, swinging it back the other way as hard as he could and dealing Sir Geoffrey an almighty clout to the side of his sallet. The older man was clearly stunned by the impact – without the helmet he would have been beheaded – and before he could gather his senses Edmund had recovered his sword, quickly repositioning his left hand part way up the blade, holding the weapon like a short spear. He made a determined lunge at his father's visor slit but Sir Geoffrey was surprisingly quick on the defence, managing to sidestep smartly to his right, pushing Edmund's blade aside and down with one gauntleted hand and smashing the pommel of his sword into the front of Edmund's helmet with the other.

The narrow, tapered end of the pommel found its way through the T-shaped opening in Edmund's barbuta, bloodying his nose and splitting his lip. One, two, three hammer blows forced Edmund to stagger back on his heels. The situation was becoming desperate. Very soon, both men would be exhausted from fighting in full armour. Under the punishing assault, Edmund managed to reverse his sword, grasping it with both hands well down the blade and holding it like a pick-axe. Before he made his move he used the distraction he had been saving.

"A fine thing, to beat your son to a pulp! Do you not know me, *father*?"

It worked. Sir Geoffrey stayed his sword hand momentarily,

frozen to the spot, looking Edmund up and down, trying to make sense of what was happening. It was all the time Edmund needed. He brought his sword round low so that the cross-guard was hooked behind Sir Geoffrey's left knee, then pulled it smartly away, dumping his father flat on his back.

Edmund was on him in a flash, throwing his main weapon to one side and drawing his dagger as he straddled the fallen knight. With his left hand he tore open Sir Geoffrey's visor, looking, for the first time in his life, into his father's intelligent, piercing blue eyes. But Edmund could feel nothing for this man he did not know. He did not care for his achievements, whatever they might be, nor did he care what alternate destiny might have been his to fulfil. This man was responsible, in Edmund's mind, for his mother's untimely and unseemly death and now it was time for retribution.

*"This is for Elaine, my mother, whom you deserted. I shall take what is rightfully mine!"* he hissed.

*Elaine.* Of course! Now Sir Geoffrey understood. But this was no time to rue past misdoings. Right now, it was kill or be killed and this young man had to die, regardless of his blood line, regardless of whether he was telling the truth. The Wardlow family must not learn the dark secret of Sir Geoffrey's past life.

The Bastard of Calais brought his dagger down, meaning to drive the point into Sir Geoffrey's eye and end the fight. But his intended victim was not ready to give in just yet, grabbing Edmund's arm with his left hand in a desperate attempt to prevent the deadly blade from doing its work. Edmund responded by applying both hands to the job of finishing his father, but that was just what the wily Sir Geoffrey, survivor of many such encounters on the battlefields of France, had hoped for. With his free right hand, he drew his own dagger and thrust it hard up into Edmund's exposed left armpit.

*"Here is your inheritance then. Take it!"* he snarled, as he pushed the narrow, stiff blade through the small area of interlocking mail rings and cloth padding that were one of the few weak spots in a fighting man's harness.

Edmund buckled under the pain, giving his father a moment to catch a breath or two before bringing his right knee smartly up into Edmund's groin, causing him to crumple further. Sir Geoffrey then shoved his murderous burden off to one side, rolling with him in order to press home his advantage. Now the older, more experienced man was on top, ready to bring the encounter to a bloody close as he in turn tried to push his dagger into his opponent's eye. Edmund resisted desperately but he was weakened by his wound. He prepared himself for pain, for death, for failure, as the sharp point came closer and closer to his face. Then, from nowhere, came the sound of trumpets close by and men shouting. But whose men? Both protagonists froze for a second as they weighed up the consequences of being discovered by a large body of enemy soldiers, then Sir Geoffrey growled, "I care not which side approaches; I cannot let you go. This ends here!" He renewed his efforts, determined to skewer Edmund and thereby extinguish any flicker of scandal from his past. A heartbeat later Sir Geoffrey Wardlow's world went black.

Edmund, by now exhausted and faint from the effects of his wound, felt his burden lift off him then land with a clattering thump on the ground beside him. His friend Girard had dealt Sir Geoffrey a massive blow to the side of his sallet with the flat hammerhead of his poll-axe. The young adventurer helped Edmund to his feet. "Come! We must make our escape!" he said in an urgent tone.

Edmund regarded the prone form of his father. Swaying a little against his friend's supporting arm, he hissed through his pain, *"Is he dead? You must finish him."*

"Leave him Edmund! There is no time. They are almost upon us. We shall be overwhelmed and captured."

Edmund looked about him, trying to take in the scene. A fierce and bloody struggle had been taking place while he had fought his father. Of his original party, only he and Girard remained alive. Bertran, his friend, was dead, as were his great uncle's servant and the three Free Company troopers. Of Sir Geoffrey's party none remained standing save for one man, who rushed to his master's aid, oblivious to the sound of approaching soldiers. He was tall and broadly built, and, as he knelt down to attend to his stricken master, he threw the two friends such a baleful look that even Edmund decided it was time to leave.

Tom Linley watched intently as the two young men turned and, with all the haste they could muster, made their way toward what they hoped would be safety. He then examined Sir Geoffrey for signs of life.

As his master and long-time friend slowly began to regain his wits, thanks to a well-made helmet worn over plenty of padding, he tried to speak. Tom leaned in closer, straining to hear his words.

*"My... family... must... not... know..."*, whispered Sir Geoffrey, gripping Tom's arm with a trained swordsman's strength. Tom laid his hand over his master's in silent acknowledgement. No further words were needed.

Scores of Yorkist troops now began to pour past, ignoring the two men in their friendly liveries and surging along on their rapid advance into the centre of town, where a surprise archery attack on King Henry's complacent central division would eventually carry the day.

As he helped his now almost fully-conscious master to his feet, Tom turned the astonishing events of the day over and over in his mind. He had served Sir Geoffrey faithfully for many years, fighting shoulder to shoulder with him on the battlefields of France, but he had never suspected there might be a son born out of wedlock. Whoever the tall, mysterious young man really was, whatever the reasons for his sudden and violent assault on the Wardlow name, Tom promised himself no-one else would find out.

# CHAPTER TWENTY-SIX

HAD KATE been able to take to the air like a majestic red kite and soar high over the countryside, serene, aloof and far above the troubles of men, she would have seen her brother's party as tiny specks below, their familiar faces only a dozen miles or so to the southwest, but separated from her by the high ridge of the Clwydian Hills, lacking horses and still twenty miles from home.

Then, wheeling on broad, outstretched wings, she might have turned northeast, flying over densely-wooded countryside until, swooping low over a forest clearing, she would have seen cold, hard faces that filled her with dread. There was one face in particular – a handsome face to be sure, but the face of a killer nevertheless. It was a face that commanded sixty mounted men stationed a mere handful of miles from everything she held dear.

# CHAPTER TWENTY-SEVEN

"MY LADY?" The woman in charge of the brewhouse, Marjorie Holmes, tentatively repeated her address to Ann Wardlow, but the mistress of the estate remained as before: stock still, positioned in the window seat and gazing fixedly out into the failing evening light.

"My lady, the hour is late and you have not eaten since midday. Please, at least take some cold meat and a little wine or you shall surely faint clean away." But still there was no response, no movement that might suggest that Ann Wardlow was connected to the world. Joan, the cook, had tried several times to entice her mistress away from the window with various supper items but without success. She had asked Marjorie to try her luck, on account of her long service with the family. The woman responsible for making the ale that sustained the entire estate had, after all, known Ann since she had arrived as Sir Geoffrey's blushing bride, eighteen years before. In spite of their long association, however, the finely-dressed woman in front of her, motionless as a statue, face pale and drawn, lips pursed, hands tightly clasped, seemed a stranger.

Marjorie understood her mistress's bravely concealed anguish only too well. Her husband Jack was one of Sir Geoffrey's full-time household retainers and he too had been gone over two weeks, marching off with the master and his retinue to goodness knew what fate. Now here was the lady of the house, her husband and son having answered the call to arms, fretting over a daughter and servant who had not returned from their ride. God was indeed testing this poor woman to her limit. Marjorie feared this most recent episode might prove too much for such a highly-strung individual.

Ann Wardlow was a firm but fair mistress, well-respected and well-liked, and the tenants and servants on the estate, many of whom were in a similar situation to Marjorie with their men gone away, had exchanged their concerns over Ann's gradual, uncharacteristic withdrawal from everyday affairs. It was whispered that her spirit was a hundred miles away, watching over her menfolk, and possibly theirs too, and that her body, increasingly drawn to the south-facing window and less and less inclined towards conversation or indeed animation, had become an empty vessel. There was even talk, among the oldest, the youngest and the most foolish women on the estate, that it was witchcraft that enabled Ann to maintain her tireless, trance-like vigil. In spite of the local church regularly filling with wives, mothers, sisters and daughters all praying earnestly for the safe return of their loved ones, any thread of hope to which they might cling was eagerly grasped, even if it flew in the face of what was acceptable.

But Ann Wardlow was oblivious to all around her. Her beloved husband and her handsome son had not returned to her and now her beautiful young daughter had been missing since just after breakfast. Though she betrayed few outward signs of the emotional turmoil inside her - other than hands that were clasped so tightly together the knuckles turned white - those around her who knew her well were in no doubt that she must be close to breaking point.

# CHAPTER TWENTY- EIGHT

Hot porridge sweetened with honey, freshly-baked bread, a hunk of cheese and a pint of small beer each: manna from Heaven for two starving girls.

Elizabeth Tanner, a plump, pretty woman in her late twenties, looked on as Kate and Jane eagerly devoured the breakfasts she had put in front of them. Her concern for their well-being was wavering between sisterly and motherly on account of the girls' ages. She turned to her husband and winked. Martin threw a slightly sad smile in return. They had longed for children of their own, but ten years of marriage had not seen them blessed. Elizabeth knew the girls were too old to have been hers, but her kindly, sympathetic nature made her wonder what anguish their mothers were going through.

Their meals finished, the girls expressed their gratitude by getting up from the table and hugging Elizabeth from both sides, their normal, ingrained mistrust of strangers having evaporated in the comforting warmth of the Tanners' kitchen.

A knock at the half-open door, followed by a rich, bass "Halloo!", signalled the timely arrival of Father Thomas.

"Ah, my benighted young daughters! I trust Elizabeth has relieved you of some of your burdens – the cold and hunger at least – for which kindness she has my heartfelt thanks. And now that you have some of your strength back, you must tell me what happened to you, then we will see about getting you home safely."

Everyone sat around the kitchen table while Kate recounted the terrifying events of the previous day. As she did so, the faces of her listeners took on expressions of shock and horror. Elizabeth cupped her hand to her mouth, her eyes wide in disbelief as the story of Edmund's dark ambition unfolded. Father Thomas and Martin exchanged grave looks, realising there might be considerable danger attached to seeing these girls home. But see them home they must; it was their Christian duty, whatever the risks. As Kate came tearfully to the end of her harrowing tale, Elizabeth comforted her and, reaching over to grasp Jane's hand, held that tightly too. Father Thomas was deep in thought, elbows on the table, hands together as if in prayer, fingertips pressed against his pursed lips, brow furrowed. Eventually he turned solemnly to Martin.

"I would ask a great favour of you, Martin. Fetch Simon, the butcher's son. Arm yourselves and protect these maids on their way home. You are both well-made lads and can look after yourselves. Will you do it?"

Martin shot a glance at Elizabeth. Both knew the journey might prove hazardous, but Elizabeth did not hesitate to give her tacit approval with a curt nod.

"Yes, Father, I will do it gladly," he replied.

The priest spoke again. "Clearly you cannot go back the same way or you will run straight into those godless beasts. Take the other main route, on the opposite side of the hills. It will be much safer."

"I know that road, Father. Elizabeth and I travelled along it when we visited family in St Asaph. It is true, the road is more open. Less woodland for scoundrels to hide in."

"It is settled then," said Father Thomas. He turned to Kate and

Jane. "Time is of the essence if you are to warn your loved ones. Your horse is rested and fed. Go with God, my daughters."

The girls knelt on the hard earth floor, their hands clasped in prayerful gratitude, as the priest laid a gentle hand on each one's head and quietly intoned a blessing. Then, a more worldly thank-you as they both embraced Elizabeth, tears in their eyes. Parcels of food and drink were prepared for the journey, swords buckled on, farewells said, then they were on their way, setting a good pace out of the village before turning north towards their destiny.

# CHAPTER TWENTY-NINE

"MORE BLOODY hills!" Edmund of Calais flung his hand across the view in a gesture of frustration. "Are we fated never to see this accursed estate?"

From the impressively lofty slope that overlooked Kate's favourite valley, he had hoped to see the Wardlow estate laid out below him, but after coaxing and coercing his panting horse over the steep, rough ground, all that greeted him to the north was the sight of the land rising up again on the other side.

He had decided to make the ascent in order to spy out the country ahead, having grown tired of seeing nothing but tree-covered slopes that seemed to hem his party in on all sides. He was accompanied by Girard, Ysabel and eight soldiers. Girard had been studying the landscape carefully while his friend vented his irritation.

"Wait," he said, then pointed. "Over there, on the other side of the valley. I can just see a track going up through the trees and some house roofs just over the brow of the hill. They must be part of Caerwys."

"Then that is where we shall head," said Edmund. Before he

turned his horse around to begin the descent, he indicated to Girard the land to the west of their vantage point. "If my father's estate is half as good as that I shall be very happy." Below them, only two or three miles away, on the perfectly flat bottom of the Vale of Clwyd, lay a patchwork of fertile fields and lush, green sheep and cow pastures.

"Beautiful," agreed Girard, "but surely prone to flooding should the river awake one morning in an ill temper. If your father's lands are higher up they may not be as lush, but you need not fear them being inundated."

"You are quite the farmer!" Edmund observed. "In any case I suspect the richest estates are tied up with the lordship of Denbigh. Whoever owns the land may rent some of it out to tenants, but I do not doubt he keeps back the best for himself."

"As would you!" laughed Girard. Edmund smiled in response, then wheeled his horse around and set off down the hillside.

Half an hour later, Edmund, his friends and his full complement of mercenaries reached the village of Caerwys.

"It seems deserted," whispered Ysabel.

"They must have seen us coming and locked themselves in their houses," Edmund replied. "I don't blame them." As they rounded a corner Ysabel suddenly sat bolt upright in her saddle.

"Look, *chéri*, a church with a tower. You could climb up it and see more from the top." Edmund looked up the street and there, indeed, was a handsome church with a very large, powerfully-built tower, the latter so sturdy, in fact, that it put him in mind of a castle.

"How clever, my love!" he remarked. "Are you feeling brave enough to accompany me to the top?"

"Oh yes, then perhaps I will see our new home!"

As the party approached the church, Edmund motioned to his scar-faced captain to position the men defensively, and then he dismounted. He, Ysabel, Girard and three soldiers entered the church warily through its stout oak door, the men with their hands on their weapons, but there was no-one inside.

Having climbed to the top of the tower, Edmund gazed out from its battlements. "Well now, *this* ascent was worth it!"

Helping Ysabel, so she could see properly, they took in the view before them. The estate appeared to occupy a high plateau, with the land dropping off on the southern and western sides. Cattle and sheep grazed quietly in the October sunshine in a multitude of small fields. He could see smoke coming from some of the scattered farm cottages, rising gently almost straight up into the calm, blue sky of a crisp autumn morning, creating an appearance of the absolute epitome of peaceful rural life.

In addition to what he could see with his own eyes, his intelligence gatherers had furnished him with more than enough to put a smile on his face. Edmund knew that there were two more villages within the estate boundary: Tremeirchion, out of sight to the west, hugging the ground sloping down the edge of the Vale of Clwyd, and Pen-y-Cefn, a little way to the northwest and once again just hidden from view by the rising ground. The hamlet of Babell marked the eastern limit of the Wardlow lands. There would, therefore, be income aplenty for the new master of the estate, what with rents from the tenants, wool-clips, milk, meat and leather from the cattle, two water-mills, woodland for timber and a stone quarry. In addition, from his earlier vantage point on the hillside, Edmund had been able to make out the sea, shimmering in the far distance like a polished sword blade. Perhaps he could even bring his wines into a nearby harbour. The whole scene filled him with excitement. Here was a place where he could spread his wings and fly.

At the farthest limit of the view from the church tower, on the high ground to the north, stood a large, recently-built red brick manor house. It was the seat of the Wardlow family, its finer features indistinct at this distance but set apart from its agricultural surroundings by virtue of its moat, formal gardens and open parkland.

"There, sweeting. There is our new home," said Edmund

squeezing Ysabel to his side as he pointed his finger across the intervening fields. "Ours for the taking!"

He was still mulling over the seemingly endless possibilities as he came back out of the church, but his reverie was interrupted by the heavy blowing of an exhausted horse as it pulled up close to his party. A tough-looking mercenary archer, wearing an open-faced sallet and a torn and grubby blue velvet-covered brigandine, jumped down from his mount and approached at a jog, his hand pressed to his scabbard to prevent the heavy falchion within from slapping his legs.

"What news, man?" asked Edmund impatiently. He had sent small scouting parties back along the routes both to the east and the west of the long ridge of the Clwydian Hills to see which road Sir Geoffrey's men had followed from Ludlow and how long it would take them to arrive. The soldier gave a shallow bow before making his report.

"My lord, we have seen them! We got within two bowshots without being spotted. They come by the road to the west and are without mounts. If they rest overnight, they cannot reach here before the ringing of vespers on the morrow."

Early evening the next day then, Edmund thought, at the same time inwardly marvelling that such a godless ruffian should be so well acquainted with the Offices of the Day. Perhaps he had learned them while looting and burning French churches during the wars.

Edmund was now torn – press on, seize the estate and consolidate his position, or turn back and fall upon his brother's small, disadvantaged band and destroy them? Here was a golden opportunity to sweep away the main opposition to his cause.

But what if it went wrong? What if he, Edmund, were killed in a desperate struggle and his plans, years in the making, came to nothing. His own force numbered three times that of Richard's, but in a battle there was always a chance for the unexpected to happen. There would be serious legal consequences, too, following a sizeable armed engagement. Allowing for Richard's men putting up a good fight - and there was no doubt in Edmund's mind that they would - there might be as many as two score of bodies lying pierced and broken; hardly a scene to escape the notice of the King's peacekeepers. If the matter were to be pursued to its conclusion it might be Edmund's own neck on the block. He pressed the cold steel of his clenched, armoured fist to his lips, deep in thought, weighing up his options.

Girard had known him long enough to read the signs. "It is a great temptation is it not, friend? Seek them out, ride them down and crush them at a stroke. We have superiority in numbers and we are mounted, but remember our advantage would be greatly diminished should your brother's men spy us first and scatter into the thickest woodland. They know this country well. We do not. We would be forced to dismount and fight on their terms. And what if they succeeded in outflanking us and reaching their villages before us? They might rouse their fellows to action and we might then be facing a larger force than our own."

Though Edmund had not been looking at Girard as he spoke, the latter knew his words had been absorbed. After a few more moments of consideration, Edmund did turn to Girard, nodding as if to confirm some unspoken decision.

"You are right of course, my friend. We must exercise prudence – it is, after all, the family motto. We will advance upon the manor house and take up a defensive position."

Though seemingly resigned to his chosen course of action, he punched the steel knuckles of one gauntlet into the leather palm of the other, tacitly expressing his frustration at having to turn his back on such a propitious juncture. He noticed the messenger, still awaiting orders.

"Good work!" he said, taking a coin from his waist pouch and pressing it into the soldier's grubby, calloused hand.

The mercenary looked at it in surprise. It was a gold half-noble, worth three shillings and four pence – a full week's pay. "My lord!?" he exclaimed, then quickly bowed and hurried back to his horse lest Edmund should change his mind. As he watched the scout depart, Edmund said to Girard. "Hah! Did you hear that? He called me 'my lord'! I have no noble title, nor have I been knighted, yet he addressed me as though I were a Duke or an Earl. I tell you Girard, a fellow could get used to this. I would do well not to let it go to my head or I may require you all to kneel in my presence!"

Girard threw back his head and laughed heartily while Ysabel stifled a giggle with the palm of her hand.

"Most gratifying dear friend, I have to agree," Girard replied, "though quite what form of address my lady, your father's widow, will employ is anybody's guess..."

Edmund's half-smile indicated that while he appreciated his friend's jest, he was not inclined to give too much time over to mirth, bearing in mind what might lay ahead. He looked soberly at Girard, then at Ysabel, his gaze lingering awhile on his sweetheart, then announced in a decisive tone. "The hour is come: our objective lies before us. Let us carry the day!"

# CHAPTER THIRTY

"*DICKON! THANK God, dear brother, you are safe!*"
Kate was almost beside herself with relief as she slowed Rollo to a walk and approached Richard Wardlow and his party of retainers. She and Jane dismounted, Kate rushing over to embrace her brother, who was completely taken aback to see her and quite lost for words. The girls and their escorts had ridden as hard as they dare without breaking the horses on a journey mercifully devoid of incident, but it was already mid-afternoon when they came across the men from their estate. Kate breathlessly introduced Martin and Simon to her brother. Richard shook them both warmly by the hand, offering heartfelt words of thanks for the safe delivery of his sister though his face still showed that he had been completely wrong-footed by her arrival, especially since she had appeared from the south, the direction he would have least expected.

"Forgive us our haste to depart, Master Richard, but we must turn for home if we are to beat the darkness," said Martin, wishing he could do more to help, but remembering that his Elizabeth would be fretting upon his return.

"You have my deepest gratitude for protecting my kin, and you are right to seek your own hearths," Richard replied. "True evil stalks the land at this time," he added, wondering how he could break the news of their father's murder to Kate, little realising that she had only recently escaped from the clutches of the perpetrator.

The girls embraced their erstwhile protectors with suitable propriety - though secretly their hearts were beating a little faster than convention would have approved of. Then they watched as the two young men spurred their mounts southwards. Turning back, Kate looked around the group in surprise. "But where are *your* horses? Have you walked all the way from Ludlow?"

"We had no time to get to them," Richard explained. "It was all but dark. Our mounts were tethered well away from the fighting lines but when our forces began to flee the field there was such an almighty crush and confusion we lost our way. By the time we had got our bearings we dared not go back to retrieve the horses lest we fell foul of the King's men who were advancing on the town. All we could do was run for our lives."

As he spoke, Richard again wrestled with the onerous task of telling Kate their father was dead. Brother and sister began to speak simultaneously, then stopped.

"You first, Sis, then you can explain how you come to be all the way out here," said Richard, glad of a few more moments to gather his thoughts.

Kate's expression became serious. "I met the man who murdered Father. His name is Edmund."

Richard looked stunned. So she already knew. And now the tall man had a name, an identity. It brought back the memory of the evil day his father had died. "I saw it, Sis. I saw it all with my own eyes from the top of a church tower. Father didn't stand a chance. What did this dog Edmund say? I'll wager he wants to steal our estate, but I don't know what his quarrel is with us. Why does he hate us so?"

Tom Linley began to shift uneasily on his feet, fearing that the time had finally come to risk his young master's displeasure and tell him all he knew about Sir Geoffrey's past and the encounter with his killer at St Albans. Mercifully, however, Kate saved him the trouble as she began to recount to her brother the details of her meeting with Edmund of Calais. This time, she told her story without tears, just a steely resolve in her voice and a determination that this murderer would not profit from her father's death.

Richard was stunned by what he heard from Kate's lips, slowly shaking his head as the tale unfolded, but in the interests of harsh practicality he did his best to put to the back of his mind all his conflicting thoughts about their father's past and what the implications were for the family. The most important thing for the moment was to get word to their mother in the hope that the villagers could organise some kind of defence, perhaps stalling Edmund's men just long enough to allow Richard and his group to get there and bolster the resistance.

"I'll go!" said Kate.

"No! I will not hear of it. It's far too dangerous," Richard replied.

"But we only have one horse between all of us and I doubt Rollo would let anyone but me... or Father... ride him."

Richard ground his teeth, knowing that Kate was probably right. He himself had never dared to mount Rollo, and he did not wish to risk one of his men being thrown and injured when he needed every pair of fighting hands.

"Very well, but you must *promise* not to try anything heroic, and if this Edmund and his mob have beaten us to it, then you will turn tail and ride straight back here, understood?"

"Yes!" said Kate, filled with an intoxicating mixture of excitement and fear.

"Follow this road until you reach a gap in the hills, then take the track to the right that passes by Bodfari," said Richard.

"Bodfari?!" Kate interrupted. "That's where Seren and Sir Caddoc live! Maybe they could raise some help or lend us some horses."

"No," said Richard, firmly. "Don't stop for anyone or anything. After Ludlow we don't know whether our friends are still our friends. They may detain you or hinder you in some way – anything is possible. For now, we can only help ourselves."

While they had been travelling through villages where they were not known, Richard and his retinue had not met any hostility, but as they neared the Wardlow homelands he wondered how the neighbouring landlords would receive him, knowing that his father had sided with the Duke of York against King Henry. Perhaps there would be barred doors, cold looks and no offers of assistance against this threat to his whole world. The thought of it made Richard feel very alone and isolated. He was glad of Tom's solid presence at his side – a living link with his dead father.

As Kate mounted up, he unfastened the rondel dagger and scabbard from his belt and handed it up to her, closing his hands over hers as she took it.

"Be careful, Sis. God go with you."

Kate nodded, tucked the dagger and scabbard into her own belt, then turned Rollo round and dug her heels into his flanks.

# CHAPTER THIRTY-ONE

EDMUND OF Calais, astride his favourite bay destrier Tiberius, with his companion-in-arms, Girard, mounted on a handsome grey courser, rode side by side at walking pace. They were at the head of an intimidating column of sixty mounted soldiers, followed by a dozen or more horse-drawn carts and wagons full of supplies, tents, equipment and belongings. Ysabel was riding close behind Edmund on Livia, her blue dun mare. The two men were resplendent in full harness; on this occasion worn just as much for dramatic effect as for personal protection. As they approached the Wardlow manor house along a wide, well-surfaced track through what appeared to be an extensive deer park studded with mature elm, oak and ash trees, the late afternoon sun glittered and dazzled off their highly-polished plate armour giving the two comrades the appearance of heroes from a chivalric romance. There was, however, scant chivalry and even less romance in Edmund's heart as he raised his right hand to bring the column to a halt, half a bowshot from the front of the house. He half-turned in his deep saddle, addressing Girard.

"Believe me, dear friend, I am as happy to see this day for

practical reasons as I am for moral ones. This rabble," he said, indicating his mercenaries with a flick of his head, "is costing me a fortune to maintain. The sooner I can get some of them settled here as tenants paying *me* rent, the better."

"That sounds like a clever way to get your investment back!" Girard replied with a wry smile. "They certainly do a fine job of frightening the locals. We haven't seen a soul since we entered the first village."

"Perhaps they are all in the church, praying to God for deliverance," observed Edmund with a grin. "I thought we would face a harder fight than this, though it must be said it would take a brave man to come out and face threescore of these ugly whores' sons with only a scythe or a pitchfork."

"Money well spent, then," laughed Girard. "But remember, though the taking may be easy, it is the keeping hold that will be the real test," he warned.

"From what I see before me it should be well worth the effort," replied Edmund, regarding his father's manor house with a critical eye.

"It is so *beautiful!*" exclaimed Ysabel.

"Then it was well-named, for I am told *Plas Anwen* means 'very beautiful palace' in Welsh," said Edmund as he took in the details of the fine dwelling that was soon to be his. His father had clearly expended a considerable amount of money and time in order to create a peaceful haven at the heart of his - of Edmund's - estate.

The approach road passed beneath a square-built, two-storey gatehouse with a battlemented three-storey octagonal tower at each corner. The material was predominantly the new and highly fashionable red brick, with the wall edges, window surrounds and door frames picked out in contrasting pale stone. Once past the gatehouse, the visitor would proceed along a short, fixed bridge over a pretty moat dotted with water lilies. The moat was perfectly square in outline, enclosing not just the house, but also the surrounding carefully-tended gardens.

The Wardlows' comfortable family seat echoed the colours of

the gatehouse, adding a profusion of diamond-latticed windows to provide ample access for the Sun to light its two storeys. At either end, protruding oriel windows ran the full height of the house, creating well-lit bays in which ladies might pursue their embroidery and the man of the house peruse the estate accounts and ledgers with his steward. The whole impression was one of comfort and elegance, well suited to the more peaceful times in which Sir Geoffrey Wardlow had latterly lived. The house, completed only three years earlier, reflected the general move away from building cold, dark, draughty fortifications and instead creating a stylish home that reflected the owner's tastes and, of course, wealth. It was an inescapable fact that, despite its moat and its battlemented gatehouse, Plas Anwen could not in any way be considered 'fortified', but that did not matter to Edmund. He thought it was perfect. If only his mother could have seen it. He turned to Ysabel and Girard.

"I believe we shall be very happy here. I am well aware that there will be obstacles in our path, not the least of them being the continued existence of my two half-siblings and their score of armed retainers and anyone else who may take pity on them and throw in their lot, but I intend to meet those obstacles suitably prepared. Wherever and however I contest my right to this estate, be it in the field or in the courts, I aim to win. Having journeyed this far I will not be denied my prize."

# CHAPTER THIRTY-TWO

ANN WARDLOW looked calmly, almost distractedly, out of an upper storey window at the large body of armed men gathered at the front of her house. She was calm because she knew what it meant and what she had to do. The point of the rondel dagger was pressing against the fine silk of her gown and through her linen chemise until she could feel its cold sharpness pricking the skin between her ribs. She had been driven beyond all reason, fretting for the safety of her family, fearing the worst, and now the arrival of Edmund and his men told her all she needed to know. She was convinced that her loved ones were all dead, murdered by the strangers outside her home, but why? Having lost everything she held dear, she did not wish to stay in the world to find out. A firm two-handed thrust and it would all be over...

*"My lady, NO!"* Marjorie screamed, rushing over to her mistress, wresting the dagger from her hands and hurling it across the chamber. Ann Wardlow sank slowly to the floor, supported by her long-time servant and companion.

"That is not the way, my lady! Do you want your body to lie

forlorn and forgotten under some bleak crossroads and your soul to wander forever in limbo? Do you wish to be truly lost?"

"I am already lost," said Ann, weakly. "At this moment I care nothing for my soul since there can be no worse place it can go than where I have been these past two weeks."

"Then let me care for it," said Marjorie, guiding her mistress to a wooden settle and pouring her a cup of wine from a flagon on the oak sideboard.

A knock came at the half-open chamber door.

"Forgive the intrusion, Mistress." It was Matthew, the steward, accompanied by two farm workers. Ann beckoned them in, slightly bemused.

"We thought you should know there are five-and-twenty of us gathered out of sight behind the house. With your leave we can unlock the storehouse and arm ourselves against the strangers. They mayhap think us cowards, having seen no-one as they approached, but we were making our way here unseen to offer you our help."

Ann stood up and smiled a tired smile. "I thank you from my heart for your loyalty, but I cannot let you face so powerful a force. They have the appearance of hardened soldiers and they are many in number. You would be throwing your lives away needlessly. It is down to me to discover their business."

"But, Mistress! What if you are attacked? What if you are killed?"

Ann looked at Matthew but her gaze seemed to go straight through him. "They cannot kill me, for I am already dead. In all likelihood my loved ones lie murdered, only the Almighty knows where, and it is a fair wager our visitors have a mind to take our property from us. You must agree, Matthew, they hardly look like the bearers of good news, do they?"

"But we cannot give up hope, my lady. We cannot know for sure what has happened to Sir Geoffrey and Master Richard. Remember they took twenty men arrayed for war with them. I'll warrant they can look after themselves if need be. As for your daughter, she has Stephen and Jane with her. I am sure they will help each other wherever they are."

"I commend your optimism, Matthew, but a chill wind blows through my heart and tells me I am alone in the world. There may be hope for your homes and property should Tom and his men return, but for the moment the only choice before us is to learn what these strangers want and to cooperate for the sake of our lives. Let me speak to them on your behalf. Alone."

"Alone? Nay, at least let us escort you, my lady. Should they try to harm you we can take a few with us on our way down," pleaded Matthew.

"No. Thank you. You still have families to care for. I do not fear them. I thought that I would, but until they either cut me down or string me up, I am still mistress here and I will not shirk my duties. It is better your men return to their homes before they are seen and perceived as a threat to our visitors."

Making it clear the conversation was at an end, Ann walked out of the chamber, her tenants moving aside to let her pass. They watched in silent admiration as she gracefully descended the stairs. At the main entrance she stopped to compose herself, then a very different Ann from the one she had been before opened the door and walked out to meet Edmund of Calais.

# CHAPTER THIRTY-THREE

"HULLO, WHAT'S this?" Edmund straightened in his saddle as a lone female figure emerged from the front door of the manor house and began to walk towards him along the bridge over the moat.

"God's teeth it must be the widow!" he exclaimed. "And she's by herself. Hellfire! Her tenants must be spineless to let her face sixty mounted men alone. I suppose I should hate her because she has lived a life of privilege denied to my mother, but by the saints I have to say I admire her courage."

"She's got balls, I'll grant her that," agreed Girard. "More than her cowering farm boys, that's for sure."

Edmund's conscience, such as it was, found itself pricked by Ann's dignity and composure. He swung himself down off his horse and did her the courtesy of advancing to meet her, unfastening his helmet as he went. He was careful, however, to remain without the gatehouse, not wishing to be cut off from his men if matters got out of hand.

Ysabel watched from her pretty blue dun mare as her lover closed with the mistress of the Wardlow estate, wondering what

117

maelstrom of emotions Ann must be fighting to control. Though she was too far away to hear what was being said, Ysabel could guess each stage of Edmund's unfolding story from Ann's behaviour. She knew exactly what Edmund had to tell her; after all, she had lived through, and been a part of, the narrative these past weeks.

First of all, she saw Ann crumple upon hearing her husband's death confirmed as fact. Ysabel's heart went out to her. Edmund caught Ann by the arms for support then appeared to carry on speaking until she pushed him angrily away and slapped him hard across the face. Ysabel assumed Edmund must at that point have admitted being personally responsible for Ann's loss.

Finally, Edmund stepped back, indicating the land around him with a slow, sweeping gesture then pointing to his troops. He hesitated for a moment before tapping an armoured finger on his chest then pointing at the manor house. Ann Wardlow sank to her knees, her head bowed, her spirit seemingly broken. He must have revealed his identity to her, wounding her to the core, the dark secret of Sir Geoffrey's past piercing her already grieving heart like an arrow. Ysabel's breath caught in her chest and tears pricked at her eyes as she witnessed Ann's despair. She knew her beloved Edmund had to see this thing through and claim what was morally his, both for his sake and that of his dead mother, but none of it was the fault of the woman with the tear-streaked face and the muddied gown, sobbing with grief and betrayal at his feet.

Her breath caught again, this time with relief, as Edmund bent down, extending Ann his hand. Ann looked at the proffered support for several moments then, seeming to have come to some kind of decision, took the hand and rose to her feet, though she could not bring herself to look upon its owner.

"I am ambitious, but not heartless," Edmund said to Ann. "You may grieve for your husband in your own chamber, pray for his soul in your own chapel. I shall not turn you out of your home at this point, but you will forgive me if I place a guard around you, for we have much to discuss when the time is right and proper. I wish to..."

Edmund suddenly fell silent, his hand moving instinctively to the hilt of his sword. From around the rear of the manor house men began to appear, armed with bills, bows, swords and axes. Slowly, warily, they advanced, forming up shoulder-to-shoulder in a body some thirty strong, crossing the moat bridge and taking up position just in front of the gatehouse. Fifty yards or so separated them from the main body of Edmund's troops.

Girard licked his dry lips while behind him a subdued clatter indicated that his comrade's seasoned mercenaries were slowly reaching for their weapons. There was a taut, strained silence broken only by the occasional snort of a horse.

*This is it*, thought Edmund. *They intend to fight for their homes after all. We are superior in number and mounted, but they have the look of men who do not care if they die, men who will sell their lives dearly. My force will be weakened, then my half-brother will arrive with his retainers and we shall be...*

Just then Ann Wardlow interrupted his train of thought in a clear, calm voice. "Neighbours, put away your weapons. There will be no blood spilled here today. There is nothing to be gained from sacrificing yourselves in a one-sided melée. Your lord, my husband, is dead. It appears the order of things is about to change. What the future now holds for myself and for those who dwell on this estate I cannot imagine, but for the present we must accept what has happened and hope to come through this with our lives."

Ann turned to Edmund, looking at him reprovingly. "You will at least leave us those?" Edmund turned to Ann, then to her tenants.

"My lady, tenants of this estate, I have come here to claim that which I believe to be mine, to possess it and to administer it. There would be no sense in depredating or despoiling something from which I intend to make a living. It is my dearest wish that the lives of those here should continue as before, the only difference being that your rents and divers other incomes of the estate shall come to me. In addition, my men have travelled far and endured much on the promise of a settled life, and so I shall make provision for them, allowing them grants of land to build houses and grow food. With careful management, tolerance and goodwill there should be room enough for all. There will, of course, be a period of adjustment, but in the long term I do not see why we cannot all live in harmony."

Harry Coverdale, one of the estate's foresters and a brawny six-footer, addressed Ann Wardlow in an angrily pleading tone. "Are we to give in thus easily, my lady? Are we simply to lie down and let these robbers and murderers take away our homes and our livelihoods?"

Ann looked steadily at Edmund as the man spoke, with an expression that seemed neither to censure nor endorse his sentiments, but nevertheless required a response.

"I have a feeling that your mistress knows there is a sensible way forward..." Edmund began, his eyes locked on Ann's.

"Well it is not *my* way!" Harry spat, launching himself across the twenty yards that separated him from Edmund, axe raised, murder in his eyes. Edmund turned and quickly drew his sword, preparing to defend himself. But moments before lethal contact, his would-be assailant was stopped in his tracks by a crossbow quarrel which slammed into his chest, burying itself right up to its wooden fletchings. Harry's body immediately stiffened with the impact, causing him to drop the axe on the sward. He made a gurgling sound in his throat, then sank to his knees before finally falling face down, dead as a doornail. Edmund looked round to see his scar-faced serjeant lowering his discharged crossbow while other mercenaries aimed their spanned ones in case of further dissent.

"Anyone else care to try their luck?" challenged Edmund, the levelled point of his sword slowly sweeping along the group of estate men. He was met with a resentful, stony silence. Half-turning his head and without taking his eyes off Ann's tenants he shouted to his troops. "Withdraw two bowshots from the house and make camp for the present. Go about your business with due care for others. Do not despoil, damage or take anything without asking and do not harass the people, particularly the women. I shall hang any man who commits rape, theft or assault."

Addressing the tenants, he added. "Return to your homes now

and do not go in fear. On the morrow, I shall speak with your lady mistress and your chosen representatives as to how matters will be conducted in the future."

Mumbling under their breath, the estate men began to break up and depart. Four of them attended to Harry Coverdale's slowly stiffening body, wrapping it in a cloak and bearing it away for washing and burial.

Satisfied that, for the time at least, some kind of understanding had been reached, Edmund put away his sword, sheathing it with a gesture of brusque finality before tipping Ann Wardlow a curt, shallow bow and stalking off back to his men.

# CHAPTER THIRTY-FOUR

WHAT HAD been a fine autumn day was coming to a spectacular close. Tattered, parallel ribbons of pink-grey cloud, edged with gold, stretched across the sky, framing the setting sun on a background of fiery orange that faded to a narrow band of intense pale blue at the horizon. Nature's artistry was lost on Kate Wardlow, however, as she slowed Rollo from a mile-eating canter to a trot, and then a walk, having reached a house on the Caerwys village whose occupants she knew well. As she approached through the failing light and lengthening shadows, a man stepped out from behind the building holding a longbow with a broadhead arrow already nocked on the string:

"*HALT!* Or my first shaft goes through your horse and my second through you." He began to draw the bow to show he meant business.

"Hold fast, Walter, it's me!" cried Kate.

"Mistress? Is it young Kate Wardlow?"

"The same," she replied. "Please put up your bow, I have grave news."

Walter Legget, one of the estate's skilled carpenters, lowered his yew bow, removing the arrow from the string and tucking it through his belt.

"Mary!" he called over his shoulder, causing a small, dark-haired woman to emerge hesitantly from the house. "'Tis the young mistress. She is alive and well!"

"Oh thank God you are safe!" cried Mary, rushing over to Kate and reaching up to clasp both her hands. "We have all been so worried since we heard you had not returned yesterday. But what of Stephen and Jane who were with you?" she asked, peering beyond Kate into the sunset's rapidly-fading afterglow.

"Jane is well and travelling home with my brother. Stephen is..." Kate fought back a lump that was rising in her throat: "Stephen is dead. He was cut down while trying to protect us from a band of Godless mercenaries. There are more of them - around threescore – on their way here to take our estate from us. They are led by the man who murdered my father."

Kate looked at the faces of Walter and Mary as she spoke her news, but apart from an expression of shock on hearing about Stephen, they showed no surprise. It was as if they already knew. Her heart sank and her blood ran cold. "They are here already, aren't they? I am too late!"

Walter let out a sigh. "Aye, Mistress. If you sought to warn us, that we might prepare our defence, you are indeed too late. We learned from one of the villagers that the strangers you speak of arrived mid-morning in front of your father's manor house, hence my precautions upon your approach. Your mother, the Lady Ann, met them alone right bravely and parleyed with them." Kate cupped her hand over her mouth in horror at the thought of her mother facing up to Edmund and his terrifying followers by herself.

"Some of the lads thought to make a stand on her behalf, but she bade them put down their weapons for fear of a massacre. She yet dwells in her own house but she is placed under guard. The strangers and their commander have pitched camp nearby. Word has it they intend to settle here alongside us, but how that is supposed to work I could not say."

"I have to see my mother!" cried Kate, starting to turn her mount northwards.

"Heavens no, girl!" pleaded Mary, her concern overriding her usual deference. "It would be far too dangerous." But her words went unheeded as Kate brought Rollo round and urged him towards the heart of the estate.

"Can you not do something husband?" she chided Walter.

"Short of bringing her horse down with an arrow and risking breaking her neck in the process... no," he replied. "She always has been a wilful one. Let us pray that fortune will continue to favour the brave."

Kate was back on home ground now and knew her way even in the gathering dusk. She cantered Rollo for a half a mile or so, then slowed to a quieter walk, all the time looking out for tell-tale campfires and listening for unfamiliar voices. Eventually, she reached a point where she decided it would be best to continue on foot, so as to make as little noise as possible. She tethered Rollo inside an old, half-ruined barn, then began to creep her way along behind hedges and through bushes towards the family home. From cover at the edge of the large, open field in which her house stood, Kate could see rows of tents and campfires surrounded by shadowy figures. She shuddered as she recalled her unscheduled visit to Edmund's previous camp. She turned and headed back into the bushes, meaning to skirt the camp and enter her house from the back. As she made her way through the woods, she heard a rustling sound close by. It started and stopped every time she did. Terrified, she froze, not daring to breathe. Moments later a strong, calloused hand was clamped firmly over her mouth, while a powerful arm encircled her chest just below her bust. A gruff voice from behind, reeking of cheap wine and slightly slurred, hissed in her ear.

*"Hah! Our leader reckons we're to farm this land. Looks like I've found a pretty furrow to plough right here."*

Kate tried to break free but her assailant's grip was too strong. The man dragged her back to where the bushes were thicker. He forced her to the ground and straddled her, bending low over her, maintaining a tight grip on a bunched fistful of Kate's gown with one hand while attempting to loosen his hose and braies with the other. It was now almost dark, meaning Kate could not clearly see her attacker, but her nostrils were filled with the smell of his unwashed body, and her hands, questing for an eye to gouge, felt the clammy, sweaty stubble of his shaved head.

"Oh, so that's your game is it?" the soldier growled, and grabbed both of Kate's wrists, pinning her to the ground. He then realised, however, that he could not finish loosening his clothing with both hands occupied, so he let one of Kate's wrists go and continued fumbling drunkenly with his garments.

Terrified though she was, Kate intended to seize the opportunity. Her free hand felt around frantically. She felt a desperate rush of gratitude as her trembling fingers closed around the spiral-carved wooden handle of Richard's dagger, overlooked by her attacker in the dark and in his haste. Gripping it tightly, she slipped it from its scabbard and with all her strength, jabbed it into the side of the soldier's face, puncturing his cheek.

*"AAAHHHH! YOU LITTLE WHORE!"* the man screamed, the sudden pain overriding the need to keep quiet. He wrested the knife from Kate's grasp, hurling it away into the undergrowth, then dealt her a punishing blow to the face with the back of his hand. Stars wheeled across her vision and she felt herself starting to slip into unconsciousness. She wondered if the end was coming: violation by a drunken mercenary, then a knife across her throat, her desecrated body tossed in a ditch to be eaten by foxes and crows.

Worried that their noise might have attracted attention, her assailant hastened towards his objective. Kate resisted with her remaining strength but the man was too strong, too angry, as the blood poured from the wound on his face.

"It'll be the first and last time you enjoy this pleasure, bitch," he snarled, hitching up Kate's dress and undershift, and bruising her with his fingers as he began to prise her legs apart. As Kate felt the last of her strength ebbing away, she thought of her family and how it had been cursed with ill fortune of late. She even wondered if it were somehow all her fault. Lost in her swirling thoughts, half-conscious, exhausted, she began to feel detached, as if she were looking down on her body without having to suffer the pain and humiliation that were about to be inflicted upon it. Then, suddenly, her attacker froze, his movements on top of her ceasing.

"One false move and you'll be bleeding like a pig on Saint Thomas's Day," said a voice in the near-darkness. The assailant felt the cold kiss of a falchion blade on the side of his neck.

"Get up slowly and turn around," continued the voice. The mercenary struggled to his feet, still panting from his efforts to subdue Kate.

"You'll swing for this, you bastard" said the voice.

Kate, who had propped herself up groggily on her elbows, could only vaguely make out the shape of the voice's owner, but she saw and heard the effect of the heavy iron pommel of his falchion as it smashed into her attacker's face, breaking his nose and knocking out two of his teeth. The mercenary staggered back, cursing, into the waiting arms of two more men who held him securely.

"Bind him well and keep a watch on him. There'll be a show tomorrow morn for sure. We can all watch him dance!"

As the two guards began to walk their prisoner away, Kate's rescuer picked up the horn-panelled copper lantern he had left on a nearby tree stump and swung it in her direction. She knew him as soon as she saw the scar on his face, picked out by the dim light, and he recognised her.

"*Christ on the Cross!* It's young Mistress Wardlow!" Edmund's serjeant exclaimed under his breath, with genuine surprise. "By Our Lady, it's the Devil's own luck we happened along when we heard a commotion, or who knows what might have happened, eh, my lady? Bring him back here a minute lads," he shouted to the other soldiers, sheathing his falchion as the prisoner was turned around and manhandled into his presence.

"You stupid shit-for-brains!" the serjeant snarled at him. "Do you realise what you've done? It's not enough for you disobey a direct order not to molest the women is it? Oh no. *You* have to try and tup the daughter of the lady of the manor just when our commander is trying to engineer a peaceful takeover."

The enormity of the prisoner's crime suddenly dawned on him, the colour draining from his battered, bleeding face in the pale lantern light.

"Ah yes, you might well be afraid now, my friend. The Master may happen to think hanging too merciful in your case. Take him away – no, wait," said the serjeant. He lashed out with his right foot, catching the mercenary squarely in the cods. The man doubled up, groaning. "*Now* you can take him away!"

The serjeant helped Kate to her feet, then offered a supporting arm as they walked towards the camp in front of the Wardlow's manor. Somewhere in her troubled mind she wondered if his saving her life had cancelled out taking Stephen's, but then, she thought, he didn't personally kill Stephen, he was only defending himself from the young groom's frenzied attack. The mental debate it threw up was far too complicated to follow at this point and, in her exhaustion, she dismissed it, deciding for the moment that any help was welcome.

"I came to see my mother," she said weakly.

"Mayhap you will, young lady, mayhap you will. But before you do, let's get some of the camp followers to look you over and tidy you up. We don't want your mother seeing you in this state."

"Thank you," was all a bruised, trembling Kate could manage by way of a reply.

"Oh, don't thank me yet," said the serjeant. "I have feeling my master will want to see you first..."

# CHAPTER THIRTY-FIVE

KATE, DAZED, aching and exhausted from the attack, offered no resistance as three of the camp's women carefully undressed her and tended to her needs. She was bathed, her hair was washed and combed out, and the mud was brushed from her gown. Her other garments were taken away to be aired outside next to a fire, and a cup of warm, spiced wine was pressed into her hands. The women, contrary to Kate's preconceptions, were sympathetic and kind despite their surface roughness. Perhaps they, too, had suffered harsh treatment at the hands of soldiers and understood the importance of female support in such a situation.

An hour later, feeling clean and warm, but still battered and bruised, especially where her attacker had struck her in the face, she was offering her heartfelt thanks to her carers when the serjeant's voice came from without the tent.

"Is the young lady respectable? The master is very keen to see her."

"Yes, Will, she's fit to present to King Henry himself!" replied Esme, one of the camp followers. "He should be so lucky!" laughed one of the others.

The women had been paying Kate a great many compliments regarding her long, red-gold tresses and after their careful tending her hair shone like freshly-polished copper.

Kate had been feeling much more herself while she had been chatting with the women, her blood warmed by the wine and the company, but now that the serjeant had arrived her heart began to pound anxiously at the thought of meeting Edmund again. This time, however, there was no Rollo on which to effect a daring escape.

"Rollo!" cried Kate suddenly. "Oh no, the poor thing will have been tethered all this time without food or drink!"

"Not so, mistress." The serjeant ducked through the tent entrance and stood in the candlelight, now far more smartly dressed than when they had first met on the road. Kate surmised that Edmund paid him well.

"We guessed from your last visit to the Master's camp that your fine beast would not be far away. He has been tended to, so do not fret for him. Fed and watered, but *not ridden*," he said, adding the last two words with a wry smile. "I have a feeling you'll be getting him back soon enough since there's no man here brave or fool enough to take him on, not even my master."

"Thank you again," said Kate, not really knowing what to make of this hard, dangerous, self-contained soldier who in spite of his previous actions had shown that he could also exhibit kindness and compassion. At least now she knew his name: Will. Kate began to think she could trust him after a fashion. She certainly felt safe as he escorted her across the camp, in spite of her recent ordeal.

Finally there it was again: Edmund's spacious blue-and-white-striped campaign tent, under whose awning she had first learned of her father's murder. Kate shuddered as she thought how drastically her life had changed over the past few days, and all of it was down to this one man. As the serjeant ushered her through the flap, she saw Edmund rising from a curule chair to greet her. Ysabel remained seated but her eyes met Kate's with a look full of sympathy and meaning. Kate dared to throw her the briefest of smiles before noticing Edmund's still-bandaged right hand. Her face tightened in alarm as she recalled Edmund's fury at being pinned to his own table.

"Fear not, sister," Edmund reassured her, having seen her discomfort. "After today's regrettable occurrence I no longer feel I can hold this against you," he said, looking at his hand and rotating it back and forth.

Will brought in another chair and Edmund motioned Kate to sit down. She took in her surroundings as she did so. A tent it may have been from the outside, but inside there were rugs on the floor, chairs and a table, various large wooden coffers bound with iron bands and, behind some thick curtains, a low wooden bed covered in luxurious-looking furs. In the centre of the living space a wrought iron charcoal brazier provided heat and light with minimal smoke. On one of the coffers there was a large salt-glazed stoneware flagon full of wine. At a nod from his master, Will took it and filled an elegant silver goblet with wine, handing it to Kate before leaving. Had Edmund proffered the drink she would have refused on principle, but coming from the man who had just saved her life she thought it churlish to decline. Encouraged by Ysabel's example she took an experimental sip of the smooth, red liquid and was both surprised by its rich, sweet, fruitiness and grateful for its restorative warmth. Edmund noticed it in her expression.

"Do you like it? It's a Burgundy from my storehouse in Calais – one of my best sellers in fact. It has travelled remarkably well."

"The wine is delicious," replied Kate, staring into the goblet, "but it does not alter the fact that you killed my father and one of your men almost killed me."

"With regard to your recent ordeal I say again: a most regrettable occurrence. I like to think I pay my men enough to obey my orders without question, but sadly it seems that isolated individuals are unable to curb their more base instincts, no matter how well rewarded. Rest assured the guilty party will pay a heavy price on the morrow. As to your... *our* father, what is done is done," said Edmund. "You would be wise now to accept what has happened and to come to terms with the changes it will bring. Your mother took a sensible and, I must say, realistic approach to recent events. She appears to have acknowledged that the *status quo* has fundamentally altered and made the wise decision not to offer any resistance to a change of governance. She has my respect for that."

"I cannot think that my mother would have given in so easily unless she believed us all to be dead. Does she know my brother and I are alive?" retorted Kate.

"I must confess I omitted to tell her the happy news," Edmund replied, casually studying the back of his hand. "Such knowledge might have given her cause to stiffen her sinews, as it were. Matters might have become, ahem, complicated."

Kate tried to imagine how her poor mother must have felt, grieving for what she believed to be the loss of her entire family. She felt outraged that her cynical, calculating half-brother would manipulate such a situation to his own advantage. She held her tongue nevertheless, wondering what Edmund had in store for her and not wishing to make things worse, but her expression gave her away.

"At least this way needless bloodshed has been avoided," Edmund pointed out, hoping to mollify her somewhat.

"Oh! So you would have been prepared to put us all to the sword had we offered any resistance?" cried Kate in dismay. Edmund was stung by her accusation. Ruthless he may have been, but he liked to think of himself as fair and reasonable too.

"You make me sound like Ghengis Khan, or perhaps Attilla the Hun!" he countered. "I am not some bloodthirsty conqueror of old, come to lay waste to all before me."

Kate looked about her, indicating her wine goblet, her chair and the comfortable surroundings of Edmund's tent. "It seems to me that you find it easy to be magnanimous now that you have what you want. I wonder what would have happened to my mother, my friends and myself had we stood up to your invading "horde". Doubtless the ordeal I suffered this day would have been pursued to its inevitable conclusion," she said, her voice faltering with emotion towards the end.

She shivered and took a sip of wine to steady herself. To her surprise Edmund seemed a little discomfited by her outburst, though he hid it well.

"It may interest you to know that the vile behaviour of one – and *only* one I hasten to add – of my men is a source of the utmost embarrassment to me. I can assure you I am not looking forward to explaining your current state to your mother, thereby suffering another tongue-lashing."

Kate touched the right side of her face experimentally and winced as her fingers traced her bruised and swollen cheek. Ysabel, unable to contain herself a moment longer, rose quickly from her chair and wrung out a square of linen in a bowl of cold water, folding it and placing it gently over Kate's bruising. Kate thanked her with a warm smile, which Ysabel readily returned.

"Yes, well," said Edmund, "we must return you to your mother before she retires for the night. I shall deliver you personally to her so that I might reassure her of my continued desire for a peaceful outcome to recent events, in spite of your appearance. Would you like to come too, my love?" he asked Ysabel.

She nodded her head enthusiastically in response, gathering up a cloak for herself and procuring a spare one for Kate from one of the coffers while Edmund ducked outside the tent to beckon Will and three other soldiers to act as an escort.

Meanwhile, Kate was feeling greatly relieved that Edmund hadn't asked if she knew where Richard was. Perhaps the evening's events had thrown him, or perhaps it had not occurred to him that they might have encountered each other on the road home – it had, indeed, been entirely due to chance that they did. She began to worry that he would ask after all, but then she remembered that Edmund would not know anything of her flight to Llanferres or her overnight stay in the church. For all he knew she and Jane had galloped straight home. She hoped her mother would not let the cat out of the bag as they walked along the track to the manor.

A few minutes later they were at the front entrance of the Wardlow house. Two bill-wielding mercenaries standing guard offered a formal salute to Edmund and the girls, and a more casual nod of acquaintance to Will. As they swung the iron-studded oak door open Kate stepped inside with mixed feelings: relief at being home again, and trepidation as to how long it would remain her home. The first familiar face she saw was Marjorie's. Her old friend and faithful servant advanced to embrace her warmly. "Oh Mistress Kate you are safe! We have been imagining all sorts of terrible things. Thank the Lord! Your poor mother has been beside herself."

Back in her own home and among friends at last, Kate was close to tears, but determined that Edmund should not see them. She buried her face in the coarse wool of Marjorie's gown, taking advantage of the intimacy to whisper in her ear. *It is vital these men do not discover I was out all night.*

Marjorie squeezed Kate a little tighter to indicate that she had understood, then examined Kate at arm's length. "Why, my dear sweet girl, however did you come by such bruises?"

"It is best I explain to my mother," said Kate.

"I shall fetch Lady Ann immediately. You must warm yourselves by the fire," replied Marjorie, before lifting her skirts and hurrying off up the stairs.

Moments later, Ann Wardlow descended the stairs, the guarded look on her face gradually changing to one of undiluted joy. She rushed over to embrace her daughter, purposely ignoring Edmund as she rocked Kate from side to side in her arms. She reacted with horror at the sight of Kate's bruised face, at which point Edmund cleared his throat and stepped in.

"My lady, I am delighted to return your daughter to you. The young lady happened upon our camp earlier this eve. Quite what she was doing out so close to twilight I cannot fathom: a little reconnaissance perhaps? She had an unfortunate experience at the hands of one odious individual who did not fully grasp the concept of obeying orders, but happily my serjeant intervened and she was saved from serious hurt."

"*Saved? Serious hurt?* Are you trying to tell me that you had to rescue her from one of your own men? How can we feel safe in our homes if this sort of thing is going to happen?" cried Ann, drawing Kate protectively into her arms as she spoke.

"I can assure you, my lady, that this was an isolated incident far out of keeping with my intentions for this place and its people. You may be certain that the full measure of justice will be meted out to the offender on the morrow."

"We have already felt the effects of your 'justice', thank you all the same," Ann replied, with bitter irony in her voice. "That is the reason I have no husband and this girl has no father. Your justice is a twisted kind indeed. I cannot understand by what authority you set yourself up to judge others and deal out death."

Edmund recoiled slightly at the ferocity of Ann's verbal onslaught, even though he had not expected the visit to go easily. He resisted the urge to answer Ann argument for argument, deciding instead to call it a night. Offering scrupulously polite farewells in the face of Ann's chilly glare, he made his escape. It was getting late and he had a man to hang in the morning. Let her vent her spleen upon some other poor fool.

# CHAPTER THIRTY-SIX

IT WAS indeed getting late, but nevertheless mother and daughter had much to talk about. Kate was surprised by her mother's apparent composure in the face of all that had happened. There were no tears, though Ann's face was pale and drawn, and the dark patches under her eyes bore witness to the strain she was under. All the same, Kate had been greatly impressed by the steely courage her mother had exhibited when facing up to Edmund. Perhaps concentrating on being strong for the sake of her children and her home was helping to distract her from grieving for her husband. She was certainly a very different person from the one her daughter had waved goodbye to only a day and a half before.

After reassuring her mother that Richard and his party were safe and well and intent on maintaining a prudent distance from the large armed force that was occupying the estate, Kate's line of conversation turned to the tall, dark-haired author of their current misfortunes.

"How much do you know of Edmund's story, Mother?" she began, wondering how much he had told her and how much he had conveniently withheld.

"Only that he is the illegitimate offspring of a former liaison of your father's and that he murdered him under the guise of "political expediency" with the intention of appropriating our land and property for himself, presumably driven by some warped notion of revenge," Ann replied.

"You have summed him up in a nutshell!" exclaimed Kate, marvelling at her mother's perspicacity.

"He is an arrogant, preening upstart who can afford to be bold with threescore of hardened mercenaries at his back," Ann continued. "For the sake of your father's memory I am not about to let our home and our lands be taken from us without a fight, though the struggle will have to be a subtle one. We must convey an outward semblance of obeisance and co-operation whilst covertly exploring every possible course of action."

Kate was still finding it hard to recognise the tough, determined woman her previously nervous, quietly-spoken mother had become. Perhaps Ann Wardlow had been living in the shadow of her self-assured, well-connected husband and only now was her true personality beginning to show. Kate had started to wonder just how hard her father's death had hit her mother, but another look at the drawn features told her that it had indeed been a heavy blow.

Ann read the concern in her daughter's expression. "I have prayed for him, child. I was not permitted to leave the house in order to visit the church, but our "benefactor" arranged for Father Philip to come here and say masses for your father's soul and we lit candles in our private chapel room. Until current matters are satisfactorily resolved that is as much as we can do. In the fullness of time we shall bring him home and commit his body to the ground with full Christian ceremony as he deserves."

Kate took the opportunity to relay to her mother Richard's message that Sir Geoffrey's body was temporarily resting with an appropriate degree of dignity in the Dwyers' family tomb just a few miles from Ludlow. Ann appeared to take great comfort from the knowledge, closing her eyes and letting out a long, deep breath as she did so. Composing herself once more, Ann Wardlow took her daughter's hands in her own and clasping them tightly said, "Richard is our hope through all of this. He faces great danger if he comes here insufficiently arrayed, therefore he must seek outside help. For that he will need money."

Releasing Kate's hands, she walked over to a large, iron-bound wooden coffer. Opening the heavy lid she delved beneath the bed linen until Kate heard a *click* and a secret drawer, subtly camouflaged within the unassuming iron furniture along the base of the chest, popped open a quarter of an inch. Gripping it with her fingernails Ann pulled it fully open to reveal a hidden compartment tightly packed with small leather bags. She took one out and untied its drawstring. She tumbled some of the contents - a glittering shower of gold coins - into her daughter's cupped hand. Kate picked one of them out and inspected it, the candlelight making it sparkle seductively as she slowly turned over it in her fingers. On the obverse was a simplistic image of King Henry standing in a ship holding a sword and shield and on the reverse was a complex design made up of a cross with a flower on the end of each arm and crowns in between, surrounded by the legend: IESUS AUTEM TRANSIENS PER MEDIUM ILLORUM IBAT, *"but Jesus, passing through the midst of them, went His way."* It was a large, heavy coin about an inch in diameter. Kate recognised it as a noble, equal to half a mark, or a third of a pound. One such coin would pay a farm labourer's wages for two whole months, and here were bags and bags of them.

As Kate continued to scrutinise the coin, fascinated by its intricate design, her mother spoke. "Look closely at the side with the cross. Do you see a letter "C" impressed in the centre?"

Kate narrowed her eyes, the better to focus in the candlelight, and nodded.

"Your father told me it signifies that the coins were struck in the King's mint in Calais. Do you not think it ironic that we may find ourselves purchasing aid against an interloper from Calais with coin from his home town?"

The eyes of mother and daughter met, and in spite of their cares they could not help but share a brief giggle.

"I can take this to Richard first thing tomorrow," Kate suggested, full of excitement and ready for another adventure.

The smile instantly fell from her mother's face. "No child, I absolutely forbid it! There is to be no more gallivanting on your part. I would have you stay close by me and be my support and my co-conspirator through these troubled times. Besides, we cannot know how far this Edmund's infuriatingly perfect manners might be tested before he loses his patience and vents his anger upon us so we must tread carefully. Once we make contact with Richard we can send the money out in instalments with the drovers and craftsmen when they take their livestock and carts to the markets at St Asaph and Denbigh. If our unwelcome visitor wishes to run 'his' new estate at a profit he cannot stand in the way of trade, can he? And if he has a mind to send a guard to watch over every movement on the estate he will soon run out of men.

"But now, daughter, it grows late. Rest if you can. I know it will be hard to find sleep, but we must at least try. God protect you and keep you. I shall pray for your father's soul before I retire," said Ann, kissing Kate tenderly.

"As will I," replied Kate, reciprocating Ann's blessing and turning to leave the chamber. She paused at the door, a tear in her eye, and gave her mother the warmest smile her bruised face could muster.

# CHAPTER THIRTY-SEVEN

SLEEP DID eventually find Kate, though her dreams were troubled. There was one particularly vivid one which caused her to wake with a start just as the departing night was giving way to a fresh dawn. In it, she was standing before her family and their tenants in the local church dressed as a bride, in a beautiful dark blue silk gown with a chaplet of woodland flowers adorning her head and her shining red-gold tresses falling to her waist. The man about to be joined with her in the sight of God and the parishioners, however, was none other than Edmund, the Bastard of Calais: her father's killer.

Disturbed by the image and not wishing to go back to sleep and risk its return Kate roused herself and padded over to the bedchamber window, unlatching the wooden shutters and gazing down at the stirrings of a new day. She shrank smartly back into the room upon hearing voices on the sward in front of the house.

Opening the window a crack and peering nervously around the shutters, she saw two of Edmund's mercenaries conversing beneath a tall elm tree not far from the house and just within earshot.

"This one'll do nicely. There's a good sturdy bough sticking out on the level; we'll use that. Master says he wants to dangle him good and high as a lesson to others. Mind, it makes no difference if you ask me. You'd hang just as surely if you was six inches off the ground as if you was twenty feet. Then again, I suppose if you was well out of reach it'd stop your mates yanking your legs to break your neck and speed your end. A long, slow choke it'd be - *grrrrrkkk...*"

"You're a cheerful sod to start the day with!" said his companion, before swinging a heavy-looking coil of rope and heaving up it at the branch. His attempt at getting the rope over it fell miserably short and he cursed loudly as the coils fell back onto his head.

"No, no, not like that, you *pillock!*" shouted the first soldier. "Here - we're going to use this."

He took off the long, narrow canvas bag that had been slung over his shoulder, untied the fastening and pulled out a yew bow. With practised ease he braced one end of the powerful longbow against his foot and began to bend it, sliding the bowstring up the wood until the loop dropped securely into a groove near the tip. He drew it experimentally a couple of times, then propped it against the elm while he took a long length of thin cord from his waist pouch. He selected an arrow from the half-dozen stuffed through his belt and proceeded to tie the thin cord around the shaft, just below the goose-feather fletchings.

"Why don't you just tie the big rope round it?" queried the second soldier.

"Because... Look, just tie the other end of the cord to the rope and be ready to haul it up once I've shot it over will you?"

Kate watched as the archer raised his bow, drawing it no more than half way so that when he loosed the arrow it flew neatly over the selected bough. As it went, it pulled the thin cord behind it, stopping in mid-flight when it met the resistance of the heavier rope. The arrow swung back down towards the soldiers, bringing it to within a few feet of the ground. The archer's accomplice attempted to grab it but fumbled the catch, swearing loudly as one of the arrowhead's acutely barbed points pricked the fleshy part of his thumb.

"*Owww!* Why didn't you use one of those blunts you keep for knocking down birds and rabbits?" he complained.

The first soldier looked at him, rubbing the stubble on his chin as if evaluating him. "You know, I can't help but think that by the time our master got round to recruiting *you,* decent mercenaries must have been a bit thin on the ground. Not much choice. Well picked over you might say. Bottom of the barrel so to speak..."

His companion glowered at him, sucking his injured thumb. "All right, all right that's enough sport at my expense," he snapped. "Let's get this over with then we can see about some breakfast. I could eat a horse."

"Well you could chew on that cussed beast of Beelzebub as belongs the young lady of the manor. Unrideable by all accounts but plenty of meat on it."

"What, the horse or the young lady?"

At this point both men roared with laughter. Kate felt distinctly uneasy at being the subject of such a coarse joke and shrank further back behind the cover of the shutters. When she dared to peer out again the soldiers were squatting down side by side. She could not see what they were doing, but eventually they both stood up, one of them hauling in the cord over the bough. As he did so, the thicker rope crept up higher and higher. A sudden chill ran through Kate as the end of the rope finally came into view, revealing a freshly-whipped, grimly businesslike noose. The soldiers secured the free end of the rope around the trunk of the tree. The uncomfortable conclusion to which she had been trying not to come for the last quarter of an hour had been confirmed. Edmund was going to hang her attacker in full view of the house.

Kate felt shaky and a little bit sick. She prayed fervently that Edmund would not come knocking at her door insisting that she and her mother witness his "justice" being done. Nevertheless, she was surprised, and a little guilty, to find that a part of her was actually flattered that this man was prepared to order another man's death on her behalf. She was horrified to feel her cheeks flush at such a notion and quickly dismissed any thoughts that Edmund might possess even the smallest measure of chivalry. He was an out-and-out murderer, and that was that.

Kate quietly closed the window shutters and went about the business of dressing herself. Normally Jane would have helped her with her clothes and her hair, but Jane was, of course, still with Richard's party, presumably somewhere the other side of Bodfari. Kate hoped that her friend and her brother were faring well.

A short while later, prepared, at least on the outside, to face the day, she resumed her vigil at the window. An insistent, penetrating drizzle was now falling from the iron-grey sky, turning the hills in the distance into vague purple smudges. A sizeable crowd had gathered; mostly Edmund's soldiers, but among them also a number of estate tenants. Kate wondered whether they had been roused from their beds at this early hour and coerced at bill-point into watching the proceedings so that Edmund could demonstrate his intention to maintain discipline among his men, while at the same time issuing a subtle warning to any locals who might be thinking of challenging his takeover. Some soldiers pushed their way through the throng carrying the components of a trestle table and two folding chairs. They set them up a few yards from the tall elm tree, just in time for Edmund, his expression as grim as the weather, to appear and take his place. He was accompanied, as always, by Girard but Kate noticed that Ysabel was nowhere to be seen. Presumably Edmund had been enough of a gentleman to spare her the grisly spectacle of a hanging. Enough of a gentleman to spare herself and her mother too, thought Kate with relief. Clearly, although the appointed place of execution was right next to the house, Edmund had at least allowed mother and daughter the choice of witnessing the event or not. Before taking his seat Edmund drew his long, narrow sword, laying the naked blade cross-ways on the table in front of him; a symbol, Kate supposed, of the military nature of the proceedings.

She winced as her attacker of the night before, dressed only in his shirt and braies, was brought before Edmund and felled to his knees by a vicious prod in the back from the butt of a bill. Though his hands were tied behind him and his face still bore the bloody evidence both of Kate's desperate defence and serjeant Will's contempt, the man seemed unbowed, even defiant. Kate strained to listen as Edmund addressed the gathering.

"I have summoned you all here this day to witness justice being done. The prisoner before this court was discovered in the act of rape, a vile pastime whose pursuit I had strictly forbidden upon our arrival. I trust that in the interests of fairness and good relations it will not be lost on my new tenants that I am executing one of my own men for a crime committed against one of their number."

*One of their number!* thought Kate. *He cannot bring himself to admit in public that it was I who was attacked though all must know by now. More manipulation, more economy of truth...*

"It is my express wish," continued Edmund, "that our two groups should learn trust and tolerance, that we might live peacefully side by side."

"Live peacefully side by side?" snorted the prisoner. "Hah! I'd rather eat my own cock!" Edmund glared at him.

"That can be arranged," he growled, in a menacing tone.

Undaunted, the mercenary continued his rant. He indicated the tenants with a gesture of his head. "These people are like sheep, ripe for shearing. We should take our plunder and move on to the next set of weaklings. We are not peasants who would settle down and till the soil. We are soldiers. We don't farm; we fight. This 'experiment' of yours will not work because you are too soft. It is doomed to fail."

The prisoner looked Edmund in the eye as if daring him to do his worst. Edmund did not disappoint him.

"And you are doomed to die! Think yourself fortunate that you will only hang today. Had the weather been more suited to the spectacle I would have had you broken on the wheel."

The mercenary's eyes suddenly widened, betraying a moment of raw fear as he pictured the alternative to a short, desperate struggle on the end of a rope. In France and in Germany 'breaking on the wheel' was a common punishment for reviled criminals. The legs and arms - and perhaps a rib or two - would be systematically smashed with an iron bar, then the pulped limbs would be threaded around the rim of a cart wheel which would be set atop a pole, leaving the wretched victim to die slowly in contorted agony. It was enough to silence the prisoner.

"It is time!" Edmund announced impatiently. "Let sentence be carried out."

A soldier placed the noose securely around the prisoner's neck while three more prepared to haul on the other end. Before the rope choked the power of speech from his throat the condemned man let out one final, defiant shout. *"I SHALL SEE YOU IN HELL, EDMUND OF CALAIS!"*

Edmund looked into the man's rolling, bulging eyes as he was hoisted into the air and replied coolly. "Indeed? Then you can save me a seat by the fire!"

There was a collective gasp from some of the tenants, shocked by such Godless language from their new landlord, but most of the soldiers merely smiled at their master's grim humour.

Their heavy burden now high in the air for all to see, the men of the lifting party secured the rope around the trunk of the tree and left it to do its deadly work. Feeling her gorge rising, Kate turned from the window in horror, closing her eyes tightly and clamping her hands over her ears. She was mercifully deaf to the condemned man's curdled gargling as the thick rope slowly strangled the life from his body, and did not see him soil himself as his bowels let go, the mess running down his dancing legs and dripping onto the grass. It took four twisting, spasming minutes to free the mercenary's soul to fly off to whatever Hell was reserved for a man who had murdered, raped and plundered his way through France for the last twenty years of his life. As the prisoner's final twitches marked the end of the morning's 'entertainment' Edmund, examining the lolling tongue and bulging eyes, seemed satisfied.

"Sentence has been carried out. Let the body remain here for a day and a night as a warning to any who would jeopardise our peace."

Kate heard Edmund's words as she tentatively took her hands from her ears. She opened her eyes but dared not look out of the window for fear of what she might see. At that moment the door to her bedchamber opened and her mother came in.

"Oh my dearest, come away from the window! How much did you see? Such horrors are not for a child to witness."

"I covered my eyes and ears, Mother. It was too terrible!" Kate ran to her mother and felt a flood of relief at her warm embrace.

"It is well that you are up and dressed betimes," Ann continued. "The hour appointed for our visitor to return draws near. The sainted Edmund will no doubt be eager to poke his nose into our accounts to see what rich rewards his new acquisition will reap. It will stick in my craw to hand over the running of our lands to that opportunistic interloper, but for the time being there is no other choice. At least Marjorie and I have managed to stow the family gold where he will not get his bloodstained hands on it. Today, and until we are in a position to wrest back our property, you must do as I do. Be outwardly courteous and cooperative, but inwardly strong, patient and discreet, though the former not too readily so, lest he think something afoot. Come, daughter, let us break our fast while we have time and put some food in our stomachs. It will likely take all our strength to keep a smile on our faces for our new lord."

# CHAPTER THIRTY-EIGHT

KATE AND her mother were not the only Wardlows breaking their fast at that moment. Less than five miles away, Richard had finished his second piece of cold mutton pie and was wiping his mouth with the back of his hand, replacing the grease and crumbs with a satisfied smile.

"My men and I are most grateful for your generous hospitality, Sir Caddoc," he said, honouring his host with a small bow of the head.

"Och, it is nothing lad. Least I can do in the circumstances," scoffed Sir Caddoc *ap* Rheged, a Welsh knight of renown and long-standing friend of Richard's father. "I wish I could do more, but you see how it is."

"You have already helped us beyond measure," Richard reassured him.

The previous evening he and his retinue, despite trying to stay out of sight, had crossed paths with Sir Caddoc out hunting with a small party of servants in the wooded hills above Bodfari. Richard had initially felt ill at ease, not knowing how he would be received after siding against their common sovereign, but Sir Caddoc had greeted him warmly and offered him and his men shelter and food. Thus it was that Richard's retainers were able to sleep in a warm, dry barn on clean straw, instead of damp woods and ditches, and taste fresh meat and good beer after days spent eating nothing but raw vegetables bought from the villages they passed through.

Richard and Tom were housed in a hastily-prepared spare room in Sir Caddoc's comfortable stone manor house, while Jane was given a warm, safe pallet in one of the female servant's quarters. After a much-needed wash, Richard and Tom enjoyed a hearty meal in the company of Sir Caddoc, his beautiful young wife, Seren, and his two sons, Twm, who was nine, and Trahern, who was seven.

"Ah! I feel thirty years younger when I look upon my blessed family!" exclaimed Sir Caddoc. His first wife had died during an unsuccessful childbirth and he had spent many lonely years coming to terms with his loss until he met Seren, twenty-five years his junior and in his eyes every bit the shining star her Welsh name proclaimed her to be. She smiled sweetly up at him as he squeezed her to his side, clearly as happy with their marriage as he was.

"My dear, loving wife," he said proudly. "And these two fine boys she bore will carry on my line when I am dust. Twm, my first-born, 'a gift from God' – how apt a name when I thought I would never dandle a child on my knees, and Trahern, 'strong as iron', a right troublesome little bugger that one. I can see him doing well at the tournaments one day."

Richard and Tom indulged the boys, privately marvelling at how well brought up they were, neither tiresomely precocious nor overly shy; just proud Welsh warriors-in-waiting.

Once the food was consumed and the table had been cleared, Seren tactfully removed herself and the boys on the pretext of putting the youngsters to bed, leaving the men to speak freely. The remainder of the evening had been spent by a roaring fire, the three friends deep in conversation. Their progressively more animated discussion was lubricated with copious amounts of good Welsh ale, the old knight preferring it to wine, as clearly evidenced by his ample paunch.

Richard was grateful for the mollifying effect of the ale, having spent the first part of the evening pacing impatiently up and down Sir Thomas's hall chewing his knuckles and demanding to know where Kate had got to.

"Why did I let that little harpy go? It has ever been her way to court trouble and danger. God alone knows what has become of her. For all we know her severed head might be stuck on a spear outside the manor and her horse boiling away in a stew pot, assuming that murderer and his mercenaries have already reached our home."

Sir Caddoc laughed out loud. "I have watched you two grow from babes and I am quite certain your sister's pretty head is at this moment still firmly attached to her shoulders. She is a nimble-witted, chary lass, if a touch impulsive at times, and can fend for herself. I'd say that at worst she has been arrested and confined to the manor house. Do not fret; I am sure she is back among friends and neighbours by now. I dare say your mother will be mightily relieved to see her."

Richard remained unconvinced, but took another draught of ale from his pewter tankard. This was not the weak, everyday "small" ale that sustained every estate in the country throughout the working day; it was best quality strong Welsh ale, brewed with care to be savoured and enjoyed. It was certainly going to Richard's head. After the emotional upheavals and physical privations of the past few days he didn't know whether to laugh or cry as he began to let out his feelings. There were tears and anger at the loss of his father, concern for his mother and sister and hatred for his half-brother, but the two older men helped him through the ordeal with comforting words and friendly assurances, until Sir Caddoc judged it was time to lighten the mood with a story or two. He motioned a servant to throw more logs on the fire.

"Did I tell you I fought for the previous King Henry at Agincourt?" he began.

Throughout his childhood years Richard had heard many of the old knight's lurid tales, but through the pleasant befuddlement of the excellent ale he was happy to hear them again and managed to make a suitably encouraging response.

Sir Caddoc smiled. "Aye, sixty-one years old I am now, so I was but a lad of seventeen - your age, Richard - when my father and I stood among King Henry's tired, ragged army on that rain-sodden field of mud, with all the power and pomp of the French nobility sneering at us, just itching to teach us a lesson.

"There were but five thousand of us against twenty thousand of them. We were convinced our time had come so every man was confessed and shriven. All that remained was to sell our lives as dearly as we could that day for we truly believed would not see another. We took up position between two parallel plantings of trees while our archers hammered in wooden stakes, sharpening the ends in the hope of impaling the French horses when they charged. Then, the worst thing that can happen in a battle happened..."

"What was that?" asked Richard, imagining all manner of nightmarish, bloody scenes.

"*Nothing!*" replied Sir Caddoc. "All keyed up we were, ready to do or die, and the bastard French just sat there, maybe three or four bowshots away, for three hours. It was sheer bloody Hell waiting. King Harry must have thought so too, for about mid-morning he gave the order '*advance banner*', and we all upped stakes and moved closer to the enemy. We stopped at the farthest range for our archers' longbows and they selected their flight arrows – the ones with the trimmed-down fletchings and smaller heads – and let fly a few volleys to gall the whoresons into doing something other than just sitting on their armoured arses looking pretty. It worked a treat. Two large bodies of mounted knights advanced to attack each of our flanks. Banners flying, armour glittering, men shouting war cries as their brightly-caparisoned horses bore down on us... Och, Richard you never *saw* such a spectacle! Hah! but their assault foundered as their mounts struggled in the mud and our archers loosed thousands of shafts into them. It was extraordinary to see the cream of the French aristocracy being shot to pieces by common bowmen standing there barefoot in a ploughed field with shit running down their legs."

"Why was that?" Richard interrupted. "Were they afraid?"

Sir Caddoc laughed out loud. "Haha! No, not afraid, lad - *terrified!* As any sane man would be. But that's not why their bowels had let go. See, they'd been marching for so long they'd run out of wine and ale, and been forced to drink from rivers and ponds and such. Disgusting habit if you ask me. No good ever came of drinking water in my opinion; gives you the Godawful runs at the very least. Why do you think Our Lord Jesus Christ turned it into wine eh? Anyway, some of the men had even thrown away their braies and hose, they were so badly soiled, but I reckon it must have gone hard for some of those French nobles that day, turning up in front of Saint Peter and having to admit they were sent there by a commoner who was naked from the waist down and covered in shit! Mind you, that was only the start of it. Shortly after the attack on our flanks the entire French centre began to advance. Well, I say advance; it was more like the ones at the rear pushing on the ones at the front in their eagerness either to slaughter the archers or capture and ransom the nobles. Right cock-up it was, no discipline at all. There was chaos everywhere; men-at-arms all squashed together unable to ply their weapons, mounted knights on arrow-maddened horses trampling their own foot soldiers, and all the while our bowmen pouring their deadly shafts into the heaving mass of French - they simply couldn't miss."

The old knight continued his epic tale but Richard's eyelids were becoming progressively heavier under the influence of his host's best ale until they closed altogether. He jolted awake just in time to hear Sir Caddoc rounding off his narrative.

"So there you are. Makes me laugh – they call it England's greatest victory but it was mostly the Welsh bowmen as won it for them!"

He looked at Richard as he struggled to appear attentive, then winked at Tom. "Time for bed I think."

Thus it was that the next morning that Richard found himself nursing a headache of epic proportions at the breakfast table while the three of them discussed his next move regarding the Wardlow estate and its unwelcome occupiers.

"I wholly understand your father, God rest his soul, supporting the Duke of York in his quarrel; after all, their friendship goes back a long way. It is unfortunate, however, that the present Duke seems to be continuing to suffer from the ill luck that has dogged his line," expounded Sir Caddoc. "Not only was his father, Richard, Earl of Cambridge, implicated in a plot and executed shortly before the previous King Henry sailed for France, but his uncle Edward, who held the title of Duke of York at that time, suffocated in his armour under a crush of bodies at Agincourt. It is a wonder the present Duke was restored to the title at all after his father's attainder for treason. He should be grateful for his privileges, and yet he still cannot resist making political waves. I do not think it will end well for Richard Plantagenet."

"They say he has fled to Ireland," said Tom. "I do not suppose he can return from there without running a grave risk of having his head struck from his shoulders."

"Leaving his faithful supporters to face the wrath of the King and find themselves under sentence of death, or attainted and landless," added Richard, a note of bitterness in his voice.

"Calm yourself lad," said Sir Caddoc. "Our King Henry is a pious and gentle man who prefers forgiveness to vengeance, provided his harridan of a wife doesn't stick her oar in. A proper vindictive one, that Margaret. 'Tis true, the most powerful of the nobles who took a stand against their sovereign will have to have their wings – or more likely their necks – clipped, but your father has already paid a high price. Far too high in my opinion, and done wholly without regard to the law of the land, but then this Edmund is a calculating venturer with no morals. As for your fears of attainder, young man, the sins of the father are not usually visited on the son and in any event you are not officially set to inherit until you reach one-and-twenty. Your mother is your father's successor for now, and I doubt a decent man like King Henry will be in a hurry to throw a respectable widow out of her home, even if that turd Edmund is. In any case, you are very unlikely to appear on any list of offenders who may be called to account for their actions, since you are not yet knighted. I mean no disrespect lad, but you are just not important enough for them to come chasing after you."

"Ah yes, my spurs," said Richard, his face falling. "I had hoped my father might present me at Court when I reached eighteen, but after openly defying King Henry's authority I think it unlikely our sovereign will be knighting me now, or at any time in the future."

"Don't despair, lad, stranger things have happened," Sir Caddoc encouraged. "You are young, with your whole life ahead of you and no-one can foresee what things will pass your way. You may perchance have the opportunity to do the King some great service when you are older and reap the rewards of his gratitude. For now, however, we must concentrate on ousting that murdering swine from your family's home, and mayhap obtaining some sweet revenge in the process."

"We need more men," said Tom. "We know that he commands threescore mercenaries, hardened veterans of the French Wars. It would be suicide to mount a direct assault to try to retake the estate."

"Besides which," added Richard, "he has my mother and sister under his 'protection'. We dare not be too obvious in our approach for fear he should turn his attentions on them."

Sir Caddoc rubbed his tangled grey beard. "The surest way to winkle him out once and for all is by due legal process. He wouldn't have a leg to stand on, but then I've known such things take ten years or more to be resolved in the courts. It would be satisfying to see his claim officially discredited by a judge once and for all, then watch him slink off home to Calais with his tail between his legs. There'd be nothing he could do after that, unless he wanted a sheriff and five hundred of the King's men knocking on his door."

"But we'd all be ten years older!" Richard exclaimed, finding it hard to hide his mounting exasperation. "There must be a quicker way."

"Well, lad, you know you can count on my support and advice for as long as I am here to give it, but as I told you last night I don't have enough men to make any great difference to your cause since my estate is considerably smaller than your father's. Didn't stop the buggers sending me a Commission of Array demanding six fully-equipped men to join the King's forces at Ludlow though. Six fully-equipped men, I ask you - the expense!"

"What did you do?" Richard enquired.

"What did I do? What I always do in matters concerning the English 'authorities'. Completely bloody ignored them, that's what I did! Now it's all blown over I doubt they'll come round here making a fuss. One thing is sure, however, you cannot stay here, much as I would enjoy having you. Your family's lands are only next door and it wouldn't be long before one of this Edmund's men saw you on his travels and worked out who you are, then there'd be trouble."

"Aye," said Tom, "it is fortunate that as yet he does not know what you look like, though should he see you at the head of twenty men wearing Wardlow livery coats, he might just gain a clue. If you were to return home someone would give you away, even though they would not mean to. We must do our best to hide our identities for now, and take great care in our movements and in the number and size of our meetings. The men are eager to see their wives and families again, but they understand the need to keep their distance for the time being. Should any of them return to their homes and it be discovered that they were with you at Ludlow there is no telling what our new friends might do to them in order to find out where you are."

Sir Caddoc nodded his head gravely in agreement, then his face suddenly brightened, his bushy eyebrows shooting up into his tangle of grey hair. He slapped the table with his right hand. "I have an idea! What about Roger Kynaston, the Constable of Denbigh Castle? You know him as a good friend both to yourself and to your father. You'd be more than safe there."

Richard recalled the long-standing friendship between his

father and Roger in spite of the difference in their ages, and also the fact that he, like his father, was a staunch ally of the Duke of York, having fought with distinction at Bloreheath in September, then set out again for Ludlow less than a fortnight later with his retinue. A truly loyal supporter, thought Richard - and then a shadow of doubt crossed his mind. "But surely, one so heavily involved in the Duke's cause as Roger is bound to be singled out for retribution after what he has done? I hear that Jasper Tudur is bent on wiping out Yorkist support in Wales and he has an army and the King's endorsement to achieve that end. Roger would doubtless be on his list. Sheltering in Denbigh would be like hiding in a hen-coop to escape the fox."

"Ha! Do not distress yourself over Jasper Tudur, lad. True, he'd do almost anything to keep well in with his half-brother, the King – I have heard he's even willing to turn on his own countrymen, let alone the English - but I very much doubt he could take Denbigh. The castle is strong, and even the town has stout walls about it, which is a pity for him, seeing as King Henry appointed *him* Constable of it two years ago in young Kynaston's place! I can't see Tudur taking up his new position in a hurry without Roger having something to say about it, can you?

"Och, that Jasper! His head has swelled so much since he was made Earl of Pembroke *and* a bloody Knight of the Garter at such a tender age, I wonder his helm still fits. He's as bad as some of the English 'royal officials' who seem to think they run things hereabouts. No offence to your father of course – as the *saesnec* go he'd have made a good Welshman and I can't pay him any higher compliment than that. Anyway these 'officials' don't molest me, see, thanks to my 'loyal and distinguished service' to our present King's father in the French Wars, but since our country became overly populated with English landlords your ordinary Welshman can expect to be harried and bullied at the whim of the sheriffs, purely for being Welsh, it would seem. I tell you, it was not so very long ago some of the poorer Welsh families were treated like chattels, to be bought and sold and owned for all of their lives. Shameful it is! A lot of it is revenge – served cold - still trickling down from the rebellion of Owain Glyndŵr, the last Welsh Prince of Wales, but that was more than fifty years since. He has more than likely been dead forty years now, I shouldn't wonder. Doesn't stop the persecution though, but then I think the English just enjoy acting like bad bastards. Well, some of them, anyway..."

Richard smiled at Sir Caddoc's closing remark then informed him of the decision he had reached during his grizzled host's persuasive discourse. "Denbigh it is then, if Tom agrees. We shall put our trust in its sturdy walls and its distinguished constable. It will serve as a safe harbour from which to direct operations against my cuckoo half-brother."

Tom nodded his assent before throwing his head back and draining the remainder of his ale.

"Splendid!" agreed Sir Caddoc. "I can provide mounts for yourself and Tom, and perhaps four of your men. I want 'em back, mind! I'm afraid the rest of your lads will have to walk there. I dare say you can find the place without my help as you've been there often enough! 'Tis not quite five miles – it will take less than half an hour on horseback and an hour and a half on foot."

"My thanks to you - my sincerest thanks," said Richard, grasping both the old knight's hands tightly. "My father chose his friends well. And we would not dream of being so churlish as to abuse your horses. It is indeed a pretty approach to Denbigh and there is little to be gained by rushing headlong into action against Edmund and his men without proper planning, though I must confess that when Kate did not return yester evening I would gladly have galloped full tilt into the midst of them and tested my sword arm."

Sir Caddoc laughed. "Your enthusiasm did not go unnoticed lad! Happily, however, you appear to be growing wiser by the hour. You have lost your father and your home in one fell swoop - a terrible blow to be sure, but if you use your head rather than your heart, you will overcome in the end. My servants will give you whatever you need for journey. God speed."

# CHAPTER THIRTY-NINE

BY MID-MORNING, the drizzle that had accompanied the execution of Kate's attacker had all but petered out, leaving in its wake a cold, damp, cheerless murk. For a few moments a thin band of brightness on the far horizon had offered a fleeting hope of deliverance from the sullen greyness, but even as Kate watched from the small side window of her bedchamber it was swallowed up by a gloomy overcast sky determined to set its leaden seal on the remainder of the day. Kate's mood matched the weather, having just returned from the private family chapel where Father Philip had said masses for her father's soul. She missed him terribly, but the task of helping her mother to deal with Edmund served to occupy her thoughts to a large extent and to prevent her from sinking into a maudlin state of mind.

One half of the front window had been left open by one of the servants to air the room, but now it was admitting an unwelcome chilly draught. Without thinking, Kate went over to close it and recoiled in shock as her gaze met the grisly spectacle of the hanged man still dangling from the elm tree. Unable to tear herself away, she found herself staring at his protruding, dead eyes and swollen, lolling tongue, listening to the hempen strands of the rope creaking gently as their eighteen-stone burden slowly swayed and twisted in response to the strengthening breeze.

The spell was broken by a reassuringly familiar sound, the chiming of her father's clock marking off the hours. Five years earlier, Sir Geoffrey had commissioned the impressive timepiece at a cost of over twelve pounds, overseeing its installation on top of the manor gatehouse, where it would not go unseen by visitors. The mechanism was ideal for the location, being one of the latest compact, spring-driven types and therefore having no need of cumbersome heavy weights suspended below it. Though he would dearly have loved to leave the complicated works of the machine on open display, he had accepted that the weather would soon have taken its toll on his investment, and compromised instead by protecting it from the elements in a small, specially-constructed brick tower and attaching a six-foot square wooden clock face to the front. The face was painted a vibrant sky blue and dotted with small white clouds, a sun and a crescent moon. Roman numerals from I to XII, picked out in gold, ran around a large gold outer circle and in each of the lower corners saintly figures in white robes blew Judgement Day trumpets. Kate had fallen in love with it from the first moment she set eyes upon it and could never understand why her father, instead of admiring its outer aspect from the approach road as she did, preferred to squeeze through the narrow trapdoor into the cramped confines of the tower, where he would while away many an hour winding, adjusting and tweaking the mechanism. It must simply be something that fathers do, she had concluded.

The clock possessed but a single large hand, to indicate the hour of the day, and upon each hour a countwheel caused a bell to be struck. The sound carried surprisingly well, regulating not only the daily comings and goings of the immediate household and the inhabitants of nearby Caerwys to the south, but also reaching as far as Pen-y-Cefn to the north, helping to justify to Father Philip Sir Geoffrey's insistence that if the estate were to have a clock it should be installed in the centrally-located manor house rather than in St.

Michael's Church at Caerwys. The inhabitants of Tremeirchion, however, separated by high ground from the rest of the estate, still relied upon the small bell at Corpus Christi Church, and upon Father Philip's lay assistant Benjamin to toll it at the appropriate times.

"... *eight, nine, ten.*" Kate counted to herself, remembering with a start that ten o' clock was when Edmund and his delegation were due at the house, no doubt to lay down his distorted idea of the law, and no doubt strip her family of the house and the lands they loved, along with anything else he could find. Her morale sank lower still as she thought of Edmund perhaps taking a shine to her father's clock and claiming it as his own, showing it off to visitors as if he himself had come up with the idea. Nevertheless, whatever her woes she had to put on a brave face. Edmund's handwritten note to Ann, delivered by a messenger half an hour after his departure the previous evening, stated quite firmly – though couched in impeccably polite language of course – that her daughter's presence was also requested at the morning meeting. Kate was not sure what she might be able to contribute to the proceedings, wondering instead whether Edmund was simply involving her out of concern for her feelings. She could not see it as anything other than perverse, however, that the man who had killed her father should take pains for her not to feel left out. *Far more likely he is afraid that I shall gallop off to seek aid, and simply wants me where he can see me,* she thought to herself as she descended the staircase and made her way to the Great Hall.

A servant bowed to her at the door, leading her past two of Edmund's burly, heavily-armed guards to one of the ten high-backed, plain oak chairs that had been arranged around the lower banqueting table in place of the usual long wooden benches. A smaller, 'high' table which would seat the Wardlow family on large, formal occasions stood on a raised dais at the far end of the hall, but Edmund had deemed it too cramped for the day's business.

On one side of the hall, the floor of which had been strewn with fresh rushes, there was a huge stone fireplace flanked by a pair of carved, seated greyhounds and on the other side four generous, full-height windows glazed with diamond-shaped leaded glass. Overhead soared a magnificent oak hammerbeam roof. The fire was doing a fine job of keeping the attendees warm, but the windows, magnificent as they were, struggled to admit sufficient light for the proceedings owing to the miserable weather outside. On Ann's orders expensive beeswax candles blazed in pewter holders, attempting to counter the sepulchral gloom that was threatening to drain all colour and life from the normally lucent room. Silver wine goblets were placed around the table, with a servant at hand nearby to fill them. Though it stuck in Ann's craw to share a table with her husband's murderer she felt obliged to offer him something to drink at least; a grudging nod to the customary hospitality that every visitor had a right to expect. She was damned if she was going to feed him though. The temptation to stir a generous helping of belladonna into his bowl of stew would have proven too strong to resist.

To Kate's acute embarrassment it seemed she was the last to arrive. Her slight flush deepened as Edmund half rose from his seat, tipping her a short bow. He had forsaken the previous day's armour for a practical but smart knee-length coat of deeply pleated, fine, dark blue woolcloth trimmed with squirrel fur, worn over a light blue and gold brocade doublet, bright red hose and ankle-length boots. On his head he wore an impressive black chaperon, consisting of a thick roll of fine woollen cloth out of which draped an elaborately-fringed cockscomb and a long tail. He looked every inch the elegant, well-heeled gentleman of leisure, but in stark defiance of the rules of entering another's house an expensive sword and a brass-hilted rondel dagger hung from either side of his belt ready for immediate use. On top of all this his sharp gaze possessed a vulpine energy that served to remind those who dealt with Edmund of Calais that he was no soft, indolent fop.

"Ah, Sister! I am happy that you are come at last. Let the meeting commence."

Kate forced a polite but flustered half-smile then settled in her seat, her gaze modestly lowered as protocol dictated, but nevertheless surreptitiously taking in the faces around the table as she nervously fiddled with the bowl of her goblet, exploring the fine repoussé and chasing with her fingertips.

Observing the seating arrangements Kate noted to her surprise that her mother, her face veiled in mourning, had been accorded the head of the table. Edmund sat on her immediate left, Matthew, the estate's steward, to her right. Girard sat next to Edmund, then came Ysabel and Will, while between Matthew and Kate were Father Philip and Thomas Pettigrew, Matthew's clerk. She wrestled with the notion of her mother being seated in the place of honour. Edmund was either being exceedingly polite or insufferably patronising, knowing that he was about to strip away the family's property and belongings. Her half-brother opened the proceedings, addressing Ann Wardlow at first, then casting his eye around the other attendees.

"I am certain that by now you are all acquainted with my history and the events which brought me to this place under these circumstances. I am here to take possession of that which I believe morally to be mine, insomuch as my recently deceased father did abandon my late mother and me without thought or provision for either of us. The purpose of this gathering is to effect the beginnings of a peaceful and efficient transference of ownership."

Edmund then began to cite a variety of justifications for his actions, followed by a list of his intentions regarding the future running of the estate.

Most of what he was saying, couched as it was in legal and financial language, went over Kate's head, with the result that as the meeting progressed she found her attention repeatedly drawn to Edmund the man, as he boldly set out the terms of his takeover. Engrossed as he was in the proceedings he appeared oblivious to her scrutiny, allowing her to make a detailed study of his features. He was indeed intriguingly handsome, the fashionable straight, shoulder-length black hair that showed under his hat contrasting with his pale skin, while his long, straight nose, chestnut-brown eyes and thin brows lent him an almost feminine delicacy that belied his martial prowess. She could see nothing of her father in his appearance but concluded that his mother must have been a great beauty. Fancifully recalling heroes from past history she compared the dark, poised Edmund with her shorter, stockier, fair-haired, blue-eyed brother: Edmund a cool, charming but calculating Saladin to Richard's open, honest, passionate Coeur-de-Lion. Such a pity, Kate mused, that Edmund had given himself over to evil.

Suddenly, her half-brother darted her a brief look that sent a shiver all the way down to her feet. She hastily dropped her gaze to the table, feeling quite unsettled at being caught out and praying that her discomfiture did not show. With mixed feelings of alarm and fascination, her thoughts returned to the dream in which she was about to wed Edmund. Her blood ran cold. Of course; that was it! Marrying her would permanently secure the estate for him, provided – here she shuddered – her mother and brother were dead. Would he do such a thing? Would he murder yet more Wardlows in cold blood to achieve his aims, not to mention setting aside the beautiful Ysabel?

It was at this point that Kate realised just how badly her beloved father's death had impaired her capacity for rational thought. Of course no marriage of the kind could take place. Edmund was her half-brother and no priest in the land would bless such a blatantly incestuous union. She must calm herself, she thought, but then the panic returned. Her mother! She bore no blood relation to Edmund, and although she was technically his stepmother the two had never met until now, never shared their lives. Given sufficient persuasion in the right ears, and perhaps a bribe or two, there might be a way for him to cement a solid claim to the estate for himself and his descendants by forcing a marriage with Ann Wardlow, then installing Ysabel in her place should Ann meet with an unfortunate 'accident'...

Kate's head began to spin with the enormity of the myriad nightmarish possibilities her fevered imagination was generating. Whichever way she looked at the situation, she and her loved ones seemed to be completely in Edmund's power and it frightened her to her very core.

When she felt able look up again, Edmund's gaze was once more directed straight at her, this time more intensely, the faintest curl of a hint of a smile playing at one corner of his mouth. Kate felt as though he were privy to her every thought, sensing her anguish and drawing sustenance from it. Had someone at that precise moment told her that Edmund possessed a warlock's power to see her naked body through her clothes, or to control the movements of her limbs as it pleased him, she would have believed them. Utterly discomfited, she rose quickly form her seat, her face flushed.

"Forgive me, I... I..."

Edmund immediately leapt to his feet, enquiring solicitously, "Why sister, whatever is the matter? Can I be of help?"

"It is nothing, just a headache, that is all. I shall go to my chamber if you will all excuse me," Kate replied gamely, managing to conceal her horror at the thought of any 'assistance' from Edmund.

Ann Wardlow was also on her feet and had by this time reached her daughter's side, cupping Kate's elbow in her hand and gently guiding her towards the door.

"I shall return when I have attended to my daughter's needs," she addressed Edmund. "In the meantime please feel free to appropriate my home and my property as you see fit."

Finding himself momentarily lacking a suitable response to Ann's biting aside, Edmund merely gave an acquiescent shrug, gesturing the two women graciously towards the door with a sweep of his hand.

Once safely past Edmund's guards, Ann took Kate into a small side room, beckoning a passing kitchen girl to bring an infusion of white willow bark for her daughter's headache. As Kate sipped the medicine Ann tenderly stroked her hand. "Do not be troubled, sweetheart. It may seem as though our lives are being taken apart nail by nail, board by board, but we can still fight for what is rightfully ours."

Kate had heard her mother express similar sentiments several times the night before. At the time she could not bring herself to believe that there was any hope for the family, but now the animated look on Ann Wardlow's face engaged her attention.

"I received word from Richard this very morning, while you were in your room!"

Kate clasped her mother's hands excitedly at the mention of her beloved brother's name.

Ann looked cautiously over her shoulder before continuing. "He, Tom and the men spent the night at the manor house in Bodfari. One of Sir Caddoc's servants rode over to Walter and Mary Legget's house early this morning and passed on the message by mouth. Richard intends to ride for Denbigh Castle and ask our friend Roger Kynaston for shelter and assistance. Edmund cannot hurt him there."

"No. Unless..." Kate's face fell as she spoke. "... Unless Edmund decides to draw Richard out from hiding using our lives as bait."

"The possibility did occur to me, which is why I have written to your brother to forbid him utterly to yield to any such low threats. We may find ourselves in grave danger, but should Richard give in to Edmund all will be lost. Rest assured, if Edmund should turn against us I will protect you to my last breath."

"And I you, dearest mother!"

The two embraced, then Ann, looking about her once more for eavesdroppers, lowered her voice to a near-whisper. "On a more cheerful note, it may please you to know that shortly before our new 'master' arrived this morning I dispatched three carts with instructions to make for Denbigh by different routes. Each is carrying one hundred marks in gold coin, hidden in sacks of wheat, flour and...", Ann wrinkled her nose in mock disgust, "barrels of salted fish!"

Kate giggled. "I dare say they will have to give the last lot a good wash before they can spend any of it!"

Her mother smiled too, then became serious. "The men I have sent on this errand are my most trusted servants. Each knows he is carrying a fortune and each knows he may face great danger, but if, with God's blessing, they arrive safely in Denbigh, Richard will have the means to pay for his keep and look after his men, and there will still remain sufficient funds to hire more soldiers should he essay to retake the estate by force." Ann paused, letting out a deep sigh. "I have also, very reluctantly, set aside three hundred marks for our beloved Edmund to "find", since he will no doubt ransack our coffers to pay his ruffians' wages. He would become highly suspicious were there nothing left to steal, though perhaps he is not expecting to find a great deal of ready coin if he believes what people say, that many of the English gentry live on loans and mortgages. He need not know how hard your father and I worked to save our fortune."

"We, meanwhile, are penniless then!" exclaimed Kate. "Is there nothing left for us to live on if Edmund should throw us out? Where will we go when Edmund moves into our house, as he surely will? Will we have to live in draughty Denbigh Castle with Richard, or will we be wandering the roads, sleeping in barns and eating berries?"

Ann tapped the side of her nose with her finger. "Do not fret my dearest. A lady should always have funds put aside for a new gown! Or in our case, food, drink and shelter. I have entrusted one hundred marks to Father Philip for just such a purpose. There are hiding places in the church that even Edmund could never guess. Nor, I suspect, would he have the stomach to look in them if he knew of them".

Kate, her overactive imagination picturing a long-dead, skeletal hand clutching a bag of gold coins in some dusty vault beneath St Michael's, thought it best not to enquire further.

Amused by the look of horror on her daughter's face, Ann continued. "In addition, I still hold the manor that was my dowry when I married your father. It is only very modest, with a stone manor house, three farms and an income of twelve pounds a year, but your father insisted it should always remain mine. It is at

Carmel, a mile or so to the north of Holy Well. You went there once as a small child."

Kate's memory was hazy, as she had only been four years old at the time, but she did remember being carried into an old, pretty, stonebuilt house with a rose garden and a view of the sea, and she recalled the family saying special prayers as she was bathed in the cool, green waters of St Winefride's Well.

"Was I ill, Mother?"

Ann stifled a sob at the memory. "You were close to death, sweetheart. Your father and I were at our wits' end as to what to do. I have always known of the supposed healing powers of the waters of the Holy Well, but it was only in desperation that I suggested it to your father. He is..., was, a modern, practical man and I did not think he would have any truck with what he might see as superstitious nonsense."

"But it worked," said Kate. "I got better."

"Yes, sweetheart, you got better, thank God in His mercy." Ann replied, wiping a tear from her cheek with the heel of her hand.

"You and your brother are more precious to me than you can possibly imagine," she continued, "and I promise you Edmund will not rob us of everything."

Kate gave a start. "Your manor, though! Edmund will discover it when he goes through the records of the estate and claim that, too."

"No child, he will not. Matthew was instructed long ago to keep the records pertaining to my manor and its income separate and well-hidden, so when Edmund inevitably presses him for details of your *father's* estate and its incomes, that is exactly what he will get. If we are discreet and careful he will never find out about Carmel. And now, if you are feeling recovered, we should return to the Great Hall, lest Edmund has by now convinced himself that we have been plotting his downfall, and that we have hired a thousand Flemish mercenaries to drive him into the sea!"

# CHAPTER FORTY

"Ah, Sister! You are yourself again I hope?" Edmund asked politely.

"Quite so, thank you," Kate replied. "I am sorry to have deprived the meeting of my mother's presence for so long."

"No matter that she was not here," said Edmund, in a light, airy tone that set Ann Wardlow seething inwardly. "Our business here is done, for now. Your good friend Matthew has furnished us with the information we need to begin to make the estate work for us *our* way."

Ann Wardlow glanced at her steward. A fleeting look passed between them which only they could understand after their many years of close friendship. It was obvious from his sagging shoulders and the downcast set of his face that Matthew had been coerced into handing over the armfuls of documents and rolls that detailed the estate's various incomes and properties, but something in his eyes told Ann that he had not revealed the existence of her manor at Carmel to Edmund.

Grateful for Matthew's courageous discretion but concealing her relief, Ann went on the attack, pricked by Edmund's smugness.

"We have functioned perfectly well these past twenty years, thank you. I do not see how a wine-seller from a Calais town house can think it possible to walk straight into a sizeable country estate and simply... run it."

Edmund rose slowly from his chair. Had Ann's barbed comment been uttered by a man, he would almost certainly have leapt to his feet, drawn his sword and more than likely used it, but though her words stung his pride he did not let her see it.

Leaning forwards, he rested both hands on the table, fixing Ann with his eyes and answering her in a controlled, patient tone. "My lady, I shall assume your remark is born of 'motherly' concern, but fear not, we are amply qualified for the task ahead of us. I, as you so acutely observed, am an experienced man of business, while my friend Girard is a lawyer of not inconsiderable talent. I also know whence I might now call upon the services of an experienced steward. In addition, may I remind you that there are threescore men in my employ who also possess a particular aptitude for the kind of work for which they are paid."

"Threescore less one," Ann interjected. "You hanged one for trying to rape and kill my daughter, remember? I do not envy you the job of keeping your hirelings in check. They must be drooling like wolves in a sheepfold, gawping at all the rich pickings around them. They will need feeding, housing and paying, too. You hold our lands only by the force of their arms. Be mindful that they do not forsake you and tear your precious new estate apart before you can start to enjoy it!"

Edmund's expression tightened, the muscles in his jaw tensing and relaxing by turns.

Kate was fretting dreadfully. Her mother had quite clearly forgotten all she had said about swallowing their pride and treating Edmund with courtesy in order to smooth their path through the present troubles, and appeared, instead, to be careering headlong into a heated confrontation, the possible outcome of which she dared not contemplate.

Mercifully, Ysabel came to the rescue. Sensing Kate's growing panic, she glided over to Edmund's side and slipped her arm through his, announcing in her sensuously liquid, heavily-accented English. "It will soon be time for the midday meal, *mon trésor.* Let us return to the camp and leave these good ladies to their preparations. *À bientôt, madame* Ann, *mademoiselle* Kate." Ysabel accorded each a small curtsey as she spoke their name, then applied a subtle but firm pressure to the inside of Edmund's elbow. After a moment's deliberation he allowed himself to be escorted gently towards the door of the Great Hall, followed by Girard and Will carrying armfuls of documents. Unfortunately for Kate, however, Ann's emotions were continuing to get the better of her and before Edmund reached the safety of the doorway she launched a parting shot at her husband's killer. "You seem very sure of your own future here, but what of ours? Did you decide our fates while we were out of the room? Are we to be kept as hostages, as pawns in your game? Are we prisoners in our own home, our lives held to ransom?" demanded Ann.

"Heavens, no, my lady!" Edmund replied testily, inwardly reeling from Ann's bombardment of questions, his midday hunger adding a sharp edge to his increasingly nettled disposition. "You are free to come and go as you please. You even have my blessing to ride pell-mell to make contact with your beloved Richard wherever he might have secreted himself, but if you do so please do not be surprised if you are followed. As you might imagine, I am most anxious to meet my dear half-brother in order to discuss... family matters."

*"Kill him, you mean!"* Ann snarled, her previously carefully-maintained facade slipping as her protective urges were roused.

A look of genuine surprise replaced the frown on Edmund's face.

"Why, no, as it happens. My grievance was against my father and the matter was dealt with under the rules of war."

*"Rules of war?"* Ann exclaimed, unable to hide her disdain. "You mean it suited you to murder my husband for personal gain then explain it away as an act of loyalty to the King!"

Edmund's expression darkened. "Under the warlike conditions prevailing at the time, summary military justice was dispensed to an enemy of the Crown," he replied, in what sounded to Ann like a well- rehearsed defence of his foul deed.

"I wonder if the courts will see it as you do," she said coldly.

"My actions will be examined and duly judged, *as will your husband's*," he replied, with carefully measured emphasis, "But for the present the fact remains that, despite unremitting provocation on your part, I neither need nor indeed wish to harm either your son, your daughter or yourself. Though looking at matters from his perspective, I am in no doubt that my dear brother would gladly skewer me on the end of his sword given half a chance. I merely seek to come to a mutual understanding now that I have what I want. I intend to keep hold of that which I consider to be my inheritance, and since, in this country, possession seems to constitute nine-tenths of the law, I would appear to have the upper hand. Granted, my task would be considerably easier were you all lying side by side in the family vault and in times gone by I might have wished it so, but however helpful your sudden demises might be to my cause, I do not relish the idea of explaining away three closely related and highly suspicious peacetime deaths to one of the King's Coroners."

Ann was momentarily silenced by Edmund's apparently sincere reassurance that she and her children were not, as she had feared, about to become food for the foxes and the ravens.

Taking subtle advantage of the lull and still determined to get him out of the house before any more trouble could brew, Ysabel once again pulled gently at Edmund's arm. This time he acquiesced, having wearied of Ann's tirades and the constant need to justify his actions to her.

*Were I my father I think I would gladly have cut my own head off just to escape from that carping witch,* he thought to himself as one of his guards opened the door of the Great Hall. He held his breath as he walked out into the corridor, bracing himself for a further outburst from Ann, then exhaled with relief when it did not come.

As Edmund and his party left the house and made their way

back to their camp, Ann Wardlow, left in the company of Kate, Matthew, Thomas and Father Philip, sank into her chair and wept bitterly, her reserves of strength and dignity sorely depleted by the morning's exchanges. Kate knelt by her side and comforted her as best she could, while the men regarded each other with grim faces, as uncertain of their futures as their mistress.

# CHAPTER FORTY-ONE

THE LAST of the wine that had travelled with Edmund all the way from Calais seemed to taste sweeter than ever as he perused, then absorbed, the information from the various rolls and parchments Matthew had given him. In the comfort of his striped campaign tent he had spent the last two hours reading deeds, accounts and ledgers, handing them to Girard as he finished with them. Ysabel sat by Edmund's side, her arms wrapped around one of his, her expression one of excited anticipation.

"Is it good news, my love?" she enquired.

"Thirteen manors in all!" he exclaimed. "Each with an average income of, oh, shall we say fourteen pounds. And then, it appears, there are the various fines and fees payable to us quarterly by divers traders. I should say that we are looking at a total income in excess of two hundred and twenty pounds per annum – enough to buy our way into the Royal court and more besides!"

"I shall need new dresses!" declared Ysabel.

"And you shall have them!" her *chevalier* replied. Edmund's mind was racing, the manifold prospects opened up by such a handsome revenue all jostling for his attention. Amid the whirlwind of new and exciting possibilities his thoughts turned to his mother, long since laid in her grave. Despite his lack of any real faith, he felt moved to give a silent prayer of thanks for his good fortune. Composing himself, he turned to Ysabel, clasping both her hands in his.

"We have spent enough time under canvas. We are no longer on campaign. The estate and the house are ours to command. I shall serve notice upon the troublesome widow and my hot-headed sister to quit the hall by the end of the week and we shall install ourselves thereafter in a manner befitting persons of property and influence."

"*Mistress of Plas Anwen*!" Ysabel proclaimed, her excitement boiling over.

"And what of you, dear friend and comrade-in-arms," queried Edmund, addressing a quiet, thoughtful-looking Girard. "What will your well-earned share of our good fortune mean for you?" Girard stroked his chin reflectively whilst slowly twirling his wine goblet to and fro in his other hand.

"I think I shall find myself an English – or Welsh – rose and settle down to a life of ease and country pursuits, punctuated by spells of legal representation when I cannot avoid working for a living. London, of course, is where lawyers are most needed."

Edmund looked dismayed. "Surely you are not planning on deserting us after all our adventures together?"

"Fie, no!" retorted Girard. "We find ourselves in uncommonly pretty country where a man can be active and free and teach his sons to ride and hunt.

I would not trade that for the clamour and stench of the city. Temporary lodgings, or a small house conveniently situated for the courts are all I would require while I am working. My home and my hearth would yet remain here. We have come far, dear friend, and this is our Canaan, our promised land."

"Flowing with milk and honey," enthused Edmund, heartily relieved at Girard's avowal, "...though sadly lacking in drinkable wine!"

# CHAPTER FORTY-TWO

THE COLD drizzle, which had dogged Richard Wardlow and his mounted advance party on their short journey across the Vale of Clwyd, finally stopped as they began to make their way slowly up the steep, narrow, winding streets that led eventually to the great bulk of Denbigh Castle rising out of the misty greyness at the top of the climb.

The lower part of the town was alive with activity as the inhabitants went about their daily chores, trying to scrape a living by any means in what were hard times for those not fortunate enough to be born into money. Over and above the chatter of people buying, selling, arguing, gossiping and complaining it was the heady mixture of smells – some pleasant, some decidedly not so – which furnished the most determined assault on the senses. The streets, with their jettied houses either side, almost meeting in the middle, seemed enveloped in a steaming, misty fug in which the sweet scents of bread-making and brewing vied with the more pungent odours of animal waste and unwashed townsfolk.

Richard's horse shied as it passed three dogs snarling and snapping over a discarded bone thrown into the road by a butcher.

Further on, geese hissed at passers-by from a wooden cage, hens cackled and clucked as they darted between people's feet, and a goat tethered near the corner of a building bleated contentedly as it emptied its bladder into the street.

Eventually Richard and his men reached the two round towers of the Burgess Gate; a sturdily-built portal that guarded the entrance to the older, walled part of the town adjacent to the castle. At the gateway burly guards holding ferociously-spiked Italian bills monitored the steady trickle of people passing in and out, demanding to know their business and checking their credentials. As Richard's party drew nearer, one of them looked up.

"Ho! It's Master Richard Wardlow! How fare you, young Sir?"

"I fare well, thank you John," Richard replied, having recognised the guard from his many visits to the castle.

"Where is your father today?" John continued.

A pang of grief shot through Richard's heart. Tom Linley came to his rescue. "Sir Geoffrey has met with ill fortune, John," he said with a meaningful look. The guard seemed to understand and returned Tom a small, quick nod of acknowledgement.

Tom continued. "We need to see your master on urgent business. May we pass?"

"Of course!" replied John. I'll take you to him myself."

Richard and his party dismounted, leading their horses along the road through the old town. The walled area was laid out in burgage plots - strips of land with, typically, a house facing onto the street and a long, narrow yard at the back, perhaps with a workshop or a storehouse at the end.

On they went, past various market stalls and the tall, slender tower of Saint Hilary's Chapel until they reached the castle's huge, imposing gatehouse with its three powerful octagonal towers, a drawbridge and several portcullises. The horses' iron shoes clopped over the wooden drawbridge then clattered on the stone floor of the main entrance passage.

Looking around and above him, taking in the numerous arrowslits and murder-holes that peppered the thick stone walls and ceiling, Richard very much doubted that anyone could ever force their way into such a well-defended place. He wished that his mother and sister were safely ensconced behind Denbigh's stout walls, but ever since Kate had galloped off into the sunset the day before he had received no word as to how they fared, well or ill.

The little party emerged from the relative gloom of the passageway into the large, open space of the castle courtyard. Richard felt immediately at home; after all, he had spent seven years of his life at the castle under Roger's guidance learning the skills of knighthood. Training with various knightly weapons had taken up much of his time, of course, but he had also been carefully tutored in reading, writing, music, dancing and even serving at the high table. One of the most honourable duties a knight could be asked to discharge during his career was to serve the king personally with his food and wine in the rarified surroundings of the royal court, where the use of proper manners and some subtle involvement in the many discreet conversations taking place around the table could see a man advancing beyond his station.

As the son of a wealthy knight, it had always been the intention that Richard should be sent away to be thoroughly schooled in the arts of war, although the abrupt cessation of hostilities against the French six years earlier, coupled with the breakdown of law and order in England and Wales, meant that the emphasis was now placed more on protecting one's local interests than on launching belligerent forays abroad. Sir Geoffrey's bailiff and old friend Walter Askham, a hoary old veteran who had served in France under King Henry V, had originally begun tutoring the lad at home. Starting at the age of five with short wooden swords and staves, young Richard practised the rudiments of attacking, parrying and countering with the sons of some of the estate's household men.

As he grew older and stronger, what had been no more than robust play began to take on a more serious aspect. Walter knew as well as Sir Geoffrey that when it came down to it, warfare was not about chivalry and shining armour, knightly manners and merciful compassion. When men met on the field, fired by the heat of battle, they survived by any means at their disposal. In the inevitable and savage hand-to-hand fighting that followed an opening exchange of missiles, the principal aim was to keep a very sharp lookout for incoming blows from whatever quarter, blocking them if possible then replying with a determined counter-attack. If your opponent was fully armoured, a well-aimed thrust with the point of a sword or a pollaxe into vulnerable areas such as the visor slit, armpit or groin might prove effective. Should you be facing less well-protected troops, the choice of targets was much greater. Arms, legs, hands, feet, faces; all provided excellent opportunities for inflicting disabling injuries.

"Put the bastard down before he does it to you, then on to the next son of a sow. Let the bloodlust take over. Relish the strength and endurance it bestows upon you, but do not let it scatter your wits. Keep a cool head while those around you are swinging and slashing wildly to no good purpose. Measure your strokes well and deal out death to your opponents. Strike them down, trample them underfoot. *God is on our side and He will forgive us our trespasses!*"

It was in this colourful fashion that old Walter encouraged Richard and the others to develop the controlled aggression and steely tenacity needed in a tight corner.

"Good manners won't get you through a fight, boy!" he would frequently remind Richard.

When Richard reached the age of nine his father entrusted the rest of his training to Roger Kynaston, nine years his senior and destined soon to be appointed constable of the castle. The boy took to castle life well, enjoying the camaraderie and tolerating the teasing of the regular garrison soldiers. As his training progressed, Richard became accustomed to fighting in more and more armour. He would practise his weapon techniques whilst wearing a variety of general issue pieces, some of them looking decidedly secondhand, borrowed from the castle stores. Over time, his bodily strength and physical endurance increased until finally, at the age of sixteen, his father had presented him with a full, made-to-measure harness of his own in the Milanese style. Words could not adequately convey

Richard's excitement and pride as each piece of armour was fastened in place, either with straps and buckles or with leather laces that attached to reinforced points on his padded arming doublet. Sam, two years his junior, acted as his squire, beginning the arming process at the feet and working his way up, finally, to the head.

As befitted the son of a knight, Richard also became a competent horseman, however, anticipating a time when Sir Geoffrey and his son might find themselves in the thick of battle, Roger introduced into Richard's training the idea of fully-armoured knights pairing up to fighting on foot. The reasons for adopting this strategy lay both in the acute vulnerability of a large target, such as a horse, to the devastating arrowstorms unleashed by the archers which made up the larger part of the armies of the day, and also the severely restricted field of view available from inside a visored sallet. With the visor down, the knight had only a narrow slit, perhaps a quarter of an inch high, through which to view the crowded and deadly confusion of the battlefield. To make matters worse the sallet was almost invariably worn along with a bevor, a shaped plate that fastened at the back of the neck and protected the throat and chin at the front. This meant the wearer could not turn his head to see attackers coming from the sides, but had to turn his whole upper body. Teaming two knights together considerably reduced this handicap and allowed a pair of fit, skilled fighters to cut a swathe through less well-protected infantry with terrifying efficiency, while at the same time watching each other's blind sides.

The favoured weapon for this type of tactic was the pollaxe, weighing around seven pounds and consisting of a six-foot wooden shaft fitted with a multi-purpose steel head. The design of the head varied but Richard's had a regular axe blade for lopping limbs on one side and a heavy, flat hammer face for bashing armour out of shape, perhaps crushing a vital joint and reducing his opponent's mobility, on the other. It also boasted two short but useful lateral spikes and a longer one on top, for thrusting into vulnerable areas of an opponent's harness to deliver the *coup de grâce*. To prevent the business end of the piece simply being chopped off, long riveted metal strips known as 'langets' extended from the head to half way down the length of the shaft, and at the end of these was a rondel which acted as a hand guard.

A heavy, two-handed weapon like the pollaxe provided the most effective means of tackling plate armour, especially when wielded in strong, well-practised hands. Richard had always approached his training with enthusiasm, hence, by the time he had returned to the family home on his seventeenth birthday, his father was satisfied that his son could more than look after himself in a battle situation and, perhaps more importantly, could be relied upon to exhibit good reliability and awareness when fighting back-to-back with a partner.

Though knighthood for Richard was still some way off, Sir Geoffrey Wardlow had wished for his son to be as well-equipped and as thoroughly prepared as possible for the bestowing of that greatest of honours. There were no worries on that score: at just turned seventeen, Richard Wardlow was a credit to his family name.

# CHAPTER FORTY-THREE

THOUGH HE had only been there a day and a night, Richard was beginning to feel trapped and restless in Denbigh Castle. He was grateful beyond measure for the protection and hospitality given by his friend Roger Kynaston, and gladdened by the sympathetic company of his former mentor, but every minute spent immured in the town's extensive and formidable stronghold was another minute during which Edmund could be tightening his grip on the Wardlow estate.

The evening of Richard's arrival had been something of a repeat of his time with Sir Caddoc, there having been a requirement for him to re-tell the story of his father's murder for Roger's benefit whilst being plied with the best drink in the castle. By the following morning, Richard was beginning to wonder, through yet another sore head, how many more times he would survive having to relate Sir Geoffrey's tale through the bleary haze induced by strong Welsh ale.

Nevertheless, he was up at first cock-crow, walking from his temporary lodgings in the Green Chambers to the gatehouse to take a little breakfast with some of the guards in the porter's lodge, though he barely spoke a word, his mind racing as he endeavoured to work out his next move. Having fed his thinking apparatus, he took a pot of small beer with him and headed up the stone stairs onto the walkway connecting the porter's lodge with the Great Kitchen Tower. From his vantage point Richard could see for miles, the most striking feature of course being the long ridge of the Clwydian Hills dominating the skyline to the east. Across the flat bottom of the river valley he could plainly see Bodfari, home of his friend Sir Caddoc, and a little way to the north, Tremeirchion, one of the villages belonging to the Wardlow estate.

Richard racked his brain until his head ached from more than just the previous night's ale. What would his father have done? What would Tom advise? He knew in his heart the word they would use: 'caution'. *To Hell with caution*, thought Richard. For all he knew his family might at this very moment be standing before his murderous half-brother barefoot, with nooses around their necks, pleading for their lives. He had to do something, and quickly. Whatever his plan, though, it could only involve Edmund and himself, since a direct attack on the estate would be doomed to bloody failure owing to Richard's force being sorely outnumbered. If he could come up with something that might exploit a weakness in his enemy - arrogance, perhaps, or vanity - he might stand a chance of isolating Edmund and making the quarrel personal. That was it! That was the answer.

He saw off the remains of his ale in a single draught, setting the pot down within one of the crenels, then turned and sprinted along the wall walk, startling a half-awake guard about to begin his morning patrol. Scampering down the steep stone stairs, then glancing around the inner ward, he made sure Tom was not around to spot him. Richard knew his serjeant would not, for one moment, go along with the idea that had sprung into his head five minutes ago, and would no doubt do his best to dissuade him for his father's sake.

Richard was utterly determined, however. It was his plan and he would see it through. He could not afford to have others interfere.

Satisfied that the coast was clear, he set off at a brisk pace in the direction of the Treasure House Tower, where the town records were kept and where he hoped a scribe could be found; a scribe who could supply him with ink, parchment and complete discretion in exchange for a little silver. He was in luck.

# CHAPTER FORTY-FOUR

GLANCING FIRST at Ysabel, then at Girard, an intrigued Edmund broke the red wax seal on the letter he had just been given. A messenger sent by Richard from Denbigh Castle had initially delivered the missive into Ann Wardlow's hand, along with a note asking that it be opened by Edmund in front of the family and their chief advisers. Ann had promptly sent word for Edmund and his friends to join her at the manor house, fretting as she did so over what her son could possibly have to say that he could not impart to her first.

Sitting at the long banqueting table in the Great Hall, Edmund carefully unfolded the letter, studied it with raised eyebrows, then handed it to Girard as if it were some strange alien artefact whose purpose he could not divine. His companion read it slowly, with a lawyer's thoroughness, before sharing the contents.

"A challenge to a trial by combat!" he exclaimed to the small, select group that had been gathered together.

Kate gasped, while Ann Wardlow's hand went to her throat in an unconscious gesture of dismay. Matthew looked gravely at

Father Philip, who responded by making a sign of the Cross, then slowly shaking his head.

Girard continued in a formal tone in keeping with the text. "I, Richard Wardlow, rightful heir to the estate of my late father, Sir Geoffrey Wardlow, recently most foully murdered, do hereby challenge Edmund of Calais, base pretender to the Wardlow family inheritance, to meet in single combat before the walls of Denbigh Castle. The fight shall be *à l'outrance*, that is to say it shall end only when one of the combatants gives up his soul - the victor to be decided according to God's judgement."

*"May the saints preserve us from such madness!"* cried Ann Wardlow, close to fainting.

As Matthew offered her a steadying hand, Father Philip, surprised by his own courage, spoke out, addressing Edmund as boldly as he would have Richard had he been present. "I need not remind you of the views of the Church regarding the fighting of duels, nor of the terrible and certain damnation of your eternal soul should you participate in such a contest."

"You are quite right, Father. You need not." Edmund replied coolly. "So..." he continued, resting his elbows on the table and pressing his pursed lips to his steepled fingers, "...my brother takes shelter in Denbigh Castle. He has some powerful friends."

Edmund raised one eyebrow as he glanced at Girard, as if seeking some kind of confirmation. Girard returned him the slightest shake of his head and Edmund nodded in acknowledgement. Taking up the letter once more he held it aloft in his right hand, waving it as he spoke to emphasise his words. "Trial by combat is indeed a quaint notion; a custom that surely died out with our great-grandfathers. And yet, and yet... how quickly matters might be settled, once and for all, by a few well-placed blows. What time, what travails, what expense, what needless bloodshed could be spared by pitting the chief litigants against each other."

Ann Wardlow shuddered inwardly, unable to grasp which way Edmund was going with his pronouncement and terrified at the thought that he might accept Richard's challenge; that she might be forced to watch her beloved son fight for his life and perhaps lose it.

Kate's emotions were see-sawing between cold fear at the possibility of losing her brother as well as her father, and raw excitement born from the knowledge that Richard was a trained fighter, skilled with sword and pollaxe. Edmund might be the taller but Richard was the broader of build. If her brother could best Edmund then perhaps the latter's mercenaries, deprived of their paymaster, might be persuaded to leave the estate peacefully and the Wardlow fortunes would be restored. Her hopes of a quick solution were dashed, however, when Edmund stopped waving the letter and tossed it back onto the table with a flick of his wrist. It slid along, spinning as it went, finally coming to rest directly under Ann Wardlow's nose.

"After due consideration I give your son my answer, and my answer is *no*," he declared firmly. Ann Wardlow let out the breath she had been holding, tears of relief welling in her eyes as she glanced down and saw her dear son's familiar signature - large and bold, if not overly scholarly in execution – at the bottom of the neat, scribe-written parchment. She knew Richard had meant every word; she knew he would have given his all in combat to avenge his father and protect his family's interests, nevertheless she offered up a silent prayer of gratitude that he would not have to – at least not on his own.

"I do not doubt that few men would fail to be attracted by the romantic ideal of settling a matter of such great import by a feat of arms," Edmund continued, "but I have waited too long and come too far to risk losing everything I have worked for in a single unguarded moment. All it would take is a slip, a stumble, a drop of sweat in the eye, an ill-considered attack or an inadequate parry, and the contest is over, quarter neither sought nor given. I would far rather pursue my case through the courts, where it can be heard and assessed by men of learning, than chance my arm on some dew-slicked castle green before an audience of gawping rustics."

Kate's disappointment battled for a few agonising moments

with her relief and she had to bite her lip to prevent herself from calling Edmund a coward, but she knew in her heart that he was no such thing. Her shoulders dropped and she slumped in her chair as she visualised what lay ahead. Of course she should have known that Edmund, having physical possession of the estate, would be more than happy to spend the next few months - years, if necessary - knee-deep in writs, claims, counter-claims and litigation, ably assisted by his lawyer friend Girard. No spark of chivalry or romance in a pile of boring old papers, but that, she supposed, had long been the thinking man's way of doing things and Edmund was nothing, if not a thinker. Richard's gambit had been so very characteristic – full of passion and commitment – but out of place in a harsh, cynical, modern world. Suddenly she missed her brother terribly. She wanted so much to talk with him about their father's death and many, many other things.

Recent events had given her the final push away from girlhood and towards becoming a young woman, and she desperately wanted to know how those same events had affected her brother; her beloved, handsome brother. It was at that point that part of the answer became apparent to her.

In offering to fight Edmund man-to-man Richard had taken a great risk, one that could have cost him his life. It was clear to all that Edmund had taken the challenge seriously and not dismissed it as mere teenage bluff and bluster. It was clear also that, although Edmund had declined to meet Richard in the field, he was no craven. His reasons for avoiding a lethal contest were flawlessly rational and impeccably prudent. Nevertheless, in some small, intangible way Richard had won this first confrontation without either meeting his adversary or drawing his sword. Kate felt certain that in the minds of those around the table in the Great Hall, the gleaming armour of the hitherto impregnable Bastard of Calais had tarnished a whit. Once word got around the estate, people - Kate and her mother included - might start to believe that Edmund was not some omnipotent, all-seeing, all-knowing demigod, but merely human after all, and that young Richard might just prove himself a worthy successor to his father by winning back what had been wrested from his family.

*Bravo Dickon!* she thought to herself, finding her strength renewed despite the seemingly negative outcome of her brother's bold challenge. Her freshly-stiffened resolve took a knock, however, as Edmund made his parting shot upon leaving the Great Hall.

"Oh, by the way, since I am the new master of this estate I think it only right and proper that I and my household should at last be appropriately accommodated. To that end I must ask that you vacate this house by the end of the week. You may take such clothes and intimate personal belongings as will fit onto two carts, but as for the furniture - the hangings, the silver, the glass, the coin - all of these will remain as part of my inheritance. Those servants who wish to remain here will enjoy the same pay and conditions as before, while those who do not are free to accompany you wherever you might go. You have five days to make your arrangements, my lady."

Though she had been expecting such a pronouncement for some time now, Ann Wardlow's face still fell, her heart sinking into her soft, delicately-stitched shoes at the thought of giving up the family home.

"Though the size of the manor would easily permit it, it is clear that harmonious cohabitation would be a goal well beyond our grasp," Edmund continued, "there being too many sources of friction to allow us to rub along even tolerably well. I do not relish the thought of being murdered in my bed. No doubt the gallant Constable of Denbigh Castle will not stand by and see ladies of quality cast into the street. I wish you well."

With that, and without waiting for any kind of response from a stunned Ann, he left.

# CHAPTER FORTY-FIVE

"IT IS my intention to make... a progress," declared Edmund over an early breakfast. "I shall use the time I have left before moving into Plas Anwen to visit all thirteen manors on the estate and make myself known to the tenants."

"How grand!" said Girard, a wry smile on his face. "You make yourself sound like royalty."

"I suppose I very nearly am," Edmund replied, unable to stifle a laugh.

"You do realise, dear friend, that like as not one or two of the peasants – I mean tenants – might just be tempted to loose the odd arrow in your direction," warned Girard. "I hardly think, given the circumstances of your arrival, that you can expect a particularly warm welcome as you make your stately way around your new domain."

"That had crossed my mind," Edmund replied. "I shall be wearing a stout brigandine under my cloak and more besides, and I shall take a score of my mercenaries along for company. You are, of course, cordially invited. Who knows, perhaps you might spy a manor that takes your fancy. On the subject of tenants, I am prepared to be forbearing should I encounter a certain coolness of reception, though should I come across outright hostility I shall not hesitate to evict potential troublemakers and replace them with such of my men as can be trusted to make a decent fist of running a farm. The less intellectually gifted among the mercenaries can help to work the land in exchange for a regular wage, should they be able to shrug off their warlike ways and settle down to country life. I need to maintain the productivity of the manors if the estate is to run profitably. Talking of which, I think we should take that Matthew fellow along. No-one seems to know the apparatus of the estate as well as he, and a familiar face should help to mollify the locals. With this early start we should be able to complete our tour before dusk. I do not wish to leave my force divided overnight nor lay myself open to ambush."

An hour later – eight o'clock, as the late Sir Geoffrey's ornate timepiece reliably informed them – Edmund and his small but well-armed party came to a halt before Plas Anwen. Ann was waiting at the entrance, having already been sent word while she was hearing Mass that he wished to see her. Dismounting from the smartly turned-out palfrey he had chosen for the day's long ride, Edmund strolled leisurely toward her, looking about him at the grounds and gardens surrounding the house as the first frost of the season made them sparkle and glitter under a bright, low sun. In the far distance the purple hills formed an encircling frame to a glorious and wide-reaching vista. Sir Geoffrey certainly had the knack of picking a good spot to build a house, Edmund mused. He gave Ann a short, formal bow.

"I shall not keep you long outdoors on such a sharp, but nevertheless beautiful morning, my lady," he began, with his usual meticulous courtesy.

"I am more than happy to walk in these gardens and enjoy the view for as long as they continue to be mine," Ann replied.

Kate came to the entrance and stood by her mother's side, linking her right arm supportively through Ann's left.

"Indeed," continued Edmund. "Then I hope you will use your

time wisely. And talking of using time wisely, I am about to make a thorough inspection of the estate that I might better understand its layout, its composition and its potential. Did you receive my message regarding - oh I see you did."

Edmund glanced across to the far end of the house to see an apprehensive-looking Matthew making his way over on a bay rouncey. Ann had been baffled and more than a little worried when Edmund's earlier message had asked for Matthew to attend dressed for a day's ride. She feared they meant to murder him along the way, but now it made perfect sense, since he was obviously going along to act as a guide.

Edmund saluted the steward. "Master Matthew, I am happy that you have joined us. Our little group is now complete and we can be on our way. My lady, Sister, I bid you good day."

Edmund bowed to the Wardlow women then turned and walked back to his horse. He remounted, but before signalling to his entourage to set off he addressed Ann once more.

"My lady, I trust you to be a person of good sense and, bearing that in mind, I do not suppose that you would endanger yourself or others by attempting to send for help while I and some of my men are absent from here. Those of my party who remain are quite capable of holding off an attack by twice their number, I can assure you."

Ann remained unmoved by Edmund's comments. She had seen Edmund's mercenaries for herself and did not doubt his bold claims regarding their prowess on the field of battle. In any case she knew in her heart that she would not risk her beloved son, her tenants or her friends, in a bloody head-on confrontation. Even if they were to prevail, the price might prove too high.

She had been thinking more along the lines of sending a single volunteer, someone who knew the lie of the land and who was an expert with the longbow or crossbow, to shadow Edmund's progress unseen, and at the right moment put an arrow or a quarrel through his snake's heart. Cut off the head of the monster and its body will die also...

Edmund's next remark interrupted Ann's train of thought as if he had been reading her mind. Her blood turned to ice.

"Furthermore, should there happen to be any attack or assault upon my person whilst I am abroad making my inspection, such that I fail to return after a certain agreed-upon interval of time, my trusted serjeant has orders to lay waste to all around him. I truly shudder to think what havoc my men might wreak given a free rein..."

The change in Ann's expression was subtle – she was trying very hard not to give herself away – but it was just enough to let Edmund know he had guessed her intention. His satisfaction showed itself in a slight upward curl at one corner of his mouth. He pulled at his right rein, turning his mount eastwards towards the tiny hamlet of Babell and, with a firm dig of his heels in its flanks, set off at a smooth but deceptively quick amble.

Ann drew Kate close and watched as Edmund's group moved away. Matthew dared a brief look back at his mistress, his face a mask of anxiety. Ann pursed her lips to stop them trembling and attempted to reassure him with a firm nod, though inside her heart was breaking for the loss of her husband and her home.

# CHAPTER FORTY-SIX

"COME, JOIN me Matthew – do not be bashful!" Edmund gestured to the steward to ride alongside him. Ysabel gently reined in her horse and dropped back beside Girard to make room in the narrow lane that led over the rise to Babell.

"We shall, after all, be working closely together for the good of the estate and should get to know each other at least a little," he continued.

Matthew dutifully coaxed his mount into the space left for him but waited politely for Edmund to continue the conversation, having formed the opinion that his new master was the sort of man who liked the sound of his own voice. He did not have to wait long for confirmation.

"There is much I hope to learn from you and I am sure, if you are honest with yourself, you have many questions for me. Ask away; I shall not be offended!"

Matthew decided he may as well find out as much about his mistress's enemy as he could, so he gathered his courage and took the plunge.

"Well, Sir, I would like to know how it is that you are able to maintain control over such a sizeable retinue of, erm..." He glanced over his shoulder at the hard, weatherworn faces of the mercenaries Edmund had picked to accompany him and chose his next words carefully in case any of them could hear him. "...shall we say, experienced and quite possibly highly excitable veterans of the recent conflicts in France."

"*Ha!*" Edmund threw back his head and laughed out loud. "You are very diplomatic Matthew! I think you meant 'murderous scum who would slit your throat for a penny'! Well, there have been occasional currents of discord along the way but I think the reasons why Girard, Ysabel and I have not ended up dead in a ditch are twofold. Firstly, I pay them well and I pay them regularly. You would be surprised how biddable such fellows become once they realise that their expectations of a shilling or two in their grubby hands every Thursday are never disappointed. Secondly I have a trusted friend in Will. I have known him for many years and he brings with him twenty well-disciplined soldiers who fought together in numerous actions in France. They form a close-knit coterie of fighters upon whom I know I can rely. Others may join us as and when the need for greater strength arises, but should there be any troublemakers among them, Will and his lads are very quick to sort them out - trust me on that!"

Having witnessed the summary execution of one of Edmund's own men the previous day, Matthew shuddered to imagine what Will's policing methods might involve, but whatever they were, they appeared to work very effectively.

"My turn now!" chirped Edmund, seeming, thought Matthew, almost childlike in his enthusiasm and excitement; an estimation strangely at odds with his actions thus far.

"What is the nearest decent-sized port?" Matthew, a little surprised at the question, considered for a moment, wondering what in Heaven's name his new master might want to bring into, or send out of, the country, before answering. "That would be Beaumaris, Sir, on Ynys Mon."

"And how far away might that be?" asked Edmund.

"Well, I would say two days for a lone traveller, with a change of horse half way," Matthew replied.

"And what if one were transporting goods by cart?"

"Then you could make that five days, or possibly a week or mayhap even ten days, depending upon the weather. Might one enquire what would be on the carts?"

Edmund fixed the steward with a look suffused with knowledge and pride. "Wines, Matthew. Wines of the finest quality from Burgundy, Gascony and elsewhere. I could supplement my incomes from the estate whilst educating the palates of the local gentry. I dread to think what slops they might be washing their meat down with at the moment."

"Indeed, sir?" queried Matthew. "You intend to continue in that area of, erm, trade?"

"It has been a long-standing family business, Matthew. We did rather well from it."

Matthew dared, inwardly, to wonder what the old, established Welsh Border families would make of a young upstart wine trader in their midst, setting himself up as a gentleman. He could not see Edmund ever being accepted locally, given his background. The thought gave him a small crumb of comfort as he ambled alongside his former master's killer.

"Do you know how many soldiers they have at Denbigh Castle?" Edmund suddenly asked Matthew, very directly. "Oh, but I doubt you would tell me if you knew, even under torture!" Matthew's face turned white momentarily, but Edmund's broad smile quickly reassured the steward that his new master had only been joking. Some joke. Edmund posed the question to Girard instead. His friend thought for a moment, then replied. "I believe our scouts, who have visited the town under cover, have estimated their strength at some four-and-twenty men, plus their womenfolk of course."

"...who could, if our Lady Ann is anything to go by, prove even more formidable adversaries than their husbands!" laughed Edmund.

Ysabel gave him a reproachful glare while Matthew privately marvelled at the alarming efficiency of Edmund's spies.

"I think the Lady Ann is a brave woman who has suffered terribly and yet shown much grace and fine breeding!" she chided.

"Just like my mother," Edmund said quietly, immediately silencing his young lover, though he had not meant his words unkindly.

Girard's face expressed dawning comprehension along with a modicum of concern. "Please tell me, friend, that you do not propose to seize Denbigh Castle and make it your own!"

Edmund laughed. "Hell's teeth no! Four-and-twenty men sheltering behind such sturdy walls would cause as much mischief as ten times that number on an open battlefield. I merely wish to appraise the strengths and inclinations of our various neighbours. It is a little worrying that my dear brother and his men will have swelled their garrison of two dozen to something approaching the size of our own force."

"It is unlikely, surely, that the Constable would strip his castle of men and leave it vulnerable to attack, even to help the son of an old friend," offered Girard.

"I hope you are right," Edmund replied thoughtfully.

The party ambled on, halting frequently in order to inspect a tenant's farm here or a brewery there, along with countless other busy little industries scattered all over the estate – pot-throwers, crock-makers, wood-turners, charcoal burners, stone quarrymen and so on – all working hard to put food on their tables. At no point did the local people exhibit any hostility towards him, his fine clothes and sizeable retinue proving more than enough to ensure a respectful reception. It was clear to Edmund that although secretly many of the tenants might view him with suspicion and resentment, they did not seem inclined to do anything about it. Indeed, the day held the occasional pleasant surprise. Edmund was unable to hide his delight upon meeting a miller who had not a single kind word to say about Sir Geoffrey, having crossed swords with him at the Manor court and come off worse on two occasions, the first of which cost him a twenty-shilling fine, the second another hefty fine plus a humiliating and uncomfortable day in the stocks. He presented the man with four silver coins for his trouble and reassured him that under the new lordship things would be different.

Everywhere he went Edmund was careful to ask people their names, hoping to build at least a small mental picture of the human aspect of the estate. After a while he turned to Matthew. "Matthew my friend, I believe you have not told me *your* surname. Please enlighten me!"

"Fletcher, sir," Matthew replied.

"Fletcher? How strange it is." Edmund retorted. "We are in Wales, yet thus far on our travels we have met not a single soul with a Welsh name. Why is this Matthew? Have you and your English friends eaten them all?"

After a short pause for thought Matthew replied. "I believe that on the whole we tend to prefer mutton, sir," with such a straight face that Edmund could not help but burst out laughing.

"Haha! I like this fellow!" he exclaimed in the direction of Girard, who was also smiling at Matthew's droll remark.

"But it *is* a little odd, is it not?" he continued, looking expectantly at Matthew for an explanation.

"I believe King Edward I had a hand in it, sir. Once he had finally subdued Wales and turned the country into an English principality, he set about populating it with English tenants. Most of the native Welsh had to flee to the hills to scrape what meagre living they could among the rocks and the ravens."

"...leaving folk with names like Ashdown, Brooker, Cheeseman and, of course, Fletcher, to enjoy the fruits of the land. They should have chiselled 'Hammer of the Scots *and* the Welsh' on his tomb!"

As the day of exploration and familiarisation wore on, so the expression on Edmund's face became more and more smug as he realised how plump, how profitable was the estate he had taken over. His had been a long journey, but now it was over and both he and his late mother could rest easier. His musings were interrupted by a glimpse of a fast-moving shape heading along the valley bottom four or five bowshots away. Edmund narrowed his eyes as the low late-afternoon sun reflected off polished metal in the distance.

"Halloo, what have we here?" said Edmund, pulling up his horse and standing in his stirrups to gain a clearer view.

Matthew followed the direction of Edmund's gaze, his eyes lighting upon the same small but rapid object, which eventually resolved itself into a horse and rider.

Turning to his party Edmund shouted, "Ho! If we but raise a canter we can head this fellow off at the joining of the roads!"

Matthew found himself carried along in the rush as the party spurred their mounts downhill. He silently cursed himself for finding his day's ride with Edmund considerably more exciting and varied than any of the duties his late master had required him to carry out and ashamed that he had allowed himself to be mesmerised by Edmund's charm and buoyed along on his infectious enthusiasm. Nevertheless the dash to the road was exhilarating and in less than a minute the group was arrayed across the main east-to-west road awaiting the arrival of the lone rider.

The horseman reined in his panting mount and despite being outnumbered by more than twenty to one announced confidently, "Sir, God give you good day. I must ask that you let me pass unhindered as I carry a message concerning the King's business."

Edmund regarded the messenger, who sat astride a good quality, well-turned-out horse and wore an expensive-looking new brigandine covered in maroon velvet and a highly-polished open-faced sallet. A falchion and a dagger hung from either side of his waist and over his shoulder was slung a tubular leather document case with the royal swan emblem picked out in white. The man looked seasoned and experienced and impressed Edmund with his apparent lack of fear in spite of the threatening presence of a score of the latter's mercenaries. He clearly placed a great deal of faith in the idea of royal messengers being untouchable. Perhaps the news he carried would be of interest.

"God give you good day also! Might one enquire where the

King's messenger is bound?" Edmund asked in the most amiable tone he could muster. The messenger, still confident of his immunity, nevertheless took a thoughtful look at the large group blocking his path before deciding that a brief reply not overly dripping with sensitive details could do no harm and might satisfy their leader so that he could be on his way.

"I am bound to deliver this letter into the hands of Sir Geoffrey Wardlow, the master of Plas Anwen," he announced, with what he hoped was the right amount of ostentation.

Edmund could not believe his luck. "It so happens that we are guests of the Lady Anne and are headed that way ourselves. Pray, let us accompany you," Edmund replied silkily.

The messenger showed the first, minute signs of unease at the mention of Sir Geoffrey's wife, but not Sir Geoffrey. He had assumed that, like most of the other rebels present at Ludlow - with the very significant exceptions of the Duke of York and the Earls of March, Gloucester, Salisbury and Warwick - Sir Geoffrey had meekly returned home to await the King's pleasure and accept such justice as the Crown saw fit to dispense. He was, of course, wrong, and as Edmund's entourage subtly closed ranks around him on the narrow valley-bottom road, his unease only grew.

His worst suspicions were confirmed as the riding party, having negotiated the climb up to and through Caerwys, reached Plas Anwen and Edmund's extensive camp hove into view. The messenger sought eye contact with Edmund in the hope that he would be enlightened as to this novel development. All of a sudden he felt a long way from the protection of the King.

Seeing the messenger's discomfort, Edmund spurred his mount until he was alongside. "Fear not my friend, you are quite safe here. I wish neither to interfere with the King's business nor to hinder those who carry it out. Indeed, I and my companions are proud to be numbered among those who mustered at Ludlow to support King Henry. Sir Geoffrey is, I regret, indisposed elsewhere for the foreseeable future, but I am sure that the Lady Anne will be most interested in the contents of your letter."

The messenger relaxed a little upon hearing Edmund's reassurances. A short while later, as the sun began to dip below the horizon, he, Edmund, Girard and Ysabel were dismounting and entering Plas Anwen. One of the kitchen boys brought wine and food for the messenger while one of the maidservants went to find her mistress.

Upon Lady Ann's arrival the messenger set down his cup and bowed deeply. "God give you good day, my lady. I trust that you are well. I have a message from His Grace King Henry to your husband, Sir Geoffrey, though I understand he is not here."

Ann Wardlow's face rapidly went through a multitude of expressions before setting cold and hard. "Sir, my husband is *dead* - murdered by that... that *man* standing behind you!"

Bewildered at the news the messenger spun round and met Edmund eye to eye. The "murderer" appeared calm and composed as he raised his open hands slightly in a gesture of futility.

"Alas, since it was I who had the sad task of informing my Lady of Sir Geoffrey's death at Ludlow, she blames me for the tragedy. Owing to the terrible shock she has suffered she becomes quite hysterical at times, but there appears little we can do to soothe her troubled heart or to contain her wild outbursts."

"Why you devious, twisting *snake!*" Ann spat, suddenly launching herself at Edmund and trying her best to claw his eyes out with her fingernails. Edmund was caught out by the speed and ferocity of her assault, but his superior strength and years of training meant that he soon had her pinioned in his arms, though she struggled mightily. He nodded to two servant girls hovering on the periphery and they hurried over, eventually managing to calm Ann sufficiently for her to be led away to her chamber sobbing quietly, her shoulders sagging in a posture of defeat.

"You see what I mean?" Edmund asked of the gawping messenger.

"It is indeed a tragedy," the messenger replied. "I have never seen such behaviour. And what of Sir Geoffrey? How did he meet his end? He must have a son and heir to whom I must now deliver this message."

Edmund affected a suitably solemn expression before replying. "Sir Geoffrey was killed in the crush at Ludford when the rebel army scattered to escape the King's wrath. Trampled by the fleeing commons and suffocated in his armour I believe; an inglorious end for such a fine man, hence my not informing you of it earlier. He leaves a son, but as to his whereabouts no-one is sure. It is thought he has gone into hiding."

"This is most unfortunate," said the messenger, rubbing his chin thoughtfully. "Clearly Sir Geoffrey's widow is in no fit state to deal with a message from the King but I cannot return with it undelivered."

"Perhaps I can be of help," Edmund offered smoothly. "I know the family well, though you might not think it from the Lady Ann's reaction, but of course she is not in her right mind at present. I could examine the letter myself then consider how best to convey the contents to her when she is recovered."

The messenger looked uncomfortable with the idea. "I fear that would be highly, erm, irregular," he said, in a voice made a little less firm than before by the proximity of Edmund's men and the lateness of the hour.

The messenger started as Edmund made a sudden move, not for the dagger that hung from his belt, but for the purse that sat next to it.

"I feel sure we can come to some arrangement, nevertheless" he said cheerily, his casual smile unnerving the messenger even more.

"I... I... cannot be bribed!" the man stammered, though with precious little conviction in his voice.

"Oh, come now!" Edmund retorted in a tone of mock offence. "You misunderstand. I would never attempt to interfere with the carrying out of the King's business. What I offer is not a bribe, more a reward for trouble taken and a job well done. You may rest assured I shall take good care of the letter and act wisely upon its contents. You will be found a bed for the night and your horse will be fed and rested for the morrow. What say you now?"

The messenger looked around him, taking in Edmund and the half dozen heavily armed mercenaries who had now joined them. He knew from the ride up to Plas Anwen that the camp outside the gates held many more. What to do? Accept a bribe, then return home and try to live with the shame he had brought to his profession, or hold to his oath and go down fighting? Either way Edmund would get his hands on the letter. He chose to live.

# CHAPTER FORTY-SEVEN

RICHARD WARDLOW cringed inwardly as his host's stern words hit home.

Roger had found out about Richard's challenge to single combat against Edmund and was busy telling his dead friend's son exactly what he thought of the whole stupid idea.

"That is not the way your father would have wanted you to pursue this matter! You cannot just throw your life away on some gallant flight of fancy."

"Throw my life away?" Richard interrupted, his pride stung. "But I would have beaten him fair and square!"

"We cannot know that. I do not doubt your skill or your bravery Richard - I helped to train you, remember - but you are responsible for your mother and sister now, not to mention those who would seek your lordship and protection on the estate. One mistake on your part and they would all be at the mercy of the snake who murdered your father."

Richard's shoulders sagged. He felt thwarted, frustrated and angry, but he knew deep down that his former mentor was right. His father would expect him to conduct himself beyond his tender years and choose a course of action that would not only demonstrate his maturity and levelheadedness by wresting the estate from the hands of the foreign interloper, but also satisfy family honour by avenging his death without transgressing the law of the land. Even in death, Sir Geoffrey Wardlow demanded much of his son.

"What do I do then, sir?"

Roger's mood softened as soon as it seemed his words had had their intended effect. "We must place our faith in the power of the King's Law," Roger replied. "Only then can we truly clip the wings of this Devil's spawn."

Out of respect, Richard stopped short of snorting his disapproval, but his host sensed his impatience.

"Remember, lad, 'though the mills of God grind slowly, yet they grind exceeding small; though with patience stands He waiting, with exactness grinds He all.'"

"But my father will be viewed as a traitor after Ludford. He is sure to be attainted and the estate declared forfeit. Legally we shall have not a leg to stand on!"

"That remains to be seen. I too will have earned the King's displeasure for my recent support for the Duke of York's cause, though whatever His Grace decides to do to me, he must prise me from my castle first. In the long run, however, the illegality of the actions of this Edmund of Calais will come to be judged, regardless of who your father or I supported, and it is in this certainty that you must put your trust. At least you now have moneys with which to finance the fight against the upstart. A little gold scattered here and there in the right places can work wonders..."

Richard relaxed a little as he remembered a number of familiar faces from the estate turning up at the castle the day before and insisting on seeing him in private. What he found secreted among the mundane market goods on their carts had given him fresh heart. It was his father's gold - bags of it. Enough gold to hire five- or six-score mercenaries of his own and bring down Edmund once and for all. Richard could already picture his half-brother's head rotting on a spike above the gatehouse of the Wardlow manor house...

Once again, however, Roger supplied the voice of reason, pointing out that although Richard was indeed in a position to mount such an operation, the potential cost in casualties and destruction of property made it self-defeating from the start, not to mention that Edmund could quite easily employ Richard's mother and sister as powerful bargaining tools. The young Wardlow heir's frustration eventually got the better of him and he had to excuse himself from the supper table with strained good manners, stalking out of the Great Hall and ascending to the wall walk, where he stared out over the valley of the Clwyd in the direction of his father's lands, his knuckles turning white as he gripped the stonework. Roger did not follow, thinking it better to allow the lad some space. He remained in his seat by the fire, rolling the stem of his silver wine goblet between his thumb and fingers, staring at the ever-changing patterns in the flames and thinking of his murdered friend.

# CHAPTER FORTY-EIGHT

IN THE privacy of his tent, illuminated by the light of a half-dozen candles in pewter holders and supplemented by the glow from two braziers, Edmund carefully unrolled the royal document he had just liberated from its tubular leather holder. Ysabel and Girard crowded in at his shoulders, undisguised excitement in their eyes, as their friend smoothed out the parchment on a small table. Edmund's lips moved silently as he read, his brain busy separating the real meat of the message from the ornate language of government. He and Girard reached the end of the letter at the same time while Ysabel lagged behind, struggling to translate the stiffly formal English.

"My, my..." said Edmund. "This is welcome news indeed! It could not have fallen better," he said with a broad grin. "For all of us," he continued, catching Ysabel's eye.

"*Pour l'amour de Dieu dites-moi, qu'est-ce que la lettre dit?*" she exclaimed, utterly perplexed.

"*Calmes-toi chérie!*" laughed Edmund. "It appears that my father's sympathy for the rebel cause has angered the King more than we could have imagined. The letter is a summons to attend a Parliament next month at which he is – *was* - to have been put on trial to answer for his treasonable actions. I have little doubt he would have been attainted and perhaps even executed. Well, we have saved Parliament one job already. Who knows, we may even get some thanks for disposing of a dangerous rebel. Attainted… His lands and property will be forfeit and his precious son will be barred from inheriting. The Wardlow name will be dishonoured forever! It only remains for us to put forward our claim to the estate, then wait for a grateful Parliament to grant us my father's lands as a reward for our loyal service to the Crown!"

Girard raised a cautionary finger. "Provided, that is, that the Crown does not fancy this particular estate for itself! I think you might stand a much better chance of success if you could secure the backing of an influential noble, someone who has the ear of the King."

Edmund was deflated somewhat at his friend's wise but troubling words. "And how, pray, might we forge such an advantageous allegiance? As yet we do not know anyone in the area," he asked.

"That I cannot answer as yet, though something may yet turn up, assuming the processes of English law run as slowly as we have been led to believe," Girard replied.

Ysabel, excited though she was at the possibilities opening up before them, failed to stifle a yawn.

"Ah, sweeting, you are tired after our long day. It is high time we all retired to our beds," said Edmund. "In the morning I shall issue my lady Ann with her marching orders. Better that she leave us sooner rather than later, since her behaviour is becoming more and more unpredictable. I do not want to risk being emasculated by a pair of sewing scissors in another of her frenzied assaults."

# CHAPTER FOURTY-NINE

THE SUN had been up barely an hour when Richard Wardlow passed through the gates of Denbigh Castle and out into the town. Accompanying him were Tom Linley and five of the household men. It was market day and traders from the surrounding area were peddling their wares from a multitude of stalls, their exhortations to buy their goods blending into a jumbled cacophony. It suited Richard, however, in that it gave his mind no single thing upon which to dwell.

He and his men ambled along the street in no particular hurry, since a look round the market would give them a welcome break from the confining gloom and dull routine of the castle. Cloth, leather, meat, spices, fruit, fish, pottery, pewterware, cutlery, ironware, needles, hats; all were given close scrutiny partly out of a desire to spin out the time away from the castle for as long as possible and partly to make some genuinely useful purchases. Many of Richard's men, for example, had worn out their shoes after the long walk from Ludlow. A few well-chosen hides bought and taken to the shoemaker in the old part of the town would see them reshod.

The married men looked wistfully at the stalls selling ribbons, brooches, combs and other feminine trinkets. They all missed their wives, but they knew that until the business with Edmund was resolved they had to stick with their master or risk scattering the only force he had to command.

It was as he was examining a silver brooch in the shape of a heart – something he knew would have caught his sister's eye – that Richard saw the man who had cut off his father's head.

# CHAPTER FIFTY

"HE HAS decided to do *what*?!" exclaimed Ann Wardlow, slamming her silver wine goblet down and denting the thin, elaborately decorated rim on the hard oak dining table in the Great Hall. "Are you sure you heard him correctly?"

Having just read of her late husband's impending attainder in the unsealed – and therefore secondhand – letter delivered at first light by one of Edmund's men, her steward's unwelcome revelation was the last straw.

Matthew steeled himself, wishing it might be anyone but he that broke the news. "I am afraid it is true, my lady."

He pushed away his pewter plate, his appetite for breakfast suddenly gone. "Edmund of Calais intends to lower the rents. All of them. The notion came to him after yesterday's progress around the estate. Every tenant is to enjoy a reduction of one-twelfth in all their obligations for the next year. And there is one more matter..." Matthew looked at the floor, his resolve withering under his mistress' fiery glare.

"Well, Matthew, whatever it is, spit it out. From your expression it agrees not with you," said Ann, impatiently.

Matthew squirmed. "He desires that I should work for him, my lady."

The heat from Ann's angry stare increased.

"As his steward, of course," he added hastily, lest his mistress should think he had been given a bow and a bill and orders to kill any defaulting tenants on sight.

"And what said you to this momentous proposal? I trust your salary will not be reduced by one-twelfth in line with the rents, that would be an insult to your many talents," Ann replied, unable to hide a touch of bitterness in her voice. Matthew had, after all, served the Wardlow family most faithfully and competently for nearly fifteen years. No-one understood the workings of the estate and how to keep it in profit better than Matthew, and Ann did not like the idea of him selling his skills to Edmund of all people.

"Ah no, my lady, no. Quite the opposite, in fact. He has suggested a remuneration of eight pounds and twelve shillings a year for my services. It is indeed a generous offer. At the same time, however, I could not help but feel that there might be unfortunate consequences were I to refuse it, though nothing to that effect was said openly. Edmund of Calais can be a very charming and persuasive man, my lady, though I suspect under his fine manners lurks a sharp and deadly edge. I find myself in a most difficult situation."

Ann, feeling her legs beginning to buckle, grasped the edge of the table with both hands and lowered herself carefully onto her chair, as if unsure whether it could bear the combined weight of herself and her relentlessly accumulating woes. Eight pounds and twelve shillings a year was a third as much again as she and her late husband had paid their steward. How could she possibly prevail against Edmund when he was clearly determined to undermine every cornerstone of the estate and its running?

Judging by the look on his face and the tone of his voice Matthew was genuinely distressed, torn between loyalty to his mistress and ensuring the safety and sustenance of his wife and three children. Ann relented, realising she could not in fairness ask him to starve for a principle. "Matthew, you have served us faithfully and well these past years, but you must do whatever you can to safeguard your livelihood so that you may provide for your loved ones. I shall not think the worse of you for it."

"My lady you are more than gracious!" Matthew exclaimed, his relief obvious. "In truth it sits ill with me that my efforts shall be directed towards putting money into the pockets of that repellent young man. If I am to reconcile myself to earning my living thus, I must tell myself daily that I am merely keeping things in good order until this estate is restored once more to its rightful owner."

"Alas, it is over, Matthew, at least for now. My daughter and I intend to quit Plas Anwen later this morning so that we might arrive at Denbigh while it is still light."

Before Matthew could draw breath to protest, one of the servants came into the hall and announced that all was ready for the departure.

Steward and mistress stood up and faced each other. Matthew took Ann's right hand, bowed deeply and placed a solemn kiss on the large ruby ring her husband had given her seventeen years earlier to celebrate the safe arrival of Richard, the first of her children to survive the ordeal of birth.

"My lady, it is with the heaviest of hearts that I am forced to witness your departure this day, but rest assured it is my firmest belief that good will prevail and Master Richard will assume his rightful place here. I shall pray for as much each and every day."

Ann was deeply touched by Matthew's little speech – so much so that she ignored convention and kissed him lightly on the cheek as tears began to run down her own.

They followed the servant outside, Ann pausing briefly to allow a tearful maid to fasten a fur-trimmed woollen riding cloak around her shoulders. A mounting block was placed next to Ann's horse, Pax, and one of the grooms helped his mistress up onto her side saddle. Once on board, Ann placed her feet on the planchette, then arranged the skirts of her dress so as to maintain a decent level of decorum. Davy Gray, one of the servants who had elected to leave with her, took up his position at beside the horse's head ready to lead it. Ann's dignified seating arrangement was not one that would permit unaided riding to any practical degree.

Kate was all ready for the off, eager to see her brother and her friend Jane again and to escape Edmund's unsettling company. Eager now, maybe, but her reddened eyes bore witness to the tears she had shed as she had taken a last look around her bedchamber before closing the door on her childhood. In stark contrast to her mother she sat astride her beloved Rollo, her long skirts almost covering her legs, but still revealing considerably more calf and ankle than Ann thought decent. Not for Kate, though, the stately dignity of being led at walking pace by a servant. She needed to feel the wind in her hair and hear the horse's hooves pounding out their beat on the road. Were it any other occasion she felt sure her mother would have issued a stern warning to her not to go galloping off ahead on her own. As it was, Kate knew she must be sensible. Amid all the grief and sadness she did not wish to add to Ann's woes by giving her further cause to worry.

The party consisted of Kate, her mother and seven servants who had elected to go with them. There were two married couples, two young sisters who had lost their parents and the young groom who was leading Ann's horse. The sisters and one of the married couples had the job of driving the two carts which held such possessions as Ann and Kate thought they could not live without, sheeted down to protect them from impending the rain which threatened to dampen their spirits even further. Ready to tag alongside Ann's horse at their usual loping gait were Sir Geoffrey's favourite greyhounds, Deimos and Phobos. Ann could never understand why her husband had called them "Terror" and "Fear" when they appeared to have such gentle natures, although he had reassured her the hares they hunted would consider them aptly named. It was his little joke, she had concluded.

Now though, with a final, tearful look at her beloved Plas Anwen, Ann instructed Davy to set off for Denbigh, leaving such memories behind. A few of the household staff and nearby tenants saw them solemnly on their way, the women sobbing into their aprons, the men standing with their heads bowed, but Ann had deliberately kept her departure time secret, fearing that a large turnout might result, as it had done previously, in potentially fatal unrest, especially if Edmund and his men turned up to gloat.

Sure enough, the little group had travelled no more than three hundred yards, leaving the manor by the back gate and taking the track to the west that would keep them as far from Edmund's camp as possible, when Edmund and his usual entourage of Girard, Ysabel and a dozen or so mercenaries hove into view with, it seemed, the intention of intercepting them before they reached the lee of the hill where they would have disappeared from sight.

*Talk of the Devil and he is presently at your elbow,* thought Ann, mortified that her tormentor should have compromised her attempt at a furtive decampment.

"God give you good day, Lady Ann, Sister!" Edmund called as soon as he was within hailing distance.

Ann cringed inwardly, dreading having to speak to a man upon whom she could barely bring herself to look.

Moments later Edmund's party had caught them up.

"Leaving so soon, my lady?" he asked, his voice tinged with almost believable concern.

Ann regarded him stony-faced, saying nothing.

"I trust you have all you need for your journey and afterwards," he continued pleasantly.

*Always so unnaturally polite,* thought Ann. *His manner sickens me. I would almost rather he chased us away at swordpoint.*

"We have all we require," Ann replied coldly. "Perhaps you would care to search our carts in case we have inadvertently packed something that might be of value. Here, you may as well have this..." She pulled the large ruby ring from the middle finger of her right hand and held it out. "It will save you the chore of hacking my hand off later."

Edmund looked genuinely shocked. "My lady!" he exclaimed, seemingly cut to the quick. "Please put it back. I am not some common thief who would waylay you on the road and make off with your jewels!"

"But you have taken everything else from us!" Ann cried. "My husband, our home…"

Edmund leaned forward in his saddle. *"My home now!* And please remember before you judge me too harshly, my lady, that I allowed you time to make such arrangements as would ease your departure. There are, I am sure, plenty of your countrymen who would have thrown you straight out of the door in your nightclothes, were they in my position."

Ann grudgingly admitted to herself that it was true. She knew of other property disputes where the women had been terrorised and the men had had their heads broken. Save for the fact that he had murdered her husband and stolen her land, Edmund had indeed behaved with surprising consideration, though it did not prevent her from hating him.

"I will grant you that much," said Ann, the words grating on her. "Now if there is no further reason for delay we must be leaving. Davy, forward!"

Edmund smiled, bowed and gestured them gallantly on their way. He let the party get fifty yards away before calling after them. *"HOLD FAST!"*

Ann twisted round in her side saddle, her face a mask of consternation, wondering what further wretchedness her *bête noir* planned to heap upon her family's blighted lives.

"I would have my sister stay awhile, that we might become better acquainted."

Kate looked aghast. Ann's face changed from alarm to anger at this last-minute outrage.

*"What? You would hold my daughter hostage? Over my dead body Edmund of Calais!"* she screamed, the words echoing through the early morning mist. Edmund said nothing. He did not need to. He glanced at the mercenaries either side of him then looked at Ann, who knew deep down that her threat was empty whereas his was not. Utterly deflated she turned to Kate and with more

tears in her eyes nodded her head to indicate that she should go to Edmund. Before doing so Kate came alongside her mother's horse and leaned over from her saddle to take both of Ann's hands in hers. Ann spoke quietly with a tremor in her voice. "Forgive me, child, for throwing you to the wolf, but I fear if we do not comply he will kill us all."

"Do not fear for me, Mother. We will prevail. Richard shall be our salvation," she replied, giving Ann's fingers a final affectionate squeeze before trotting over to join Edmund's party.

She made straight for Ysabel, who greeted her with the smallest of smiles lest Edmund should see, then turned Rollo around in order to watch her mother's party as it slowly made its way towards an uncertain future. Kate had never felt so forlorn in all her life.

# CHAPTER FIFTY-ONE

THE MERCENARY who had dealt Sir Geoffrey Wardlow his death blow had never laid eyes on his victim's son, therefore he did not recognise the broad, well-built young man charging towards him across the busy street. What he did recognise, however, was the look in his eyes. It was a look he had seen several times before on French battlefields, and it said *"I am going to kill you!"*

For a moment, the wily, seasoned fighter thought of drawing his dagger, sticking his attacker in the guts and then disappearing into the crowd. The boy looked strong but he appeared to have lost his wits, making himself any easy target for someone who could keep a cool head. It was when the mercenary noticed the six other men approaching rapidly behind the lad that he realised he was sorely outnumbered and running was his only option. He turned and fled, his eyes frantically searching for a suitably narrow alley down which to make his escape. As he headed full pelt down a gloomy little side street where the houses overhung the road, almost meeting in the middle, it dawned on him that the boy must be Richard Wardlow and the other men his retainers.

He grinned to himself. The spying mission for his master, Edmund, aimed at finding out what Richard actually looked like, had been successful, perhaps a little too successful, given the proximity of his pursuers. The idea of being caught and "questioned" about his activities did not appeal to the mercenary and lent a spur to his pace. It did him little good. Richard, having spent much of his childhood in Denbigh, knew every short cut there was. Just as the fleeing spy thought he had given Richard's household men the slip, he was brought crashing down by a determined tackle around the shins. Instinctively he twisted over onto his back and kicked out, catching Richard in the mouth and cutting his lip. Richard scrabbled his way up the man's thrashing legs until he was able to grab the folds of his grubby woollen coat. The soldier frantically beat his calloused fists against the boy's head, fighting like a cornered granary rat. Richard kept tight hold of the man's coat, weathering the vicious blows until he was in position, then whipped his head back and dealt the mercenary a shattering headbutt, which broke his nose and left him only half-conscious.

Richard's dagger was out of its sheath in the blink of an eye. He raised his right arm, ready to plunge the blade into the throat of his father's executioner, but it was caught in a vice-like grip. Try as he might he could not break free. He snapped his head round to see who dared to deny him his revenge, the look of a wild animal in his eyes. He heard Tom's voice. "Master Richard, hold fast! Do not kill the scum now! He may have much to tell us of Edmund's strength and disposition. I am sure he will be happy to talk to Master Roger, eventually."

Richard continued to struggle against the hand wrapped around his wrist but the hand belonged to an archer and his efforts were in vain. Finally he relaxed, reluctantly acknowledging the good sense in Tom's reasoning. He waited until his companions had the mercenary under control, then stood up and sheathed his dagger, his eyes fixed on the soldier. Lacking any rope to bind him, two of the household men held the prisoner firmly by the arms and wrists and frogmarched him off to the castle. Not a word was spoken by anyone as they walked along the streets eventually passing through the castle's mighty triple-towered gateway.

Tom glanced sideways at his young master. Pure hatred was etched on Richard's face as his eyes bored into the prisoner's back.

*Better not have the lad in charge of the interrogation or the prisoner will be in a dozen pieces before we've even got his name out of him,* thought Tom, still taken aback by the wild look he had seen in Richard's eyes. Tom had seen the boy's father in action on many a French battlefield and, yes, he had seen him take many a man's life, but always with skill and a cool head. He began to wonder what kind of master Richard would make with his fiery temperament, but before his musings could provide him with any kind of answer they had reached the inner bailey where they found the constable, Roger Kynaston, chatting with his falconer. They were idly watching the progress of two carpenters who were repairing one of the wooden buildings that fringed the large courtyard. Breaking off from his conversation he regarded Richard's party with some surprise.

"Well, well, what have we here? They sell all sorts at the market these days!" he remarked, on noticing the bloodied prisoner. "Richard, who is this fellow?"

Richard spoke slowly, his voice was thick with emotion. "This is the very dog-hearted craven who struck off my father's head when he could not defend himself."

Realising he was looking upon the low-born scum who had visited an ignominious death upon his old friend, Roger's stare hardened. "In that case I dare say the two of you will have much to discuss. Take him to the basement in the Prison Tower. The guards there will know what to do. An application of red-hot iron is sure to get the conversation flowing."

Richard nodded grimly to Roger then turned in the direction of the prison, but whatever hopes he had of extracting a grisly revenge were to be blighted. The two household men followed him, holding the prisoner by the wrists and arms as before, but less tightly now, since they had reached the security of the castle and their charge still appeared groggy from Richard's assault. The mercenary was anything but, however, his wits having returned very smartly at the mention of red-hot iron. As they walked, he waited for the right moment then lashed out sideways with his right foot, catching his guard painfully on the shin. It was just enough of a distraction for him to be able to wrench his right arm free. With a lightning speed born of desperation, he swung round to his left and dealt the other guard a mighty clout with the heel of his hand, flattening the man's nose. Free at last he pelted off towards the main gate, bent on escape. Richard's mind was racing. The prisoner had a head start on him and the two guards at the main entrance were busy checking a cartload of building materials. There was an outside chance his father's murderer might make it to freedom after all. He looked frantically about him until his eyes lit upon a short, heavy axe one of the carpenters had been using. Snatching it up, he hurled it with all his strength at the fleeing man, now some twenty or thirty yards away. It flew straight and true, whickering through the air end-over-end, until the blade bit deep into the mercenary's skull, killing him instantly.

*"EVEN AS YOU TOOK MY FATHER'S LIFE WITH A COMMON AXE, SO SHALL YOURS BE TAKEN!"* Richard screamed, his anguished voice echoing off the walls of the castle. He slumped to his knees, buried his face in his hands and wept. People going about their business stopped and stared, open-mouthed, struggling to believe what they had just seen. Tom and Roger exchanged troubled glances, the latter slowly shaking his head.

# CHAPTER FIFTY-TWO

ANN WARDLOW'S small party slowly made its way towards Denbigh, plodding in dejected silence along one of the many small tracks that criss-crossed the estate. Ann had elected to pass by Tremeirchion, rather than take the more major road through Bodfari, thereby avoiding a chance meeting with Sir Caddoc ap Rheged. Though he was an old and valued friend she could not bear the thought of him seeing her in her ignominy and disgrace. All she wanted to do, assuming Roger Kynaston had space at the castle for her and her modest entourage, was to throw her arms around her beloved son before walling herself up in the smallest room in the highest tower and never coming out.

She berated herself for letting Edmund take her daughter as a hostage but she knew resistance would quite possibly have led to bloodshed. Nevertheless, something told her that Edmund would not be in any hurry to harm Kate, though the thought did little to lift her spirits.

The weather, perhaps sensing Ann's downcast mood, charitably remained fine and, for the time of year, mild, making the four-hour journey less of a trial of endurance than it would have been had the heavens opened on her cheerless little group.

At last, around mid-afternoon, Ann and her servants found themselves on the long climb that led up Denbigh High Street to the castle's imposing gatehouse. One of the group had gone ahead to warn Roger of Ann's imminent arrival and the young constable had been busy preparing to receive his guest.

It was in the Great Hall that mother and son were finally reunited after almost a month. Richard knelt down, took both of Ann's hands in his and kissed them. Ann raised him up and they exchanged formal greetings in accordance with etiquette as the rest of the castle looked on. There would be plenty of time for private conversations after supper, one of which would certainly centre on Kate's absence from the group. Richard was anxious for her and furious at Edmund, but not particularly surprised at the idea of his half-brother electing to take a hostage. He had better treat her kindly for his own sake.

They were accorded places of honour to the left and right of the constable at the supper table, Roger having no wife to sit by his side since his Elizabeth died six years before. There was much to discuss with regard not just to Sir Geoffrey's cold-blooded murder and the loss of the Wardlow estate, but also to the general state of the country since the events at Ludford Bridge. Such subjects, however, were not appropriate for the supper table and would have to wait until after the meal.

Roger had not yet been attainted, nor had he heard that he was likely to be. Indeed, he was somewhat taken aback to hear of the speed with which Sir Geoffrey's impending attainder had arrived, though he would have been the first to admit that the older Sir Geoffrey was far better known to, and trusted by, King Henry than he was and therefore far more likely to incur his displeasure as a result of his defiance. In any case, whatever the judgement upon himself for his part at Ludford, Roger had confidence in the stout walls of his castle. The King would not be able to winkle him out of his refuge easily and in the meantime he was happy to offer shelter and assistance to any Yorkist sympathisers who happened to knock at his gate. In view of his long friendship with Sir Geoffrey, offering food, a roaring fire and comfortable chambers to his widow and son was the least he could do.

The meal over, Ann, Richard and Roger retired to the privacy and comfort of Roger's apartment in the Green Chambers, where their conversation became more earnest, more confidential. Richard was keen, almost aggressive, in his eagerness to find out all he could about his mortal enemy, Edmund. Indeed, Ann found Richard's relentless interrogation and bitter impatience hard to bear. She had set great store by their reunion, hoping to derive some comfort from the proximity of her beloved first-born, but all she could see and hear was a man who looked like her son, spitting venom and vowing to wreak bloody vengeance on the head of their persecutor at whatever cost. Granted, she would be only too happy herself to see the hated Edmund ascend the scaffold and place his neck on the axeman's block, but she had decided to place her faith in the due processes of law, especially since her daughter was now a hostage. Richard, however, rather than having donned the mantle of responsibility now that his father was dead, appeared instead to be teetering on the very edge of self-control. If he were to undertake some rash, spur-of-the-moment venture, such as an all-out armed attack on the estate, who knew what might happen to Kate, or indeed any of them?

Ann, assisted by Roger, tried to calm him, tried to reason with him, but he seemed hell-bent on revenge without a thought to the consequences.

It was with immeasurable sadness that Ann finally came to the conclusion that she had lost not only her beloved husband, but her son, too. When Richard had departed for Ludlow with his father he had been his usual cheerful, loving self. She remembered how he had kissed her goodbye, mounted his horse, ridden it ten yards and then jumped off it so he could run back and kiss her again, squeezing the breath from her with his strong arms. Tears welled in her eyes at the memory, even though Richard was at that moment sitting mere feet from her. She felt she did not know this haunted, vengeful shell of a man. All she could do was fervently pray that once matters had been resolved she could have her son back; her *real* son.

Exhausted and utterly downcast, she made her excuses and retired to the warm, comfortable room Roger had prepared for her in the upper part of the White Chamber Tower. At Ann's personal request, Jane, who had been at the castle ever since the fateful night Kate had galloped off to Plas Anwen, accompanied her. As she helped her mistress out of her heavy formal clothes and into her nightdress, Jane expressed her concern for Kate's safety. Ann tried to quell her anxieties as best she could, but given her own fears regarding her daughter she was sure her reassurances must have sounded flimsy. Before retiring to the straw pallet that had been placed at the foot of her mistress's bed, Jane snuffed out the chandelier, leaving them a single candle on an iron pricket for company. Roger had been considerate enough to endow the room with best beeswax candles, rather than smoky, smelly tallow ones, and as the solitary night light burned it gave off a sweet scent which made Ann feel drowsy. As she watched the bright yellow flame dance and flicker her tangled thoughts began to unravel and her eyelids started to droop. A few feet away she could hear Jane's steady breathing while from outside, beyond the circle of the candle's soft, comforting glow and muted by the heavy curtains around her bed, came the sounds of the castle as its inhabitants settled down for the night: watchmen declaring that all was well as they passed each other on the wall walk; a dog barking plaintively to be let in; a sudden, distant burst of laughter from the guardhouse. Unable to keep her eyes open any longer, Ann said a final prayer, crossed herself, kissed the jewelled crucifix around her neck and sank into a troubled sleep.

# CHAPTER FIFTY-THREE

Breakfast at Denbigh Castle was a quiet, subdued affair. Richard appeared to be suffering from an excess of ale and wine from the previous night and it was not long before he mumbled his apologies and went off to clear his head on the wall walk. Roger gave Ann a knowing, sympathetic glance but he felt there was little he could do to ease the tension between mother and son. Having eaten her fill Ann graciously thanked her host then announced that she was going to St. Hilary's Chapel, on the green just outside the castle gates, to pray and to think. Roger got up from his chair and bowed, nodding to Jane, who had been serving their meal, to accompany Ann back to her apartment.

As she passed through the castle gate and stepped out alone onto the green, Ann pulled her cloak more tightly around her. A chill wind, laced with stinging rain, had sprung up as a reminder that autumn was giving way to winter. The days would soon shorten and everyone would be looking to their supplies of food and fuel to ensure they had enough put by to survive the ravages of the coming months. Looking back briefly in the direction of the castle something caught her eye high up on the battlements. It was Richard, his shoulders hunched against the elements, looking quite forlorn as he watched her from his lofty post. Her mother's heart went out to her unhappy boy and instantly forgave him the previous night's transgressions, but after holding his gaze for a few moments she turned and carried on. She needed time to herself in order to decide upon her next move.

She found the chapel cold and empty, but peaceful. She walked to the end of the nave, genuflected towards the altar then knelt on the hard stone steps that led to the chancel. She began to pray for strength and wisdom for herself, and salvation for the soul of her beloved dead husband. She also beseeched her Father in Heaven to keep her daughter and son safe and to see the Wardlow family restored to their rightful place, if that were His will.

After perhaps a further quarter of an hour reflecting on the more prosaic choices that now lay before her Ann suddenly opened her eyes, as if she had had a revelation. As she made to rise from her intentionally uncomfortable station she heard the click of the chapel door latch. Looking around, she saw Richard. He strode towards her and she made her way to him as best she could, her legs stiff after kneeling on the cold floor. They embraced, saying nothing, for no words were needed at that point. It was only as Richard tenderly escorted his mother back across the green, lending her an arm for support which she did not need but was delighted to accept, that she spoke of the decision she had reached whilst deep in prayer.

"I think it best for all concerned if my servants and I repair to my manor and farms at Carmel. Edmund does not know of their existence and I am sure I can survive quite comfortably there. It will take some of the burden off Roger's shoulders. He has you and your men to feed after all."

Richard made to interrupt but Ann continued. "Yes, my son, I know full well that you pay your way fair and square, after all it was I who arranged for our money to be sent to you here, nevertheless extra bodies mean extra work for Roger and his household. It is true what you say, that you and your men must stick together otherwise the estate will see its only fighting force dissolved. So long as Roger continues to be a generous host the castle is the safest place for you all – for now."

Richard considered his mother's words for a few moments then said, "I agree with what you say, Mother. Granted I, like you, am sorely concerned for my sister's safety but I fear there is nothing we can do for the present that would not put her life in great danger."

Ann sagged with relief upon hearing her son come to his senses at last. She could retreat to Carmel now confident that Richard would handle things cautiously and not go charging in, sword drawn, and bring down tragedy on their heads.

"I shall, of course, escort you there myself," he announced.

Ann shook her head slowly. "It is too dangerous. One of our great advantages is that Edmund does not know what you look like. If he or his spies were to see you in my company they would eventually put two and two together and you would be a marked man. He knows you are sheltering in the castle and we have already seen that his agents move freely and unknown through the streets and markets of the town. If he discovered your identity I would not rule out a cowardly assassination as one of the many devious tools our dear Edmund would happily use to achieve his end."

Richard's disappointment was impossible to conceal, but he knew his mother was right. Roger would be sure to offer an armed escort for Ann and her small party, and if they travelled far enough north on their way to Carmel, perhaps passing through Rhuddlan rather than St. Asaph, they would be more likely to avoid the attention of Edmund's roving pickets. A measure of disguise would not go amiss either, anything to throw the enemy off their scent. Ann took Richard's hands in hers, leaned forward and kissed him lightly on the cheek.

"I shall go and inform our good friend Roger of my plans. I intend to depart for Carmel as soon as I can. I shall do my best to stay in touch, that we might both remain apprised of important developments, but we must at all cost avoid having our communications intercepted, therefore do not think ill of me if I write but infrequently. I leave the future of our lands and our home in your hands, my son. Do this for your father."

"For my father," Richard replied, choking back a sob as he embraced his mother.

# CHAPTER FIFTY-FOUR

TWO WEEKS had passed since Kate's mother and her small party had departed for Denbigh Castle, reluctantly leaving her to Edmund's tender mercy. In fairness he had treated her well during that time, even allowing her to keep her own bedchamber. After a tentative beginning she had made proper friends with Ysabel, finding her to be delightful company and a godsend in her current situation, though their conversation rarely touched on the subject of Plas Anwen's new master. It wasn't, Kate decided, that Ysabel was afraid of Edmund, more that she felt she was being loyal by keeping his secrets secret.

In stark contrast to Edmund's dealings with Kate's mother, there was little or no friction between him and his half-sister. Once he had made it clear to Kate that she was *not* to attempt to gallop off to join her brother at Denbigh, lest he be forced to implement drastic measures, and she in return had made it clear to him that she understood perfectly, he was as charming as always. Kate was free to wander at will provided she did not stray too far. She was not allowed to ride a horse, however, and access to Rollo in particular was on a strictly social basis. Wherever she went she was under the watchful eyes of Edmund's men, leading even her to conclude very quickly that any escape attempt would be ill-considered. She had already seen her half-brother's darker side and did not want the ominous shadow of his authority to fall across her path.

On a more cheerful note, it was clear to Kate that Edmund derived great joy and satisfaction from throwing himself wholeheartedly into the running of the estate. Seeing him breezing in and out of the house, his cheeks flushed from a morning ride to one of the manors, a ready smile on his face and a glass of wine in his hand, Kate found herself almost liking him - almost, although it was not long before his true colours shone through causing her to change her opinion back again.

It was early November and upon the feast of Martinmas, as on several other occasions during the year, the lord of the manor traditionally held a court at which he passed formal judgement on the many and varied matters concerning the tenants and their disputes. Since the King's centre of power was so far away from most country estates it was accepted by all that the lords of the manor had the authority to act as judge, jury and, on occasion, executioner in all matters concerning their tenants. This system saved the King's officers no end of work, not to mention travelling, but it was, of course, open to the most appalling abuse, and upon witnessing the handling and outcomes of the first day's cases Kate was beginning to suspect that Edmund was going to prove just as susceptible to the allure of absolute power as any of his peers. The most immediately noticeable aspect of the court held in the spacious, but nevertheless packed, nave of the church of St Michael in Caerwys, was the fact that the twelve-strong jury consisted of eleven of Edmund's men and one rather apprehensive-looking tenant. At previous sessions, her father had, as always, ensured that judgements would be made by a broad cross-section of the local inhabitants and had selected the jury accordingly. Punishments for those who had broken the law were no less harsh under Sir Geoffrey than those being meted out by the new master of the estate, but at least the defendants knew they were getting a fair hearing.

Strangely, however, Edmund did appear to be giving serious consideration to the cases brought before him and his 'jury'. Judging by the wide range of expressions on his face, Kate thought, even he was surprised and intrigued by the variety and complexity of the tenants' complaints and the passion with which those he would no doubt regard as 'ordinary' argued their corner.

In many instances the misdemeanours were very minor and the issuing of a modest fine served both to chasten the offender and mollify the plaintiff. Girard seemed to be acting as a legal 'go-between' the whole time, ferrying whispered messages and instructions from Edmund to the jury. None of the tenants dared complain of malpractice, of course, owing to the presence of another two dozen of Edmund's men, heavily armed and stationed around the perimeter of the nave, but so far, in Kate's eyes, there had been none. The faces on the jury were different from those of previous years, bar one, but she had to admit to herself that Edmund was handling matters much as her father would have done. Indeed he seemed to have quite an eye for spotting those whose testimonies might be suspect, or those whose complaints were spurious, brought falsely against a neighbour out of spite.

Judging by the lack of grumbling among the tenants, most of the jury's - that is to say Edmund's - rulings seemed to meet with their approval. It was only when the more serious cases came up - those involving inheritance disputes, arguments over land rights and rent arrears - that Kate saw how her half-brother intended to misuse his authority.

Upon his arrival at Plas Anwen, Edmund had had threescore mercenaries in tow to back up his claim. He needed to keep them close by in order to maintain his iron grip on the estate and to achieve that end his men must all be permanently housed. Kate had seen evidence of house building on the edges of Caerwys and in other places nearby, but not sufficient for sixty souls and not progressing quickly enough to provide warm homes before the winter came. Now it was time for Edmund's calculating ruthlessness to be given free rein.

Wherever there was a serious breach of the agreement laid down binding landlord and tenant, Edmund came down hard. By the end of the first day of the court sessions he had thrown seven families out of their homes for falling into serious arrears with their rent. Another two had their homes taken from them when neither could agree who had the right to graze their livestock on one particularly hotly disputed field. Kate could see at once that the newly-vacated properties would prove highly convenient for accommodating at least some of Edmund's soldiers, but the tenants did not appear to catch on quite so quickly. In their eyes the day's court proceedings seemed to have been, on the whole, conducted fairly. No doubt some of them might have thought some of the judgements a little harsh but the law was the law and the new master was applying it to the letter, as he was entitled to do and as they expected him to do. There was, possibly, another reason for their collective acquiescence. They had all seen the large military camp close to Plas Anwen and had all slept uneasily in their beds dreaming of the horrors that sixty battle-hardened soldiers might visit upon peaceful country folk. It was infinitely more desirable to have their disputes resolved by a stroke from a clerk's quill, rather than a mercenary's sword.

To the astute Kate, however, it was just another of Edmund's clever ways of getting what he wanted. Rather than ejecting people forcibly from their homes upon his arrival and risking a violent backlash from the tenantry while they were still in a state of upheaval, he had bided his time until he could achieve his end legally. None of the villagers who had witnessed the court's decision-making process could truthfully say they had seen any dishonesty, under-hand dealing or evidence of corruption save, perhaps, for the composition of the 'jury'. Edmund had managed to put himself well and truly in charge. *How clever and how typical,* thought Kate.

The court was closed an hour before dusk to give those who had attended time to get home before darkness fell. Even so, as Kate stepped out of the church the sky was already the colour of

Welsh slate and a steady, penetrating rain was sweeping across the estate, driven by a keen north-westerly wind.

Edmund had thoughtfully provided a covered cart for Ysabel and Kate and although progress along the road back to Plas Anwen was slow and bumpy at least the girls stayed dry. Edmund rode alongside Girard while his mercenaries walked back to their camp in loose order. He seemed oblivious to the worsening weather, conversing animatedly with his friend as they discussed how the day's proceedings had gone.

There was little talk inside the covered cart, however. Kate sat in silence, her knees drawn up to her chin and her hands clasped around her shins, staring into space. Ysabel longed to reach out to her, but did not know what to say or do. Today Kate had been no more than a spectator, her family's power on the estate broken and their tenants under another's authority. How must that feel?

Back at Plas Anwen, Kate saw that news had travelled fast. Several of the campaign tents belonging to Edmund's mercenaries were in the process of being struck; no doubt their owners would be eager to move out of the cold wind and into the newly-vacated houses. As she alighted from the cart the rain turned to sleet, signalling the arrival of winter, and she wondered what the evicted families, all of whom she knew, would do now.

Inside the manor house there were piles of wooden boxes and numerous mysterious bundles wrapped in canvas. It turned out that Edmund had sent to Calais for some of his personal belongings as soon as he had moved in to the house, hoping that they would get there before the worsening weather transformed the local roads into a muddy, rutted, waterlogged mess.

The next morning more items were delivered; this time they had legs and wings. So sure was Edmund of his permanency at Plas Anwen that he had ordered three hunting dogs and two falcons. Kate fell in love straight away with the former: two greyhounds, both of which immediately made friends with her, licking her hand and reminding her poignantly of her father's dogs who had trotted off to Denbigh beside her mother's horse, and a bloodhound.

The falcons were a rather more intimidating prospect with their cruel beaks and beady eyes. There was a small, pretty Merlin and a much larger, very regal-looking Gerfalcon. Edmund had even hired a trainer to help him to get to grips with handling the birds. Having lived his whole life thus far in a crowded, smelly town it was obvious that he meant to embrace what he saw as 'healthy country living' to the full and that was what he did. In the days following the arrival of his menagerie, he and Girard would set out as often as they could, regardless of the weather, hunting or hawking anything that moved. They would frequently return with their clothes wet through but their spirits high, enthusiastically recounting tales of their exploits as the servants struggled with their long riding boots in front of a roaring fire and the dogs shook themselves all over Kate and Ysabel.

It was at those times, when her worries had been eased by a glass or two of mulled wine and Girard had perhaps caught her eye and flashed her one of his dazzling smiles, that Kate found herself looking upon the two friends as just a pair of exuberant – and very handsome – boys. Regrettably, though, it was never long after such moments that reality intruded into her thoughts and reminded her that she was in the company of her father's murderer and his accomplice.

# CHAPTER FIFTY-FIVE

A S THE ever-shortening days passed, talk turned to preparations for Christmas, only three weeks away. It depressed Kate enormously to think of spending the feast apart from her family. Tired of being a prisoner in a gilded cage she longed to embrace her mother and fight with her brother. She thought of writing a letter to her mother, not knowing that Ann was now comfortably settled with her servants at Carmel, but her fear of Edmund finding out stopped her. She wondered how long it would be before she would see them again, if indeed she ever would. The events of the following few days only served to deepen her despondency.

First of all, another Royal messenger arrived at Plas Anwen. After accepting the traditionally proffered refreshment he solemnly informed Edmund that at a recent session of Parliament the proposed attainder of Sir Geoffrey Wardlow had been passed. His line of inheritance was now declared void and his property and estate forfeited to the Crown. It was only partly what Edmund had wanted to hear, though no great surprise. He had always known he would have to fight to keep what he had worked so hard to obtain, be it on the field of battle against an armed and armoured opponent, or in a court against the expert legal advisers of a grasping and acquisitive King Henry. He made his position clear to the messenger.

"I do not wish to inconvenience his Grace the King, but I happen to be the new master of Plas Anwen and its associated lands."

The messenger accorded Edmund a polite bow in acknowledgement, tinged, Edmund thought, with the merest hint of sarcasm. "Of course, sir, if you feel you have a strong and valid claim then you are entitled to petition the King and have your case heard in the courts."

Edmund's confidence had taken a knock at the thought of perhaps losing his prize, but he rallied admirably, even though he was not sure of his ground at that particular moment.

"You may be sure that I shall speak most eloquently at the appointed time. I am sure King Henry will judge me to be a faithful and deserving servant."

The messenger offered various routine pleasantries then went on his way.

Edmund caught Girard's eye and indicated with a nod of his head that he wished to have a council of war in private. Ysabel and Kate made their excuses and left the two friends, now in sombre mood, to come up with a watertight legal plan for protecting Edmund's 'inheritance'.

Edmund's general demeanour remained dour for several days until one morning fresh intelligence arrived that put the smile back on his face in no small measure. He, Ysabel and Kate were part way through their midday meal when Girard, who had been on a business errand, burst into the room, almost unable to contain himself.

"*MOMENTOUS NEWS!*" he began breathlessly. His state of agitation was such that Edmund got up from his chair, poured a glass of wine and pressed it into his friend's hand, at the same time placing a firm, steadying hand on his shoulder.

"Calm yourself, Girard! Whatever can it be that has caused you such excitement?"

Girard downed his wine in one draught, set his glass down on the table, then grasped Edmund by both shoulders.

"I had heard it noised about of late that Jasper Tudur, Earl of Pembroke, was on his way with an army to invest Denbigh Castle and take his rightful place as its constable. At the time I dismissed it as the idle gossip of bored soldiers, but this very morning rumour has given way to fact. He is *here,* Edmund, come with a thousand men to lay siege to the castle in the King's cause!"

Edmund's eyes blazed as his mind raced through the implications.

"It would appear that Saint Nicholas has brought us an early Christmas gift! We could not have wished for better. A siege, eh? That will keep my dear brother out of our hair for a while. I wonder how he will like the taste of cats and rats when his regular fare has run out?"

He turned round to see Kate jump up from her seat and run to her room in floods of tears.

Ysabel followed her, a look of extreme concern on her face.

Shrugging at the seemingly unfathomable ways of women, Edmund switched his attention back to Girard. His friend was highly animated and his enthusiasm was infectious. They recharged their glasses, clinked them together in a toast then laughed loud and long.

As they celebrated the news with wine and more wine, an idea suddenly sprang into Girard's mind. He immediately shared it with Edmund. "Jasper Tudur is the King's half-brother and a very influential figure. Why not approach him with the aim of securing his support for your claim on the estate?"

"My friend, you are a genius!" Edmund replied. His face lit up at the prospect of gaining such a powerful ally. "We must arrange an audience with him as soon as possible."

# CHAPTER FIFTY-SIX

RICHARD'S INSIDES performed a somersault at the sight that greeted him below. He had bounded up the stairway onto the wall walk in response to the frenzied shouts from the guards. He was joined moments later by Roger. Soon after that it seemed as if the entire garrison had turned out to look.

There was nothing out of the ordinary to see as far as the town walls, but beyond the Burgess Gate, coming up the long main street of the new town was an army. Banners fluttered and sunlight reflected off the heads of hundreds of polearms. Thanks to their scout patrols the inhabitants of the castle had known of the approach of the host for two days, but it was still a shock to see such a force arriving on their doorstep.

"Jesus Christ!" muttered Roger under his breath. "It's Jasper Tudur."

Richard regarded the slow-moving mass, reckoning there to be at least a thousand men.

"Can we keep them out?" he asked, his voice a little unsteady.

Roger carefully scanned Jasper's army before answering. "For now, yes. Certainly he will just walk in and occupy the new town, but taking the walled burgh will not be so straightforward and then he has these to scale," he said, patting the stone battlements of the castle. "Let us hope he has not brought gunpowder artillery. If he has no cannon my guess is that he will play a waiting game and try to starve us out."

"And I and my men will be a score of extra mouths using up your reserves of food!" Richard cried in dismay. "We should have left with my mother. I knew we should prove to be a burden on you."

"Stop!" Roger said firmly. "You and your fellows are not a burden, you are twenty extra sword arms which may prove decisive when it comes to keeping the foe from passing through our gates." Richard relaxed a little, then pointed suddenly towards the Burgess Gate, part of the town wall and the principal entrance to the burgh. The main body of the army had come to a halt, drawn up in close order for almost the entire length of the main street and looking, he thought, utterly terrifying.

As the host stood by a party of half-a-dozen horsemen, one of whom was carrying a plain white flag, trotted towards the town gate and held a conversation with the guards. Moments later, a guard descended from the gate tower and ran in the direction of the castle. Roger tapped Richard on the arm, indicating that he should accompany him. The two of them hurried down to the castle gatehouse and went out to meet the running guard.

"My lord!" he began breathlessly. "The Earl of Pembroke requests that you parley with his representative under a flag of truce."

"I'll wager ten marks to a bucket of night soil he is not here to discuss the weather," Roger coolly remarked to Richard, who was impressed by his calmness in such a serious situation. But then, Richard recalled, this was the same Roger Kynaston who less than three months earlier had counter-charged the Lancastrian cavalry at Bloreheath and personally killed its commander, Lord Audley. Jasper Tudur might have his work cut out, army or no army.

Not wishing to fall victim to an enemy ruse Roger stayed out of sight behind the massive stonework of the Burgess Gate until he had received a nod from his guard signalling that nothing appeared to be amiss.

Looking over the parapet he saw two colourfully-attired heralds, three men-at-arms and an impressive figure wearing a full harness of expensive armour. All six were well-mounted. Regarding the host in the distance Roger noted that they had stopped well out of arrow range. Clearly there had been no dishonourable intention of luring him onto the walls then shooting him down. He addressed the figure in full armour – most likely one of Jasper's lieutenants.

"I am Roger Kynaston, Constable of Denbigh Castle. God give you good day, sir. Forgive us if we do not invite you in to sup with us, only I fear we should struggle to feed you all!"

The armoured rider, satisfied that he was not about to be picked off by one of the archers stationed on the town wall, lifted the visor of his armet. He offered a polite bow, as far as his full harness and high war saddle would allow, then responded. "God give you good day also, sir. I am Roger Puleston and I have been granted my lord of Pembroke's authority to treat on his behalf. I thank you for your consideration but I fancy your victuals will be used up soon enough unless you agree to surrender this castle to its appointed Constable, Jasper Tudur."

The other Roger laughed as he responded. "Why, it so happens that I, too, am Constable of Denbigh! Surely the castle, having one perfectly good constable, does not need another? Pray respectfully inform the Earl of Pembroke that he need not trouble himself with a tiresome siege. I doubt that he will derive much pleasure from banging his head against a stone wall and in any case I am sure a man of his station has far more important matters to attend to."

"I ask you to reconsider your position," Roger Puleston said gravely. "I shall return upon the morrow that you might sleep upon the matter."

"No need for that," Roger Kynaston replied. "My answer would be the same whether you came to me tomorrow or in six weeks' time. I beg his lordship's pardon for the inconvenience but I will not give up my castle, not today nor any day."

"Then God be your help. Prepare yourselves to be tested to the very utmost!" Roger Puleston offered a curt parting salutation before wheeling his horse around and making his way back to the Earl of Pembroke and his waiting army.

Roger Kynaston looked at Richard, his expression taut with uncertainty. "You and your men can leave now with no loss of honour. This fight is mine, not yours."

"No!" Richard replied. "We shall stand with you to the end. It is the least we can do to repay your kindness."

"Very well," Roger declared, "our first move is to study our most recent inventory and ration our food accordingly. Our enemy does not yet have us surrounded so we can bring in extra supplies through the postern gate until they do but we will have to be quick. Those living in the burgh who wish to leave may do so and those who are able and willing to fight can assist our cause. We do not yet know how they intend to conduct the siege, whether it be through starvation or bombardment, but over the coming days we shall see what their intentions are and tailor our own actions to suit." Richard nodded his assent.

"I shall go straight and tell my men what I expect of them. You may count upon our best support – it is what my father would have done were he here now."

Roger placed his hands on his young friend's broad shoulders. "I know he would be proud Richard."

# CHAPTER FIFTY-SEVEN

ONLY FOUR days after first hearing of the siege, Edmund was in Denbigh at Jasper Tudur's invitation, seeing with his own eyes the preparations the would-be besieger had been making.

The streets were thronged with soldiers wearing the liveries not only of the Earl of Pembroke but also of other noblemen who were supporting his cause. Edmund had arrived with a modest bodyguard of ten of his soldiers, including Will, their serjeant. He had not seen the point of taking too many of his men with him. He feared no attack from Richard's party, holed up and surrounded as they were, and he did not wish for Girard, left in charge at Plas Anwen, to be undermanned. In any event, even if he had brought along all of his mercenaries there was nothing he and his threescore followers could possibly do against an army, so he had no choice but to answer the questions thrown at him by Jasper's guards at the town gates and comply with their instructions.

From what he could see as he and his men were escorted through the narrow side streets, Edmund deduced that so far Jasper had taken over the new part of the town – a relatively easy task as it had little in the way of formal defences – and was now preparing to concentrate his efforts against the older, walled burgh that surrounded the castle.

Eventually the group reached a large, well-appointed merchant's house which Edmund guessed Jasper had requisitioned to serve as his centre of operations. Will and the men were ordered to give up their arms, then pointed in the direction of a nearby tavern. There were no complaints. Edmund, too, unbuckled his swordbelt as directed and handed it to a waiting man-at-arms before entering the house and being shown through to a large, richly-furnished hall. Around one end of a long table, warmed by an impressive log fire, sat a council of war consisting of some half-dozen finely dressed men that Edmund assumed to be nobles. Two men-at-arms remained at the door, pollaxes at the ready, their eyes never leaving Edmund's back. The figure at the head of the table, dressed even more richly than the others though perhaps only three or four years older than Edmund himself, beckoned with his hand. His expression appeared friendly but curious. As Edmund approached he studied the young man's face, noting the long, slender nose, thin-lipped smile and pale, calculating eyes. They seemed to hint at a mind perhaps lacking in fire or passion, but coldly efficient nevertheless.

"Be welcome. I am Jasper Tudur, Earl of Pembroke, for my troubles, and these are my friends," the young man began. The minor nobles each accorded Edmund a vague, disinterested nod by way of courtesy. They had already concluded he was just another petitioner looking for a favour.

"God save you and give you good day, my lord," Edmund responded, executing a deep, respectful bow.

"Come closer and speak your business. I may be able to help you if you are willing to be of service to me in return."

The tone seemed well-practised and Edmund began to wonder whether he had done the right thing in coming to see a man in Jasper Tudur's lofty position. He must have seen and heard it all before; after all, he was King Henry's half-brother.

"My name is Edmund of Calais, my lord, and I seek your support in making a claim upon a property which I believe to be mine by right."

At this, one or two of the nobles rolled their eyes towards the ceiling. Edmund felt uneasy, almost foolish, but Jasper had the good manners to let him continue.

"The knight who previously held the land turned traitor, taking up arms against the King at Ludford. I was fortunate to be able to capture him as he fled the field."

Jasper leaned forward in his chair, his interest suddenly aroused. His nobles also pricked up their ears. This was not the way most petitioners' stories began.

"*Do* continue!" Jasper urged.

Edmund's heart was pounding. He was taking a gamble which, if it went wrong, could see him on trial for murder, but he desperately needed help and could see no other way of obtaining it. He was pinning his hopes on one military man understanding and condoning the actions of another in a war situation.

"He was executed as a traitor the following day on my orders," was all Edmund was prepared to say, thinking it sufficient for them to make a judgement one way or the other.

"*Ah!*" exclaimed Jasper, smacking both of his hands down on the arms of his chair. Edmund detected the merest curl of a smile on the Earl's lips and dared to hope.

"Decisive action - I like that!" The nobles nodded in agreement with something approaching enthusiasm, perhaps even approval, Edmund thought. He relaxed a little inwardly but the strain still showed on his face. Jasper noticed it. He leaned forward, steepling his fingers and pressing them against his lips, suddenly looking much older and wiser than his youthful appearance suggested. He studied Edmund with intense interest. Not wishing to seem abashed or overawed, Edmund maintained eye contact with Jasper, but was careful not to make himself appear arrogant or disrespectful.

After an uneasy silence Jasper continued. "And where are these disputed lands might I ask?"

"Plas Anwen at Caerwys, along with a dozen or so surrounding manors, my lord," Edmund replied.

"Ah, the Wardlow estate. That is close by here. I heard of Sir Geoffrey's attainder; now I know why he was not there to hear the bill being read!"

The minor nobles laughed politely at their master's remark. At the mention of his father's name Edmund's nerves began to jangle.

Jasper remained equable, though his expression became more searching.

"Was there by any chance some feud between yourself and Sir Geoffrey which might have coloured your judgement and contributed to his speedy execution? I do not wish to be seen encouraging personal vendettas."

Edmund, not wishing to reveal the whole story, tried to keep it simple without appearing too transparent. The young Earl was no fool.

"My lord, Sir Geoffrey was known to me prior to the events at Ludford, but only distantly. It is common knowledge that he took up arms against King Henry four years ago at St Albans. The King was gracious on that occasion, pardoning him for his treason in the interests of harmony, yet at Ludford he chose once again to defy the sacred authority of the Crown. There can be no forgiveness a second time. It was God's will that he should fall into my hands. I was merely the instrument through which a useful service could be performed in removing a threat to the King's peace."

"You have also done me a service by ridding me of a potentially troublesome neighbour," Jasper added. "I intend to make Denbigh my centre of operations for the time being. I shall rest easier in my bed knowing that I do not have an ardent Yorkist living next door. All in all, given the circumstances surrounding your actions and the favourable consequences thereof, it is my personal opinion that your judgement was sound on this occasion."

Relief flooded through Edmund's body as Jasper continued.

"The enemies of the King are everywhere, causing mischief up and down the country wheresoever and howsoever they can.

Only a firm hand will bring them to heel. Do you know why I am here, Edmund? I am here because some months ago King Henry bestowed upon me the honour of Constable of Denbigh Castle. Unfortunately, the present Constable, Roger Kynaston, friend to the Duke of York and therefore an enemy of the King, refuses to part with it. Can you imagine how irksome and indeed embarrassing such a hindrance is to a man in my position? It is as if someone had made you a gift of a fine horse, yet you were obliged to watch another man riding it, to the amusement of those who were not your friends. Hence my bringing an army to invest the castle and starve Kynaston into seeing the error of his ways.

"Whether I shall follow your bold example and cut off his head should he dare to show it above the battlements I cannot say at this point, but I *will* have my castle! As to the matter of Sir Geoffrey's estate, you may count upon my support should you need it."

Edmund made another deep bow. "My lord you are most gracious. Pray tell me how I might repay the great favour you have shown me."

Jasper smiled. "How many men do you have under your command, Edmund?"

"Approaching threescore, my lord," Edmund replied. "All veterans of the French Wars and hardened fighters who can be relied upon in a tight corner. We have travelled a long way together."

Jasper seemed impressed. "Indeed? You could be a useful ally then, though you need do nothing as yet. I have men enough to retake the castle if the current situation does not alter. We shall simply play a waiting game. I do not wish to waste the lives of my men in futile assaults, nor do I as yet wish to bring up artillery to batter my own castle into rubble. Where would be the sense in that? All I ask is that if I should call upon you and your men in my hour of need, you will hasten to my side immediately and without question. These are troubled times and we cannot be sure that the King's enemies will not band together at some future date to propagate disharmony and misrule."

"We shall serve you willingly with our bodies and our lives, my lord," Edmund declared earnestly. *But not if we can avoid it,* he thought to himself as he bowed and turned to leave, the young Earl having subtly indicated that the audience was at an end.

He had almost reached the door when Jasper spoke again. "Oh, there *is* one more thing. Sir Geoffrey was your father, was he not?"

Edmund froze. *What game is he playing now?* he thought. He glanced furtively at the two guards on the door. They stared fixedly ahead, but Edmund noticed their fingers tightening almost imperceptibly around their weapons. He felt like a cornered rat.

Knowing escape was out of the question he slowly turned to face Jasper, fearing his newly-forged alliance was about to turn sour. He fought to maintain a calm expression but his heart was pounding and his mouth was dry. The young Earl noticed his discomfiture and quickly waved his hand in a reassuring gesture.

"Pray do not be alarmed, my friend. A man in my position must have *all* the facts if he is to keep his head above water in these troubled times.

My intelligence gatherers are reliable, well-informed and everywhere. I do not accuse you of dissembling - I merely wish to confirm the full story behind your journey here."

Edmund realised he had no choice but to be completely honest. The fact that he had, so far, not *actually* lied to Jasper would make things easier to explain.

"It is true, my lord. Sir Geoffrey *was* my father, though I do not carry his name. I was his bastard but he chose to turn his back on me, abandoning my mother and playing no part in my upbringing. It is both for my sake and for my mother's sacred memory that I have come to claim the inheritance I feel is due to me."

Jasper seemed genuinely enthralled, as though he were listening to a travelling storyteller recounting some great romance around the hall fire.

"A most compelling tale!" he exclaimed. "To be sure, I do not know where circumstances now place you regarding Sir Geoffrey's attainder. Certainly as his bastard you had no claim on his estate in the normal run of things, so conversely I cannot see that you could be excluded now that the attainder is in place. The courts may view you as an outsider with as much right to make a claim on his property as anyone else, provided the King does not snap it up first. It will be most interesting to see how the case turns out."

"Indeed it will, my lord", said Edmund, with masterly understatement. His dry comment was not lost on Jasper:

"Haha! Yes, especially for you, Edmund, but remember that I will be happy to lend my support and such influence as I have to your endeavour so long as you are willing to place yourself and your men at my call."

"We have an accord, my lord", Edmund replied, bowing again. Jasper nodded in acknowledgement.

Pleased at the outcome of the audience, but relieved to be on his way, Edmund breezed past the guards, fastened on his sword belt and set off to prise his men out of the tavern.

On the journey back to Plas Anwen, Edmund reflected upon the events of the last two months. At first he had been happy to use the unrest between the houses of Lancaster and York as a smokescreen for obtaining what he wanted, but he was quickly coming to realise that if he wished to hold on to what he had won he would have no choice but to become personally involved. There were some very powerful players in this deadly game and in order to survive Edmund would have to take sides, especially as one particular act in the overall drama was taking place on his doorstep.

He needed Jasper Tudur's 'good lordship' but it came at a price. Whether he liked it or not, Edmund was now a committed Lancastrian. Not such a bad thing perhaps, he mused. The Yorkists had suffered a devastating reverse at Ludford, their army was scattered to the four winds and their leaders had run off to cower in Ireland and Calais with their collective tails between their legs. Granted, there were still pockets of resistance such as that being put up by an obstinate Roger Kynaston at Denbigh Castle, but they would soon be crushed. There was undoubtedly a sense of satisfaction to be gained from choosing the winning side, Edmund thought.

His musings were cut short when he was met by Girard and two of Will's men. Girard appeared uneasy as he pulled up his horse.

"What is it, friend?" Edmund asked. "You look as though you bear ill tidings."

Girard knew Edmund well enough to come straight to the point. "We have lost twenty mercenaries! It seems they packed their gear and left at first light, led by a friend of the man you hanged. Apparently they had become restless, preferring fighting to farming."

"Where will they go?" asked Edmund.

"My guess is the Scottish Borders, Master," one of Will's band replied. "There is always violence and unrest there, enough to satisfy the most warlike of men."

Edmund did not doubt the truth of the man's statement.

"We still outnumber your brother's retainers and they can do little against us while the Earl of Pembroke has them surrounded," Girard continued. "Nevertheless it would be imprudent to sit back and rely upon a weakened force to defend our interests."

"...and I have just secured Jasper Tudur's support for my claim in exchange for a promise to provide him with sixty mercenaries should he need them," Edmund added. "We must replace them with all urgency. Let us hasten back to Plas Anwen. I have an idea."

Back at the manor house, Girard, joined by Ysabel and Kate, looked on as Edmund conducted a thorough search of his travelling chests and document satchels. After several minutes of enthusiastic rummaging Edmund turned to his small audience, a small, rather battered letter in his hand and an expression of triumph on his face.

"Haha! I knew I had it somewhere," he announced. "Herein lies the answer to the problem of our disappearing mercenaries."

Ysabel looked at Girard to see if he knew what was going on but all he could do was shrug.

Seeing their bewilderment Edmund offered an explanation. "This is a letter from a man – a Fleming - whose acquaintance I made whilst learning to use the great sword in the Talhoffer *Fechtschule*. He fared well enough in the fencing classes but handgonnes are his real passion. We spent many an evening in the taverns around the *Fechtschule* putting the world to rights."

"What was, or rather is, his name?" asked Girard. "You may have mentioned such an associate before but I do not believe I ever met him myself."

"It was before you and I became friends. His name is Balthazar van Herck," Edmund replied.

"What a flamboyant sounding name!" exclaimed Ysabel. "He could be one of the three Wise Men."

Edmund laughed. "Wise Men? Haha! He is certainly wise on the subject of gunpowder and its uses, but he can be a little, shall we say, eccentric. I doubt very much if he would have been allowed anywhere near Bethlehem with or without a gift, especially after a night on the wine!"

"So how will this Balthazar help us in regard to filling the gaps in our force?" asked Girard. "Does he perchance have a private army?"

"Not quite," Edmund replied, smiling, "but after we finished at the *Fechtschule* he said that he planned to form a small company of handgonners, to be available for hire by whoever needed them. This letter, written only a year ago, confirms that he has realized his intention. He speaks of making a good living at his craft. Balthazar is convinced that gunpowder weapons represent the future, and that their intelligent use will revolutionise warfare."

Girard's face seemed undecided as to whether to express cynicism or wonder. It settled somewhere between the two. "You intend, then, to hire a company of Flemish handgonners? What good will they be? As far as I am aware handgonnes have been in common use for a hundred years now, but I still see far more archers employed than gonners. If they were so marvellous surely we would be surrounded them by now?"

His words of caution were lost on Edmund, who seemed to have a faraway look in his eyes, as if he were already imagining a thunderous volley from a company of handgonners, the air of the battlefield impressively shrouded in dense white smoke as scores of enemy soldiers instantly fell dead, their breastplates easily penetrated by the speeding lead balls spewed from the muzzles of the gonners' weapons.

"I am convinced that employing Balthazar and his company would be a shrewd move," Edmund finally announced when he had finally stirred himself from his little reverie.

"But what happens when they run out of powder and shot? Do they make their excuses and sail back to Flanders?" Girard asked, still not persuaded that Edmund's faith was well-placed.

"Why, they put down their gonnes, take up their swords and bucklers and fight alongside us as capably as any regular soldier. They are all trained in close-quarter fighting otherwise their usefulness would be short-lived, as indeed would they," Edmund countered enthusiastically.

At this, Girard gradually began to come round to his friend's way of thinking. Such a company might prove an effective shock weapon in a battlefield situation, especially if Balthazar's men could also be relied upon to fight hand-to-hand once the customary initial exchange of missiles had turned into a melée.

"Very well, you have my approval," he declared, "though I have a feeling you would have engaged his services come what may!"

Edmund smiled. "In that happy case I shall write to him immediately and enquire as to whether he is available for hire. It may strengthen our new-found friendship with our lord of Pembroke if we were to appear in Denbigh at the head of a score or so of handgonners."

# CHAPTER FIFTY-EIGHT

TWO WEEKS went by during which time Jasper Tudur had steadily consolidated his position at Denbigh, having surrounded the castle and the walled burgh and then contented himself with playing a waiting game, knowing that no food could make it through his cordon of a thousand archers and men-at-arms. His army had no problem finding supplies since there was a whole town from which they could help themselves and when they had stripped it bare there was the countryside beyond.

It was a different story within the strong walls of Denbigh Castle, however, as the celebration of Christ's birth approached. There would be no Christmas feasting for Richard and Roger, just the same plain fare as their men, carefully measured out so as to last as long as possible. They were by no means reduced to eating cats and rats, but they were being careful all the same. Roger had whittled down the complement within the walls as far as he dare, sending traders, craftsmen, women, children and the old and infirm on their way to find shelter with friends or relatives in the nearby villages. Only the fit, fighting men remained: twenty to garrison the castle and another forty on constant patrol up on the walls of the burgh, where they knew the initial attack must come.

Richard felt for the men of the Wardlow estate who had accompanied him to Ludlow and stayed by his side ever since. They had not seen their wives since the beginning of October and there would certainly be no chance of them celebrating Christmas together. There was even a possibility that they might never see them again if the Earl of Pembroke decided to step up the siege and stage an all-out assault.

Richard tried to put such thoughts from his mind as he ate his simple meal, but again and again he found himself wondering how his mother was faring at Carmel and above all how his hated half-brother was treating Kate.

He need not have worried on the latter score. Edmund had decided to make his first Christmas at Plas Anwen a memorable one and had gone to some considerable expense to ensure that there was more than enough to eat and drink on the eve of the Saviour's birthday. The largest of the barns near the manor house had been given over to feasting, with benches and trestle tables to accommodate those tenants whose desire to take advantage of the offer of free food and ale had outweighed any uncomfortable notions of disloyalty to the Wardlow family.

Kate was surprised and a little dismayed to see the torch-lit building almost filled with laughing revellers, stuffing their faces with Edmund's offerings and dancing to the music of the players he had hired.

*How soon people forget,* she thought, but then life was hard and especially so through the long, dark, unforgiving winter. Certainly, among the poorer tenants, there would be precious few who would pass up the opportunity to stave off the constant, gnawing hunger that shadowed their lives, even if only for a day.

The following morning, as she and her family had always done on Christmas Day, Kate went to the church at Caerwys. She was very grateful for the company – on this occasion Ysabel, who had been most insistent that they should go together – but a little disturbed that neither Edmund nor Girard had stirred from their beds on this holiest of days. In fact, she noted privately, she had never seen them in church unless it was on a matter of business. She found their apparent godlessness more disconcerting than any of their other unsavoury personal traits. It worried her to think what excesses such men might be capable of, if really pushed. Her father had been a firm dealer of justice on the estate and a seasoned warrior on the battlefields of France, no doubt with the blood of numerous enemies on his hands, but at least he had feared God. If Edmund were not actually in league with the Devil, they knew each other by sight, Kate concluded.

Ann Wardlow was also at church that morning, at St. Winefride's in Holywell, praying hard for her children and berating herself for not doing more to protect them. She prayed, too, for the soul of her beloved husband, whose body still lay cold and homeless in a faraway vault that bore another family's name. How she longed to bring him home and give him a decent Christian burial, but that was out of the question while Edmund was in charge at Plas Anwen. *Because of him even the dead can find no rest,* she thought bitterly.

# CHAPTER FIFTY-NINE

CHRISTMAS DAY for Edmund and Girard may have been a hazy affair, due entirely to the amount of wine and ale they had consumed while hosting the previous night's revelries, but the following day was infinitely more memorable, made so by the arrival of Balthazar van Herck and his Flemish mercenaries.

What made it even more momentous was the fact that, in addition to a company of fifteen handgonners there was a cannon, drawn along by four horses on its own wheeled carriage, with a crew of five men. Edmund was agog, almost lost for words as the column of men, beasts and wagons clattered up to the gates of the Plas Anwen. He ran out to meet Balthazar, who vaulted from his horse and embraced Edmund like a long-lost friend. They exchanged greetings then walked towards the door of the house, their arms around each others' shoulders. When they reached the entrance, Girard stepped forward and shook Balthazar's hand. Ysabel and Kate were standing just behind and when the visitor saw the young ladies he snatched off his red and black chaperon, to reveal a completely bald head, seemingly polished to a high gloss.

As he executed a deep bow, he flashed the girls a wide, glittering smile with a mouthful of gold teeth.

He chuckled to himself at the girls' reaction to his appearance then turned to Edmund, tapping his costly dentition. "As I told you, business has been good!"

Edmund laughed. "Either that or your rates are too high!"

"We can discuss such matters over supper," Girard added, "but before we eat I would be very interested in looking over your artillery piece."

"You mean *Eloise?*" asked Balthazar, brimming with pride at the mention of his favourite ordnance.

"What a delightful name!" cried Edmund. "I am sure the defenders of Denbigh Castle will be unable to resist her charms for long."

Balthazar smiled a sly smile. "Oh, Eloise has her wiles. She is not one to take 'no' for an answer!"

Kate shrank back into the house unnoticed and hurried up to her room in tears, her alarm increasing by the minute as she thought of the growing multitude of brutal assailants her brother now faced.

Ysabel looked around too late to see her friend depart, but was herself beginning to feel like an overlooked spare part in the midst of all the man-talk that was flying back and forth. She decided to visit the kitchen and organize the food for later, knowing she would feel infinitely more at home with Cicely the cook than she would with a gunpowder-obsessed crackpot with golden teeth.

Outside, the men were oblivious to their absence. Edmund and Girard positively fizzed with excitement as they followed Balthazar to the back of the wagon train. There before them stood Eloise, simple, elegant and deadly. Mounted on a slim wooden carriage suspended from a pair of cart-sized wheels, she had a seven-foot-long bronze barrel with a six-inch bore and a pair of curved supports with a series of holes into which pegs could be inserted to raise or lower the gun's trajectory. Balthazar explained that, although loosely speaking Eloise could be called a cannon, she was really a serpentine.

"I thought the big guns were far more cumbersome than this," Girard remarked.

"Yes," Edmund agreed. "She looks very manoeuvrable compared to the clumsy bombards I have seen. But will she still pack a hefty enough punch to worry the defenders of Denbigh Castle?"

"Fear not," Balthazar replied. "She may be only a slender serpentine, but like a snake she has a lethal bite!"

Edmund indicated a spot some distance from the house at the edge of his own mercenaries' camp and suggested that Balthazar's men pitch their tents there. Balthazar himself would be billeted in the manor house. The column set off clanking and clattering while the three friends turned and strolled back to Plas Anwen.

"Any chance of a demonstration on the morrow?" Edmund asked tentatively.

"I should think we can make some loud noises and scare the locals!" Balthazar replied. "We must limit ourselves to one discharge from the serpentine and a half-dozen or so shots from the handgonnes in order to conserve our supply of powder but I have a feeling you will be impressed."

"I had better be impressed," laughed Edmund, "for I, too, have a feeling: a feeling that I shall be paying royally for the privilege!"

"As your wise friend Girard pointed out, we can discuss my rates over supper and a good wine. Wine is the grease that lubricates the wheels of commerce!" exclaimed Balthazar.

"Or in your case makes them so slippery that you career off the road headfirst into a ditch!" Edmund added, remembering Balthazar's past antics and making a mental note not to get too drunk in case he ended up agreeing to pay an outlandish sum in return for the gonners' services.

The following morning, Edmund and Girard met with Balthazar and his mercenaries. The two friends had been obliged to wait until, much to Edmund's amazement, the entire company of Flemings, its leader included, had been to St Michael's to hear

Mass. His former classmate at the *Fechtschule* was a changed man, Edmund concluded, though not so changed as to refuse the many refills offered him the night before whilst negotiating a fee that left Edmund in no doubt as to how he could have afforded a mouth full of gold teeth.

After a brief discussion, a suitable piece of open ground was selected and an old cart from one of Plas Anwen's barns placed some eighty yards from where Eloise had been towed and set up by her crew.

"She can hurl a thirty-pound iron ball a thousand yards with ease and can knock a hole through the wall of a normal house at five hundred," Balthazar proudly announced. *"We just want to make sure we can hit our target today to show you what she can do."

"Remarkable!" Edmund replied, "but what can she *do* against the walls of Denbigh Castle? They must be ten feet thick in places."

"We shall not waste our shot where the walls are thickest," said Balthazar, tapping the side of his nose conspiratorially. "Every fortress, no matter how mighty, has its weaknesses and we pride ourselves on seeking them out. The fact that Eloise is so much easier to move about than a clumsy old bombard makes our task a great deal easier." Satisfied for the moment, Edmund, along with Girard, watched with interest as the crew busied themselves around Eloise, chattering away to each other in Flemish as they prepared her for the demonstration. The first task was to estimate the range and set the elevation of the gun to suit, using the curved supports and pegs that allowed the barrel and the bed in which it lay to move in relation to the wheeled carriage and trail.

At only eighty yards the trajectory to the target was almost horizontal.

Since Eloise was a breech-loader, one of the crew cut open a linen bag with a measured charge of powder and poured it into what looked like an extremely sturdy iron tankard. As he held it steady, another man hammered a softwood plug into the mouth of the tankard to seal it. The charge was placed in the gap in the breech so that it fitted snugly inside a lip in the barrel, then a wooden wedge was driven tightly in behind it to hold it in place. An iron ball was loaded the usual way, down the muzzle of the gun and rammed home. The touch-hole in the charge was pricked clear with a piece of wire and finally a little powder was poured into the priming pan. All was now ready.

Balthazar motioned to Edmund and Girard to withdraw a few paces in case of a mishap, then introduced a glowing match, wrapped around a six-foot linstock, to the touch hole, shouting *"HAVE A CARE!"* as he did so.

There was a brief, blinding flash from the powder in the pan, then a second later came a deafening *'BOOM!'* and the ground shook as Eloise spat out her iron ball, recoiling several feet as she did so.

Every bird in the vicinity took to the air in fright, the crows in particular cawing their disgust as they vacated their trees in one huge, black, flapping cloud. A dense plume of white smoke billowed out behind the shot as it flew from the gun's muzzle but it did not prevent Edmund from seeing the target cart being smashed to pieces as the ball struck home, sending splinters of wood flying in all directions in a satisfying orgy of destruction. He and Girard laughed like a pair of excited schoolboys as they witnessed the spectacle.

"We can manage a shot a minute from Eloise if there is need," said Balthazar, "or three minutes to be sure of the best accuracy. But wait, there is more. Watch this."

One of his men took an old breastplate and set it up against a post thirty or so yards away. Another mercenary stepped forward and took a lead ball a little under an inch in diameter from his waist pouch. Undoing a powder flask made from a cow's horn, he tipped out just enough to cover the ball, which he then picked out and put between his teeth. He poured the powder down the muzzle of his gonne, then finally dropped the ball in and rammed everything home with an iron rod.

The gonne consisted of an iron tube reinforced with hoops

along its two-foot length, mounted on a shoulder stock much like that of a crossbow. An S-shaped lever, when depressed, brought the slow match down onto the priming pan and that was all there was to it. The gonner blew on his match to make it glow, then took aim as best he could, being, Edmund noted, very careful to keep his face back from the priming pan. Having witnessed the flash from Eloise, Edmund could understand why. The man nodded to Balthazar to indicate that he was ready, then the latter called out *"GIVE FIRE!"*

In contrast to the bass thunder of the serpentine, the sound of the handgonne discharging was more of a short *'crack'*. The weapon kicked back violently into the shooter's shoulder and a second later there was a dull thud as the ball hit its target. The crows, having just returned indignantly to their perches, chose to ignore the proceedings this time.

Edmund, however, could not ignore the effects of the shot. The lead ball had punched straight through the steel breastplate with ease. At the same distance a well-trained archer shooting the most powerful of longbows might hope to achieve penetration with a short bodkin arrowhead, but it could not always be guaranteed. In contrast, a simple handgonne, operable by anyone, seemed to promise certain death at close range, even for an opponent clad in armour. Edmund was sold.

"I cannot wait to bring these impressive weapons to bear on our friends at Denbigh," he said, grinning at Balthazar, who returned the compliment with a flash of gold.

# CHAPTER SIXTY

THE DEFENDERS of Denbigh Castle were, as yet, unacquainted with the terrors of an artillery bombardment. Roger had correctly surmised that Jasper Tudur would be reluctant to damage what he viewed as his own castle in order to take possession of it, only to have to expend time and money on repairs once he had.

At first, Jasper had confined himself to small, probing raids on sections of the burgh wall, but as his men discovered the weakest points of its defences, and also the limits of the thinly-stretched defenders, it was only a matter of time before an all-out assault broke through into the old town and Roger's men had to fall back as fast as their legs could carry them into the protection of the castle's thick walls. It was a grim-faced Roger who addressed his men at a meeting he had called during a lull in the proceedings.

"As you all know, the enemy is now without. The burgh has fallen into their hands and will provide the ideal base from which to launch a determined attack. We have lost six good men and another eight lie wounded, but we still have these stout walls, from behind which we can make nuisances of ourselves. Jasper Tudur's army is now making itself comfortable in the burgh, but its very proximity puts many of his men within bowshot. I want all archers to take up position on the west wall and do their utmost to disrupt the enemy's preparations with well-placed shots. We are not short of a few arrows in the store. Make every one count though, but without making a target of yourself. There are far more of them than there are of us, so you have more to shoot at. In any case, once they get inside the fighting will be hand-to-hand, with little room to ply a bow, so you may as well use up your arrows before then."

"Once they get inside?" Richard queried, a little disconcerted by Roger's closing remark. "Are you so sure the castle will fall?"

Roger gave a resigned shrug. "We are on our own, Richard. There is no-one to come to our aid, no reinforcements marching up the Vale of Clwyd. Jasper means to take 'his' castle as not to do so would be a black mark on his honour. And my honour depends on keeping it from him for as long as I can because that is the promise I made to my friend, Richard Plantagenet, Duke of York.

"Whether I shall be cut down in the final assault, or forced to surrender to spare my men a miserable death by starvation, I do not know, but at this moment we have an opportunity to pare down the odds, if only a little. As long as we have archers left on the walls and arrows in the store any soldier of Tudur's foolish enough to venture out sight-seeing around the burgh will be skewered like a rabbit on a spit. I want them to be afraid to leave their billets."

# CHAPTER SIXTY-ONE

THE NEW year was almost two months old when Ysabel found herself standing at the door to Plas Anwen, watching anxiously as an impressive-looking column comprising Edmund, Girard, Balthazar and his gonners, and twenty of Edmund's own mercenaries set out for Denbigh. Jasper Tudur had grown tired of playing a waiting game and had decided to step up his efforts to wrest the castle from Roger Kynaston and his adherents. Needing all the help he could get for the final, decisive assault he had called upon Edmund who, anxious to please, had immediately sprung into action, hoping the appearance of his modern, mobile artillery company would impress the young Earl of Pembroke.

Edmund had not been in the best of tempers when he had set out, owing to the fact that Kate, his bargaining chip should Richard prove hard to prise from his stony retreat, was not standing beside her friend Ysabel to see him off. Only the day before she had, to his great annoyance, managed to slip away on her accursed black horse. The details were sketchy but Ysabel recalled Kate excusing herself from the sewing with which they were passing the time that afternoon, saying she had a headache. The next thing Ysabel could remember was a commotion outside Plas Anwen about half an hour later, as two of Edmund's soldiers arrived supporting a third who had been hit on the back of the head with a shovel while on guard duty near the stables.

Edmund had been livid. He had fined the unfortunate guard a month's pay, but there was little he could do to remedy the situation. His half-sister had clearly been paying far closer attention to his lengthy preparations for Denbigh than he had realized, having chosen the perfect moment when he, Girard and Will had been at their most distracted, marshalling the men and organising the equipment and provisions ready for the off.

Three weeks earlier Kate's mother had, at great risk, managed to get a letter to her telling her of her flight to Carmel and entreating her not to try to join her lest Edmund should find out and vent his anger upon her, or worse still, follow her to Carmel and vent it upon them both. Kate read it and then, as Ann Wardlow had instructed, held it in the flame of her bedside candle. As the paper caught fire so did Kate's imagination. Ignoring her mother's pleadings, her mind blazed as she weighed up her chances of escape. It had to be soon. All she needed was a window of opportunity and it only had to be open the merest crack for her to slip through and free herself from Edmund's clutches. The consequences of having his soldiers follow her to Carmel did not bear thinking about which was why, as she threw herself over Rollo's broad back that late February afternoon, dug her heels into his flanks and revelled once more in his silky power, she decided to head straight for Bodfari.

Kate managed to avoid being detected by Edmund's soldiers but once clear of Plas Anwen and the mercenaries she made sure several tenants saw her gallop by, hoping that they would, if questioned, swear by all that was holy that she must have been making for the safety of Sir Caddoc ap Rheged's manor house, from where Edmund could not hope to extract her without causing a major incident, since the old knight was highly thought of by King Henry.

Only when she was completely sure she was not being pursued did Kate pull on Rollo's reins to steer him onto an overgrown, little-used woodland track that would eventually lead her to Carmel. She prayed that the daylight would last long enough to see her over Halkyn Mountain and down the other side to her mother.

# CHAPTER SIXTY-TWO

THE SITUATION at Denbigh Castle was becoming desperate. Roger's tactic of using his archers as marksmen to harry the attackers as they swarmed through the streets of the burgh below the castle walls had met with initial success, but was less effective once Jasper's men had secured and manned the town wall. The wall met the castle itself at the Postern Tower on the south side at a narrow angle, allowing the besiegers to rake the defenders stationed between there and the White Chamber Tower with arrows, crossbow quarrels and handgonne fire. The Postern Tower looked set to become the focal point for any serious attempt to take the castle but Roger's men, positioned both on the battlements adjoining the White Chamber Tower and on the protecting wall that jutted out from the other side of the Postern Tower, were able to return fire from both sides.

Richard was sheltering momentarily behind a merlon, spanning a powerful crossbow with a goat's foot lever, a quarrel clamped in his mouth ready to load. He was no expert with the weapon but the range was relatively short and there were plenty of targets at which to aim.

Just as the thick hempen string clicked over the iron nut, locking it in place, he felt a tap on his shoulder. He turned his head to see a grim-faced Roger.

"It is time for you to go, Richard. The castle is all but lost. We cannot hope to hold out against so many. Once our defences are breached, and they surely will be, I shall order my men to put down their weapons and we shall throw ourselves upon the mercy of our lord of Pembroke. You and your men, on the other hand, would do better to slip away while you can, back to your families." Richard spat the quarrel onto the floor and propped his crossbow against the wall.

"But that would make us guilty of the lowest cowardice!" he protested. "Neither I nor my men would hear of it. We would rather defend this castle to the death and take our chances alongside you."

Roger shook his head slowly. "I am touched by your loyalty, Richard, but I do not intend to die here if I can help it. My promise to the Duke of York was to hold this castle for as long as I was able, and that I have done. With only a handful of men we have tied up a large and potent Lancastrian force for several weeks, with the result that it could not usefully be deployed elsewhere. I do not think the Duke expects any more of us for the present and provided Jasper does not have us all executed the moment he sets foot inside the castle, we will live to serve our master another day. There is another good reason for you to leave before the castle falls."

Richard knew what Roger was going to say.

"Edmund, my half-brother? Do you think he might have thrown in his lot with Jasper Tudur?"

"It is quite possible. If I were he and a major incident such as this were taking place almost on my doorstep I would at least want to see what was going on, and perhaps even make myself known in case I could form some kind of mutually beneficial alliance. The Earl of Pembroke is the King's half-brother and a very influential man. Assuming Edmund manages to make himself useful in some way he may be able to secure some very powerful support. If he is among the besiegers he will surely come looking for you when we are taken prisoner."

Richard frowned. "If he found me he would show no mercy. My head would be struck off before you could say Jack Cade. Very well my friend, we will do as you ask, but reluctantly. How can we make our escape though? Surely we are surrounded?"

"Not entirely," said Roger. "Jasper has concentrated his entire force on the east side as he prepares for a final assault. There seems to be little or no activity to the west. Below the Bishop's Tower there is a sally-port that leads through the outer mantlet wall and down to the road. The track is very steep and rough, but it is your only avenue now. I suggest you gather your men together and do not tarry. I cannot be certain that you have enough time left to wait for nightfall. Better you were on your way now."

Richard's throat was tight with emotion as he clasped Roger's hands. As he thanked him for his generosity and protection he wondered if they would ever meet again. Looking down, he saw the spanned crossbow still propped against the wall.

"It would be a shame to waste this," he said, managing a grin.

Roger watched from his shelter as Richard placed a quarrel in the bolt channel, shouldered the weapon and peeped out from behind the merlon, taking care to expose only the minimum of himself to any like-minded opponent. He took aim and squeezed the tiller. There was a *thwack* as the string flew forwards followed by the *whirr* of the nut as it spun in its housing. Fifty yards away a lightly-protected footsoldier staggered back as Richard's quarrel struck him in the chest and passed with ease through his mail shirt and linen padding, burying itself deep between his ribs.

"One less for you to deal with!" Richard announced in jubilation.

Roger nodded his appreciation, then gestured to Richard that he should make haste. The latter put down his bow and set off towards the steps that led to the inner bailey.

*"Go with God!"* Roger shouted, above the din of the fighting. Richard turned and looked at his friend and mentor one last time.

*"And may God and all His saints keep you safe!"* he replied, his words curdling with emotion.

# CHAPTER SIXTY-THREE

TO HIS great relief, Edmund had arrived at Denbigh in time to make a contribution to the siege. He would have been mortified had he come too late to take part and lost Jasper's goodwill. As it turned out, the young Earl was very keen to see what Edmund's men could do; in particular the colourful Balthazar van Herck and his artillery company. Jasper explained to Edmund that if necessary he could call upon several large bombards to pound the castle walls, but they were heavy, slow and ponderous and the damage they would do would take weeks to repair. The best opportunity for seizing victory whilst preserving the fabric of the castle seemed to be presenting itself between the Postern Tower and the White Chamber Tower, where there was a small postern gate set into the wall, but the terrain there was unsuitable for large guns. The other, more formidable hurdle to be overcome was the lethal concentration of crossfire being laid down by the defenders on the ground between the two towers. Undaunted, Balthazar boasted of Eloise's mobility and hitting power and requested that he and his men be allowed to try their luck on the gate. Jasper assented willingly and placed fifty archers under Edmund's temporary command, with orders to shield the gonners and lay down their own covering fire as the Flemings manoeuvred and served their piece. Edmund immediately had an idea. He grabbed a nearby pavise – a tall, rectangular shield that could be propped up for a crossbowman to shelter behind whilst reloading - and held it above another, making a shield that was effectively eight feet high.

"We can use these like the Romans did!" he exclaimed.

Girard also picked up a pavise, gesturing to the borrowed soldiers to do likewise. With a little shuffling, and rather more swearing, they managed to form something resembling the leading edge of a *testudo*, behind which the gunners would be able to ply their trade safely until, at the moment of firing, the shield wall would part to allow Eloise's shot to spew forth.

Having shown Jasper's men what he wanted them to do, Edmund kept a firm grip on his pavise. Danger or no, he intended that the young Earl should see him leading by example and placing himself in the thick of the fighting. Besides, he wanted to be among the first into the castle so that he could get his hands on Richard, assuming he was still alive.

After Eloise had been loaded the unwieldy-looking ensemble began to make its way into the mouth of Hell: the killing ground in the narrow angle between the town wall and that of the castle. A dozen or so pavises protected the gun while eight of Balthazar's mercenaries manhandled it to a firing position close enough to guarantee a direct hit. As Edmund and Girard shuffled forward shoulder-to-shoulder they heard and felt the repeated *thunk* of arrows and quarrels smacking into their shields.

*"It is like advancing into a hornets' nest!"* Edmund shouted to his friend.

*"Then let us pray we do not get too badly stung!"* Girard replied.

Just then one of Jasper's soldiers on the end of the shield formation stumbled, shot in the face by an arrow that had passed through a space between the pavises.

*"KEEP THOSE DAMNED SHIELDS TOGETHER!"* bawled Edmund, as one of the accompanying archers threw down

his longbow, grabbed the fallen man's shield and made good the gap.

Balthazar had been keeping a sharp eye out for the small postern gate at the foot of the White Chamber tower and now he could see it clearly. It was just a wooden door, but made of thick oak and undoubtedly very sturdy. Jasper's men would have been shot to pieces from both sides before they could have battered it down with a conventional ram.

He indicated to everyone that he wished to stop and set up Eloise ready for firing. Sighting his gun through a narrow slit in a wall of shields, in constant danger of being skewered by an enemy shaft, Balthazar felt alive. He flashed Edmund a golden grin from beneath his open-faced sallet.

*"We are ready when you are – let us knock and see if anyone is at home!"*

Edmund nodded to his opposite numbers and the entire shield wall shuffled unsteadily in two directions, leaving a three-foot gap in the middle, from which Eloise's flared bronze muzzle now protruded.

*"HAVE A CARE!"* cried Balthazar as he offered his slow match to the priming pan. There was a flash, then *'BOOM!'*, the iron ball was on its way. At a range of only sixty yards Balthazar was confident as to the outcome, and indeed as the thirty-pound shot struck home the postern door shattered into a thousand splinters. But the way was still not clear. Behind the wooden door was a strong grille made from a lattice of inch-thick wrought-iron bars, still firmly attached to its hinges.

"Bugger it!" snarled Balthazar to himself, then above the din of battle he shouted, *"CLOSE UP, CLOSE UP. WE HAVE TO RELOAD!"*

Edmund's ears were ringing from the battering that Eloise's discharge had just given them, but he duly closed up the gap in the shield wall to allow the Flemings to hurry through their loading duties. In less than two minutes there was another almighty *crack* as a second missile sped towards its target. This time the impact was

270

accompanied by a resounding *clang* as the wrought-iron grille was ripped from its mountings and sent flying through the air.

Balthazar clapped Edmund on the shoulder. "Our key appears to fit. After you, my friend!"

Edmund nodded, then closed the visor on his new armet, threw down his pavise and sounded the charge. The entire company ran forward until they were at the ruined gate, but before anyone attempted to pass through into the castle Balthazar had a half-dozen of his handgonners fire a volley into the swirling cloud of fine mortar dust still hanging in the passageway, just as a precaution. From his rearward position, Jasper had been watching with intense interest. Sensing that the moment of victory was close at hand he ordered half of his men forward in support of Edmund, with orders that they should advance through the breach and open the main gates as soon as they could. Mounting his horse and drawing his sword he cried out to the remainder of his force, "Let us take the day! We shall march round to their front door and make a proper entrance."

Back at the postern gate, Edmund took a firm grip on his two-handed warhammer and strode impatiently through the thick curtain of white smoke left by the handgonners' volley. Bursting out of it into the castle yard he had only one thing on his mind: fight his way through the enemy until he found Richard Wardlow and then kill him. He had never seen his father's legitimate heir face to face, but he felt they would know each other at once. If not, he would happily slaughter every last man in the castle just to make sure Richard did not escape.

He was greatly surprised, therefore, to find a mere two dozen or so exhausted-looking defenders, many of them wounded, throwing down their weapons and taking off their helmets. They all wore the equipment of common footsoldiers save for one, dressed in a rich blue brigandine supplemented with plate armour on his arms and legs, and it was this man who stepped forward to address him. He looked ten years too old to be Richard Wardlow.

"I am Roger Kynaston, Constable of this castle, though not,

I suspect, for much longer. I am ready to surrender the keys to my lord of Pembroke in the hope that he might spare our lives."

Roger's words, however, barely registered with Edmund. Raising his visor he looked all around him before fixing Roger with an angry stare. When he spoke, his voice had a threatening, steely edge. "I have it on good authority that a certain Richard Wardlow was lately assisting in the defence of this castle. I claim him as my prisoner. Where is he?"

"He departed some hours ago at my insistence," Roger replied calmly. "You must be Edmund of Calais," he added.

Edmund was livid at losing his quarry after expending so much time, money and effort to pin him down. Without warning, he grabbed Roger by the throat with one steel-gloved hand and pressed him against the castle wall. As one, Roger's men made to go to his aid, but they were held back by the levelled bill points and threatening handgonnes of Edmund's mercenaries.

*"TELL ME WHERE HE WENT!"* Edmund screamed, his eyes glowing like hot coals, the sharp spike on top of his warhammer an inch away from Roger's face. "Tell me or so help me I shall nail your head to the wall!"

"I.. swear before.. God.. I do not.. know!" Roger replied with some difficulty, as Edmund's vice-like grip squeezed his windpipe and the edges of the joints on his steel gauntlet dug into his flesh. "I asked him not to tell me where he was headed so that if such a situation as this arose, you would not discover his whereabouts, even if you were to kill me."

Edmund's grip tightened until Roger's eyes began to bulge. His warhammer moved slowly forward until the cruelly sharp top spike was pressing on Roger's lower eyelid.

"One last chance," Edmund snarled. "Where is Richard Wardlow?"

*"HOLD, EDMUND, LET HIM GO!"* ordered a commanding voice.

Looking round but not relaxing his grip, Edmund saw Jasper in all his lordly finery astride a costly warhorse. Realizing the game was up, he pushed Roger roughly aside in disgust. As the latter rubbed his bruised throat, Jasper dismounted and strode triumphantly over to Edmund, clapping him on the back.

"You and your men have won the day for us Edmund. Your valuable service will not go unrecognised."

Edmund, seething inwardly over Richard's timely escape, nevertheless managed to put on a show of enthusiasm for his benefactor. Though the day had brought him the bitter taste of disappointment, he was sure another opportunity to eliminate his half-brother would arise at some point. In the meantime he might as well enjoy whatever rewards Jasper felt inclined to bestow upon him for his labours.

Turning to the dispirited Roger, Jasper magnanimously declared, "Roger Kynaston! You have been the cause of much delay and consternation. A proper nuisance in fact. I should hang you from your own gatehouse as an example. However, had you been *my* constable defending *my* castle I would have expected you to conduct no less stout a defence. I cannot bring myself to judge you so harshly simply for doing your duty. Your men are free to return to their homes."

"What, then, is to be my fate, my lord?" Roger asked nervously, wondering if the bruising on his neck from Edmund's fingers was about to become the least of his worries.

"Unlike some of my peers I do not believe that gentlemen should murder other gentlemen after a battle," Jasper replied. "You, my obstinate friend, are to dine this night at my table as a guest in *my* castle."

"My lord of Pembroke is most gracious," replied a very relieved Roger, bowing deeply, "though I fear after so many weeks under siege we have little left in our pantry that would tempt your palate."

Jasper laughed. "I daresay that is the case, but I am sure we can cobble up a feast of sorts with what I have. You, Edmund, will sit at my right hand, for tonight I wish to show my gratitude for your efforts in securing the castle."

Edmund bowed graciously, though his thoughts were still fixed on discovering Richard's whereabouts.

# CHAPTER SIXTY-FOUR

AN HOUR before Edmund and his men had begun manhandling Eloise into her firing position, Richard Wardlow and his men had already reached the relative safety of St Asaph, a small cathedral and market town a few miles to the west of the Wardlow estate. Richard addressed his men, some carrying injuries from the recent fighting and all of them weary, in sight of the cathedral. He had great difficulty getting his words out, such was the emotion of the occasion, but his loyal followers hung onto every one he uttered.

"Friends, neighbours, tenants - it is over. You have supported me faithfully through the long months since the events at Ludford Bridge and you have stood at my side as we helped to defend Denbigh Castle for a very dear friend. You have been separated from your wives and families for long enough now. I can ask no more of you. It appears Edmund had won and I have lost everything, in spite of the best help I could have wished for. My father would turn in his grave, if he had one. Fare you well and go with God."

As he finished Richard began to sob unashamedly. Tom put a comforting arm around his shoulder. "We have all seen how you conducted yourself during these most difficult times, Master Richard, and none of us harbours anything but admiration for you. We were outnumbered at every stage of this devilish game but we all gave of our best and should be proud to be standing here together. Let us not scatter ourselves, let us follow you to Carmel so that we might remain a fighting unit. You may be able to call upon other friends of your father for help."

"No, Tom," Richard replied grimly. "My father's Yorkist allies are in the south and east of the country, many miles away, and in any case with Jasper's army of a thousand men ready to spill out of Denbigh Castle at a moment's notice I doubt even the most loyal of his friends would dare to come out of hiding. Go back to your homes with my blessing and my eternal gratitude."

Tom nodded slowly, realizing that the time had indeed come to call it a day. With Jasper firmly in control of a large part of Wales and King Henry's court party ruling from London, a Yorkist was a dangerous thing to be.

"We shall return in dribs and drabs, Master Richard, so as to attract only the minimum of attention. I doubt Edmund knows every face on the estate, so a few more appearing over the next few days should not alarm him unduly."

"If he is even there," Richard observed bitterly. "Perhaps he will stay a few days in Denbigh with his new friend, the Earl of Pembroke, to celebrate their victory. I felt sure he was there, planning his moves so he could take me prisoner."

"I think you are right on that score, Master Richard," said Tom. "Rest assured, though, we shall not give you away if he comes asking questions."

Richard looked alarmed. "No, Tom! All of you! I will not have you suffer on my behalf. If my brother turns inquisitor and you find yourselves or your families being threatened to reveal my whereabouts then tell him. I care not what happens to me now. If he comes to Carmel I shall arm myself and fight him to my last breath for my father's sake. That is, if he does not hide behind his mercenaries as he has done so far. In any event, I do not think he would harm my mother or my sister now that he has possession of the estate. If he wishes anyone harm, it is me he is after so that he can extinguish my father's bloodline. But enough – it is time to return to your families."

Richard's little retinue shuffled past him one by one, shaking his hand and mumbling emotional words of support before heading off home in various directions. Soon only Tom remained. He had been watching his dead master's son with a heavy heart. At just turned eighteen – the anniversary marked by a low-key celebration during the early days of the siege – Richard looked a broken man. Tom thought once more about offering to accompany Richard to Carmel, but he knew his words would fall on deaf ears. Only Richard Wardlow could decide what Richard Wardlow would do next. Tom worried about his young friend sinking into a slough of despair, but then he remembered how strong Ann had been whilst under Edmund's iron fist. She would keep him from drowning in self-pity.

No words were spoken as Tom and Richard embraced. At first they parted without looking back, but before Tom reached the turn in the road that would put them out of sight of each other he took one last glance at his master. Richard's back and shoulders were sagging in a posture of utter despair, but at least he was walking in the direction of the place where Tom had told him he could hire a horse for the eight-mile journey to Carmel. Tom said a prayer for him and set off home.

# CHAPTER SIXTY-FIVE

DESPITE THE departure of the servants at the beginning of the siege, the Great Hall of Denbigh Castle still offered a warm, welcoming atmosphere once the fires were lit and hot food brought to the long trestle tables at which Jasper's serjeants and men-at-arms were filling their faces. Jasper sat in the chair of honour at the top table, with Roger on his left and Edmund on his right. Various minor nobles occupied the remaining seats, their regard for Edmund now greatly improved since their first encounter in the merchant's house. Balthazar had also been accorded a place and was competing with the chandeliers, lighting up the room with his golden grin. The drink was flowing freely and Edmund was struck by Jasper's magnanimity towards his former adversary. He very much doubted whether he would have extended Roger Kynaston such courtesy had he been in a similar position.

After everyone had at least eaten, if not yet drunk, their fill, Jasper stood up and banged loudly on the table to attract attention.

"Gentlemen! I would have your ears for a moment. We celebrate this night the delivering into our hands of the castle at whose walls we have thrown ourselves for so many weeks. This dangerous work was brought to a speedy conclusion thanks to the contribution of our friend Edmund, who brought along Balthazar and his cannon to smash down the door and provide a convenient way in."

At the mention of their names both men half rose from their seats and bowed politely to the assembly.

"I think this the perfect opportunity to express our gratitude. Firstly, Master Gonner Balthazar, please accept this small token of our appreciation." Jasper produced two bulging leather pouches that chinked with the sweet music of hammered gold coin and handed it to the grinning Fleming.

"One hundred marks for yourself and another hundred for your gonners to share, with our blessings and thanks."

Amid loud cheers from the diners Balthazar bowed so low he almost knocked his tankard over, then smiled a dazzling, gilded smile that made Edmund wonder which held the more gold – Jasper's purse or Balthazar's mouth.

The young Earl's next announcement almost made Edmund's heart stop.

# CHAPTER SIXTY-SIX

RICHARD WARDLOW sat slumped in his chair, his face buried in his hands. He had arrived at Carmel two hours earlier, just as it was getting dark, soaked to the skin from a heavy shower and looking utterly dejected. Neither the roaring fire in the modest hall of the manor house at Carmel, nor the ale he had thrown down his neck, did much to warm his spirits. Not even an emotional - on her part - reunion with his beloved sister could stir him from his misery.

As the dregs of his drink trickled out of his overturned pewter tankard onto the floor, he addressed his mother in a faltering voice thick with choked-backed tears. "I have failed our family, Mother. Firstly, I have allowed my father's murderer to steal the very roof from over our heads without so much as drawing my sword. Secondly, I have run away from a fight leaving a good friend in God knows what danger. To cap it all, I now find myself cowering in hiding with the womenfolk and servants."

"The last part is unfair!" cried Kate. "Mother never cowered. She stood up to Edmund."

"And I did not? Is that what you are saying, Sister?"

"No, no!" Kate replied. "I did not mean for my words to be taken thus. It was better that you stayed at Denbigh. Edmund would have killed you otherwise."

"Perhaps it would have been for the best," Richard observed bitterly, righting his tankard, picking up the large pitcher next to his chair and pouring himself another drink.

"Children! Have you forgotten I am here?" Ann interrupted. "I will not have you bicker amongst yourselves. It will only serve to divide us to our detriment and Edmund's gain. If the only thing left to us is our dignity then let us all do our utmost to preserve it. And Richard – the answers to our problems are not to be found at the bottom of an ale pot! Would you throw what money we have left down your neck and turn yourself into a contemptible souse? You are still your father's son, my son. You have a strong sword arm, a good brain and a tongue in your head. We must use what resources we have to carry on our fight. Between us we can prepare a case to put before the King."

Richard groaned. "Mother, my father was attainted by Parliament. Do you not understand? His name – our name – is Mud until Judgement Day as far as those in power are concerned. They will not listen to our pleas."

"I cannot and will not believe that there is nothing we can do to reclaim what is rightfully ours," Ann continued.

Richard was not in the mood for a serious discussion. "Tomorrow, then, Mother. Let us speak of this again tomorrow. Tonight I am going out to the alehouse I saw on the way here."

Ann looked horrified. "But what if some of Edmund's spies are there? You must be careful where you show your face!"

"I no longer care, Mother. If there are ten of his agents there, let them see me, let them take me. They can hack off my head and use it as a football if they wish, I shall not oppose them."

Ann's face began to crease as she struggled to hold back her tears. "Go then, foolish boy! Put yourself in mortal danger and leave your sister and I to the wolves, all for the sake of a belly full of ale." Before Ann's emotional blackmail could work on him Richard had grabbed a cloak and was out of the door, striding through the pelting rain, leaving a speechless Kate to comfort their weeping mother.

# CHAPTER SIXTY-SEVEN

JASPER TUDUR, Earl of Pembroke, motioned to Edmund to join him at one end of the dais. Another gesture brought a soldier hurrying up with a red velvet covered cushion which he placed on the floor, while a second soldier handed Jasper his sword in its richly decorated scabbard.

"You should bare your head for this, Edmund," he said in a low voice. Edmund took off both his black chaperon and the linen coif he was wearing underneath it and handed them to the waiting trooper.

"Now, if you would be so kind as to kneel," the Earl continued. Edmund's mind was racing.

*Christ on the Cross, if this is what I think it is...*

Jasper made sure he had everyone's attention before drawing his sword from its scabbard and holding it up in the air. The hall fell silent.

"Edmund of Calais, do you swear to be without fear in the face of your enemies and to be brave and upright that God may love thee? Do you swear to speak the truth always, even if it leads to your death, and to safeguard the helpless and do no wrong?"

Edmund's heart was pounding with excitement as he replied in the firmest, clearest voice he could manage. "I do solemnly swear it."

"Then by the authority vested in me by my brother King Henry, and in recognition of your outstanding service on the field of battle this momentous day, I dub thee knight."

Jasper tapped Edmund lightly on the right shoulder, then the left, then once more on the right.

"Arise, Sir Edmund of Calais!"

Edmund was brimming with pride as he rose, a fleeting image of his mother crossing his mind as he thought how happy she would have been. He was now standing face-to-face with Jasper, who had exchanged his sword for a leather glove. The Earl dealt him a measured slap across the face, saying as he did so, "This is the last blow you will suffer without redress."

He then kissed Edmund on the mouth and embraced him like a brother. A deafening roar of approval shot up from the assembly, but Jasper silenced the clamour with a wave of his hand.

"As a further token of my appreciation I wish you to have this."

The cushion bearer returned but now on the red velvet lay something glittering and metallic; a silver livery chain. As the Earl lifted up the chain, placed it over Edmund's head and arranged it around his shoulders, Edmund could see that it comprised the letter "S", exquisitely wrought and repeated over and over. The two ends met in a trefoil ring, with a rope-twist circle of silver hanging from its bottom lobe. Edmund was in a daze as he followed Jasper back to his seat at the feasting table.

"The night, as they say, is still young," Jasper announced to the room. "Let us drink to our success!"

He saw off his wine in one draught, then held his silver goblet out to a servant for more. He leaned in close to Edmund and, in a confidential tone, said, "One more thing – after your exemplary conduct in the field I think it might be safe to regard the estate at Plas Anwen as yours. I shall write to my brother, the King, and make such representations are necessary to achieve that end." For the first time in his life Edmund was completely and utterly lost for words.

# CHAPTER SIXTY-EIGHT

TWO DAYS later, Edmund returned in triumph to Plas Anwen. The enthusiastic welcome he received from Ysabel, merely for returning in one piece, turned to almost uncontrollable joy once his young lover learned that her *beau* was now a *véritable chevalier*, dubbed by none other than King Henry's half-brother.

Edmund wasted no time in capitalising on his recent successes, lifting his sweetheart up in his strong arms on the doorstep of the manor house and declaring, "A knight should have a lady by his side to advise and comfort him. We shall be married as soon as I can arrange it!"

As Ysabel clung to him in her excitement he said, "Give me a son and we shall make our mark upon this land I swear it!"

Ysabel responded in words that only Edmund could hear, blushing slightly as she did so, then the two of them took their leave, hurrying up to their bedchamber and bolting the door, leaving a bemused entourage of mercenaries and servants in their wake.

Girard dismounted, handing the reins of his horse to a servant. He walked over to Will, who had been left in charge of the estate while Edmund had been away, and gave him a nudge in the ribs.

"A wedding and a christening in rapid succession then, it would appear…"

Will laughed, a wry smile creasing his face. "No-one could accuse Master Edmund - forgive me, *Sir* Edmund – of shirking his knightly duties!"

Edmund did indeed attend to his duties with great enthusiasm in the days that followed, especially those concerning the establishment of a future dynasty. Once the routine affairs of the estate had been dealt with it was a quick supper and an early night for the lord and lady of the manor, the pattern continuing for a week or so until the pair appeared satisfied that they had achieved what they had set out to do, though how they could be so sure of success after such a short time no-one knew. Of course there were those among both the giddy young maidservants and the crotchety older women of the household who firmly believed that witchcraft was involved, but Girard and Will put their faith in Mother Nature's wondrous processes. As men of the world it was their opinion that the seeds of Edmund's future must be well and truly planted by now, though the terms in which they had expressed it over a jug or two of ale had been considerably more ribald.

# CHAPTER SIXTY-NINE

TWO DAYS after Edmund had finally resurfaced, somewhat dishevelled, from performing his husbandly 'chores', he called a meeting attended only by Girard and Matthew. He was in fine form as he addressed the intimate gathering.

"I wish to arrange a wedding between myself and my beloved Ysabel as quickly as possible. Matthew, how much do we have in our coffers? I want the best for my sweetheart but I do not want to bring her home to the life of a pauper afterwards!"

Matthew looked through the estate account books that Edmund had asked him to bring and nodded brightly. "The financial situation is reasonable, my lord. I cannot foresee any great problems if you wish to have only a modest ceremony."

Edmund was a little taken aback. "Reasonable, Matthew? What, might I ask, is '*reasonable*' when it is at home?"

"Well, ahem", Matthew coughed, "your finances did take something of a beating what with hiring Master Gunner Balthazar and his entourage. As you know, their services did not come cheap. However, the balance *will* recover, and nicely, once spring gets underway and your flocks start to return wool and new lambs. At present we find ourselves in a traditionally lean time, at least until the better weather brings farming and industry back to life."

Edmund looked thoughtful, then spoke out as if he had come to a decision. "Then we shall wait until I can hold the kind of wedding that Ysabel deserves. Yes, a June ceremony perhaps, with the sun shining on us all as we celebrate and feast. It will be an event to remember!"

Matthew looked relieved. "That would make a great deal of sense, in terms of both business and pleasure, sir."

"I shall make enquiries of the Bishop of St Asaph with regard to us being wed in his cathedral. I am sure a generous donation to the Church will smooth the way." Edmund noticed that Girard was smiling to himself. "And what, pray, has tickled you my friend?"

"Just the thought of you in a place of worship, that is all. Can you be absolutely sure you will not burst into flames the moment your feet touch hallowed ground?"

Girard had known Edmund a long time, but had never had him down as being even remotely religious, let alone the kind of fellow who would hobnob with a bishop.

Edmund saw the joke, but felt the need to correct his old friend. "You are right, of course, Girard. My faith in God died at about the same time as my dear mother, to be sure. Religion is a game for fools, just a collection of empty reassurances and false miracles cobbled up by parasitic charlatans in order to control the minds of the weak."

At this utterance, Matthew's spectacles fell off his nose and clattered onto the table. He apologized for the interruption whilst inwardly picturing his new master impaled on a giant toasting fork, turning slowly above a lake of fire for all eternity in the hottest pit of Hell. He had never heard such blasphemy at first hand.

Undaunted, Edmund continued. "I do believe, however, that now I have joined the ranks of the knighthood it behoves me at least to be *seen* to be embracing the Church as part of my knightly vows. I also want the world to witness mine and Ysabel's union so that our children can be born without the taint of bastardy that

I bore through my early life, and can enjoy all the privileges that legitimacy bestows. Now that I hold this estate I intend to establish a blood-line that will endure long after I have turned to dust. *I am here to stay, Matthew!*"

The steward could not help recoiling at Edmund's final sentence. To Matthew it was almost as though the words had been spoken by Beelzebub himself. The estate had been taken over by one of the Devil's familiars, or so it would seem. At that moment his private hopes of an upturn in the fortunes of the Wardlow family sank to an all-time low.

# CHAPTER SEVENTY

AS THE weeks wore on, the weather improved. The flowers in the gardens and hedgerows began to bloom and so did Ysabel. Edmund was beside himself over her condition, treating her with the utmost delicacy until she complained that he was embarrassing her with his excessive solicitousness.

"As soon as she is safely through her first delivery and properly rested, I plan to have another, and then another, then another!", he told Girard excitedly as the two friends ambled round the estate on an inspection one bright May morning.

Girard raised an eyebrow in jest. "Do you indeed? Then you have your work cut out for a few years yet! Perhaps you should employ a deputy to run the estate while you are otherwise occupied!" Edmund laughed. "That will not be necessary. Matthew does a fine job of managing the books, even though I am sure he loathes me with every fibre of his being, and I know I can rely upon you, my good friend, to look after things should I be, ahem, *busy...*"

Girard chuckled and they walked their horses on for a while until Edmund suddenly held up his hand indicating that they should stop immediately.

"*There!*" he hissed, pointing to a man holding a woodcutter's axe. "I know that man. *He was at St Albans!*"

The object of Edmund's interest was standing less than twenty yards away. He seemed uncomfortable at having attracted Edmund's attention, but had nowhere to run to and no option but to submit to Edmund's examination as the latter encouraged his mount forward.

"You, woodcutter or forester or whatever you purport to be, what is your name?" Edmund asked curtly.

"Tom Linley, if it please your lordship." The forced courtesy stuck in Tom's throat, but he was doing all he could to remain anonymous. His hopes were soon dashed.

"No, it does not please me. It does not please me at all. You came between me and my father at St Albans and prevented me from finishing him off!"

There was little Tom could say or do. His fingers tightened on the haft of his axe and he tensed himself, ready to strike a blow for his dead master if Edmund were to draw his sword.

Edmund's next words took him aback. "Put away your axe, Tom Linley. I have no quarrel with you now. I had my suspicions that the men who were at Denbigh along with my dear brother must have slipped quietly back to their families and you are the proof. If you are all working and paying me rent then there is no reason to harry any of you. The war is over. Your former master's overlords are scattered to the four winds, never to return. The power of the Duke of York is broken and the King's Court calls the tune now."

Tom relaxed for a moment but then he saw Edmund's face narrow.

"But what of Richard Wardlow? Would his father be proud of a drunken sot who cowers behind his mother's skirts and chases common village girls? My sources tell me he has sunk to a sorry pass. It is not even worth me sullying my hands and having my agents dispose of him, such is the depth of his fall."

At Edmund's needling provocation Tom shifted his axe into a

threatening position, happy for Girard to cut him down so long as he could kill Edmund first.

"Ha!" Edmund sneered. "Still carrying the standard for him I see. I shall have to keep a watch on you after all. Hear me and hear me well, Tom Linley. My brother has no friends to turn to and would do himself a great favour by keeping a low profile, as would you. Live quietly and you will come to no harm. Stir up trouble and…" He looked at Tom's mutilated right hand, "…we shall cut off the fingers the French saw fit to leave you, followed by *your head!*"

Tom was forced to jump back as Edmund spurred his horse forward. Girard gave him a baleful look as he followed his friend back to the manor house, leaving Sir Geoffrey Wardlow's former serjeant to reflect on the fickle ways of Fate.

# CHAPTER SEVENTY-ONE

HAVING MOLLIFIED Thomas Bird, the somewhat intimidating Bishop of St Asaph, with the promise of a generous donation towards God's works, Edmund finally succeeded in arranging for his marriage to Ysabel to take place on St Alban's Day. He felt there was a certain resonance about the timing, not to mention a good chance of some hot June sunshine to lend extra cheer to the celebrations.

In addition, Edmund had taken a surname. The Bishop had made it clear that it would simplify affairs greatly if the groom had a proper appellation by which he, his wife and his future offspring could be known. Without hesitation Edmund chose his mother's surname, le Corbeau, leaving the Bishop to sort out the details. As a further homage to his mother, he came up with a design for a livery jacket based on her coat of arms and had enough made up for himself and all his mercenaries in time for the big occasion. Not only would Will and the guard of honour look the part on the day, but thereafter the uniform would serve to emphasise Edmund's status as a knight of the land and a man of wealth and power.

When the Feast of St Alban finally arrived, Tom Linley

watched the wedding party pass by on its way to the cathedral. He took careful note of Edmund's livery colours, committing them to memory lest he should ever see them on a field of battle, though that seemed very unlikely now. Quartered sky blue and yellow – *azure et or* to a herald - with a black raven, *le corbeau*, embroidered on the breast and back. Tom thought of his own dark blue Wardlow livery coat with a silver greyhound badge, shamefully hidden from sight at the bottom of his wife's linen chest, and hung his head.

As Edmund stood beside his sweetheart in the compact but beautiful nave of St Asaph's Cathedral, his heart swelled with love, pride and ambition. His beloved mother, too, was constantly in his thoughts as he and Ysabel, resplendent in her dark blue silk gown and chaplet of summer flowers, repeated their solemn vows and exchanged golden rings.

Jasper Tudur was there, at Edmund's special request, to give Ysabel away and no expense had been spared in bedecking the cathedral with flowers and hiring choristers to sing joyous hymns. At last, the formalities were dispensed with and after a long but laughter-filled ride back to Plas Anwen in a horse-litter the feasting and merriment began in earnest.

On that warm June night the tenants ate and drank their fill, then danced their cares away, having seemingly forsaken their former allegiance to the Wardlow family. Now the estate was administered by a dazzling young couple with their whole lives before them, willing to lower rents, put on feasts and help ordinary folk forget their troubles. Everyone was happy. Everyone, that is, apart from Tom Linley and Matthew Fletcher. As the merriments proceeded around them they discussed in low tones the possibility of their dead master's son retaking the estate, but their dour faces betrayed their lack of hope, contrasting starkly with Edmund's joyous expression as he danced the night away with his new bride.

# CHAPTER SEVENTY-TWO

LITTLE DID Edmund - almost stupidly content with his new life as a married man of property and position - or his drunken, despairing half-brother Richard realize that a lone messenger, spurring his horse over the Welsh border one muggy, thunder-threatening mid-July morning, was carrying news that would profoundly affect them both. As the information was disseminated, spreading like a growing stain across the county, the two men learned independently what had come to pass.

On the tenth day of that month, in the rain-sodden grounds of Delapré Abbey just outside Northampton, Yorkist forces led by Richard Neville, Earl of Warwick, had overwhelmed King Henry's Lancastrian army and taken the King himself prisoner while Margaret, his queen, had been forced to flee to Wales in disguise to seek shelter under the protection of Jasper Tudur. The Yorkists were assisted greatly by the shameless treachery of Lord Grey of Ruthin, who allowed Warwick's troops to pass unhindered through the complex defences that had been set up. In exchange, he had been promised the Duke of York's backing in a property dispute with Lord Fanhope. Warwick, recently returned from Calais and warmly welcomed in London, wasted no time in capitalizing on his success and laying the foundations for the triumphant return of his master, the Duke of York, from his exile in Ireland.

One of Warwick's primary aims was to send a sizeable Yorkist army into Wales to subdue any Lancastrian resistance, in particular those forces loyal to Jasper, Earl of Pembroke. It was this intelligence that both sent a wave of apprehension and disbelief through Edmund le Corbeau and that jolted Ann Wardlow out of her usual early morning despondency.

"Richard, awake! Great things are afoot!", Ann Wardlow cried at the snoring form still apparently sleeping off the effects of the previous night's carousing.

Her frustration at her son's continuing indolence reached boiling point and she snatched up the ewer from beside the bed and hurled the contents in his unshaven face.

Richard spluttered and swore until he realized it was his mother that had orchestrated his rude awakening. He stared groggily at her, attempting to focus on her face and read its expression, the better to understand what manner of tirade might be coming next.

"What is it, Mother? Are the Scots invading? Or perhaps the French?" he enquired irritably. "Kate will see them off single-handed, I have no doubt of that. The poor buggers won't stand a chance." Ann, ignoring her son's slurred protestations, was already pulling the covers off the bed, inwardly disgusted to see that Richard had spent the night with his boots on.

"It is as well that you are already shod. Mayhap you will be riding to Plas Anwen erelong to reclaim our property!"

At this utterance the lingering mists of Richard's hangover suddenly evaporated. At once he was all ears.

"Go on, Mother. What has happened?"

Ann told him the news that had arrived that morning and as the story of Northampton unfolded Richard's expression hardened until his mother was sure she had her son, her fighting son, back.

Richard thought for a while, then declared, "I must ride out to meet this army! I can direct them to Denbigh Castle and show them its weak points, and on the way they can sweep my brother aside and open the way for us back to our home."

Ann hugged her son until he was forced to push her away for fear of being suffocated.

"Enough, Mother! I cannot ride with broken ribs. Let me gather an escort and make my preparations then I will seize this opportunity and take back our pride. I know I have broken your heart over and over these past months but now is the time to repay the debt I owe both to you and to my father. Let Edmund flee or be cut down, I care not. We shall dine at Plas Anwen before the month is out!"

A few miles away, a smashed wine glass bore mute witness to Edmund's rage at the thought that all that he had worked so hard for might suddenly be taken away.

"How many are they? Can we make a stand against them?" he enquired of Will, his mercenary captain.

Will scratched his head before offering a tentative reply. "It would appear from our spies that the force sent to clear Lancastrian sympathizers out of Wales numbers in the thousands," he suggested, bracing himself for an outburst from his master.

"I must send to the Earl of Pembroke and seek his advice!" Edmund declared. "Time is of the essence – Will, dispatch a messenger at once."

Will executed a curt nod and hastened off to do his master's bidding, secretly thinking that beating a hasty retreat might be the best course of action.

A little over an hour later, Edmund had Jasper's reply in his hands, his brow deeply furrowed as he read it. The Earl, stating the obvious, said that should Edmund offer any resistance to so large a force unaided, the only thing he could be sure of was a violent death. That was something he wished to avoid, he said, as he considered Edmund a true friend and a useful ally. Edmund was then stunned to learn that Queen Margaret, who had fled to the west after her husband had been captured, was now under Jasper's protection at Denbigh. In view of the fact that an enemy army was now advancing in precisely that direction, however, the Earl had decided that it would be much safer to remove her royal personage to his fortress at Harlech, some fifty miles away. This increased protection he now offered to Edmund, his pregnant wife and such of his friends and mercenaries as wished to throw in their lot with him and swell his fighting numbers in the turbulent times to come.

Jasper's generosity afforded Edmund a way out, but as a proud, fighting man he hesitated to accept until a swollen but glowing Ysabel, accompanied by a maidservant, made her way carefully downstairs to ask what was going on. At that moment he realized, reluctantly, that it was his future, if not the place in which it would unfold, that he must protect.

# CHAPTER SEVENTY-THREE

TWO DAYS later, Richard stood at the threshold of the small manor house at Carmel. There were tears of pride in Ann Wardlow's eyes as her son, resplendent in shining full harness, albeit borrowed, and four armed men from their modest household, set off in the direction of the advancing Yorkist army. Kate also looked on in admiration, overjoyed that her brother had finally thrown off the yoke of dormancy and taken up their father's cause once more.

It was after only half a day's ride that Richard and his men encountered an advance party of the main Yorkist army carrying the Royal Standard before them as they marched through the town of Wrexham. To his unbridled delight Richard spotted his friend from Denbigh Castle, its former constable, Roger Kynaston. He spurred his horse over the cobbles, then turned it sharply so as to fall in alongside Roger at the head of five hundred or so mounted archers, men-at-arms and footsoldiers. The two men greeted each other joyously, each having many questions to ask of the other since their last parting. The principal subject of conversation was of course the reason for Roger's appearance at the head of so many troops.

"This is just the vanguard," he told Richard. There are many more men behind me, led by Richard Corbet, and in the mid- and south Marches Walter Devereux and others are also heading into Wales with their hosts. Those Lancastrians who hold strategic castles have been ordered to surrender them by the Earl of Warwick, who has seized the reins of government. It is all part of paving the way for the Duke of York's return from Ireland."

Richard could not hide his excitement. "I could never have dreamed that such a day as this would arrive!" he exclaimed.

Roger could easily guess what was going in his young friend's mind. "Aye, Richard, the wheel of Fortune will soon be turning to our advantage and many a Lancastrian who thought he had his feet firmly under the table will be out on his ear! I see no reason why you and your family should not reclaim your home, the same as I intend to have my castle back. We may have to fight for them, or we may find some of our Lancastrian friends willing to strike a deal to save their skins, who knows?"

The two friends rode on, Richard's heart thumping under his steel breastplate as he realized after a few more hours that they had just turned onto the road that would eventually lead them straight to his beloved Plas Anwen.

Would he finally come face-to-face with Edmund, his hated half-brother? Would he get the chance to strike him down in a fair fight and avenge his father's shameful death?

Roger sensed Richard's mood and gave him a brief nod to show that he understood what the lad was thinking.

"I have been commissioned by my superiors," Roger began, "to demand the surrender of Denbigh Castle and take over the constableship once more. It will give me great satisfaction to have Roger Puleston hand me back the keys!"

This much Richard already knew.

"However," he continued, "It occurs to me that if I were to advance on Denbigh with three-score or so of our friend Edmund's mercenaries still at my back, I might well get bitten on the arse. I therefore propose to drive this nuisance from the area before continuing on my way."

Richard could not believe his ears. "You can do that?" he asked, incredulous. "What will your superiors say if you deviate from your purpose?"

Roger laughed. "Mayhap I would be doing you a favour but I would be doing myself one also. I do not suppose my commanders would think very highly of me if I did not protect my rearguard from attack! In this way we can kill two birds with one stone, as it were. If we can wrest your house and estate from Edmund and send him to Hell in the process I would consider it payment to you for your help in defending my castle when it was besieged by Jasper Tudur."

Richard's heart swelled at the idea of taking back his home, but one dark thought clouded his excitement. "Oh, but what about my father's attainder? Might they give the estate away to some nobleman while our claim is overlooked?"

Roger shook his head. "I do not think that will happen. Your father was attainted by his enemies, but it is his friends who are running the country now. He knew the Duke of York closely and served with him in France, did he not? A few words in the right ears and the attainder could be reversed."

Real, genuine hope surged through Richard now as he imagined the Wardlow family legally reinstated in their rightful home and the usurping Edmund dead or banished. His thoughts were tinged with sadness, too, as he realized it would mean that his father's body could at last be brought back from its temporary resting place and decently interred in the family tomb.

# CHAPTER SEVENTY-FOUR

IT WAS a very different scene in the household of the recently-knighted, recently-married Sir Edmund le Corbeau. There was something akin to panic in the air, though that was not a state Edmund willingly chose to entertain. He was doing his best to maintain order, sprinting hither and thither as he directed the packing of his effects, but he was so torn between fleeing to the protection of Harlech Castle and actually staying to fight that more often than not the poor servants would find themselves being given an order, only to have it countermanded moments later. It was not until Girard seized him by the shoulders and shouted at him to stop for a moment, that he finally, reluctantly had to face the inevitable.

"Friend, the situation is hopeless! We *must* leave as soon as possible. Our scouts have reported a body of some five hundred men less than an hour's march from here. We had but forty mercenaries after Balthazar's gonners went home. Now half of those have run away rather than face an army."

Edmund recalled how secure he had felt only four short months ago. He had decided back then that he no longer needed to maintain such a large, expensive mercenary force now that his life was settled and the security of his position at Plas Anwen seemed assured. Now, however, all the profits from the estate for a whole year would not buy him enough men to stand successfully against an army of five hundred, with more on the way if the latest reports reaching him were accurate.

Never mind the five hundred, though, he thought. There would surely be one among them who by himself would present the same danger to Edmund as twenty men. Richard Wardlow was sure to seize the opportunity that such a sudden political reversal presented. If he turned up on the doorstep with an army at his back, there would be no chance of negotiating a peaceful withdrawal. The only way out for Edmund would be in several pieces in a wooden box, though he harboured doubts as to whether his vengeful brother would even accord him the dignity of a coffin.

Edmund very quickly decided that living with Ysabel and watching their children grow up was infinitely preferable to having his guts ripped out on the end of a bill as a smiling Richard Wardlow looked on. It went against his fierce pride and all his martial training to flee from the field of battle, but this was a question of pure survival; not just for him, but for the family - the bloodline - that he and Ysabel had begun to create. He would take whatever action was necessary to preserve the name of le Corbeau and in doing so honour his mother's memory.

"Yes, Girard, let us go. Let us make all haste and quit this place. I shall return one day and claim it back, but right now we must save our skins! Where is Ysabel? Her litter is ready."

# CHAPTER SEVENTY-FIVE

TEARS OF joy streamed down Richard Wardlow's face as he greeted friends and servants with equal enthusiasm. He, Roger and the Yorkist soldiers had marched directly upon Plas Anwen only to find that Edmund and his entourage had departed by a margin sufficiently wide as to make it difficult to overhaul them.

"No matter," Roger declared. "Your estate is once more in the hands of a Wardlow, and a worthy one at that. Now, I must be on my way. I have a castle to reclaim!"

Richard begged to be allowed to accompany him, but Roger shook his head. "You have much to do here, friend, as well as much to undo. I would suggest that sending a messenger to your mother with the good news might be your first priority." Richard shook his friend's hand warmly and watched as the Yorkist vanguard responded to various shouts and trumpet calls and slowly wheeled its way round in the direction of Denbigh. He could not help but wonder where Edmund had slipped off to. Denbigh was the obvious choice, but it was about to be surrounded, so where else could he go? It was a question he would have to address later. Wales was rich in hiding places, but now that the Duke of York's faction held political sway once more it would not profit Edmund to follow any other course than to keep an extremely low profile.

To his relief, as he surveyed the familiar features of his father's estate – *his* estate now – he could see little evidence of his half-brother's recent occupation. The large mercenary camp Kate had described had disappeared without trace, save for a few circles of ash where there had been cooking fires, and the house itself was just as he remembered it from that fateful day when he and Sir Geoffrey had set out for Ludlow nine long, eventful months earlier. Nine months, but he felt nine years older. So much had happened: loss, gain, defeat, victory. Sharp tears of regret pricked his eyes as he remembered what he had put his dear mother through these last few months. He determined to make it up to her.

Word soon got around the estate regarding the sudden change of ownership and it was not long before Richard was exchanging the warmest of greetings with his two most trusted lieutenants, Matthew Fletcher and Tom Linley. Reassuring him that they could handle matters satisfactorily in his temporary absence, they urged him to ride to Carmel and bring his mother and sister home in triumph. Edmund had been obliged to leave in such haste, Matthew imparted, that he had only had time to take such of the estate's wealth as he could carry in two saddlebags. There was plenty left to pay for a celebration.

# CHAPTER SEVENTY-SIX

EDMUND HAD never in his life been in the presence of someone so utterly *regal*. He was down on both knees in the middle of being presented to Queen Margaret, shortly after his arrival at Denbigh castle, and frankly he did not know what to do or say. Jasper had tutored him briefly with regard to the etiquette of meeting the wife of the King of England, but nevertheless Edmund was feeling distinctly uncomfortable. Queen Margaret's reputation preceded her and Edmund was in the perfect position to confirm that she was indeed all at once beautiful, arrogant and cold. For a fleeting moment he wondered what she was like in bed, but her perfunctory acknowledgement of his fealty soon cooled his ardour.

Normally there would have been music and feasting in the Queen's honour, but the Yorkist army was on its way and time was of the essence. Jasper and Edmund busied themselves preparing their respective entourages for departure, the latter wondering what adventures had befallen Queen Margaret on her flight from Northampton, as she did not appear to have been travelling with a large company, far from it. Perhaps if Ysabel were privileged to be admitted to the royal circle of womenfolk in the days to come she might winkle out an interesting tale or two.

At last they were ready to leave. Edmund, Ysabel, Girard, Will and the twenty remaining mercenaries fell in behind Jasper, Queen Margaret and a bodyguard of one hundred soldiers. Another fifty of Jasper's men kept a distance of half a mile to act as a rearguard and warn the main party should the enemy army look like catching them up.

Having disbanded most of his thousand-strong attacking force once the castle had fallen five months earlier, Jasper had only a further fifty men to leave under the command of his deputy, Roger Puleston, who had orders to hold Denbigh for as long as he could. As they made their way westwards out of the town Edmund kept glancing back over his shoulder, his face pale and his expression taut, looking as though Death himself were stalking him.

# CHAPTER SEVENTY-SEVEN

IT WAS almost sunset by the time Ann and Kate Wardlow stepped once more through the door of Plas Anwen to be greeted by tearful servants and an equally emotional Matthew. A late supper had been hastily prepared and as many familiar faces from the estate as could be squeezed in were seated around the large table in the Great Hall. Wine and ale flowed freely, although Richard, mindful of what he had put his mother through recently, was careful to exercise moderation. After the meal, music was played and the mercurial locals danced the evening away, delighted that the Wardlows were back in their rightful place.

The following morning, Richard, Matthew and Tom made a tour of the villages to see what harm Edmund had caused during his brief occupation, but in the main his half-brother had treated the tenants fairly and few had any complaints. Personal feelings against Edmund were still strong, however, in regard to his brutal disposal of Sir Geoffrey. No-one was prepared to forgive that transgression, no matter how well they had been looked after by their temporary landlord. Richard was indeed moved by the number of messages of condolence he received as he made his way around the estate and several of the villagers to whom he spoke agreed that bringing his father's body home for a decent burial should be a priority.

Tom was of the same mind as his neighbours on that score but he urged caution, reminding Richard that the current situation, both political and military, was still unsettled. Long journeys such as the one to Ludlow should not be undertaken without considerable thought, given the uncertainty of the times.

Richard took his serjeant's advice, satisfied that they still had perhaps three more months before the weather made the roads difficult to travel. In the meantime, he, his mother and Matthew held many a meeting in the Great Hall to sort out the estate's finances and find out where they stood, Ann having been forced to spend a good deal of the money she had taken to Denbigh simply to get by. She was not surprised to find that her steward had done a fine job in her absence, although it irked her considerably to learn that Edmund had introduced one or two innovations which had improved the efficiency, and thus the profitability, of the estate. Uncomfortable though she was with the notion of continuing with his ideas, she had to admit, reluctantly, that they did actually work. In the end she was able to reconcile herself to keeping his modifications in place by telling herself that he was effectively putting money in her coffers.

Over the next few weeks, everyone settled down into their old routines as the corn began to ripen and the villagers prepared to tackle the harvesting. In the meantime, Richard had recalled the members of the regular household soldiery, increasing their numbers to twenty in view of recent events and holding frequent training sessions to maintain their effectiveness. He also recruited and armed a further thirty men from the villages who would down tools and fight at a moment's notice if it were ever necessary.

With a force of fifty behind him Richard felt a little safer than before, but nevertheless he was glad that his Yorkist overlords currently thought it prudent to continue to maintain a sizeable military presence in Wales. One reason for their circumspection was the fact that Queen Margaret was still in the country. According to the reports that filtered through from time to time she had moved on from Harlech Castle, still under the protection of the ever-loyal Jasper, and was now safely ensconced behind the truly massive walls of his fortress at Pembroke along with, it was rumoured, a large force commanded by the Duke of Exeter. Richard was relieved that she and her followers were tucked away in the far south-western corner of the country, several days' ride away, but as he went about his business he never let his guard down and politely interrogated every stranger that rode through the villages, eager for news of any fresh developments.

He regularly visited his friend Roger Kynaston, billeted in Denbigh on what the latter described as 'the wrong side of the walls', but there was little for him to do. Roger was simply copying what Jasper had done by playing a waiting game. He was quietly confident that the castle would be his by the autumn.

As August wore on, Richard made up his mind to bring his father home. He felt it safe enough now to undertake the journey to the little village close to Ludlow where the Dwyer family vault still housed Sir Geoffrey's earthly remains. Sensing that the trip would be something of an ordeal for the boy, Tom volunteered to accompany him. Richard was glad of the support. He took only six other men along, to act more as a guard of honour for the dead than a bodyguard for the living now that things had quietened down. The plan was to ride down on horseback, buy a cart to carry the coffin, drape them both appropriately in the black material his mother had procured from the market in St Asaph, then hitch up two of the horses to take Sir Geoffrey back to Plas Anwen.

The operation went smoothly, though it hit Richard hard to see once again the church from whose tower he had witnessed his father's execution. He went inside to pray, then settled generous donations upon both the church and the local priory, whose monks had said daily masses for his father's soul. Tom held him back from going inside the Dwyer vault, leaving Sir Francis, the head of that family, to direct the removal of Sir Geoffrey's remains. After showering Sir Francis with thanks and offering him payment which was gallantly refused, Richard took up position behind the hearse and the little funeral party began its sad journey home.

# CHAPTER SEVENTY-EIGHT

"A POX on this stinking weather!" Edmund snarled, as the pitching and rolling of '*Le Dauphin*' caused him to spill wine on his hose for a third time.

"The way this cog travels through a rough sea I think '*Le Brique*' would have been a more fitting name!" he exclaimed, as he did his best to brush away the offending liquid.

Ysabel looked wearily up at him, one hand pressed to her swollen stomach, the other clapped over her mouth. She dared not utter a word in reply in case the effort should tip her over the edge and cause her to lose what little food she had been able to keep down.

Edmund looked at her and his expression softened. His sweetheart was finding the crossing to Calais quite an ordeal and he feared for her safety and that of the child she was carrying. He glanced across at Girard, who appeared smugly at ease in spite of the violent motion of the small merchant vessel they had chartered in Pembroke.

"Ha! You would make a good pirate, Girard!" Edmund quipped.

"Perhaps that is a career choice I might consider now that we are effectively *personae non gratae* in England," his friend replied.

Edmund drained the remains of his wine so as to avoid further spillages and set his mind to trying to ignore the messages that the ship's movements were sending to his stomach. He thought back to the conversations he had with Jasper at Harlech and later at Pembroke. His patron had been at pains to point out that there was little Edmund could do to help further the Lancastrian cause at present, especially now the lack of income from his lost estate had severely impaired his ability to maintain a sizeable retinue of mercenaries. Upon learning that Edmund still had a wine business in Calais the Earl had suggested that the best course of action might be for him to go back there and assess what resources he had at his disposal, gather his strength and return in force as and when circumstances dictated. Edmund had no real argument with which to counter Jasper's logic, hence his presence on the small merchant ship which at that moment was mercifully close to docking in Calais harbour one breezy day in late August.

As the ship approached the quayside, Edmund gently helped Ysabel to her feet. He looked once again at Girard. "I hope for his own sake that Caspar has been running my business properly. If I find out he has been fleecing me, God help me I shall sew his balls to his chin!"

Girard laughed, almost hoping that Caspar *had* been cooking the books, thus providing an interesting spectacle for his first night back in Calais.

As it turned out, upon returning to the town house in which his great uncle had taught him so much about the world, Edmund was initially more perplexed than angry.

Striding from room to room in an effort to find his deputy so that he could interrogate him regarding the current health of the business, he was eventually amazed to discover that the sole occupant of the house was a boy of no more than ten years old, sitting with his feet up on the counting-house table, whittling a piece of wood into the shape of what looked vaguely like a full set of male genitalia.

The boy jumped out of his skin at the sight of the richly-attired, stern-faced Edmund, dropping his work and leaping to his feet, knocking over his chair as he did so.

"And just who, in the name of Satan's reeking hole, might you be?" Edmund snarled, surveying the shaking lad as the latter attempted to pluck up the courage to reply. He appeared clean – as clean as a boy of that age could be kept at any rate - and respectably dressed. Not a thief then, Edmund concluded.

"B-begging your p-pardon, Your Honour, sir, my lord," he stammered, "I was just w-watching over things while my master went out into the t-town." Edmund saw a picture emerging.

"And your master; might his name be Caspar, by any chance?"

"Yes, Your Majesty, Caspar Moreau. This is his wine business."

At first Edmund didn't know whether to laugh or fly into a rage, but he chose the former. "Haha, *his* wine business? He has done well for himself then! Well, young..."

"Ector, Your Grace."

"...Ector, we are, ahem, *friends* of your master. We have travelled far and my wife, as you can see, is heavy with child. Is there food and drink in the house that we might be refreshed while we await your father's return?"

"But of course, monsieur! Please find yourselves a seat and I will prepare something."

Whatever he thought of Ector's absent master at that moment, Edmund could not help but smile at the boy's good manners and eagerness to please, not to mention his extensive vocabulary of polite terms of address.

After a hastily-cobbled but welcome meal, Ector showed Ysabel to a spare bedchamber where she could rest. When he came back downstairs Girard was holding the obscene-looking piece of wood the lad had been whittling earlier.

"And this is, *what*, exactly?"

Ector ran excitedly to a nearby cupboard and opened a drawer.

315

He pulled out a long, narrow piece of polished metal a little over a foot long and placed it on the table in front of Girard, who offered up the piece of wood.

"See, monsieur? It is a handle for my dagger. The smith made me the blade after I ran a few errands for him."

"Aha! Your first bollock dagger eh? Just needs a hole for the tang and a round plate at the end to hold it all together. It's coming along nicely."

The two men found it easy to like Ector, but the indulgent smile on Edmund's face vanished in an instant when the door to the room opened and Caspar walked in.

# CHAPTER SEVENTY-NINE

UPON RECOGNIZING Edmund, Casper cursed under his breath and turned smartly on his heels hoping to make a hasty exit, thereby confirming Edmund's suspicions.

Girard was too quick for the deputy, however, and barred the way to the door. Caspar's face was a mask of cornered panic, but he was no match for the younger man, who motioned to him to sit in the nearest chair. Knowing what he would see if he turned around he hesitated, occasioning Girard to grab a handful of his doublet and guide him forcefully to his seat.

"Ah! Caspar, my *trusted* friend. How has life been treating you? And how does your - I should say *my* - business fare?"

Caspar squirmed in his seat, unwilling to look Edmund in the eye. "Well, Master Edmund, very well on both counts!"

"Then let us see *how* well," suggested Edmund, with just a hint of menace.

"And it's *Sir* Edmund now!" Girard added, further, cowing the deputy as it quickly became clear to the latter that a large number of his chickens had come home to roost at once. Realising young Ector was still present Edmund sent him on an errand down the street, thinking that should his interrogation of Caspar become a little heavy-handed the boy would not be there to witness it.

First of all, Girard tied the deputy's hands behind his back, such that he was firmly secured to the chair. Next, Edmund rifled through the old, familiar desks and coffers until he found the accounts for the period he had been absent. He read them thoroughly, noting every aberration large or small. As he did so, Caspar grew more and more agitated, knowing that he could not hope to hide anything from a man who had grown up in the wine trade and was as familiar with book-keeping as he was with breathing.

Edmund shut the last book with a sudden *'clap'* that made Caspar jump. As his master got up from his chair and walked slowly towards him, the deputy struggled in vain against his bonds. Edmund's face was white with anger. He did not like to be fleeced.

"You know what you have done. I have now seen what you have done. I estimate my profits to be down by some five or six hundred marks over the eleven months I have been away. I cannot believe that my customers have suddenly taken a great dislike to my wine, so *where is my money?!*"

Caspar was shaking with fear but managed a stumbling reply. "I... I do not have it any more. What I took is all spent."

*"SPENT?"* Edmund roared. "Spent on what? Harlots? Horses? Houses? Or indeed anything beginning with "H" that costs more than you earn? I thought I paid you fairly, but it appears I have underestimated your worth. Forgive me for driving you to this. Clearly the fault is mine!" Caspar cringed as Edmund lashed him with bitter sarcasm. From somewhere he summoned the courage to speak. "I assumed you would be killed in a battle. I did not see how you could survive for long in a country simmering on the brink of war."

"Well I am sorry to disappoint you, my friend, but I *did* survive and now I am home and I want what is mine. Unfortunately, you cannot furnish me with it, so I must seek redress in some other form. Girard, hold his head."

Girard did as he was ordered, seizing a large handful of Caspar's thick, dark hair while Edmund drew his keen-edged rondel dagger. Caspar struggled but Girard was too strong.

"This is for stealing my money!" he snarled, grabbing the deputy's right ear, slicing it clean off and hurling it into the fireplace. He hoped Caspar's agonized screams would not wake Ysabel, but he was too intent on retribution to stop now.

"And this is to let others know what sort of a man you are. I wish you luck in finding employment anywhere now!"

As he spoke, Edmund pinched Caspar's nose tight and cut through the fleshy tip. As the blood poured from the deputy's wounds his tormentor snatched up a linen hand towel from the table and thrust it at him.

"You have done me enough harm. Kindly do not compound your mischief by bleeding on my floor! Now, begone. Be out of this town before nightfall otherwise I may call upon the services of certain 'acquaintances' who would make my actions seem like a kindness. Rest assured you do not want to meet them."

Groaning in pain, Caspar stumbled through the door and out into the street. A few minutes later, Ector returned carrying a basket of provisions. He stared open mouthed at the blood on the chair, table and floor.

"Monsieur Caspar had an, erm, accident," Edmund offered unconvincingly. Ector seemed unperturbed.

"I did not care for him. He gave me all the worst jobs and he used to beat me whenever he came home drunk. Did you kill him? I wish I could have watched!"

Though still a little shaky himself, Edmund could not help but laugh out loud. "No, Ector, we spared his miserable life but we certainly gave him a stern talking-to then sent him on his way. We must hang on to this lad Girard! He has qualities that I admire."

Girard smiled in reply, then walked over to Ector, lifted him up by his armpits and set him on the table. "My friend here seems to like you and my friend here is a knight. Perhaps he will make you his squire and then you will have a sword and buckler to go with your dagger!"

Ector's face lit up and he grinned from ear to ear.

# CHAPTER EIGHTY

IT TOOK Edmund some weeks, but eventually he was back in the old Calais routine, talking with other traders and ships' captains, courting potential customers, keeping existing ones happy and writing business letters to France, Burgundy and England. Each time a ship set sail across *La Manche*, however, he could not help but think of the beautiful estate he had left behind in Wales. He was determined to win it back whatever it took.

In the meantime, he worked hard at improving his business so as to repair some of the damage done by the accursed Caspar. He had enough money left to get by, but all his grand designs would have to wait until his coffers had swelled enough to match Ysabel. She was still a month away from her confinement but her walk had now become a waddle. Edmund felt a surge of love and pride every time he saw her, the thought of a son to carry on the le Corbeau name becoming the driving force behind his every action.

"But *chérie*, what if I should give you a daughter?" Ysabel enquired one night. "Would you be *so* disappointed?"

"Of course not, my love! We would dress her like a princess and teach her the manners of a queen. She would have suitors beating

321

a path to her door and we would let her choose the richest and handsomest of them."

Ysabel sighed then said sleepily, "I miss Plas Anwen."

Edmund tenderly kissed her hair and silently agreed.

# CHAPTER EIGHTY-ONE

THE NEWS that reached Richard Wardlow's ears in the autumn of 1460 was sensational to say the least. Richard Plantagenet, Duke of York, had sailed from Ireland and put ashore at Redcliffe in Lancashire. He had then made his way through his Welsh Border heartlands, visiting Shrewsbury, Ludlow and Hereford. Satisfied that he could count on sufficient support, his next port of call was London, which he reached in early October. What had happened after that was even more amazing.

At a session of Parliament in Westminster Hall, after years of professing his loyalty to King Henry, York had publicly announced his claim to the throne. It was his, he said, by right of descent from King Edward III through his son Edmund of Langley, 1st Duke of York.

Parliament was taken aback and even York's own supporters thought it an unwise move. It led to frantic discussions among the nobles of both factions, eventually resulting in the passing of the Act of Accord. This ruled that Henry should remain King for life, but upon his death York, now appointed Protector, or his heirs, would succeed.

While these momentous events were unfolding, Queen Margaret had sailed from Pembroke to Scotland in order to establish a new centre of operations. She was not best pleased upon hearing the news that her seven-year-old son Edward was to be disinherited to make way for her bitterest enemy and his Devil's brood and vowed from that moment on to fight to the very end to preserve his birthright. She would not rest until Richard Plantagenet and his bloodline had been wiped from the pages of history. It would not be long before the houses of Lancaster and York took up arms once more.

In Calais, another significant event had taken place. On 2$^{nd}$ November, the Feast of All Souls, Ysabel was safely delivered of a son. Edmund was beside himself. He named the boy Benoît - 'blessed one' - and after a christening in the church of Nôtre Dame the proud father threw open his town house to as many of his friends and employees as could be squeezed in. No expense was spared and his tables groaned with every conceivable delicacy, not to mention the finest wines his long experience in the trade could source. Looking around the extensive company Girard felt that a considerable wealth of pearls was being cast before a sizeable number of swine, but if his friend was happy, that was all that mattered.

The celebrations went on for two days, at the end of which clear heads were at a premium, but Edmund was without a care in the world, other than a burning desire that his newborn son should one day inherit a certain estate in Wales.

# CHAPTER EIGHTY-TWO

A S THE days shortened so did the odds on the country's uneasy peace being shattered, though the signs were well-hidden. The Wardlows, like those who were similarly fortunate, had celebrated Christmas in fine style at Plas Anwen. There had been sadness mixed in with the joy, however. Before the feasting could begin on the Saviour's birthday, prayers were offered and special masses said at Sir Geoffrey's tomb at St Michael's church in Caerwys.

Ann, Richard and Kate bowed their heads in unison as Father Philip pleaded in Latin for God to have mercy on the soul of the departed knight and grant him peace everlasting, and to guide the living along the path of forgiveness, although Richard was thinking more of vengeance than forbearance.

One hundred miles away, Richard Plantagenet, Duke of York, had cobbled together a Christmas feast with such supplies as he could scrape from the storerooms of his castle at Sandal. After that, his men would have to go out searching for food if they were to survive into the new year. He had marched north from London to assess the security of his Yorkshire estates, having sent his eighteen-year-old son Edward, Earl of March, off to Wales to deal with a potential new threat from the ever-troublesome Jasper Tudur. The Earl of Warwick remained in London, guarding the hapless King Henry.

York knew that a number of sizeable bodies of Lancastrian troops were said to be lurking in the woodland in the vicinity of his family seat but for reasons unknown, when one of his foraging parties came under attack he sallied forth from his stronghold and went to their aid. It was to be the last mistake he would ever make. Queen Margaret had flooded the area with troops in far greater numbers than York could have imagined. By the time he realized his error it was too late. He was no more than a quarter of a mile from his stronghold when he was surrounded and cut down, fighting valiantly to the last to preserve his name.

One of his sons, the Earl of Rutland, was killed in the rout that followed and the Earl of Salisbury, Warwick's father, was captured and beheaded the following day. It was a disaster of gargantuan proportions for the Yorkist cause. Queen Margaret celebrated her victory by having the heads of York, Salisbury and Rutland impaled on spikes on Micklegate Bar, in the city of York.

The colour drained from Richard Wardlow's face upon hearing the messenger's dismal report five days after the debacle. Once again his family's tenure of Plas Anwen might come under threat, now that the political *status quo* had been turned on its head. Edmund, wherever he was, would no doubt be rubbing his hands with glee.

# CHAPTER EIGHTY-THREE

THE LIFE Edmund le Corbeau had been leading as the new year unfurled was one to which he might easily have become accustomed. He was comfortably ensconced in a fine, spacious town house with a beautiful young wife, a healthy baby son and a business burgeoning once more after its earlier setback. His interest in affairs over the water, however, was still keen. The news of the sudden and violent demise of the head of the House of York had piqued his interest and the captain of each and every ship that set forth for England was promised a little extra remuneration for any reliable intelligence they might bring back.

Ysabel was torn. She loved having her husband close by, instead of risking his life in military adventures, and was delighted with the attention he lavished upon little Benoît. But she, too, had known the thrill of being Lady of the Manor. She had tasted freedom and power and she liked how it felt. A part of her wanted Edmund to go back and claim an inheritance for their son. Edmund, on the other hand, was a little more circumspect than his wife.

Yet again he played a waiting game, watching as the various political pieces moved around the board, trying to second-guess his half-brother's actions and work out the right time to make his own move.

At the time the Duke of York had been hacked down outside Sandal Castle, his first son, Edward, the young Earl of March, had been in Gloucester. At first, upon hearing the devastating news of his father's death, he and his army had set out for London in order to link up with the Earl of Warwick and discuss battle plans. Before Edward had got very far, however, his sources had reported a large body of enemy troops, commanded by the ever-active Jasper, also making its way eastwards.

Not wishing to suffer an attack from the rear Edward had marched northwards to face his enemy, eventually meeting Jasper's force on the 2nd February at Mortimer's Cross, close to Leominster. The resulting battle went very much in Edward's favour. Jasper managed to escape but his father, Owen, who was famous for having married the widow of Henry V, was taken and beheaded in Hereford market square along with numerous other Lancastrian nobles.

The Wardlows held their collective breath, initially ecstatic at Edward's pivotal victory but fretting a little over a fortnight later when they learned of Warwick's ignominious defeat at St Albans, the second time a battle had been fought on its streets.

As Warwick fled westwards to unite with Edward's eastbound forces, Queen Margaret's unruly Scottish mercenaries sacked the town and freed King Henry. Unable to enter London, due to stout resistance from the city's militia, the Lancastrian host headed for York, spoiling and pillaging as they went.

Edward, on the other hand, eventually entered London to wild cheering in late February. After earnest consultation with the Yorkist nobles, it was agreed that now King Henry was at large the only way Edward could command authority was to claim the crown for himself. This he did on 4th March 1461. Now the realm had two kings. The stakes were enormous, with everything to play for and everything to lose. The rival factions of York and Lancaster were headed for a final, all-out confrontation which would settle matters for good.

# CHAPTER EIGHTY-FOUR

EDMUND RECALLED Ysabel's tears as he had boarded a ship bound for England, but they both knew that if they were to succeed to the Wardlow estate he would have to play his part in the drama to come. Reports strongly suggested that the armies of the newly-proclaimed, but as yet uncrowned, King Edward were heading northwards for a likely *dénouement* somewhere near York, where King Henry's forces were concentrating. It was vital that Edmund should be seen to be supporting the Lancastrian cause so that if the day went in King Henry's favour and rewards were forthcoming to those who had fought well, he might be near the front of the queue and regain his estate.

There was also the smallest outside chance that he might at last cross swords in person with Richard Wardlow. But given the vast numbers that were said to be mustering ahead of the inevitable battle, Edmund was not overly optimistic as to the possibility of such an encounter. Nevertheless, if the opportunity came along to smash a warhammer into his half-brother's skull and claim his inheritance beyond any shadow of a doubt, he would gladly take it.

There were tears at Plas Anwen, too, as Ann Wardlow proudly

bade her son farewell. Richard was equipped once more in the armour his father had bought him, having reclaimed the missing pieces when he returned to Ludlow for Sir Geoffrey's body. Over it, he proudly wore the Wardlow livery of a silver greyhound on a dark blue background. The thirty men of the estate who were trained in the art of war accompanied him, their wives' and sweethearts' faces pale as they waved their goodbyes. They were answering a muster call sent out by King Edward to all the shires asking for as many armed men as possible to join him on his march northwards.

All of them knew that they were heading for a decisive battle, a bloody Armageddon, the like of which the country had never seen before. There would be no mercy shown on the field, each of the rival kings bent on utterly destroying the other's army and thus breaking their power. It would be very much a case of winner takes all.

# CHAPTER EIGHTY-FIVE

RICHARD, TOM and the household men had been travelling for what seemed like an eternity, encouraging their shivering horses through snow, ice, slush and mud for mile after wearying mile, but they had finally arrived at the place which in a few short hours would become a battlefield but for now would have to serve as a camp. A bitter northerly wind, carrying sleet and snow before it as it scoured the open countryside, cut them to the bone. Their feet ached with cold and their hands had become so numb that they could barely perform the simple tasks their owners asked of them as they secured their tired mounts in the makeshift baggage park.

Food and fuel were in short supply and as an early dusk gathered the men steeled themselves for a miserable, soul-chilling night out in the open. Only the very highest-ranking nobles and knights had been able to procure proper lodgings, billeting themselves in the deserted cottages and inns of the surrounding villages. The locals had thought it prudent not to stay and watch.

Earlier that day, an advance party of Yorkists, commanded by Warwick's uncle, Lord Fauconberg, had crossed the River Aire and fought a small but bloody encounter with Lancastrian troops under Lord Clifford. Clifford was killed in the clash and his men routed, allowing King Edward to move his entire force over the river.

As they looked around them in the descending gloom, punctuated here and there by the camp fires of those fortunate enough to have found something to burn, Richard and his men were awestruck by the sheer size of the army of which they were but a tiny part. Thousands upon thousands of soldiers had arrived, and kept on arriving, to pass the night on the same freezing fields. They all prayed hard as they pondered what the morrow might bring.

# CHAPTER EIGHTY-SIX

A S DAWN broke on Palm Sunday, 29<sup>th</sup> March 1461, some twenty to thirty thousand Yorkist soldiers began to awaken, cursing their aching limbs and their grumbling, empty bellies.

It had been such a bitterly cold night that there were more than a few who never stirred from their slumbers, their stiff, frozen corpses bearing pathetic witness to the harshness of the weather and the bleakness of the chosen battleground. Richard Wardlow checked his small contingent and was relieved to find them all alive, at least. Before long, serjeants and captains of some of the large royal and noble retinues started making their way through the innumerable small companies, indicating how they should set out their archers and other troops when the time came, and which drum rolls, trumpet calls and shouted orders they should obey.

Richard wondered how such a vast array of people could possibly be subject to any kind of control, but an hour or so later the colossal mass of men, recruited from all corners of the land and knitted together hastily to form three great battles or divisions, began to move forward with one grim intent.

Across a shallow valley just to the south of the village of Towton the Lancastrian army, under the overall command of the Duke of Somerset, had fared somewhat better overnight. They had established their camp after a short march from York with the result that they were less weary and footsore than their opponents and many had enjoyed the luxury of a tent to shelter them from the worst excesses of the weather.

Their captains, too, began to manoeuvre their equally vast force into what they judged was a favourable position.

As he and his men slowly advanced northwards, Richard noticed a lone hawthorn tree starkly silhouetted against the pale winter sky, a solitary landmark in an otherwise featureless waste. It was shortly after passing this tree that the cold, tired, hungry Yorkist army first laid eyes on their enemy.

*"Oh Sweet Jesus will you just look at that!"* exclaimed one of the younger recruits from the Wardlow estate, upon seeing the massed ranks of Lancastrian soldiery. "We don't have a hope in Hell!"

Tom clouted him soundly across the back of his open-faced sallet, causing him to stumble forward.

"Keep such talk to yourself, lad! We cannot afford to believe in anything but outright victory or else we are lost."

"I'm scared to my very soul, Tom," the boy replied.

"So am I, lad, so am I. Bloody near shitting myself if the truth be known. But we have to do our duty for King Edward and for Master Richard and make our families proud. We'll all look out for each other when it all kicks off, don't you fret."

At last the two armies faced each other, drawn up in full battle order some three hundred yards apart. Across the shallow vale, noble gazed upon noble, commoner upon commoner. Never had two such mighty hosts gathered to settle the fate of the country. It was a staggering sight. On either side, for almost two thousand yards, rank upon rank of archers, billmen, footsoldiers and men-at-arms stood ready to do or die. There was a lengthy pause as the men of both armies said their final prayers and confessed their sins en masse to the accompanying shivering priests, then a dread silence fell upon the entire field, broken only by the sound of pennants, standards and banners flapping and snapping in the damp, chill wind.

As the commanders-in-chief considered their opening moves, the sky darkened and the wind strengthened, heralding a snowstorm. The biting northerly of the night before, however, had now swung round so as to come from the south. As the stinging flakes of the incoming squall started to lash both armies it was the Lancastrians who got by far the worst of it as it was blowing straight in their faces.

Sensing a golden opportunity to seize an early advantage, Lord Fauconberg ordered the Yorkist archers to step forward and loose a single volley into the blizzard. Richard's bowmen positioned themselves accordingly on the open ground in front of the battle lines along with countless others. Upon command they drew their bows back to their ears and let fly. Ten, perhaps twelve, thousand arrows were launched into the swirling white-out. Carried high, borne along by the stiff southerly wind, they flew forty or fifty yards further than usual before slamming into the unsuspecting Lancastrian ranks with devastating results. Men screamed and fell in their hundreds. Those not killed outright by a strike to the face or throat were either disabled or thrown into disarray. It was the Devil's own job to restore any kind of order, but against all the odds that is what the Lancastrian captains managed to do. Before long, the familiar commands were being shouted out above the buffeting wind and blinding snow.

*"Nock, draw, LOOSE!"*

Volley after vengeful volley of arrows sailed up from the Lancastrian front line, their shooters almost feeling pity for the men on the receiving end as they plied their simple but deadly weapons. They need not have worried, however. Lord Fauconberg had judged the wind strength wisely and the Yorkist archers began to shout and jeer as they saw wave after wave of enemy shafts fall short by as much distance as theirs had gained, their effectiveness blunted by the stiff southerly. Eventually, having reckoned the

Lancastrians' stocks to be exhausted, Fauconberg ordered his own bowmen to advance, shooting as they went and eventually plucking their enemies' shafts from the hard ground and sending them flying back whence they came.

The Lancastrian commanders could not allow their men to suffer such harsh punishment for long and so to the beat of many drums a general advance was ordered across the slippery, snow-covered ground.

As the opposing armies drew ever closer, the lightly-armoured Yorkist archers hurried back to take up position behind their own men-at-arms. These heavily-armoured troops would do their best to absorb the shock as the two massive bodies of men crashed into each other. As he waited for the impact, Richard's mouth was so dry that he bent down and scooped up a handful of snow to slake his thirst. It made his teeth ache as it melted, but he ignored the pain as he concentrated his mind on the coming battle that was now so close he could read the individual expressions on the faces of the approaching enemy soldiers. He glanced briefly to his right to see Tom Linley, drawn sword in one hand and the Wardlow standard gripped tightly in the other. The large family banner, on its eight-foot ash pole, would serve both as a rallying point in the heaving melée that was about to ensue and also as a visible encouragement to household men and tenants alike to stand firm against all odds. Carrying it into battle was a great honour and as Richard's eyes met Tom's determined gaze he knew he could not have picked a better man for the task.

As the two armies finally met a great shout went up from both sides to bolster their confidence. All sense of the wider picture now disappeared and it became purely a question of staying alive. For Richard the agony of waiting and the fear of dying had evaporated, replaced now by the visceral joy of smashing, slashing and stabbing other human beings. This was what he was born and trained to do and he did it well.

The clatter of steel striking steel over and over again offered a constant and deafening accompaniment to the sounds of men shouting, screaming and swearing as they vented their fear and their anger. Bills, swords, pollaxes, maces, war hammers and battleaxes were plied with deadly effectiveness. A favourite tactic on the front line was for the billmen to keep their weapons held low, raking and stabbing at the often unarmoured shins of their enemies, felling them to the ground so that the following footsoldiers could dispatch them with a thrust of a dagger or a blow from a maul while they themselves went on to wreak further havoc.

The battlefield soon became a slaughterhouse. Richard found himself having to step over piles of bodies in order to get at his next opponent. The snow that lay on the ground was dyed red with the blood of the slain. Chaos reigned and only the strongest, the wiliest and above all the luckiest would survive the day.

Over and over again Richard swung or thrust his pollaxe according to the amount of space around him. One moment he would have room to aim a powerful sideways blow at an enemy's head; the next the breath would almost be crushed from his lungs as the seething mass of men surged one way or the other according to the ebb and flow of the battle. It was mayhem and it was exhausting, but he fought and fought for his father and for his new King.

Every so often, following the example of others and not feeling a coward for doing so, he forced his way to the rear of the *melée* where there was open space and he could get his breath back. It was during one of these brief respites that he received a powerful blow on his right shoulder. He spun round in an instant, ready to skewer the perpetrator, but was astonished to see a tall, impressive-looking figure wearing a livery jacket bearing the arms of England. It was the young King Edward himself. Richard fell to his knees, bowing his head in homage.

"You fight well for our cause, young man!" Edward exclaimed. "I swear we would need but a hundred of you to see our enemy clear off the field. What is your name?"

"Wardlow, Sire. Richard Wardlow. Son of Sir Geoffrey, lately murdered."

"A murky business to be sure! Our fathers were friends," Edward shouted above the din. Richard nodded by way of reply.

"Well, now you are *Sir* Richard Wardlow, in recognition of your outstanding service to the Crown!" Edward helped Richard to his feet, clapped him on the shoulder once more and set off back into the *melée,* accompanied by several men-at-arms. Richard did likewise, seeking out the greyhound banner that indicated where his men were.

"Well deserved, young Master!" Tom was the first to offer his congratulations at Richard's summary knighting in the field, though the honour appeared to be lost on its recipient for the present, fired up as he was with the heat of battle. It was not long, however, before Tom's jubilant smile evaporated.

*"I don't believe it! In all this hellish crowd! Over there, Richard. There's the bastard that murdered your father. Let's have him!"*

Richard looked along Tom's outstretched arm and caught a fleeting glimpse of the blue and yellow livery his friend had described earlier. Edmund and his retinue appeared to be in the thick of some particularly savage fighting.

Pushing and shoving their way through the press of men, Richard and Tom finally found themselves close to a small group fighting for their lives, clad in blue and yellow livery with the badge of a raven blazoned on the breast and back. One of the men bore a standard displaying the same design. This had to be his hated half-brother's entourage, though it appeared sadly depleted, no doubt as a result of the brutally unequal archery exchange at the start of the battle.

Within the group there were two men clad in expensive armour, either of whom might have been Edmund. At that point in time Richard did not particularly care, and went for the nearest one. His quarry happened to be otherwise occupied, fending off an attack from an axe-wielding Yorkist archer. Ignoring the rules of chivalry he gripped his pollaxe tightly and delivered a determined thrust to the area just under the rim of his opponent's sallet. The long, sharp point of his weapon went straight through the rings of his target's mail collar and into his neck. The man buckled at the knees then sank, to rise no more. The other armoured man, upon seeing what had happened, cried out in an anguished voice, muffled by the visor of his sallet, *"GIRARD! NO!"*

Richard had at last found his man. After more than a year of cat-and-mouse games here they were, two yards apart. Neither had set eyes upon the other in all that time, and yet they felt they knew each other well - far too well.

Edmund was carrying the two–handed war hammer he had wielded as he strode through the gates of Denbigh castle, supremely confident in its destructive capabilities. As they weighed each other up both men had difficulty in keeping their footing, partly because of the six-inch covering of snow that had by now been trampled to a treacherously slippery, bloody slush and partly because of the number of battered, twisted corpses that encumbered the arena in which they were attempting to fight.

Ignoring his martial training Richard lifted his visor to get a better look at his nemesis. Edmund did likewise, so that the blue eyes of the Wardlows were once again staring into the brown ones of *la famille le Corbeau* on a field of battle. They tightened their hold on their weapons as they prepared to engage. Each man constantly assessed the other, looking for a weakness, waiting for an error. Time itself seemed to stand still as they squared up for a fight to the death, oblivious to the mayhem all around them, each determined to destroy the other and keep their family name alive.

*"SO IT HAS COME TO THIS, DEAR BROTHER! WE ARE TO DETERMINE OUR FATE IN A SNOWSTORM,"* cried Edmund above the din of the fighting. *"I AM AMAZED OUR PATHS CROSSED IN THIS VAST, WHITE WASTE."*

*"THEY SAY 'BE SURE YOUR SIN WILL FIND YOU OUT', AND IT DID!"* Richard shouted back. *"I WAS ALWAYS GOING TO TRACK YOU DOWN AND MAKE YOU PAY FOR MURDERING MY FATHER NO MATTER WHETHER YOU HID IN A BLIZZARD OR IN A BURNING DESERT."* Edmund thought of his abandoned mother as he replied.

*"SINCE WE ARE DISCUSSING SIN, LET HE AMONG YOU THAT IS WITHOUT IT CAST THE FIRST STONE! YOUR FATHER STARTED THIS FEUD. HAD HE NOT ILL-USED MY MOTHER WE WOULD NOT BE HERE."*

Richard had no verbal counter for Edmund's riposte, but he had a physical one. As the gargantuan conflict raged around them, Edmund and Richard traded blows, parrying and thrusting until their arms ached and their ribs were sore from struggling for breath in their heavy plate armour.

And then, finally, it happened. Edmund stumbled backwards over the mutilated corpse of some unfortunate wretch, offering Richard the chance to end it all with one determined downward blow. At the critical moment, however, Richard's aim was spoiled when an enemy footsoldier, engaged in a desperate battle of his own, blundered into him, knocking him off balance. Furious at being denied, he turned around and drove the sharp point of his pollaxe through the man's padded jack, between his ribs and into his lungs, granting him a relatively speedy death as he drowned in his own blood.

Meanwhile, Edmund had regained his feet and was about to bring the deadly curved crow's beak of his heavy war hammer crashing down into the middle of Richard's back. Before he could deliver the lethal blow, however, an already badly-wounded Tom Linley, still desperately clutching the Wardlow standard, threw himself between the two men, taking the full force of the attack. The cruel point of Edmund's weapon punctured the side of Tom's sallet and entered his brain, ending his life in an instant. Edmund wrenched his hammer free from Tom's skull, releasing a fountain of crimson blood. Tom collapsed on the spot and for a brief moment the greyhound banner fell from his hand onto the slushy, muddy ground but it was speedily rescued by the young recruit he had reassured at the start of the battle.

Ignoring the boy for the moment, Edmund quickly turned his attention back to Richard and readied himself for another attack. Richard, having spun round and seen his best friend's demise, went berserk. With a guttural scream he lunged at Edmund with a strength born of desperation, and stabbed his pollaxe at one of the gaps in his half-brother's armour. Edmund, near-exhausted and unprepared for the savagery of the attack, staggered back, his body pierced, as chance would have it, through the mail covering his left armpit. Richard's point, however, went far deeper than his father's had done at St Albans.

Now, once again, Richard had the upper hand, but he was to be thwarted by his own side. He was within a hairsbreadth of finishing the matter once and for all when finally, after hours of bloody fighting in the bitter cold and the blinding, swirling snow, the Yorkist army smelled victory. As the closely-packed mass of men moved in a new direction the sudden surge lifted him off his feet and carried him away from his quarry.

Richard cried out in frustration, powerless to land the killing blow. He watched, helpless, as a fugitive human tide swept the wounded Edmund off towards Cock Beck. He peered into the rapidly-gathering dusk, desperate to locate his target and finish him off, but all he could see was a sea of reinvigorated Yorkist soldiers plying their weapons with fresh savagery against their fleeing adversaries now that fortune had favoured them and the day was almost won.

As he followed in the direction of the fiercest fighting, Richard strove to keep his footing on the steeply-sloping, snow-covered ground. The merciless pursuers gradually hacked, slashed, stabbed and battered their vengeful way downhill towards the chill waters of the swollen river. Amid the screaming and shouting and the endless clanging and clashing of steel upon steel Richard somehow managed to elbow his way through the murderous crowd until he reached the edge of the beck. All around him, war hammers, pollaxes, swords, daggers and mauls rose and fell in a frenzied orgy of killing. There would be no 'sparing the commons' this day, Richard thought. King Edward, out for revenge for the slaughter of his father at Sandal Castle, clearly aimed to smash the Lancastrian army once and for all, dealing it a terrible blow from which it would never recover.

Stabbing the spiked butt of his own pollaxe into the frozen ground and using it as a brace to prevent his being pushed into the Cock Beck's icy spate, Richard surveyed the surrounding carnage for any sight of his adversary. All the while, routed Lancastrian troops slipped or fell headlong into the swollen beck to be skewered by victorious Yorkists, or trampled and drowned under the boots of their fleeing fellows. It was truly a scene from Hell as hundreds of bloody corpses began to choke the little river, the first few drifting face down on the strong current in the direction of Tadcaster to make a supremely ironic escape from the battlefield, the rest quickly forming an enormous, gruesome logjam of broken bodies over which it was now possible to cross the blood-stained water dry shod. But of Edmund there was no sign.

Richard's heart sank as it began to dawn on him that vengeance would not be wrought by his hand this day. His half-brother surely could not have escaped the slaughter, injured as he was and clad in full harness. If the Yorkists' determined footsoldiers had not overtaken him and cut him down during the rout, then their mounted, lance-wielding 'prickers' certainly would as the pursuit stretched out over the white fields.

Richard knew he would not stand a chance of finding Edmund's body among the bloody tangle of victims while the fighting was still going on. He cursed his luck and he cursed the day, vowing to return the following morning at first light to scour the mangled heaps of dead, hoping that the snow would not have completely obscured the battle's terrible aftermath, hoping for a sight of the blue and yellow livery that would lead him to Edmund's corpse. Only then, when he could gaze upon his half-brother's pale, frozen face and look into his glassy, lifeless eyes, would he be sure that it was over, that his father's murder had been avenged and the Wardlow family could once again live in peace.

# CHAPTER EIGHTY-SEVEN

THAT NIGHT, after a cobbled-together meal of whatever was to hand - which was very little - and a sizeable share in a barrel of 'liberated' ale, Richard Wardlow eased his bruised and battered body onto a straw-filled mattress in a farmhouse billet on the edge of Saxton village. The other five soldiers with whom he was sharing the room were happy to carry on enjoying the unmitigated luxury of a roaring fire in the hearth, but Richard was more than ready to settle down and try to close his eyes on the horrors of the day. He had little success, however, his mind dwelling particularly on the brutal death of his best friend Tom and his last sighting of Edmund as the fleeing Lancastrian army swept his half-brother away to an unknown fate.

As he stared up at the ceiling, Richard's troubled thoughts wrote themselves in a fiery hand upon the crude, smoke-blackened beams:

*"I will find you..."*

# ᴛʜᴇCLAIMANT

## *SIMON ANDERSON*

For as long as he can remember Simon has been fascinated by the medieval world, in particular the glorious triumphs and shattering reverses of the period in English history known as the Wars of the Roses. He has undertaken extensive research on the subject in both England and Wales visiting castles, battlefields, churches and tombs. Although not a member of any official re-enactment group, Simon has practiced archery using an English longbow, amassed a modest collection of reproduction weapons and armour and occasionally worn a complete outfit of 15th century clothes. He sees this as the best way get a true feel for the people of those times and give his writing extra authenticity.

# MadeGlobal Publishing

## Non-Fiction History

- Illustrated Kings and Queens of England - **Claire Ridgway**
- The Fall of Anne Boleyn - **Claire Ridgway**
- George Boleyn: Tudor Poet, Courtier & Diplomat
  - **Claire Ridgway**
- The Anne Boleyn Collection - **Claire Ridgway**
- The Anne Boleyn Collection II - **Claire Ridgway**
- On This Day in Tudor History - **Claire Ridgway**
- Katherine Howard: A New History - **Conor Byrne**
- Two Gentleman Poets at the Court of Henry VIII
  - **Edmond Bapst**
- A Mountain Road - **Douglas Weddell Thompson**

## Historical Fiction

- The Truth of the Line - **Melanie V. Taylor**
- Cor Rotto: A Novel of Catherine Carey - **Adrienne Dillard**
- The Merry Wives of Henry VIII - **Ann Nonny**

## Other Books

- Easy Alternate Day Fasting - **Beth Christian**
- 100 Under 500 Calorie Meals - **Beth Christian**
- 100 Under 200 Calorie Desserts - **Beth Christian**
- 100 Under 500 Calorie Vegetarian Meals
  - **Beth Christian**
- Interviews with Indie Authors - **Claire Ridgway**
- Popular - **Gareth Russell**
- The Immaculate Deception - **Gareth Russell**
- Talia's Adventures (English|Spanish)- **Verity Ridgway**

## Please Leave a Review

If you enjoyed this book, *please* leave a review at the book seller where you purchased it. There is no better way to thank the author and it really does make a huge difference! *Thank you in advance.*

CPSIA information can be obtained at www.ICGtesting.com
Printed in the USA
BVOW05s0219081214

378410BV00003B/224/P